Death at
the Durbar

Books by Arjun Raj Gaind

The Maharaja Mysteries
A Very Pukka Murder
Death at the Durbar

Death at the Durbar

A Maharaja Mystery

Arjun Raj Gaind

Poisoned Pen Press

Copyright © 2018 by Arjun Raj Gaind

First Edition 2018

10 9 8 7 6 5 4 3 2 1

Library of Congress Control Number: 2017938960

ISBN: 9781464209208   Trade Paperback
ISBN: 9781464209215   Ebook

Poisoned Pen Press
4014 N. Goldwater Blvd., #201
Scottsdale, AZ 85251
www.poisonedpenpress.com
info@poisonedpenpress.com

Printed in the United States of America

For my father, who left us far too soon.

Acknowledgments

First and foremost, I must thank my mother. Not only has she stalwartly supported me through my often difficult journey as a writer, but it was she who first kindled my interest in history. In many ways, I think she represents all that is best about the people of Punjab—manners, elegance and character, all of which she possesses in vast excess. I can only hope that she is as proud of being my mother as I am of being her son.

I am deeply indebted to Shobha De for her generosity. I am also very grateful to my agent and friend Kanishka Gupta. Not only did he help me find a home for the Maharaja Mysteries, but he was always more than willing to lend a sympathetic ear to my frequent tirades during the editing process for both A Very Pukka Murder and this book.

I am very fortunate that Harper Collins India and Ananth Padmanabhan have placed enough faith in my work to acquire three Sikander books. It takes a great deal of pressure off an author's shoulders to know that a quality publisher is backing him to the hilt. Of course, none of this would have been possible if not for Manasi Subramaniam, without whose perspicacity the Maharaja Mysteries would never have seen the light of day.

This time around, I have had the pleasure of working with not one, but three exceptional editors—Diya Kar Hazra, Swati Daftuar, and Bidisha Srivastava. I cannot thank you enough. Not only was it a pleasure to interact with you, but a privilege I hope to enjoy many times in the future.

I am also very lucky to have had another opportunity to collaborate with Barbara Peters and Robert Rosenwald from Poisoned Pen Press for the American edition of this book. I am very grateful to Barbara for her guidance and to Beth Deveny for her valiant efforts to make sure the book was free of errors. I am also very thankful to Diane Di Biase and Holli Roach for all their help.

I would like to thank Vivek Shinde for his amazing artwork, and Jamal Sheikh and Hindustan Times Brunch for being kind enough to allow us to re-purpose Vivek's imagery and use it for the cover of our American edition.

I am also extremely grateful to Rohit Agarwal, who very generously shared much of his extensive Durbar research with me, and to Jeffery Bates from Bates and Hindmarch, who was kind enough to provide me with a copy of the layout of the various Durbar encampments.

I am truly blessed to have a friend like Amitabh Nanda. It is his handsome face you see on the cover, and I will always owe him an insurmountable debt for his unflinching support of every one of my idiosyncrasies.

Last but not least, thank you, Pooja Vir, for all the hours you spent listening to me prattle on while I was writing this book. Thank you for letting me read you random passages on the phone and for allowing me to vent my myriad frustrations with such gentle and enduring grace. Thank you for your clever suggestions and for being such a grammar Nazi, and for taking the time to proof read my first draft for me. I was blessed to have you in my life, however briefly, and I want you to know that this is as much your book as it is mine.

Chapter One

On most days, Maharaja Sikander Singh held a lackluster opinion of the English.

Shakespeare bored him, Dickens was too depressing, and Miss Austen had always managed to give him a resounding migraine. Elgar was...well, too loud, and the raucous lures of music-hall held no appeal for a man of his education and elegance. Cricket he found bewildering, since he had always failed to see the attraction of standing beneath the noonday sun and flailing about with a piece of polished willow. As for tea, it was not his drink. He much preferred coffee, preferably of the Yemeni variety. And, frankly, as far as he was concerned, the British couldn't bottle a good wine if Dionysus himself came down from Olympus and taught them how.

For Sikander, the one great contribution the Angrezi Sahibs had managed to make to world culture was the music of Henry Purcell.

When it came to Baroque music, people were quick to praise Handel and Bach, but it was Purcell, a relatively ignored composer, that Sikander had come to admire the most. True, Bach was magnificent more often than not, and some of Handel's work could elevate a man's soul toward that rare state of transcendence that al-Ghazali had described as *tanzih*, but with Purcell, the anguish in his music, the palpable longing, appealed to Sikander's intrinsically romantic nature.

Each evening, he followed a well-established ritual. Before retiring for the night, he would spend at least an hour at his piano, inevitably polishing off the better part of a bottle of champagne while caressing its ivory keys. It was a habit that dated back to his childhood, when he had first learned to play seated upon his mother's lap, and one he continued even as he approached the ripe old age of forty. In many ways, it was his favorite part of each day. For these few moments, he was not the Maharaja of Rajpore. He was free, identified only by whatever music his slender fingers wrought, liberated from the web of duty and obligation and responsibility within which his birth had trapped him.

On this particular evening, swaddled in a bronze silk *banyan* jacket, his feet comfortably ensconced in a pair of woolen socks to fend off the chill, Sikander had spent two and a half hours trying to transcribe one of Purcell's finest compositions, the aria "The Cold Song." He had heard it performed by a fine soprano in London, and it had haunted him since—a bewildering piece of music, tragic to the point of heartbreaking.

Sadly, in spite of his prodigious technical abilities, he found himself unable to master its intricacy. Every note was perfect, for Sikander was very nearly as skilled as a virtuoso. Still, something remained missing, that ephemeral rapture that Byron had described so well as the "echo of the spheres." It was unsettling, to say the least. Perhaps it was the fact that he was in Delhi, a city he had always loathed, that was throwing off his rhythm so thoroughly, or that he was playing a strange instrument, a brand new Vertegrand upright that felt very different from the concert grand he normally preferred. To his dismay, the music was proving incapable of calming his restlessness.

Finally, Sikander could bear it no longer. Unable to restrain his mounting frustration, he thwacked shut the piano's lid. Rising to his feet, he crossed to a side table where a bottle of Abele was chilling in a Baccarat crystal ice bucket. As he began to pour himself a fresh tulip, it dawned on him that he was being watched by a pair of cold eyes, stony with disapproval.

The bust was exquisite, a Rodin carved from brown-veined porphyry, but despite its elegance, it failed to capture even a glimmer of his mother's essence. Maharani Amrita Devi had been diminutive in stature, barely five feet tall, but she had possessed such exuberance, such vitality, that her presence had filled every room she entered. It was from her that Sikander had inherited his pale eyes, which were as gray as a thunderstorm, and his love of everything French. Most of all, it was from his mother that he had received that insatiable sense of curiosity which so defined him as a person.

It isn't my fault, Mother, he thought apologetically. *It's just that I am so dreadfully bored.*

How could he deny it? It was not in Sikander's nature to be inactive. Like a shark, he needed to keep moving. If forced to stop, even for a moment, it felt to him he was drowning. That was what had made this past week even more difficult to endure. The inertia of sitting around and twiddling his thumbs, waiting for the King to arrive and for the Coronation celebrations to commence, had managed to leave him on the very brink of despair.

Once again, as he was prone to do at least eight or nine times each day, Sikander felt a familiar stirring of wanderlust in his gut. It was so tempting to call for his faithful manservant, Charan Singh, and command him to pack their bags immediately and make arrangements to hop aboard the first mail train going south, no matter what the destination, just as long as it took them far away from Delhi and the miasma of the blasted Durbar encampment.

Sadly, Sikander was far too pragmatic to give in to such a cavalier impulse. Stifling his impatience, he raised his glass in mock salutation to his mother's effigy.

It should have been you here, not me, Ma. You would have made a far better king than I can ever hope to be.

Before he could take a sip, though, he was interrupted most rudely.

The door slammed open, and a pair of Englishmen came barging into the room.

"Are you Sikander Singh of Rajpore?" the first of them asked rather too forcefully, strutting to a stop directly to his right.

The brusqueness of his manner nettled the Maharaja, causing him to scowl. Who did the silly bugger think he was talking to? Not so much as an "excuse me" or a "pardon the interruption." How dare he just barge in and address Sikander in such a high-handed fashion, as if he were a common *khidmutgar*?

Sikander swiveled his neck to glare up at the man. He did not have too far to turn, for the gentleman was immense, as wide as a wall, with hulking shoulders. A soldier, Sikander deduced. That much was obvious, for not only was his posture as stiff as a marionette's, but he was dressed in one of the new khaki serge uniforms that the English regiments had recently adopted to replace their traditional red coats. A quick glance at his epaulets revealed a single cluster, which meant the man was a lowly second lieutenant. From a Highland regiment, Sikander surmised, judging by the tartan cockade pinned to his lapel. Yes, definitely a Scotsman, he concluded, for though his head was razored clean to his skull, he sported a very ginger beard, in obvious imitation of the new King.

Stifling his irritation, Sikander decided to ignore the obtrusive lieutenant. Turning his attention back to the glass in his hand, he brought it to his mouth, but to his dismay, the champagne had gone rather flat.

"Didn't you hear what I said?" The lieutenant barked even more belligerently. "Or are you deaf?"

The Maharaja pursed his lips, trying to restrain his annoyance. How had the fool even managed to get past the door? Casting an irate glance towards the entrance, he waited for his manservant to show his face. Where in God's name was he, the damnable oaf? This was precisely his job, to bar such unwarranted intrusions. A slow minute elapsed, then another, but still Charan Singh did not appear. Sikander's irritation turned to concern. Ordinarily, the old Sikh was as immovable as a sphinx, and it was highly unlikely that he was drunk or asleep on duty. That left only one possibility: something or someone was forcibly preventing him from doing his job. Sikander's temper stirred at that thought. He loved the old man like a member of his own family, and if either of these two upstarts had dared to hurt even one hair on his head, there would be hell to pay, he promised himself.

"Oh, do go away, you silly lout," he snarled, "before I lose my temper and do something I regret!"

Naturally, a dismissal this contemptuous was not at all well received. Bristling visibly, the large lieutenant's face darkened. Very deliberately, he let one hand move to his belt, coming to rest atop the holster. To his surprise, Sikander noticed that he was armed, in absolute contravention of the Viceregal order that there were to be no weapons worn publicly at the Durbar, except on the parade ground.

Thankfully, before the situation could escalate any further, the lieutenant's companion surged forward, placing one warning hand on his compatriot's bulging shoulder to restrain him.

"Do pardon Lieutenant Munro's coarse behaviour," he apologized. "He comes from Irish stock, and Hibernian blood, as I am sure you understand, is easily inflamed."

Ignoring the poisonous glare the lieutenant shot in his direction, the man bowed slightly at the waist and offered Sikander a dazzling smile. The Maharaja studied him, not quite sure what to make of him. Unlike his companion, he was tall and very slim, with an aristocratic jaw and a fine pair of whiskers in the fashion known as the Imperial, as made popular by the Kaiser some years previously. On a heavier man, such a style might have seemed pugnacious, but in this case, it gave him a rather piratical air.

While the lieutenant was rather pale, this man, a Captain, Sikander surmised as he spied the triple pips decorating his shoulders, was almost as brown as an Indian, a fact which suggested he wasn't just a campground soldier. In India, you could tell the veterans from the griffins by the color of their skin, which was soon tanned to old leather by the hours spent under the glare of the sun while on campaign. This inference was strengthened by the way he moved, with that languid nonchalance that came from countless hours spent practicing with a sword. Sikander's eyes widened as they flickered across the regimental insignia embossed on the brass buckle of the man's Sam Browne belt. It was an emblem he recognized immediately, an eight-pointed starburst with a Latin motto emblazoned atop it, which read: *Honi soit qui mal y pense*—Evil be to him who evil thinks.

A Lilywhite! Sikander thought, letting out a surprised gasp. This fine fellow wasn't just any run-of-the-mill trooper. He was a guardsman, a member of the legendary Coldstream Guards. Perhaps the oldest and most prestigious regiment in the British Army, the Coldstream was ranked second in precedence, surmounted only by the Grenadier Guards. They were about as elite as elite soldiers could be, tasked with protecting the King and Queen themselves, and permanently posted as the household garrison at Windsor.

What on earth was a Lilywhite Captain doing in Delhi, turning up at the Majestic Hotel at six in the bloody evening? And what dire emergency could have induced such a severe breach of protocol that he had chosen to come barging into a Maharaja's private boudoir without so much as an invitation?

Whatever it was, Sikander thought, his curiosity aroused, it had to be something well and truly interesting.

"Who exactly are you?" he said imperiously, "and what the blooming hell do you want?"

The Captain's smile flickered with a hint of annoyance at being spoken down to with such disdain, but he managed to recover admirably.

"Allow me to introduce myself. I am Arthur Campbell, at your service. Unlike the lieutenant, I hail from Argyll, and we are careful never to forget our manners."

Sikander rolled his eyes, refusing to be beguiled by this excess of civility. A more naïve man might have bought into Campbell's carefully orchestrated bonhomie, but Sikander could see it for what it was—a tactic intended to put him off his guard. Why, he had used it often enough himself during difficult interrogations, acting the gentleman while his manservant played the brute.

"Forgive our intrusion, but could you confirm that are you, indeed, the Maharaja of Rajpore?"

"I should hope so," Sikander growled. "If I wasn't, what would I bloody well be doing in his bedroom, eh?"

While Lieutenant Munro remained unmoved by this jest, Campbell let out a low chuckle.

"In that case, Your Majesty, I would be very grateful if you would be so kind as to accompany us. It is a matter of the utmost imperative, I assure you."

Sikander looked at him, unsure of how to respond. On a whim, he decided the Captain was not to be trusted. He was too handsome, for one, and decidedly overly familiar, a trait which Sikander had always found distasteful. And then, of course, there was the way his smile never quite reached his eyes, which remained watchful, calculating, almost reptilian.

"I think not. Not only have you quite ruined my evening, but your manners are nothing short of deplorable. I have a pressing appointment with the Viceroy himself tomorrow morning, and you can be certain I shall inform him about your unforgivable behavior. Good evening! You may see yourself out."

If he had imagined such blatant name-dropping would be quite enough to cow this pair, Sikander was sorely disappointed. The two gentlemen reacted very differently. Predictably, the large lieutenant, already rather displeased, started to bunch those immense shoulders of his, like an ox preparing to charge.

"Enough of this rubbish!" he snarled. "We haven't time to waste on games, sir. Our orders were explicit. Let's just drag the fellow back by his boot-heels."

"Calm down, old boy," Campbell admonished. "Do try and remember you're a gentleman, not a blasted slogger, won't you?"

Turning back to Sikander, the Captain sighed and offered another one of those infuriating grins, as if to suggest he knew something the Maharaja did not.

"Might I have a drink, Your Highness?"

Sikander could not but help be amused by the man's effrontery. In spite of the fact that every one of his instincts was telling him not to trust the Captain one bit, he found himself beginning to like this Campbell fellow. True, he was too presumptuous, but the man had a devil-may-care style to him, a cocky charm that Sikander could appreciate. He was astute enough to recognize a kindred spirit when he saw one. More than once, he had been called a rogue and a knave, and now, he saw the same quality in Captain Campbell—that willingness to ignore what anyone thought and march to the beat of your own drum.

"Aren't you on duty, Captain? Is it not forbidden to indulge in spirits while in uniform?"

"Ordinarily, I would agree, but this once, let us make an exception." He rubbed at his throat. "I am afraid the ride over has left me quite parched, and frankly, I won't tell if you don't."

"In that case, by all means, help yourself!" Sikander nodded, gesturing one hand towards the bottle of Abele.

His lips could not help but curve into a smile as the Captain made a great show of picking up the bottle and sniffing its contents. After clucking his tongue appreciatively, he decanted a very generous measure into a slim tulip.

"To the unknown, sir," he exclaimed before quaffing the entire glassful in one Herculean swig.

"What about your friend?' Sikander pointed at the lieutenant, who was watching them with a dangerous glower, obviously still ticked off at having been spoken to like a child. "Wouldn't he care for a glass?"

"Oh, I doubt it," Campbell replied. "Young Munro has a very narrow view of duty, I am sorry to report. He is a devil for always doing the right thing."

"And you are not?"

"I have my moments, sir, but, not unlike yourself, I am a pragmatist, first and last."

With that declaration, he proceeded to pour himself another glass of wine.

"The gentleman who sent us to fetch you warned me you would not agree to come along quite so meekly. If that was the case, then I was instructed to say," Campbell straightened up, and recited in a lilting baritone, "'You must fathom the ocean; it contains all you need and desire. Why soil your hands searching the little ponds?'"

Sikander's back stiffened, and his smile wilted. He recognized that particular couplet all too well. It was a quotation from one of his favorite poets, the great Sufi mystic Farid, describing the difficult path a seeker after truth must follow, explaining how he must learn to ignore the obvious and teach himself to recognize the greater, higher meanings hidden beneath the mundane.

Not only was it a fine stanza, but in this case, it offered a palpable clue as to who had dispatched these two officers. There was only one man who was aware of Sikander's love of Farid's poetry, and who had the wherewithal to send a Coldstream Captain scurrying about like a errand boy. And the worst part was that Sikander owed him a damn favor, which meant he could not in good conscience ignore this summons, no matter how intrusive it might be.

He felt his insatiable curiosity flare to life, a ravenous anticipation gnawing at the pit of his stomach. This was Sikander's most telling weakness, his greatest vice. Gold he was content to leave to the Nizam of Hyderabad, wine to the Gaekwad boys, polo ponies to his cousin Bhupinder of Patiala, and fast women to his dearest friend, Jagatjit of Kapurthala.

But when it came to riddles, try as he might, Sikander just could not resist. They tantalized him, the way the slightest scent of a Château d'Yquem could move an oenophile to tears, or the merest taste of an Istrian truffle elevate a gourmand to ecstasy. The unknown, the enigmatic, the arcane, they sang to him, a litany quite as compelling as Circe's song.

If my guess about the identity of the man behind this cryptic message is indeed correct, he thought, *then there was only one logical explanation why this mismatched pair had been sent to get me.*

It did not take a detective to deduce that some sort of *garbar* was afoot, but the fact that his particular abilities were required could only mean one thing:

Someone was dead.

And, judging by the urgency, he thought, *it had to be someone rather important.*

Chapter Two

"Very well, gentlemen," Sikander said. "I will play your game."

"Wonderful!" Captain Campbell chuckled. "Oh, this is going to be a right bit of fun." Grinning, he raised the bottle of Abele in mock toast. "I assure you, sir, you have made the right choice. Here's to whatever twists and turns that may await as we travel down the path of adventure together!"

Sikander resisted the urge to snort at such a florid declamation.

"Would you mind stepping outside while I change into something more suitable?"

"Ah, I am afraid there just isn't time for that." Discarding the now-empty bottle, Captain Campbell gave Munro a brisk nod, and the hulking lieutenant brusquely fetched a dun woolen Norfolk overcoat from a nearby coat-hanger, holding it out it toward Sikander. "As my friend said, we have our orders."

"This is ridiculous," Sikander exclaimed. "I cannot possibly go traipsing about in my pajamas. It's downright uncivilized."

"I apologize, sir," Campbell responded, but it was patent from the glib expression on his face that he did not mean a word he was saying. For a moment, Sikander was tempted to stand his ground and refuse to cooperate with the man, if only to see if he was truly brash enough to make good on his threat to have him dragged away.

In the end, however, it was his curiosity, ever profane, which won out. With ill grace, Sikander took the proffered coat, shrugging it on over his *banyan* and buckling the belt around his waist. Feeling a proper fool, he hurriedly exchanged his bedroom slippers for a pair of suede *veldskoen* boots. A quick glance at a nearby mirror reassured him that even in such outlandish garb, he still managed to cut a strikingly elegant figure. He was not a handsome man, not with that nose of his, which was as massive as the Matterhorn and quite managed to ruin the symmetry of his features, but even in a drab overcoat, it was obvious he was every bit a king. His hair was cut very short, and his beard trimmed into a neat *pick-devant*, in the style sometimes called the Charlie, as made famous by the first Charles. Ordinarily, he would have taken the trouble to don a *pugree* in the Sikh style, but since time was short, he helped himself to a felt homburg with a wide brim, placing it atop his head at rather a raffish angle.

Examining himself cursorily, Sikander let out a satisfied grunt. Behind him, he saw Captain Campbell watching him, one inquisitive brow arched questioningly, his lips twisted into a bemused smirk.

"If you are quite done admiring yourself, sir, we are on the clock," he said, holding up his fob watch.

He gave Munro a nod, and the large lieutenant wrenched open the door with an exaggerated bow.

Sikander swept past him, only to come juddering to a halt right outside. It took just a moment for him to understand exactly why his manservant had failed to prevent this pair of obstreperous Englishmen from intruding upon his privacy. Charan Singh was a big man, almost six and a half feet tall, not counting his peaked pugree, and it had taken not one, but three guardsmen, to restrain him, keeping him pinioned firmly in place by holding his arms, which were manacled together at the wrists.

When he saw his master, Charan Singh began to thrash about violently, trying to break free.

"Huzoor, have these baboons hurt you?"

Sikander's patience, already fraying, came to an end as he noticed the deplorable condition his manservant was in. Obviously, the old Sikh had not failed to put up a valiant resistance. His left eye was swollen and his lip split, leaving him looking as battered as a prizefighter who had gone fifteen rounds with John L. Sullivan himself.

"What is the meaning of this?" he snarled. "How dare you restrain my man?" He took one purposeful step towards the men holding Charan Singh. "Release him this instant."

It was a laughable sight. Sikander was a small man, just over five and a half feet tall, but his bearing was so regal it managed to intimidate the trio of guardsmen quite completely. Even though they were each a foot taller than he, they recoiled, taking an involuntary step backwards and releasing Charan Singh with the utmost alacrity.

"Unshackle him," Campbell barked. Munro stepped forward to oblige, unlocking Charan Singh's restraints, but not before giving the big Sikh a sullen sneer, which made Sikander realise that he was most likely the one who had dared to treat his manservant so roughly. He swore beneath his breath, promising himself that he would find a way to get even with Lieutenant Munro, to pay him back double for every indignity heaped upon his faithful friend.

As soon as he was free, the big Sikh let out a growl, and shuffled forward, clenching his fists. The sight of him advancing with such menace, as large as a battleship, would have been enough to make most men break into a sweat, but to Munro's credit, he refused to retreat, hunching forward slightly, like a full-back preparing to take a tackle.

For a heartbeat, Sikander was tempted to see how it played out. Charan Singh was as strong as an elephant, but judging by his width, the lieutenant seemed half a handful himself. If the two came to blows, Sikander mused, who would come out on top? He would always wager on Charan Singh to be the victor, but he had a feeling that Munro was not the sort to roll over and play dead. It could be quite a battle, he thought with a grin, as good as any exhibition bout.

Sadly, before anything untoward could ensue, Campbell decided to intervene.

"Back in your cage, Munro!" Turning to Charan Singh, he offered him a bow. "On behalf of my compatriot, I owe you an apology. Lieutenant Munro has tested you abominably and for that breach of good manners, I am truly sorry."

Charan Singh let out a sniff. His face remained stern, but he unclenched his fists and gave Campbell a brisk nod, mollified by his attempts at conciliation. Sikander found himself reevaluating his opinion of the Captain, if only by a smidgen. True, he was brash and his manner was tiresomely cocksure, but it was rare for any Occidental to show an Indian any courtesy, especially a servant. Perhaps there was more to him than met the eye.

"Are you all right, you old bullock?" he inquired in Punjabi, but his tone was more worried than critical. The Sikh had always been more than a servant to Sikander. Although he maintained a careful distance in public, as befitted his position, Charan Singh was akin to a father to him. He had been his personal aide since his childhood, and was the one person Sikander trusted above all others, which explained his concern for the old Sikh's well-being.

"I am fine, sahib." Charan Singh's battered mouth twisted into a parody of a grin. "I am not so old that these boys could cause me any real harm."

"Are you sure?" Sikander joked. "I mean, at your age, it is so easy to break a hip."

The Sikh snorted volubly. "Speak for yourself, sahib!" He looked Sikander up and down with a critical sneer, his lip curling. "And where, may I ask, are you off to dressed so shabbily?"

"I am going to accompany these fine gentlemen for a bit."

"Surely you cannot be serious, huzoor." His eyes widened

with disbelief. "I do not trust these..." he punctuated this admonition by giving Munro a particularly poisonous look, "...these sweaty white apes one bit."

"I should warn you, my dear fellow, some of us sweaty white apes speak rather decent Punjabi," Campbell interjected, his accent perfect. He offered the Sikh a raffish grin. "Do not worry, old man. I will take good care of your master and ensure he comes to no harm. You have my word on that, as an officer and a gentleman."

From the expression of dubiety that flickered across Charan Singh's face, it was clear he regarded Campbell neither as an officer, nor as a gentleman.

"Perhaps I should accompany you," he said.

"I am afraid that is not possible," the Captain replied before Sikander could, tapping his nose with one forefinger. "Hush hush, need to know, and all that!"

"It will be fine. You stay here, old man. Decant a bottle of wine for me, a nice Romanée-Conti, I think. I should be back before the sediment has had time to settle." He looked toward the Captain. "Have you a vehicle, or shall I have my driver ready my Rolls-Royce?"

"We came prepared, sir," Campbell replied. He led Sikander out of the hotel, where a car was waiting nearby, its engine idling with a throaty murmur. Sikander paused for a moment and gave it an admiring once-over. It was a Landaulet Tourer with an elongated coach, manufactured by the Standard Motor Company of London. This particular one was painted a striking shade of royal blue, with red lines around the windows, and a gilded crown emblazoned on both the driver's door and the bonnet.

"Is this the twenty hp, or the fifteen?" Sikander asked, making a slow circuit of the vehicle.

"I have no clue," Campbell retorted, holding open the passenger door. "Shall we, sir? Time, as they say, is of the utmost essence."

He waited until Sikander had taken one of the finely upholstered seats, which were covered in matching blue leather, before settling in beside the Maharaja, hemming him in neatly. Dour Lieutenant Munro mounted the driver's seat, his weight making the carriage springs rock.

"*Chalo, chalo,*" the Captain exclaimed, knocking on the roof. "*Jaldi karo,* Munro! Get moving, will you? We are already too bloody late!"

As the car sped into motion, Campbell did not try to engage Sikander in further conversation. Instead, he leaned back and closed his eyes. It was only a matter of minutes before he let out a thunderous snore. Sikander cast an envious glance in his direction. He felt much too keyed up to rest. Instead, he peered out the window, watching his hotel recede, soon left behind. As names went, the Majestic was a misnomer, for there was certainly nothing even remotely majestic about the place. It was rather a drab affair, a cramped complex of four small bungalows surrounding a larger circuit house. There were cobwebs everywhere, the furniture was tattered, the beds musty, and the curtains needed a proper dusting. As for the bathrooms, the less said the better.

Still, the Majestic had one very distinct advantage, which was, of course, its location. It was perfectly placed at the very heart of the Civil Lines, just across the road from the far grander Cecil Hotel and almost equidistant from the old walled city of Shahjahanabad and the sprawling Durbar camp, which lay about eight kilometers to the north, on the opposite side of the Delhi Ridge. It was also very close to the Delhi Club, and just a stone's throw away from the railway station, where the King was due to arrive, and the Rajpur Road, along which he would make his grand procession toward the Coronation Amphitheater.

Sikander had expected the car to turn north along the Alipur Road and then cross the ridge at the Flagstaff Tower. Instead, to his surprise, they looped to the west, taking the Ludlow Castle

Road, which took them directly past the old British Residency. A breeze fanned against his face. Sikander wrinkled his nose as the noxious scent of the old city wafted into his nostrils. Cities, he had always thought, smelled like women. Paris, his favorite, was a courtesan, perfumed with mystery. London was an aging dowager, filled with secrets and regret. But Delhi smelled like a corpse long-buried, redolent of rot and decay and death.

Of all the cities in India, Sikander loathed Delhi the most. Calcutta had an Imperial charm, and he did not mind Bombay, although its bustling energy felt a touch too mercantile for his tastes. Delhi, however, was a cold mausoleum, more a city of the dead than the living. There was an old legend about the city, that whichever dynasty anointed Delhi as its capital would be doomed to fall. Nine times that had come to pass—Hastinapur, Surajkund, Lalkot, Quila Rai Pithora, Jahapanah, Firozabad, Siri, Tughlakabad, and of course, Shahjahanbad. And each time, the curse had struck, leaving only ruins everywhere you turned, the remnants of empires long fallen, and kingdoms turned to dust.

As the Standard maneuvered onto the Rajpur Road, Sikander found himself wondering if the English were even aware of this curse? Had they considered it when they had chosen this as the site for their great gathering? Most likely, they had disregarded it as mere superstition, as they were wont to do with most Indian beliefs. Sikander, however, despite his thoroughly modern attitudes, was not quite so quick to be dismissive. Where some men saw dogma, others chose to see truth. What was that line from *Hamlet*? "There are more things in heaven and earth, Horatio, than are dreamt of in your philosophy."

While he disliked the city, Sikander was smart enough to realise that it possessed an innately symbolic value, especially for the English. Not only was Delhi where the Silk Road ultimately ended, the culmination of Sher Shah Suri's Sadak-e-Azam, but it had been the capital of the Mughal Empire for almost two hundred years. Most of all, this was where the Great Mutiny of 1857 had decisively been quashed, when the Siege of Delhi had culminated in the defeat of the rebels and poor old Bahadur Shah Zafar, the last of the Mughal emperors, had been toppled from the Peacock Throne.

That meant that, to the British, there was no place with greater symbolic significance in the sub-continent, not even Plassey, which was exactly why Lord Lytton had chosen Delhi as the location for the first Durbar in 1877. In India, the tradition of holding Durbars was an ancient one. Essentially, it was an assembly of vassals and satraps coming together to pay homage and swear fealty to their overlord. While the practise had fallen out of favor with the splintering of the Mughal Empire, the English had decided to revive it. The pretext, of course, had been to commemorate Victoria's coronation as the Empress of India, but the reality had been somewhat more political. After the tumult of the Great Mutiny, the English had been eager to reinforce their hold on India, particularly over the native principalities, and thus, under the guise of officially transferring power from the East India Company to the Crown, what had actually occurred was a grand exercise in saber-rattling meant to intimidate any potential rebels.

Compared to the second Durbar, the first had been rather a muted, lackluster affair. In 1903, Lord Curzon had decided to hold a requiem celebration, ostensibly to fete the succession of Edward VII to the throne. While the King had refused to travel out to India, his brother, the Duke of Connaught, had been dispatched to attend, and what had ensued was a wastefully extravagant display of pomp and circumstance so dazzling it had nearly bankrupted the government. In typical Curzonian fashion, it had been a grand excuse for him to lord himself about, and he had done just that, mounting a caparisoned howdah atop an elephant like some sultan of old, and forcing the Princes of India to congregate in the heat and dust while he acted even more self-important than usual.

Nobody had expected a third Durbar, but then, when Edward had died and George V had ascended to the throne, the new King had commanded one final extravaganza, deciding this time around to be the first British monarch to travel out to India and accept homage from the Native Princes in person. As a result, once more the Maharajas and Nawabs of India had been summoned from across the length and breadth of the sub-continent, a collection of the wealthiest and most ancient bloodlines in the world, forced to bow and scrape like common *khidmutgars* to appease the ego of a King whose ancestors had been little better than pig farmers in Bavaria.

Personally, Sikander disapproved of *tamasha* in general, and this Durbar was about as big a *tamasha* as they came. The British had declared it a celebration of Empire, but Sikander was smart enough to recognise it for what it really was, little more than showing off on a grand scale, designed mainly to discourage the Russians and the Germans from casting their greedy eyes toward the jewel in England's crown. That was what rankled him most, not that he was being forced to be part of the King's show, but the fact that he had no choice in the matter. It was anathema to his very nature to acquiesce without resistance, but on this occasion, he had been forced to do exactly that. He had to put what was best for Rajpore before his own preferences, even if it meant being paraded around like a prize heifer.

Still, he thought, leaning forward as the car crested the Ridge, whatever else their flaws, you certainly had to give the English credit for their organizational skills. Below, as far as the eye could see, a million twinkling lights were arrayed neatly, as if the stars themselves had fallen to Earth. This was the Durbar camp, an expanse that covered almost twenty-five square miles.

Until a few months ago, this had been sylvan countryside, dotted by an assortment of settlements and acres of arid farmland. But then, the Corps of Engineers, ever-efficient, had descended like a plague of proverbial locusts. Their task had been a mammoth one. A grand total of fifty square miles had been earmarked for the celebrations. As a result, almost forty villages had been leveled, and their inhabitants resettled. Vast expanses of swampy marshland had been drained, and the River Jumna embanked to create an artificial plain just north of the ancient walls of Shajahanbad. A hundred miles of metaled roadway had been excavated, and forty-four miles of railway track laid, including ten miles of narrow-gauge. Twenty-nine new stations had been built, including the complete renovation of the Selimgarh Station, where the King was due to make his arrival.

Several hospitals had been erected, two exclusively for Europeans and three segregated ones, not to mention a veterinary hospital for animals of all kinds. An ambulance corps of a hundred men had been raised, and a fire brigade deployed, to combat the ever-present threat of fire. Close to one-hundred-twenty miles of pipeline had been laid to provide an adequate supply of clean water, and more than a hundred miles of telephone cable strung. And, of course, the *pièce de résistance*: more than a one-hundred-fifty miles of electric wire had been erected to provide the entire camp with electric lights. And all of this had been achieved amid the blazing heat of summer while battling the plague and an unseasonable drought.

The end result of all this furious labor? A vast tent city had sprung out of nothingness, a sea of canvas, like some fantastical mirage come to life. At the extreme northern edge was the Coronation Amphitheater and the Review Ground, where the King would view a march past of the fifty-thousand soldiers in attendance. From the Ampitheater, two roads led southwards, the Princes Road and the Kingsway, bisected by the Mall. Surrounding these thoroughfares, one hundred-seventy-five separate encampments had been laid out. To the south of the Mall lay the English camps, over two hundred individual encampments, which included separate areas earmarked for each state and several sporting grounds, as well as the vast expanse of the King Emperor's camp, which covered almost seventy-two acres immediately abutting Delhi Ridge.

North of the Mall, arranged in a rough isosceles, lay the camps assigned to the Native Princes. While the senior potentates had been given the plum plots next to the central causeway, the appropriately named Coronation Road, the lesser Maharajas had been given space at the distant fringes, very near the Najafgarh Canal and the Wazirpur *nullah*. Sikander's own encampment was at the distant corner of the Princes' enclosure, very near the horse mews, with a bad water supply and the constant smell of dung, so far removed, it barely qualified to be considered Delhi at all, which was exactly why he had decided to decamp to the Majestic, a decision he was yet to regret.

A discreet cough intruded upon his reverie. Swiveling his neck, Sikander discovered that he was being watched. Captain Campbell had only been feigning sleep, it seemed, for his eyes were now wide open, fixed upon Sikander with an unblinking intensity, his expression a mixture of curiosity and something more indistinguishable, suspicion perhaps, or wariness, he could not quite tell.

"It is an honor to be working with you, Mr. Singh," he said. "I have heard great things about you and your abilities."

"Is that so?"

"Yes." His mouth split into a thoroughly insincere grin. "John Simpson is a great friend of mine. He speaks of you very highly."

Sikander's eyes narrowed. Simpson was the newest Resident officer of Rajpore. He had been transferred there some two years previously, actually arriving to investigate Sikander after the previous Resident had died under mysterious circumstances. Rather than hampering Sikander's investigations, Simpson had been of invaluable assistance then, and several times after. As a result, he was a man Sikander had come to count on as a friend, one of the few Englishmen he trusted. In fact, he found himself wishing Simpson were here now. He could use a friend to watch his back, but sadly, Simpson, along with Ismail Bhakht, Sikander's Chief Minister, had been selected to be part of the contingent that had traveled out to Bombay to greet the King upon the arrival of his ship, the *Medina*.

Still, the fact that Simpson was a friend of this Captain's made Sikander's frigid opinion of the man thaw, if only by a whit.

"Well, Captain," he murmured, "don't you think it is high time you told me where you are taking me?"

Campbell responded to this question with another, even more sanguine smile.

"Aren't you the legendary detective, sir? Why don't you tell me?"

Sikander pursed his lips. "Very well, if that is how you want to play it," he said, deciding to take up the gauntlet, if only to spite Campbell. "You may think you are very clever, Captain, but unknowingly, you have already given me more than enough clues for me to make a calculated deduction about our destination."

"Is that so?" Campbell replied, his voice as smooth as silk. "Please, do enlighten me."

"Well, first there is the matter of your regimental affiliations. Your lieutenant is of the Black Watch, and you, Campbell, are from an even more illustrious regiment, the Coldstream Guards, which can only mean that you must be attached to an important personage, indeed. Then, of course, there is the small matter of this vehicle. This is the twenty hp Standard Landaulet, not the ten, and while there are more than fifty Standards here at the Durbar for British use, only two of them, as far as I am aware, are of this particular model. Last, there is the simple fact that you have chosen to take the same route the Durbar procession will follow, up the Rajpur Road toward the Kingsway. That can only mean one thing. You are taking me to one of the British encampments, most likely the Commander in Chief's camp."

Sikander challenged the Captain: "Am I correct?"

Campbell did not reply, either to confirm or deny. Instead, he sat back, closing his eyes once again.

"Just a wee bit longer, sir. You shall find out for yourself, soon enough."

Chapter Three

"Here we are," Campbell said some twenty minutes later. The car came to a halt, and he hopped off with boundless agility. Sikander dismounted at a statelier pace. He made a great show of stretching his back as Campbell paused to instruct Lieutenant Munro to remain with the vehicle, but it was all an excuse. Instead, he used this delay to take a surreptitious look around, studying his surroundings, which seemed to be the epicenter of a neat encampment. Some distance behind them, loomed a massive archway shaped like a flaming star, illuminated brilliantly. Before it, a vast oval lawn stretched into the distance, bordered by three intersecting roads. At the crossroads, on Sikander's immediate right, stood a flat topped *shamiana*-style reception tent, as massive as a barn, its frontage lined by a long row of white and gold pillars. Beyond it, he saw two even larger tents arranged in a rough L, at the junction of which four other automobiles were parked, surrounded by what seemed to be half a *paltan* of soldiers, all looking very alert, and all members of the Black Watch as well, judging by their kilts.

"This way," the Captain said, as he led Sikander past the reception tent, making his way up a gentle slope toward a small circuit house, a nondescript cottage with a tin roof and a broad verandah, like a *dak bangla*. Arrayed around it were six large tents, in two rows of three, adjoining a neatly trimmed rose garden.

As Campbell came to a stop in front of the first row of tents, the sickly sweet scent of the roses inundated Sikander's senses, and he realised with a shudder exactly where he was.

"This is not the Commander in Chief's camp, is it?"

"Indeed, it is not," Campbell laughed. "It is nice to see that even the legendary Sikander Singh can be fallible from time to time."

Crossing over to the tent in the middle, he leaned forward and pulled open its flap.

"They are waiting for you, Mr. Singh." He offered Sikander an insolent grin. "And do try to be a bit more impressive, if you can manage it. The gentlemen in there, they are not quite as friendly as I am."

Squaring his shoulders, Sikander fought off a clenching at the pit of his stomach. Striding past Campbell, he entered the tent to find himself in a formal meeting room—what the Continentals described as a salon.

It was richly appointed in splendor, its blinding panoply of gilt and brocade so ornate that it made Sikander, a man more than accustomed to luxury, blink disbelievingly. Dumbfounded, he could not help but cast a stunned eye about him. While he had certainly been prepared for opulence, given that this was the King Emperor's reception pavilion, this was very nearly gauche. It was difficult even to believe he was in a tent, if not for the whispering sighing of the canvas roof above. The floors underfoot were not packed earth or bare brick, but rather Persian marble. The walls were royal blue silk, festooned with brocade tapestries, which looked to be genuine Gobelins, or at least excellent imitations. Directly to his left, he saw a triptych of paintings that looked to be original Gainsboroughs, beneath which stood a *pietra dura* cabinet, and a large Breguet regulator clock. To his right, he noticed a very handsome mahogany and ivory tableau atop which sat a chess set in jade and mother of pearl, flanked by two gilded *fauteuils* and a well-upholstered *duchesse brisée* chaise.

Sikander was forced to cut short his appreciation of the décor as he noticed the cluster of people at the far end of the room, watching him intently.

It was a decidedly curious assemblage. There were five of them, four gentlemen of the Occidental persuasion and one native. The English he did not recognize, but something about the Indian seemed very familiar. It took Sikander a moment to place the face—it had been some years since their paths had crossed, and he had changed almost beyond recognition, but undoubtedly, this was the very man who had sent him such a cryptic summons.

It was impossible to live in Punjab and not be aware of who Malik Umar Hayat Khan was. His grandfather had begun his career as John Nicholson's personal interpreter but, over time, had risen from obscurity to become one of the largest land-owners in North India, his services deemed so invaluable to the *burra* sahibs in Simla that they had made him first a Nawab and then a peer of the realm. The grandson, who faced Sikander now, had been his contemporary at school briefly before Malik had departed for Harrow and he for Eton. He remembered a rather podgy pudding of a boy who had always been dreadfully homesick. They had never quite managed to be friends, but on more than occasion, Sikander had rescued him from the grim attentions of their seniors, not because of any shared affinity, but rather because he had felt sorry for Malik Umar, who had been quite as awkward as Tom Brown.

All that had changed, of course. The shy, bumbling creature so willing to burst into tears at the drop of a hat was long gone. Instead, the man staring back at him was very nearly a stranger, tall, slim, exceedingly urbane with his carefully trimmed moustache and pomade-slicked hair, dressed in a simple black *achkan* so elegant it made Sikander feel like a pauper.

He wracked his memory, trying to recollect what gossip he had heard over the years. He knew that Malik Umar had earned a reputation as quite a soldier, and that he was one of the new

King's personal aides, which was why he had been appointed as the Durbar's herald, a fact that made him perhaps the most powerful Indian in the camps—senior, technically, even to the Nizam, though he was but a mere Captain in rank.

It was apparent from his self-assured demeanor that Malik Umar was only too comfortable playing this role. At first, there was no warmth on his face as he eyed Sikander, no flicker of recognition. Instead, all Sikander saw reflected there was a cold hauteur, that habitual calculation of a man of wealth and quality experiences when he encounters another of his ilk.

But then, after a heartbeat, a quite astounding transformation took place.

"Ah, here he is at last!" Malik Umar exclaimed, and everything about him seemed to undergo a metamorphosis. It was unnerving, to say the least. In the blink of an eye, it was like Malik had become another person, throwing open his arms genially, his thin lips splitting into a reptilian smile as he came forward to greet Sikander.

"It has been far too long, old friend. How good of you to come!"

The greeting was much too brittle to be anything but contrived. Sikander shivered, his paranoia, never far from the surface, flaring to wary life. Malik Umar was making far too much of their relationship, which had been tenuous at best. It was obviously for the benefit of the Englishmen, which could only mean one thing—something rotten was afoot and his old classmate intended, no doubt, to land him squarely arse-first in it.

"It's not as though I had much of a choice," Sikander replied, pointedly ignoring Malik Umar's outstretched hand. "Your baboons insisted on dragging me here like I was a common criminal."

"Come now, don't be so melodramatic. You aren't in any trouble, I promise you. Forgive the hugger-mugger, but I am sure you understand we could not take the risk you were seen coming here, not without raising too many suspicions."

"Enough prevarication, Malik Umar. What exactly do you want from me?"

"Actually, I was hoping you could do me a favour." Malik Umar's face tightened, as if to suggest he was not happy having to put himself so squarely in Sikander's debt.

"What sort of favour?"

"In a moment. But first come along, let me make a few introductions, yes?"

Placing one perfectly manicured hand on Sikander's wrist, he gently steered him toward the quartet of Englishmen who had been watching their exchange.

"This," Malik Umar said, gesturing at the closest man, a squat solemn-faced fellow clad in the accouterment of a military policeman, "is the deputy commissioner of the Punjab, Mr. Edward Lee French."

The gentleman made no move to offer Sikander any felicitations, merely a hostile scowl that seemed to begin somewhere near his navel. Here was an enemy, Sikander thought instinctively, a man who would do everything in his power to obstruct him.

As was his habit, rather than feel intimidated by such a display of naked antagonism, he offered the man a purposefully cheeky grin.

"Mr. French," he said, ignoring his rank if only to needle the man, "how very interesting to meet you!"

"I wish I could say the same," the commissioner replied with a sniff and deliberately turned away, a calculated rebuff.

"Have we met before?"

"No, but my nephew, Jardine, was your superintendent in Rajpore."

That certainly explained the man's hostile demeanor, Sikander thought. Until a year or so ago, Jardine had been the head of the Rajpore Constabulary. However, his enduring incompetence had caused Sikander to request the new Resident, John Simpson, to impeach him. The last he had heard, Jardine had returned to his native Gloucester, his career in India all but over, but apparently not before managing to fill his uncle's ears against Sikander quite thoroughly.

As if to illustrate this very thought, the commissioner turned to the second man, and appealed to him plaintively.

"Must we have him here? The Punjab Police can handle this, I assure you." The commissioner's sneer was withering. "Good heavens, just look at him. He has not even taken the trouble to dress appropriately."

Sikander's face reddened. The commissioner's salvo had hit far too close to home for comfort. By nature, he was an exceedingly fastidious man, and in spite of his best attempts to seem diffident, he could not help but fight back a frisson of embarrassment. What a fool he must look!

"Come now, Colonel," interjected the second man, a handsome, well-proportioned gentleman with a bristling handlebar moustache and silver hair that was receding into a widow's peak, "let us not be hasty. After all, never judge a book and all that, eh?" He offered Sikander an impish grin. "Louis Dane," he offered by way of introduction. "Thank you for answering our invitation so promptly, and please, do let me apologize for the commissioner's rudeness."

Sikander's eyes widened. The great Dane himself! Now that was a surprise. This was the lieutenant governor of the Punjab, perhaps the second most powerful man in the whole hierarchy of British India, answering only to the Viceroy himself. Not only was he powerful enough to make and break Maharajas with a single stroke of his pen, he was also rumored to be unimpeachably honest, an Englishman of the old school, as Sikander's venerable minister, Ismail Bhakht had described him admiringly. However, that was not what made it so startling to see him here, knee-deep in whatever nefarious mess had compelled Malik Umar to summon Sikander in such a hasty fashion. No, it was unexpected because the Great Dane had a reputation for being a man who went to great lengths to keep a low profile. In fact, he was said to be so shy of publicity that he had never consented to have his portrait painted, nor allowed himself to be photographed.

So this was the man who had single-handedly made a seemingly impossible endeavor like the Durbar possible, Sikander thought, giving him an appreciative nod. He had expected a paunchy old relic, but the Great Dane exuded vitality, as energetic as a greyhound.

"And I am O'Dwyer," the man next him said. A stout, steel-jawed specimen with cold eyes, and prematurely graying hair worn high and tight with a side parting, he made no effort to shake the Maharaja's hand, nor did he bow.

Sikander eyed him warily. Their paths had never crossed before, but he had heard of Michael O'Dwyer. He was said to be an up-and-comer, one of Curzon's chosen boys, with a great gift for problem-solving and a knack for turning up when things went bad. He was also a bigot and, if rumor was to be believed, very handy with his fists, a halfway decent prizefighter who had won several bouts in his youth. All in all, a very dangerous man, Sikander thought, and undoubtedly, one on whose good side it was best to stay firmly planted.

Unfortunately, that was a bridge, it seemed, that had been well and truly burned. Sikander was accustomed to the fact that people reacted to him rather strongly. Either they found him intriguing, or they tended to take an immediate aversion. In this instance, it looked to be the latter, judging by the expression of naked antipathy on O'Dwyer's face as he returned Sikander's scrutiny without blinking, like a lion eyeing a rival.

"I am afraid I must agree with the commissioner," he said, deferring to the last of the group, the only gentleman of the lot who was seated. "Despite his formidable reputation, we simply cannot allow Mr. Singh to poke about. What if the news were to get out? We just cannot risk a scandal, not this close to His Majesty's impending arrival. No, the risk is far too great."

The seated man leaned forward, and Sikander got his first

good look at his face. Until that moment, it had been obscured from his sight by the swooping back of his chosen chair, but now, Sikander saw that he was a handsome older man, with a slim moustache worn *en brosse* and piercing eyes. Abruptly, recognition dawned. While he had never met this gentleman before, he had seen his photograph often enough, on the front page of every broadsheet for the last few months.

This was none other than the Viceroy of India himself, Lord Hardinge, the highest ranked Englishman in India, second in power only to the Earl of Crewe in London.

Unlike his predecessors, Curzon, who had been a vain peacock of a man, and Lord Minto, who had been rather a nonentity, Charles Hardinge was said to be a sensible, conservative sort. A career diplomat who had previously been the permanent Under Secretary at the Foreign Office, his tenure as Viceroy had certainly begun well, with the implementation of several reforms and an earnest attempt to support Indian immigrants in South Africa. Unlike Curzon, he was not given to ostentatious displays and was said to be a straight-shooter, preferring a more private, businesslike approach to administration, which was very much in line with what Asquith and the Liberals desired. And, while there was a pernicious rumor that Hardinge disliked Indians, thinking them inferior to Europeans, Sikander could not help but admit a flicker of admiration for the man. Most people would have gone mad trying to put together as mammoth an exercise as the Delhi Durbar, but somehow Lord Hardinge had managed to bring the whole thing together, managing not just the logistics of shipping in fifty regiments and the engineering obstacles of uprooting entire villages, but also juggling the capricious egos of more than a hundred Indian princes, a breed that was not renowned for being cooperative.

Being confronted by Hardinge himself was the last thing Sikander had expected. His mind raced frantically. Malik Umar had been insistent he was not in any trouble, but could he have been lying? No, he concluded, he had been on his very best behavior for months, which meant this gathering was not about him. This was something else, something altogether more dire to have brought men of such stature together for a secret meeting. The cloak and dagger suggested it was something they wanted kept quiet, which could only mean it threatened the Durbar, and the fact that they had brought him into the royal encampment in such a clandestine fashion could only mean there was a mystery that needed to be solved. A murder most likely, but who? Who could it be?

"I take it, Mr. Singh, that you know who I am," Lord Hardinge said, rising to his feet wearily.

"I do, indeed." Though he was more than a little intimidated, Sikander was determined to brazen it out, although he was well aware that the bedraggled overcoat he wore made a less-than-arresting first impression.

"John Simpson speaks very highly of you, as does Mr. Hayat Khan here," Hardinge said, sounding entirely unconvinced.

Sikander offered Malik Umar a very cool look. "I was not aware that I was important enough to be discussed by such exalted personages."

Hardinge remained unmoved by his sarcasm. "You are said to be very talented at finding answers that elude most men. Tell me, is it true that you possess mystic powers, that you are able to perceive that which others cannot?"

O'Dwyer let out an audible snort. "Balderdash!" He exclaimed, in a voice so acidic it could have melted steel. "Utter tripe!"

"Mr. O'Dwyer is quite right," Sikander smiled. "What some men consider magic or mysticism is merely a matter of keen observation, the skill of a well-trained eye. For example, it does not take a magician to see that Mr. Dane here is an avid philatelist or that Mr. O'Dwyer needs less beef and more vegetables in his diet, or that you, Your Lordship, had a bowl of asparagus soup for lunch."

"He's right," Dane declared, his eyes widening with amazement. "I do collect stamps! In fact, I was just organizing one of my albums when you sent for me. How on earth did you guess that?"

"It was a simple enough deduction, sir," Sikander said, enjoying being the center of attention as he always did. "When you shook hands with me, I felt the gummy residue on your thumb and forefinger, which my nose quickly recognized as stamp adhesive. As for my conjecture that Lord Hardinge imbibed asparagus soup, once again, we can thank my nose. Asparagus, you see, has a very distinctive odor that is easily discernible. And your Mr. O'Dwyer, I can tell from his posture and his inability to stand still for too long, that he suffers from a case of piles, which is why I suggested he imbibe more fiber and less meat."

"Oh, very well done!" The Great Dane stifled an amused snigger. As for O'Dwyer, he turned red as a beet. Sikander cursed himself for letting his sharp tongue get away from him. If he had any doubt that O'Dwyer disliked him, that was erased by the poisonous glare now directed at him. Once again, his brashness had made him an enemy, and he had a feeling O'Dwyer was not the sort of man who forgot a slight or forgave one.

"It was asparagus tart, but yes, I can see Mr. Hayat Khan was dead on." With that declaration, Lord Hardinge finally offered the Maharaja a rather morose smile. "You are, indeed, perfect for the job, Mr. Singh."

"And what job might that be, Your Lordship?"

"All in due time." The Viceroy's brow furrowed. "First, I need your word, as a prince and a gentleman, that you will keep what you are about to see and hear completely confidential."

Sikander resisted the urge to roll his eyes. *My word*, indeed, he wanted to snort. To a man like Hardinge, with a predictably Victorian world view, a man's word may have held great value.

But to someone like Sikander, who was pragmatic enough to understand that if there was one great and universal truth in the world, it was that all men lied, which meant that any assurances he offered the Viceroy would be exactly that, mere words.

But at the same time, he was also astute enough to realise that if he did not at least go through the motions, his curiosity, which was now fully aroused, would go unsatisfied.

"Consider my lips sealed."

"This is no joking matter, Mr. Singh. Let me make this clear. If you breathe one word, if there is one leak in the newspapers, I shall not rest until you are rewarded with the direst of consequences. Is that understood?"

His cold eyes bored into Sikander's own, and for once, it was the Maharaja who blinked first.

"I understand," he said, an involuntary shiver running down his spine. Hardinge's ominous, no-nonsense reputation as someone not to be trifled with was well deserved, it seemed. From the looks of it, the man's sense of humor had been clinically excised. "You have my word, sir, on my honor and Rajpore's."

"Very well." Hardinge gave Malik Umar a curt nod. "Go on, then. Show him."

Chapter Four

"You must excuse me, gentlemen. Matters of state await." Lord Hardinge fixed Sikander with a stern scowl. "Mr. Singh, I will leave you to your devices, but not without a warning. Do not muck this up. You simply have to resolve this affair at the very latest by tomorrow evening, before the King and his entourage arrive. Is that clear?"

The Viceroy turned and hurried away, followed closely by Louis Dane, who paused long enough to offer Sikander a sympathetic grin. "Good luck! You are going to need it, I think."

Malik Umar stepped up, taking Sikander by the arm. "Come along then, old man! Let us get started, shall we?"

"I cannot help but repeat my objections, Mr. Khan," Commissioner French exclaimed. "I still think the Punjab Police can handle this matter without the Maharaja of Rajpore's help."

"I agree," O'Dwyer chimed in a moment later. "The police are professionals. Mr. Singh, while undoubtedly clever, is merely a dilettante."

Malik Umar grimaced, looking from one gentleman to the next, his nostrils flaring with barely repressed exasperation.

"The Punjab Police, while undoubtedly competent, are a blunt instrument. What we need now is precision, subtlety, circumspection. We cannot afford a public investigation, not with half the newspaper *wallahs* in India sniffing about for a story.

No, what we need is a discreet investigation, and from what I know of Mr. Singh, his cleverness, as you put it so succinctly, is exceeded only by his good sense."

"But still, Mr. Khan, he is an outsider," the commissioner protested.

Malik Umar cut him off with a most unsubtle grunt. "Enough! We have wasted far too much time already."

Turning back to Sikander, he beckoned for him to follow, leading him not toward the exit so recently used by Hardinge, but rather to a curtained portal at the back of the room that he had not noticed earlier.

"This way!" Malik Umar pulled back the curtain and ushered Sikander into the next room. It was a much smaller enclosure than the first, the Diwan-i-Khas, Sikander guessed, the King's private sanctum, as opposed to the Diwan-I-Am, the public reception hall. Here, he saw none of the regal opulence that had so blinded him previously. Instead, the room had an almost utilitarian feel. There was an open fire crackling beneath a cast-iron chimney. Hanging from a chain above, a cast-iron electric chandelier swayed gently. The carpets underfoot were not expensive silk, but rather woven Bikaner durries, and the furniture was very homely, more suited to a traveling officer's quarters than the chambers assigned to the King of England.

At the far end of the room hung two paintings. The first was the usual portrait of Queen Victoria and her husband, looking like a pair of pugnacious horses. Next to it hung what was undoubtedly a Stubbs, a rather grisly piece that was not quite to Sikander's taste, depicting a lion attacking a horse, chosen, no doubt, to give the place a Colonial flavor.

However, that was not what engaged Sikander's attention. What caught his eye was the dead woman hanging from one of the tent's rafters, swaying back and forth gently, even though there was no hint of a breeze.

"Now you see the cause for our urgency," Malik Umar explained. "She was found this morning, just after reveille.

Nobody can understand or explain how she got here, inside the King's private atelier." He shuddered. "We have been very lucky so far. Can you imagine what a disaster it would be if the press *wallahs* found out? What a godawful scandal that on the very eve of His Majesty's Coronation celebration, a dead girl should be found in his personal chambers?"

Sikander pursed his lips. Malik Umar was certainly right about that. There were far too many newspaper *wallahs* sniffing about, not to mention the film contingent, all of whom had come to cover the Grand Durbar, some from as far away as America. To call what would ensue if something like this became public a mere scandal was the grossest of understatements. Not only would it be a severe embarrassment to the Royal family, but this was just the sort of mess that could shake the very foundation of the British Empire itself, perhaps even topple the incumbent Liberal government, not to mention that it would irrevocably ruin a very expensive spectacle on which Hardinge had already spent over a hundred thousand pounds.

"I made certain no one touched the corpse. They wanted to cut her down, but I insisted that the crime scene remained pristine." He offered Sikander a grimace. "What do you think happened here, old man?"

"Give me a moment to take a look around," Sikander said. With those words, his face seemed to change, a dispassionate mask descending. From the inside pocket of his jacket, he pulled a pair of gloves, slipping them carefully onto his hands. However, rather than approaching the body directly, he chose to made a slow circuit of the room, touching a tapestry here, caressing a piece of marble statuary there.

To those unfamiliar with his techniques, it might have looked like Sikander was wasting time, but this was actually a vital part of his process, a ritual he had devised in imitation of the legendary Eugene Vidocq. In his opinion, there was no better way to get a sense of the scene, to discern if there were any clues worth recording, any traces left behind by the killer that might offer an indication of his identity. To Sikander's chagrin, nothing seemed particularly out of the ordinary. There was no mess, no blood, no signs of a struggle. Even the rug beneath the corpse, a Savonnerie, he noted absently, was unwrinkled.

Out of the periphery of his vision, he noticed that Commissioner French and O'Dwyer had followed him into the room. They stood by the door, whispering to each other, eyeing him with nearly identical expressions of smirking contempt. Frowning, Sikander bit back his irritation and finally approached the corpse. Rather than examining it directly, he came to a stop behind it, some two feet away. Closing his eyes, he tried to clear his mind, to sharpen his ephemeral senses to a razor's edge, seeking that elusive state of clarity that Fichte and the German Idealists had described as higher intuition.

"What on earth is he doing?" the commissioner's voice exclaimed behind him. "Is he working some kind of *fakir's* trick?"

"This is a waste of time, I declare," O'Dwyer's deep bass chimed in. "The man is a *poseur*."

"Shhh, don't distract him." Malik Umar spoke this time, offering encouragement. "Go on, old boy, work your magic."

Sikander took a deep breath, trying his mightiest to ignore their carping. As always, the usual desolation he felt when faced with a corpse gripped him. How could he not but surrender to tragedy? Just yesterday, this had been a living, breathing human being, but now, all that remained was rotting meat, all its dreams and hopes snuffed out, extinguished in one fell stroke.

This melancholy did not last long. Very quickly, it was transformed into a familiar tingling, the excitement that always seized him when he was about to begin an investigation, followed by a pang of regret as he chastised himself for being such a ghoul.

Delicately, like a sculptor making his first cut, Sikander reached out and turned the body until it faced him. She was little more than a girl, really, not more than nineteen, her arms still soft with pubescent fat. In life, she must have been very beautiful. He could detect some vestiges of that beauty, since below the neck she was entirely naked, except for a belt of gold *mohurs* surrounding her hips. Her breasts were perfect, dark-nippled and as voluptuous as ripe mangoes, her stomach taut, crowned by a pearl ensconced in her navel, her waist so tiny that he could have encompassed it with one hand, and her legs supple, as strong and slender as willow branches.

Above the shoulders, sadly, she was a monstrosity. The pashmina scarf bound around her neck had bitten deep into her throat, leaving her face suffused, bloated to almost twice its size, her mouth twisted open in a raw scream of horror. From between her teeth, her tongue protruded, swollen as fat as a slug. But it was her eyes that made Sikander gasp, so filled with accusation that, involuntarily, he broke his own cardinal rule and reached out to gently ease shut her eyelids, to block out the recrimination in those awful, staring eyes.

Unexpectedly, the balsamic scent of whatever unguents she had used to oil her body filled his nostrils, combining with the faint scent of putrefaction to make him feel more than a little dizzy. Sikander let out a groan. From his breast pocket, he extracted a small pen knife, and folded it open with a click. Stepping forward, he wrapped one arm around the girl's waist, hefting her meager weight easily, even as he stretched out and sawed the sharp blade back and forth, until the scarf's woolen material came apart and she sagged down into his embrace.

As reverently as a priest performing last rites, he eased the girl's corpse to the ground. Shrugging off his coat, he draped it across her face to obscure her grotesque features, before straightening up and swiveling to face the trio of gentlemen who had been watching him expectantly.

"I have seen all that I need to," he declared, shaking his head sorrowfully.

"What on earth?" Commissioner French erupted. "Aren't you going to poke around a bit? Take some samples and so forth. Isn't that what you detective fellows are supposed to do?"

"What a crock!" O'Dwyer scoffed, making no effort to hide his dubiety. "They say you are a veritable magician, Mr. Singh. Go on then, dazzle the lot of us, if you can, unless of course you're a rank pretender."

O'Dwyer's words stung at him, making his hackles rise. He knew it was silly to take such obvious bait, but for once, suppressing his better instincts, Sikander decided to show off a bit, if for no other reason than to put the ponderous Irishman in his place.

"Very well, if you insist! The girl is about eighteen, of Kashmiri origin, and she was very definitely murdered."

"Are you certain of that?" The Commissioner interjected. "She could have killed herself, yes?"

"No, she was strangled, of that I am certain. Not more than ten hours ago, most likely a little before dawn this very morning. Also, the killer is a man, not more than thirty-five years old, between five-foot-eight and six feet tall. He is a meat-eater, I reckon, most likely either a soldier or sailor with broad shoulders and a strong build. Also, he was her lover. I am almost definite on that."

This analysis was greeted by a stunned silence, broken only by a loud snort from the commissioner.

"Good God, are you making all that up?" He gave Sikander a piercing scowl. "Would you care to explain yourself, Mr. Singh? How have you arrived at these outlandish conclusions?"

"I doubt you would understand me, Mr. French. You don't seem terribly bright."

"Oh, do stop needling the commissioner, Sikander," Malik Umar chimed in, unable to hide a smile.

"Please, Mr. Singh," O'Dwyer added, "for those of us who are amateurs, would you kindly elaborate?"

"Very well! Let us begin with the fact that she was strangled. That much is really quite obvious from the livid ligature marks circling her throat and neck. If you take a careful look, beneath the striations left by the pashmina, you will see the imprint of a man's fingers, left behind when the killer throttled the life from her. Even though he most likely strung her up precisely to disguise what had truly occurred, thankfully he could not erase every trace left behind."

"As for the time of death, the lividity of the girl's flesh suggests she was killed within the last twenty hours, and since her skin is still supple and rigor mortis has only now begun to set in, I can conclude that she died very recently, most likely early this morning."

"Now, to the identity of her killer. It had to be a man who throttled her. She was young, in her prime and considerably healthy, judging by her physique, which means the killer had to be someone larger and stronger than her, not a woman. And of course, we must consider the violence of the crime. The imprints around her neck are quite widely spaced, which indicates the killer had large hands and a strong grip, which makes me believe he was either a sailor or a soldier, someone with fingers tempered to steel, whether from handling ropes or reins. Also, the poor child's neck was broken, not just in one place, but two, which in turn suggests that the person who did this is uncommonly strong, and most likely a young man. Strangulation is a crime of heat and passion. Old men rarely act on such savage impulses, and even then, they are rarely quite so vicious."

"As for the inference to his height, she is almost five and a half feet tall. However, the inclination of the marks around her neck are angled downwards, which suggests that her murderer was taller. This is what I think happened. I believe that our killer overpowered her, and while he was throttling the life from her, he lifted her bodily off the ground, and that is when her neck broke, killing her instantly. Do you see?"

"But how did you conclude that he was her lover?" O'Dwyer inquired.

"That was a piece of carefully calculated guesswork," Sikander replied. "I deduced that from the fact that she is in a state of *déshabille*, and because I can still smell the sour scent of musk and sweat on her, faint, yes, but perceptible to a nose as discerning as my own."

"Pure conjecture!" the Commissioner growled. "Perhaps she was undressing when the killer took her by surprise. Maybe he despoiled her, eh? Some sort of lust-crazed madman? Did you even consider that?"

"Ah, but then where are the defensive wounds? There are no bruises on her wrists and arms, no blood under her fingernails, which can only mean that she did not fight him. That suggests that the killer was known to her, that she felt she had naught to fear from him—a belief, alas, which I think was the very thing that led to her murder."

O'Dwyer looked about ready to offer argument, to mount another diatribe, but when he realized that there were no refutations he could offer without looking foolish, he snapped his mouth shut, with such speed that his jaw clicked audibly.

Commissioner Lee French was not quite so graceful. "That is all well and good, but nothing that a good policeman could not have pieced together as well. Besides, you don't have a shred of evidence, do you, not one clue not a single lead to chase down?"

"No, I do not." Even as the commissioner puffed up, Sikander gave him a stiff smile. "However, there is a very good reason for that. The girl was not killed here, in this room."

"What makes you so sure of that?"

"Have you heard of Locard's Principle, Mr. French? An interesting fellow, Monsieur Locard. I met him while I was studying in France. As a matter of fact, he was Alexandre Lacassagne's assistant for some years. He postulated a theory to me once, that every contact leaves behind a trace, that wherever a criminal steps, whatever he touches, whatever he leaves behind, even unconsciously, can be found by an observant investigator and used ultimately as a silent witness against him."

"What does that have to do with this poor girl's murder?"

"Patience, Commissioner! Just take a look around. Do you see anything out of place? Any signs of a struggle? A girl was strangled to death. Where are the torn tapestries, the broken vases, the shattered furniture? This place is absolutely pristine, is it not?"

The commissioner shrugged. "Maybe the killer cleaned up after himself, and got rid of any incriminating evidence!"

"No, I doubt he had the time." Sikander's jaw hardened. "I suspect that she was killed elsewhere and that the body was moved to this location. But why this particular tent? Why this particular camp? Those are the real questions we must find the answers to."

"Why would anyone want to embarrass the King and ruin the Durbar?"

Chapter Five

A stilted silence greeted this declaration, broken only when Malik Umar clapped his hands in approbation.

"Well, that was quite impressive, I must say, Sikander! I can see your reputation is truly well deserved!"

Unfortunately, judging by the identically sour expressions that continued to decorate both Commissioner French's and Mr. O'Dwyer's faces, they did not seem to share the same opinion.

"I still say we just sweep this whole mess under the rug, Mr. Khan," O'Dwyer said, "and be done with it. We cannot afford to run the risk of having Mr. Singh blundering about, not with the King's arrival so imminent."

"I have to agree," the commissioner chimed in. "Frankly, who is going to give a damn if a whore turns up dead, just as long as we dump the body somewhere far away?"

Sikander clenched his teeth, scowling. It was a commonly held misconception, particularly by the British, that *nautch* girls were little more than prostitutes. This was an egregious and pejorative misconception. In reality, *nautch* girls, especially the *tawaifs* of Lucknow and Lahore, were courtesans of the highest quality, skillful performers educated from a young age in not merely the art of *ada* and *andaz*, but also *tehfeez* and *tehmeez*, culture and etiquette.

It was a tradition as ancient as India itself, one that had

traveled to the subcontinent from Persia via the Silk Road, reaching the peak of fashion during the age of the Mughals. Legend had it that a *nautch* girl named Anarkali had very nearly managed to cause Akbar to lose his throne, driving his son Jahangir, who became besotted with her beauty, to open revolt. Another legend was that of Rupmati, who had risen to become the queen of Malwa, possessed of such legendary grace that Akbar had invaded her husband Baz Bahadur's kingdom just so that he could watch her perform. In the Punjab, too, there had been no shortage of famous, or rather, infamous *nautch* girls. Maharaja Ranjit Singh had taken not one but two to be his consorts, the fabled Moran Sarkar and of course, Jindan, the Messalina of India, who had hocked the Sikh Empire to the English.

In many ways, they were the Indian equivalent of Japanese *geishas*, trained to captivate and entrance men, not merely titillate them. It was common practice in Nawabi India for the wealthy to send their sons to their salons, not to be taught the ways of lovemaking, but to be educated in courtly manners and acquire good taste. It was the *nautch* girls who were the purveyors of art and culture in the Urdu world, the proponents of music and poetry. In fact, it was at their *mehfils* that the golden age of *shayeri* had flourished, at least until the English had annexed Avadh. After that, the tradition had been condemned because it clashed with Victorian morality, and the *tawaif* class had acquired a seedy reputation, defamed as whores and tarts of the lowest order, branded as *bayederes*, or street dancers, as the Portuguese called them.

It was precisely this regressive attitude Sikander saw writ upon the commissioner's face, a leering contempt that set his teeth on edge.

"She is not a whore," he growled. "Her name is Zahra, and she is a dancer."

"How could you possibly know that?" O'Dwyer offered Sikander a suspicious frown.

"I saw her perform once a long time ago," Sikander murmured absently, still looking down at the dead girl's lifeless form apprehensively. "She was exquisite, a rare and beautiful thing."

"What difference does it make? Whore or dancing girl, let's just bury her and be done with the whole mess." Commissioner French mimed washing his hands.

"Lord Hardinge was quite explicit about his orders," Malik Umar responded, making no effort to hide his disgust at such a duplicitous suggestion. "He wished for Sikander here to investigate, and that is exactly what I intend to let him do. If you have any disagreement, then I suggest you take it up with the Viceroy directly."

"I shall do just that," the commissioner sniffed, giving Sikander one last black look before storming away.

O'Dwyer made to follow, but not before approaching Sikander first. "This is not over, Mr. Singh, mark my words. As it says in the book of Isaiah, 'According to their deeds, so He will repay, Wrath to His adversaries, recompense to His enemies.' Remember that!"

"Don't pay O'Dwyer any attention," Malik Umar interjected as the Irishman strode off. "He is an Ulsterman, and they are all full of biblical wrath and judgment. It's all just hot air. Come along, let's get out of this morbid place."

He led Sikander back into the sumptuous parlor where he had met the Viceroy, pausing to pull a chased gold flask from his pocket. Uncapping it, he brought it to his lips with a most ungentlemanly eagerness.

"I did not take you for a drinking man, Malik Umar."

"On most days, I am not. But today, after what we just saw in there," he shivered, "I cannot help but need a bit of liquid courage to fortify my resolve."

He proffered the flask to Sikander, who accepted it, taking a quick swig. To his surprise, it turned out to be a very decent anisette, a Del Mono, he guessed from the rich depth of flavor.

Ordinarily, Sikander did not enjoy sweet liqueurs, but this once, he found himself relishing the warmth that spread through his chest. It went a long way toward dispelling the icy sorrow that had seized his heart when he had gazed down at Zahra's face.

"Do have some more!" Malik Umar said. "Don't be shy!"

Sikander obliged readily, taking another, more generous sip as Malik ushered them to a nearby chaise.

"You said you knew the girl. Would you care to elaborate?"

Sikander closed his eyes.

"*Zahra* means blossom in Persian, did you know?" Tiredly, he massaged the bridge of his nose, assailed by a welter of disparate memories. A slender throat, the sinuous curve of a neck, a naïve laugh as brittle as freshly blown glass, the melodious clink of jeweled anklets, a fan of dull ochre blood sprayed across a red terra-cotta tile, two pale brown eyes, once bright, then dead, unseeing.

"It was a long time ago," he exhaled. "Before Paris, before my father died, before my mother was…" his voice caught in his throat, the wound of her loss still raw, in spite of the passage of time "…before she was taken from us so unexpectedly. I had just returned to India after rather an unfulfilling sojourn at Eton. One evening, I had become rather intoxicated in the company of a very intoxicating barmaid only to be caught by one of the beaks trying to sneak her into my garret, a misunderstanding that had ended with me being sent down for ungentlemanly behavior.

"My father was not at all pleased, as you can imagine." Sikander shuddered. To say that the *Burra* Maharaja had been displeased was an utter understatement. His father had threatened to cut him off, and the only thing that had prevented him from whipping Sikander with a belt was the intervention of his mother, who had come to his rescue, as she had always done whenever he got into an adolescent scrape.

"I was a very different person back then, Malik Umar, just a boy, all knees and garters, you understand, filled with the fire and madness of youth. I was constantly getting into trouble. I confess I searched it out with the eagerness that only a child who believes he is indestructible possesses. All that has changed now. I would like to say that I am wiser, but the truth, I fear, is that caution comes with the crown. I have no stomach for controversy any longer, even though often enough it manages to seek me out.

"Anyway, my father was determined not to let me out of his sight. As a result, rather than being permitted to travel to Simla to attend the season, I was forced to accompany him to Bikaner, to Gajner for the annual grouse hunt hosted by Maharaja Ganga Singh."

Sikander's smile evaporated. "There were six of us there that year, my father and myself, Rajinder Singh of Patiala, Jagatjit of Kapurthala of course, who was banned from Simla after that mess he got into with Curzon's sister, the Sahibzada of Malerkotla, and the young prince of Alwar."

The moue of distaste that flickered across his features as he said the last of those names was reflected on Malik Umar's face.

"Do you mean Jey Singh?"

"Yes!" Sikander's frown deepened. Jey Singh, now the Maharaja of Alwar, had been one year behind them in school. Even back then, he had been legendary for his unnatural inclinations, overly fond of torturing animals, dogs and cats mainly, but once Sikander had caught him in the act of ripping the wings off a crow. Sikander believed himself to be a difficult man to scare, but he had never forgotten the expression on Jey Singh's face as he had torn that poor creature to pieces. It had been horrifying, a rapture, like something one saw on the face of a worshiper in a church.

Once again, he found himself assailed by the bitter after-taste of memories half-forgotten, as sour in his mouth as milk that has turned. A child's face, red, streaked by tears, her mouth open, screaming, but no sound to be heard but a broken click-ing. A hand, each finger curled into a question mark. A matted strand of hair from which curved a rivulet of blood, so unbearably red.

"Was that was where you met this girl, in Bikaner?" Malik Umar asked, interrupting the macabre drift of his thoughts.

"In a manner of speaking," Sikander took a deep breath, struggling to regain his composure. "It turned out that was a bad year for grouse and after a week of shooting at everything from vultures to monkeys, we were all about bored enough to scream. That was when Jagatjit decided that what we needed was some culture to divert us."

"Oh, God!" Malik Umar rolled his eyes. Obviously, he knew enough of Kapurthala's reputation to understand that whatever entertainments he had come up with had to have been nothing short of scandalous.

"Exactly!" Sikander chuckled. "In typical Jagatjit fashion, he sent off for a coterie of dancing girls, and when they arrived, we were treated to what turned out to be quite a dramatic evening."

His eyes misted over once more. "One of them, the lead performer, she was quite famous at the time. A Watul gypsy who performed by the name of Wazeeran. Perhaps you may have heard of her?"

Malik Umar shook his head.

"It doesn't matter." Sikander smiled wistfully. "She was spectacular, as pale and ethereal as a wisp of moonlight, barely taller than a child but with the kind of statuesque figure that moves poets to epiphany. And those eyes! I did not realise what enticing really means until I gazed into those eyes of hers." His shoulders quivered as an involuntary spasm of embarrassment gripped him. "I am not the sort of man who considers paying for a woman's affections, Malik Umar, but for once, when I set eyes on Wazeeran, even I was tempted. I admit it."

"That night, we were treated to her signature performance, which was a snake dance, performed in the gypsy style. It was quite magnificent, watching her swirl and shimmer and sway, clad in six layers of veiled silk and translucent muslin, almost as intoxicating as a drug. About halfway through the show, her daughter came out and joined her, this little imp of a thing who could not have been more than four or five years old, leaping and prancing about with great *chutzpah*. She was the mongoose, you see, just as Wazeeran was a cobra. They had rehearsed it until it was quite electrifying. First one would rush forward, and immediately the other would back away, and then the reverse, back and forth, as blindingly quick as any real snake and mongoose locked in battle."

"And that child was?" Malik Umar bobbed his neck in the direction of room where the dead girl lay, seeking affirmation.

Sikander nodded. "When the performance was over, very briefly, I contemplated making an overture toward Wazeeran. We all did, I think, but I couldn't go through with it. Perhaps it was my natural reticence, or the fact that she was accompanied by a child, but I decided to retire for the evening and drown my amorous intentions in a jeroboam of Dom Pérignon.

"A little after four in the morning, I was roused by a piercing scream. Naturally, I rushed to see what had happened. It seemed to have emanated from the servants' quarters, and when I reached there, to my dismay, I found..." He paused, his voice catching in his throat. "It was Wazeeran. She had been murdered most brutally. I think she had been ravaged first. Her clothes were torn, and she was naked from the waist down." His voice remained quite deadpan, as if he was reading aloud from a report. "The list of her other injuries was really quite shocking. Both her wrists had been bound, and she had been beaten quite severely, her cheekbones and her jaw cracked in three places. There were knife cuts all over her arms and face, which led me to believe that the killer had tortured her for some time before finally slitting her neck and leaving her to bleed to death.

"We found the child hiding nearby, inside a trunk filled with stage props and costumes. I believe that Wazeeran must have secreted her there, and that the poor thing had witnessed the whole sordid event, crouched there, watching her mother being tortured and beaten and then murdered." He shivered. "I tried to question her, but she had quite lost her voice, stricken dumb from the trauma of what she had endured."

The disgust on Malik Umar's face matched Sikander's own. "Who was the murderer? Did you manage to track him down?"

Sikander let out an anguished groan. "That's just it. I never did find out. Don't get me wrong. I dearly wanted to chase down who had killed her. With every breath in my chest, I wanted to apprehend the culprit who had wreaked such horrors on Wazeeran, if for no other reason than to protect the daughter from his cruel attentions. Sadly, who would let a nineteen-year-old carry out a murder investigation? I protested, I begged, I even tried to threaten to go to the press, but it was all to no avail. Ganga Singhji, who has no stomach for even a hint of scandal, wanted the matter swept under the rug immediately. By the time the sun rose, his men had disposed of the corpse, the dance troupe had been paid handsomely to hold their tongues and packed off back to Lahore, and this poor creature," he let out a weary sigh, "she was long gone."

Grimacing, he rose and crossed to the door that led to the inner chamber, his features distorted by an expression of pure regret. "That was the last time I saw her, but now, in a way, I cannot help but feel I am to blame that she is lying here today, such a broken wreck."

"It most certainly is not! How could you have prevented her demise, Sikander? You are only human, after all."

"I could have saved her, Malik Umar. I should have tried harder. I could have rescued her from this life. I could have made sure she never became a *nautch-wali*. I could have apprehended her mother's murderer. I could have done so much, but I did not." Sikander's face contorted with guilt. "I failed her, my friend. I am responsible for her death as much as the man who actually performed the deed."

"You are being too hard on yourself, Sikander. She made her own choices. You could no more have saved her than I could."

Sikander shook his head, as stubborn as a child. "No, this is my fault, at least partially. I could not help her when I had the chance. But I promise you, I will not permit her death to go unavenged. I will find the man who killed her, I swear it, or my name is not Sikander Singh."

Chapter Six

"Very well, Sikander, I shall try to assist you as best as I can. Tell me, what do you need from me?"

"I think the first thing we must ascertain, Malik Umar, is how a *nautch* girl came to be in the royal compound in the first place. I mean, she didn't just wander in here. Someone had to have brought her here, someone with influence enough to gain access to such a closely guarded enclosure."

"Perhaps I can help with that," a voice said from behind them.

Captain Campbell stood framed in the entrance-way, wearing that annoyingly sardonic smile that Sikander had so come to loathe, even though he had known the man for a matter of hours.

"Ah, Campbell, good man! I was just about to send for you. Sikander, I take it the two of you have met."

"Indeed, we have," Sikander replied, his voice so wintry it could have frozen water to ice.

"Capital! Captain, answer the Maharaja of Rajpore's question, if you please."

"Certainly!" Campbell offered Sikander a rather an ironic salute. "You see, Your Majesty, I am the one who brought her here."

"What? You and Zahra were involved?" Sikander squawked, jumping to the most obvious conclusion.

"Oh, no!" He shook his head. "She was a gift, sir, for the King from the Maharaja of Kapurthala."

Sikander frowned, bewildered. Why on earth would Jagatjit Singh send the King of England a *nautch* girl, of all things? It was true that the Maharajas and Nawabs of India were all going a little mad trying to outdo each other offering the King Emperor the most expensive tokens of admiration they could afford, but a dancer? That was a decidedly odd choice, even given Jagatjit's picturesque reputation for eccentricity.

Campbell seemed to read his mind, because he proceeded to offer an explanation. "When the Duke of Connaught made his tour of India some years ago, he had the opportunity to watch a bevy of Kashmiri girls perform, and had been quite enchanted. As a result, months ago, while the plans for the Durbar were being finalized, the King had made a passing aside expressing his desire to witness something similar. I imagine that when the Maharaja heard about this, he purchased the *nautch* girl as a small token of his affection for the King."

It was a reasonable enough explanation, but somehow, it did not quite sit well with Sikander. Still, he realized he had no choice but to accept it at face value, at least not until he had the time to ask Jagatjit a few questions face to face.

"Tell me, Malik Umar," he asked, turning to his old classmate, "who is in charge of camp security?"

"Why, that would be me," Campbell said, butting in once again, to Sikander's vexation. He looked to Malik Umar for confirmation, and received a curt nod of affirmation in return.

"In that case, Captain Campbell, I would like to speak with whoever was the Officer of the Day yesterday. I need to know how many visitors Zahara had, and exactly who they were."

Campbell gave Sikander another of his cocksure grins. "As it happens, I anticipated just such a request. Your Majesty, Mr. Khan, would you excuse me for a moment?"

Turning, he swept out of the room, as theatrical as Iago departing the stage. Sikander rolled his eyes, and gave Malik Umar a withering frown.

"I really do not like that fellow."

"Well, that's just too bad, Sikander," Malik Umar responded with a twinkle in his eye. "It seems that you are going to be stuck with him, at least for the duration."

Sikander's frown deepened into a scowl. "Whatever do you mean?"

"I am sorry to say, my friend, that the Captain will be accompanying you on your investigations."

This declaration made Sikander sit bolt upright. "I should think not," he snarled, bristling with indignation. "I have no need for either an assistant or a babysitter, Malik Umar. I will not stand for it."

"Unfortunately, this time around, you have no choice in the matter. Lord Hardinge was quite insistent. In fact, he made that the condition for your involvement, that you have an English officer as your shadow. After all, we can't have you traipsing about through the encampments without someone to watch over you, now can we?" He offered Sikander a sarcastic smile. "Besides, don't write off Captain Campbell so quickly. I think you will find him very useful. He's quite the wag about camp, I'm told. Not only does he know damn nearly everyone, he is a very personable chap, I assure you."

"Is that so? From the way he talks and acts, I thought him a bit of a blackguard."

"Oh, no, actually, he is rather the opposite." Malik Umar leaned forward. "Surely you have heard the story of the Honorable Bastard?"

Sikander shook his head. "I have not, but do tell."

Malik Umar grinned, delighted by the prospect of sharing a bit of gossip that Sikander did not already know.

"He's a hell of a soldier. Was up for the VC during the Boer War. Won a French Legion of Honor in China, and was one of the first through the wall at Gyantse Dzong. Mentioned in regimental despatches seventeen times, which is a staggering number."

"Is that why they call him the Honorable Bastard, because of his battlefield prowess?"

"Not quite." Malik Umar lowered his voice to a conspiratorial murmur. "That particular sobriquet is because of the stories surrounding his parenthood. You see, when the Duke of Connaught was commanding the Bombay garrison, rumor has it he became rather enamored of a beautiful young Scotswoman named Hannah Campbell, the daughter of a well-to-do cotton merchant. In fact, it was said that they maintained a discreet liaison, that she was his mistress briefly until he returned to England."

"You mean to say…?"

"Yes, if the grapevine is to be believed, then our dear Captain has royal blood. Illegitimately, of course—the Duke has never acknowledged him publicly—but he is as much a Hanoverian as our new King."

"Is there any proof of that?" Sikander said, not bothering to hide his skepticism.

"Not really. Unless of course you consider the fact that he began as a humble infantry lieutenant, but was then offered a commission as a Captain in the Coldstream Guards not five years ago. Not to mention that he has been appointed the steward in charge of camp security, in spite of several finer-born and better-connected candidates. How do you think he managed to swing that honor, eh?"

Sikander scowled. As evidence went, while not one hundred percent, it was certainly persuasive. Officers of the line did not suddenly gain offers to transfer to elite regiments, especially those based in England. Not only was it highly irregular, it was a bloody expensive enterprise, to boot, and most men could never afford it, not without patronage. There were only two reasons Sikander could conceive to explain Campbell's sudden and unexpected advancement. Either the man had the greatest of good fortune, or he had powerful connections watching over him.

"Whoever his antecedents may be, I do not want or need him. I work best alone," Sikander said, his face mulish.

"This is not a request, I am afraid. Either you take Campbell, or you can return to your hotel, and Commissioner French shall be granted his wish." Malik Umar's shoulders twitched, a sympathetic shrug. "The choice is yours, Sikander."

The unequivocal tone of his voice made it clear to Sikander that he meant business. For a moment, he was tempted to call Malik Umar out, to march away and wash his hands of the whole mess. But in the end, as always, it was his curiosity that won out.

"Very well." He let out a frustrated sigh. "I'll take him, but make sure he knows to stay out of my way."

"Excellent!" Malik Umar gave him a knowing smile, as if he had been sure this was exactly how things would turn out. "Personally, I think you will be glad to have him around. I have been told he can handle himself. In fact, that was why I accepted his offer when he volunteered."

"He volunteered?" Sikander said, his lips compressing, but before Malik Umar could answer, he was cut short by the Captain's triumphant return.

"Do forgive the delay, gentlemen," Campbell said, holding open the flap of the tent behind him. "Come in, Sergeant, won't you?"

In response to this command, a soldier came marching in, high-stepping like one of the Life Guards on parade. He was a grizzled specimen, about forty years old, wearing the sash of a regimental sergeant-major. Another Scotsman, Sikander inferred, since he was clad in kilt and sporran, a member of Gordon's Highlanders, judging from the blue-and-green pattern of his tartan.

He halted opposite Sikander and Malik Umar, his hobnailed boots clattering as he came to attention. However, he did not snap out a salute, perhaps because they were natives, an omission which caused Malik Umar's cheeks to darken with obvious displeasure.

"This is Sergeant Major Macgregor," Campbell said by way of introduction. "As it happens, he was on duty yesterday, serving as the commandant of the guard."

"Ah, excellent!" Sikander said. "I have a few questions for you, Sergeant. Tell me, did the *nautch* girl Zahra have very many visitors yesterday?"

To his surprise, the man did not respond. Instead, his gaze stayed fixed straight ahead, staring blankly into the middle distance, as expressionless as a statue.

"I asked you a question, Sergeant."

Once more, the man remained obdurate, so stiff he may well have been carved of stone.

"Are you impaired in some way?" Malik Umar hissed, his temper fraying. "Answer the Maharaja, damn you."

"He will not speak to you, sir," Campbell spoke up. "He's from Selkirk, and these Souters, they are legendary for their close-mouthedness."

"Well, how am I expected to question him if he will not answer my questions?"

"Let me have a go, will you?"

Without waiting for permission, Campbell approached the sergeant.

"I am a traveler, Brother Macgregor, from the west."

The sergeant reacted to this cryptic declaration with a furrowing of his brow. "And what is it that you are seeking?" He said in a lilting brogue, breaking his silence.

"I have come east, searching for illumination."

With that, Campbell held out his left hand, splaying his fingers. After a moment's hesitation, the sergeant took it, a complicated grip where he placed his thumb between the Captain's first and second knuckles and enveloped his palm in his fist.

"What the bloody hell is going on?" Malik Umar murmured.

"The sergeant is a Mason, and so is the Captain, it seems," Sikander replied, recognizing the handshake for what it was, the greeting shared by two masters of the craft.

"See," Malik Umar said, "he is proving useful already."

The Captain released the sergeant's hand and turned to face him. "I think you will find the Sergeant slightly more cooperative now, Your Majesty."

Sikander bit back a snort, and said, "Well, Sergeant?"

"The young lady you mentioned had several official visitors. Six, to be precise."

"Would you happen to recall the identity of these visitors?"

"I recorded them in the visitors' ledger, as I was instructed to do."

"And where is this ledger now?"

"I have it right here." He held up a brown canvas-bound register, offering it to Campbell, rather than Sikander, much to the Maharaja's annoyance.

"Let's have a look." Campbell took the book and opened it, leafing through the pages slowly, biting his lower lip.

"Give it to me," Sikander growled, snapping his fingers impatiently.

"Just a moment, sir. Ah, here we are!" The Captain ran one finger down the page. "The Nizam of Hyderabad. The Maharaja of Patiala. The Maharaja of Alwar. The Maharaja of Gwalior. The Maharani of Bharatpur. And, last but not least, there was a journalist of some kind, a Mr. Urban, who had a letter of introduction from the Home Office." He let out a low whistle, proffering the book at Sikander. "That is quite a list."

"Yes," Sikander said, "it most certainly is." He scanned the page, his brow wrinkled with dismay. If these were his suspects, he thought, he was in for a thoroughly tumultuous investigation. Not only were these some of the senior-most potentates in India, but each of them could buy and sell a minor monarch like himself several times over. Frankly, he doubted he would be able to get in to see most of them, much less interrogate them as potential murderers.

Even as he mulled over how to overcome that obstacle, a pang of acid in his gut reminded him that he was missing something, something important.

"Hold on a minute," Campbell said. "Tell me, Sergeant, did the girl have any unofficial visitors?"

Sikander gave the Captain a sour look. That was the very question he had been about to ask, but the cheeky bastard had beaten him to it.

The sergeant looked reluctant to answer, his pupils widening with dismay.

"Don't worry," Campbell interjected, beating Sikander to the draw once again. "You are amongst friends here. There will be no repercussions or recriminations, I assure you."

"There was a *munshi*, sir, from the Maharaja of Kashmir. He had a letter for the young lady, which he insisted on delivering personally. There was another native as well, an elderly fellow who claimed to be her uncle, who asked to meet with her briefly. And there were two English *memsahibs*, one of whom, a young lady, insisted on speaking with her in person." The sergeant's face reddened, as if he was embarrassed, and he offered Campbell an apologetic look. "That is all I know, Captain."

"Thank you, Brother Macgregor. You have been very helpful."

He turned to Sikander, seeking his agreement.

"Yes, you may go, Sergeant. Return to your duties."

This time, the sergeant snapped out a curt salute, so crisp it could have felled a redwood. As he swiveled and marched away, Campbell let out a sigh. "Well, this is quite a pickle, isn't it? Should we consider all of the people in the register suspects, sir?"

"Perhaps," Sikander replied, pursing his lips. "We certainly cannot be sure they are not involved until we speak to each of them and ascertain why they came to see the girl."

"Well, I for one, do not envy you that task, Sikander," Malik Umar rose to his feet, stretching his back with a groan. "If you will excuse me, I will leave you to get on with it. Captain, do try not to irritate the Maharaja too much, will you? As for you, Sikander, give the lad a chance, and try not to stir up too much trouble, for once.

"Good luck, gentlemen. Now, if you will excuse me, the King, it seems, is unwilling to mount an elephant, which means I must go and find him a suitable nag to ride."

Chapter Seven

"Well, Mr. Singh," Campbell said, offering Sikander a comradely grin, "it looks like we are stuck with each other!"

The easy familiarity with which he said the word "we" rankled Sikander. There is no "we," he wanted to shout. Like the Mariner, I am burdened with you. You are the proverbial albatross around my neck.

It took all of his willpower to hold his tongue. The Captain was a difficult man to dislike, with his handsome features and affable grin, but that was exactly why Sikander found it easy to distrust the man so readily. In his experience, it was the fellows who were overly confident of themselves who turned out to be the most fickle in character. Those were the ones who always chose their interests over anyone else's, who inevitably left you hanging when push came to shove.

"So," Campbell continued, apparently immune to the antipathy being exuded from Sikander's every pore, "where would you like to begin?"

Damn the man. Why did he have to be so earnest, so enthusiastic? It was bloody well annoying. Biting back a surge of irritation, Sikander considered this question. The logical approach would be to question each of the visitors that the sergeant had mentioned, but given the lateness of the hour, he simply could not go calling on such luminaries as the Nizam and the Maharaja of Kashmir, nor could he charge in mob-handed to question Bhupinder or any of the others, not without alerting every press *wallah* west of Aden. No, that would have to wait until morning, which meant there was only one choice for him for the present.

"As I mentioned to Malik Umar, the girl was not killed here. What we must do next is locate the actual site of the murder. Tell me, Captain, where was the girl being quartered? I assume she was not being kept here, in this very tent."

"No, not at all. We had placed her in the servants' enclave, just across the compound."

"Don't tell me, man. Show me."

"Yes, of course!" Spinning on one heel, he nearly tripped in his haste to oblige Sikander. The Maharaja stifled a smile, following Campbell as he hurried back out of the reception pavilion, scurrying across the pristinely manicured lawn, before taking an abrupt left turn onto a narrow path which culminated in a small cluster of tents located directly behind the Circuit House, hidden away from plain sight in the shadow of a large water cistern. This must be where the servants were housed, Sikander assumed, for they were little more than military bell-tents laid out in a neat row.

Campbell led him to the last of the tents, a solitary grey one that seemed out of place amid its dun neighbors, as though it had been thrown up rather hastily.

"In there. That is where she was staying."

Sikander ducked into the tent. Inside, it was shadowy, cool, surprisingly quiet, the thick canvas very successfully managing to block out the hustle and bustle of camp life. Campbell was about to enter behind him, but Sikander forestalled him with a gesture.

"Give me a moment," he said. "I have a system I like to follow." Standing perfectly still, he soaked in his surroundings. The tent was small, about twelve feet by fifteen, with a peaked roof and a tarpaulin covered floor. A muslin curtain divided the space into two small rooms: a tiny reception area with a folding table and two camp chairs, and a sleeping area furnished with a low campaign bed and a chest of drawers and a lantern.

At the base of the bed, three Ross and Company steamer trunks were stacked in an untidy heap. Sikander approached them, kneeling down to examine their base, squinting with intense concentration.

"This is where she was killed."

"What makes you think that?" Campbell said from the doorway.

"The dust, Captain! Look at the dust beneath the bed and the dresser. It is the insignificant things that say the most."

"What am I supposed to be seeing?" Campbell asked, dutifully gazing where Sikander was pointing.

"Scuff marks, there and there. You can see that the furniture has been moved around. And the tarpaulin base-sheet does not quite line up properly, not like it should." He frowned. "This, I surmise, is where the girl was strangled. There was a struggle, and while the murderer tried to tidy up afterwards, I suspect he was hurried, and missed a thing or two."

"Are you sure?" Campbell sounded entirely unconvinced.

"An educated guess, but yes, I am almost certain. Just as I am certain that the killer had to be someone who knew her, or was known to her."

"What makes you say that?"

"She let him in here, didn't she? That can only mean that she knew the man, or that she did not think he would harm her."

The doubt in Campbell's voice was palpable. "I don't know, sir. I am no expert, but it all seems a bit far-fetched to me."

Sikander ignored the Captain's questioning tone.

"That is the one thing we agree about, Captain, that you are no expert." Sikander let out a sniff and rose back to his feet. "Tell me, Campbell, where is her entourage? These *nautch-wallis* always have a staff they travel with, a maid, a coterie of musicians, a guard or two. Go track them down for me, will you? I wish to have a word with them."

"Ah." Campbell's grin returned, twice as wide as before. "I am glad to say that I predicted that eventuality as well."

Bringing his thumb and forefinger to his lips, he let out a piercing whistle. A moment later, a very curious duo was ushered into the tent, herded along by none other than the taciturn sergeant.

The first was a girl, not more than fifteen, a pale wraith clad in a rather tight embroidered bodice and a loose skirt. While her figure was nicely rounded in all the appropriate places, sadly she had been cursed with exceptionally protuberant teeth, plus her eyes were placed much too far apart, rather giving her the look of a surprised frog.

The second person was a *mirasi*, Sikander guessed, an itinerant minstrel. He was certainly dressed like one. His lanky frame was draped in a red silk *kurta* and a tight mirrored silver waistcoat, with a bracelet made of bells clinking on one wrist. His age was about twenty or thereabouts and he was narrow-faced like a fox, with drooping eyes and carefully oiled hair.

"You are the maid, I am guessing," Sikander said to the girl, deciding to address her first.

She did not reply, keeping her head pointed firmly downwards, refusing to meet either his eye or the Captain's.

"Didn't you hear the Maharaja?" Campbell echoed, his voice rising several octaves. "Answer him, damn you!"

"She cannot, sahib," the boy piped up. "She is a mute. She cannot communicate in words, only with signs."

"And you understand these signs?"

"I do." The boy made a ham-handed attempt at a courtly bow. "I am Salim, master of the *tabla* and, on occasion, also the flute. I am at your service, huzoor."

"Tell me, Salim, were you the only musician in Zahra's service?"

"I was not in her service, huzoor. I am a free player, and I was contracted to perform in accompaniment with her, along with two others, a *shehnai-wala* and a *sarangi-ustad*. They are due to arrive this evening."

Sikander wrinkled his brow. It was not an uncommon practise for musicians to be contracted for a single performance,
which meant that the boy would likely be of little use as a
witness.

The girl, on the other hand, could prove to be more helpful.

"I am going to ask her several questions," Sikander said,
turning to face the maid once more, "and you will translate her
answers for me."

He held up a handful of coins, offering them to Salim the
musician, who accepted them eagerly.

"As you command, Your Majesty. I am at your service."

"I want a verbatim translation. Word for word. Is that clear?"

"Of course!" Salim replied with a wounded expression, as if
he were horrified that Sikander would assume he was anything
less than honest.

"You are Zahra's maid, yes?"

The girl nodded, accompanied by a gesture of affirmation
that needed no translation.

"How long have you served her?"

"Several months," Salim translated as the girl gesticulated.
"I was taken into her service when her last contract ran out.
My cousin served her before that, and she recommended me
because of my skill at braiding hair."

"Tell me, was your mistress involved with anyone?"

"Involved, sir?" Her fingers danced out in reply, feigning
confusion.

"Did she have a gentleman caller?" Sikander said, fascinated
by the nimble intricacy of the girl's gestures. "A lover?"

The girl blushed, a deep crimson. "How can I answer that?"
This time, though, there was the slightest hesitation, an imperceptible tremor to her motions that told Sikander that she was
hiding something quite as loudly as if she had shouted it out.

"Come now, my dear, you are not telling me the whole
truth. You servants, you see and hear everything. Your mistress
was a beautiful woman, and I doubt she led a life of celibacy.

And let us be honest. There is no way your mistress could have taken a lover without you being aware of it." He fixed her with a stern look. "Stop trying to protect her. She is gone, and unless you want her murderer to go free, you must tell me everything you know, the unvarnished truth."

The girl blanched, and then shook her head. "There was a man, I think," she sighed. "The mistress seemed much happier lately, like she was in love. And she told me, a few days ago, that she would soon be leaving this life and settling down, and promised to take me with her."

"Who was he? Was he a native, or an *Angrez*?"

"I do not know his identity, sir. I never met him. The mistress was very discreet."

Sikander bit back a curse. It would have been too easy if the girl had known who Zahra's mystery lover was. "When was the last time you saw your mistress?"

Again, the girl wavered slightly, darting a nervous glance first at Salim, and then quite surprisingly, toward Sergeant Macgregor before shyly answering with her hands.

"Yesterday, sahib," the musician interjected, "just after two. I can corroborate that. We went to the *badshashi mela* together to see the acrobats."

He gave the girl a nod, as if to insinuate the two of them were involved. Sikander raised an inquiring brow, and she flushed, confirming his suspicions.

"What time did you return?"

"Very late, huzoor," the boy replied too quickly, "after dark."

Something about his manner struck Sikander as much too glib. "Is what he is saying true?" he asked the girl.

Rather than replying, once again, she turned to the musician. Her fingers blurred through a rapid sequence of signs, and she moaned, a shrill half-sound, as if to signify her frustration.

"What did she say?"

"She agrees with me, huzoor," the boy insisted.

"That is not what she said," Sikander growled. "As it happens, I can read enough of the signs to deduce that much."

The Captain bunched his fists menacingly and took one half step forward. Salim backed away, but to Sikander's surprise, his eyes shifted to the sergeant, giving him a wide-eyed look, utterly brimming with desperation.

"What are you hiding, Salim? And how is the sergeant involved in this?"

"Help me, sahib," Salim squealed at Macgregor. "You promised us we would be safe."

He fell to his knees, starting to blubber like a child caught cheating. "Forgive me, huzoor. It is not my fault. He forced us. We had no choice."

Both Sikander and Campbell turned to face Macgregor, who looked about ready to bolt.

"What is the meaning of this, Macgregor?" Campbell hissed.

The Scotsman hung his head in shame. "I fear I have not been entirely honest with you. Something else happened yesterday involving the young lady, something I did not mention to you earlier." He wrung his hands, his face drawn into a piteous grimace. "There was a private performance, sir, where the young lady danced for several gentlemen. I was assigned to arrange it, and commanded to keep it a secret."

"What? Who were these gentlemen?"

"I am reluctant to reveal their identities, sir." He gave Sikander a despairing look. "They can destroy me in the blink of an eye."

"If you do not tell me their names," Sikander snarled, "I will destroy you, I assure you of that. I shall have you stripped of your rank and clapped into irons if you do not tell us every last thing you know, damn you!"

The sergeant blanched, but remained obdurate. "I cannot help you," he bleated. "They are too powerful."

"Hold on a minute," Captain Campbell said. "I think I know who he is protecting. There is only one group of gentlemen who could scare someone like our sergeant here quite so thoroughly." He turned to Macgregor. "You don't have to say a word, Sergeant. Just nod if I am correct. Tell me, are you speaking of the Guppies? Are they the ones who had Zahra stage a private *nautch* last evening?"

Macgregor remained stock still, as rigid as a golem for a long minute, until finally, he gave the slightest dip of his chin, a tremor so reluctant it was nearly imperceptible.

"And who, pray tell, are these Guppies?" Sikander asked Campbell, as the Captain turned to him, beaming triumphantly.

"Oh, there are six or seven of them. Boy Hardinge and of course Prince Battenberg, and an assortment of well-born hangers-on. They are the boys about town, the *beau monde* of the Durbar, as it were."

"But the Guppies? I don't understand."

"Ah, of course! Let me explain. They are the sons of powerful men, you see, the big fish, the scions who will inherit the reins of power and steer the Empire one day." His voice sounded bitter. "That makes them the little fish, hence the Guppies. They are a raucous, madcap bunch, and have been raising holy hell these last few days, running as wild as a pack of jackals without their parents to rein them in."

"Well then let us go and have a chat with these little fish of yours right now, shall we?" Sikander dusted his hands, struggling to restrain his excitement. "Where do you surmise we can find them at this late hour? The Club perhaps? Or the Viceregal Camp?"

"Actually, sir, I think they shall be in the Old City. That is where they go to play cards each evening."

"Excellent! Then it is to the Old City we shall go as well, and with the greatest of haste."

"One moment, sir! What about Macgregor? What shall I do with him?"

"I don't really care," Sikander said with a snort. "At last, we have a lead, and a very proper one at that."

Chapter Eight

Despite having spent a good deal of time in England, both as a student and as an adult, there were still a great many things about the British which Sikander found extremely bewildering—their reluctance to bathe every day, for one, and their refusal to drink tea without milk and sugar. The way they seemed to become ever more polite as they grew angry, and their fascination with baked beans and roast beef, not to mention their constant preoccupation with the weather. But if there was one thing that truly confounded him, it was their peculiarly adjustable sense of morality. Take the British attitude toward gambling, which was quite as double a standard as their acceptance of prostitution. While the Church considered it a venial sin to gamble, with priests preaching eternal damnation from their pulpits for any who dared to make a wager, amongst the *beau monde* in London, particularly the younger generation, gambling was a way of life. In fact, amongst certain circles of the aristocracy, a man was not considered a gentleman until he knew how to gracefully lose at cards.

In India, the state of affairs was not much different. While wagering was, of course, forbidden within the cantonments, the English authorities had been quick to realise that soldiers needed to indulge themselves, to blow off steam, so to speak, and as a result, wherever a British encampment was to be found, a host of bordellos and gaming dens could be sure to be doing a roaring trade nearby.

In the case of the Durbar, the planning commission had been quite stymied as to how to manage such extracurricular activities. With such a large number of visitors gathered in the same place, close to a hundred thousand people, it was certain that the festive atmosphere would attract more than the usual number of charlatans, gamblers, and swindlers. There was obviously no way to prevent it, but the authorities had deemed that if such goings-on were permitted to occur openly in public, it would be offensive to Their Majesties. As a result, a Viceregal Proclamation had been widely circulated, prohibiting all gambling, with the exception of backgammon, within the Durbar camps, and banning the consumption of liquor except at mess halls and clubs.

All this edict had managed to achieve was the creation of a shadowy enclave some miles to the south, very near the Ajmeri Gate. It was here that the Cimmerian arts of dusk were being practised and purveyed by the whores and cardsharps who had set up shop and were doing brisk business catering to the many visitors who had come from far and wide to view the King's grand State entry. This was what locals had come to describe picturesquely as the Kala Bazaar, the Market of the Night.

It was to this haven of disrepute that Major Campbell led Sikander.

Their destination was tucked away deep at the heart of the maze of gullies adjoining the Chandni Chowk. Here an enterprising Jew named Roger Solomon, once a waiter at White's in London, had rented a *kothi* and founded his own version of a British gentleman's establishment, the curiously named Golden Bough.

Though dusk had long since descended, the streets of Shahjahanabad were still crowded. A festive mood seemed to have seized the city in anticipation of the King's arrival. Every corner, every *chowk*, was teeming with people, a restless throng of soldiers and street-vendors and tourists and traders and hawkers and pickpockets. As a result, they were forced to abandon the Standard not far from the Lahori Gate, and make the last quarter mile of their journey on foot.

From the outside, the Golden Bough seemed innocuous, a rickety two-storey building that looked like it would collapse if buffeted by a stiff breeze. The only remarkable detail about the place was its door, painted a garish shade of red, as carmine as a *traje de flamenca*.

"This is where we will find the Guppies," Major Campbell said. "I am sure of it."

Inside, Sikander could not help but be a touch disappointed by what greeted him. He had expected a tavern-like atmosphere, but this place was as squalid as a dockyard hell, with sawdust floors and bare brick walls and dim lighting that did little to hide the general air of disrepute. A musty fug hung in the air, the atmosphere thick with cheap tobacco smoke. There was no furniture. Instead, the patrons, who were largely native *sepoys*, squatted on their haunches, shouting and arguing raucously each time a pair of dice was rolled.

"Follow me," Campbell said, and elbowed through the crowd, threading his way toward an exit at the back of the room.

"Through here," he explained, pulling back the thick curtain.

Now this is more like it, Sikander thought as he stepped through and found himself standing in a handsomely appointed lounge. Someone had gone to a great deal of trouble to try to recreate the very epitome of a Victorian gentleman's club, one of those exalted establishments surrounding Hanover Square. The floors were carpeted with Turkish rugs, the walls festooned with imitation Gobelin tapestries, and overhead, a mural depicted what seemed to be Zeus, Poseidon, and Hades casting lots in the heavens.

There was, of course, a bar, an oak-paneled expanse in one corner, but most of the space was dominated by an array of gaming tables. On the right, they were dedicated to backgammon and hazard, but on the left, there were several spirited card games under way, mainly whist and faro.

"There they are!" Campbell whispered, coming up beside him. He made a faint bob of his head, nodding toward a private table in the far corner of the room, tucked away behind a birchwood-and-silk screen.

Sikander crossed to the bar, seeking a better vantage point.

"Do you know how to make a Bijou?" He asked the bartender, a tall Goan with a slim moustache and a receding hairline.

"I am afraid not, sir," the man replied.

"Take three equal parts of Gordon's, Cinzano, and Chartreuse and mix them up well. Stirred, not shaken, and serve it up in a coupe glass with a twist of lemon."

"Very good, sir!" He turned to the Captain. "And for you?"

Captain Campbell grinned, as if to suggest he admired Sikander's style. "I will have the same."

Leaving the bartender to get to work, Sikander transferred his attention back to the Englishmen surrounding the table Campbell had indicated, studying them intently. They seemed little more than boys, really, children play-acting at being all grown up, laughing and braying and having a gay old time without a care in the world.

"What can you tell me about them?"

"The tall one is the leader." Campbell nodded at the man seated at the center of the table, a lean, elegantly proportioned fellow with a supercilious expression on his face that made Sikander dislike him immediately. "George Battenberg, the King's second cousin. Rather a pompous sort, really. He thinks very highly of himself, and is said to be somewhat of a genius, a fact he is only too quick to tell you. And, oh yes, he has quite a collection of vintage erotica, I believe."

"Now how could you possibly know that?"

"I have found that even the wildest of rumors, sir," Campbell retorted, "are almost always based on a kernel of truth. Anyway, on to the large fellow next to him, hanging on his every word…" He pointed at a broad-shouldered specimen standing in Battenberg's shadow. "That is George Cholmondeley, the Earl of Rocksavage. He is here as one of the Viceroy's aides, but spends most of his time playing tennis or chasing after officers' wives. Curiously enough, he is a bit of an expert on penmanship, I have heard."

"The Corinthian standing behind him…" Campbell looked at the young man leaning against a nearby pillar, a handsome fellow wearing an expression of practiced boredom. "…is Boy Hardinge, the Viceroy's elder son. A smart fellow, but the only things he cares about are the cut of his suit, and who is buying his next drink. A disappointment to his father, in more ways than one."

"Those two," he said indicating a similar-looking pair standing off to the left, both with matching pale hair, both wearing lieutenant's bars, "are the Pelham brothers, the sons of the Earl of Yarborough. The one on the right is Sackville, a good fellow, really, though he drinks rather too much. The other is the elder, Charles. He was just married recently, and if rumor is to be believed, the wife is quite a shrew, which is why he spends every waking hour either at the club or here, gambling away his dowry."

"The bulldog on the left is Grenville Peek." Campbell pointed at a squat fellow with a bushy unkempt moustache. "He's a bit of a nonentity. Said to be a hell of a soldier, a proper Wellesley in the making, but lately, he has been reduced to being a hanger-on with the swish set. A nasty specimen after a couple of drinks, from what I have heard, who likes to use his fists as often as his tongue."

"And that," Campbell hissed, indicating the last of the crowd, a tall, ugly goblin with protuberant ears and uneven teeth and the look of a rat, wearing the insignia of the Skinner's Horse regiment, "is the infamous Fruity Metcalfe. He is the worst kind of sycophant, very chummy with the horse and hound set, makes sure he shows up wherever the action is. They say there isn't a sin in the Good Book that old Fruity has not mastered."

Campbell turned to Sikander, giving him a hesitant smile. "Be very careful, Your Majesty. I know these chaps. They have no fear of consequences, of recriminations. They believe themselves untouchable, and have never been taught otherwise. That makes them very, very dangerous. Do you understand?"

Sikander was curiously touched by his concern.

"Don't you worry, Campbell. The day I cannot handle a bunch of overbred brats, I shall abdicate my throne and go into exile."

The bartender chose that moment to return with their cocktails. Sikander picked up the proffered coupe and took a hesitant sip. Campbell aped him, his eyes widening with amazed delight.

"That's bloody astonishing."

"It's not bad," Sikander agreed. "It could use a touch more of the bitters, but a very passable effort. Well done!" He generously tipped the bartender a golden coin, and the man's face split into a beatific smile.

"Come," Sikander said, taking another sip of his cocktail, "let us go and introduce ourselves."

He led the way, coming to a stop a few meters away from the table. By the look of it, the Guppies were in the middle of a spirited round of faro. Judging by the heap of coins stacked in front of him, it was Battenberg who was winning, and by a sizable margin. But was that luck, or skill, or something altogether more iniquitous at play? Rather than barging in like a rhinoceros, Sikander spared a moment to study the game. It did not take him long to comprehend exactly what was going on. The dealer, who was the gargoyle named Metcalfe, was rigging the deck, making sure that Battenberg always got the best cards. He was actually bloody good at it, skilled enough at sleight of hand not to get caught dealing from the bottom of the deck, but Sikander, with his trained eye, saw it soon enough. What he did not see, though, was any sign that Battenberg knew what was going on, which made him wonder if it was Battenberg who was cheating, or Metcalfe who was letting him win.

Without asking permission, Sikander pulled out a chair and sat down at the table. The Guppies all reacted differently. The leader, Battenberg, offered him a cool grin, while the brow of his large shadow, Cholmondeley, darkened with furious outrage. Boy Hardinge looked him up and down, before letting out a curt sniff. The Pelham brothers looked equally offended, and Grenville Peek merely glared at him, an evaluative frown, like a soldier surveying the enemy for the first time. As for Fruity Metcalfe, he never stopped smiling. It was rather unnerving, but Sikander noticed his eyes remained cold, as hard as agates.

"Hello, gentlemen. I was hoping we could have a bit of a chat."

"Oh, go away, Blackie," Battenberg exclaimed, not even bothering to look up from his cards, "and take the bastard with you!"

"Ha ha!" Metcalfe chimed in, "Blackie, Blackie, be gone."

Immediately, a spate of sniggers broke out, and the others took up the chant.

"Blackie, Blackie, be gone. Blackie, Blackie, be gone."

Sikander was a hard man to embarrass, but as the laughter spread around the room like wildfire, he felt his cheeks heating up. Almost all the people here were white, and they joined in readily, eager to humble any Indian, even a Maharaja. It occurred to him just how far out of his depth he was. It was different investigating a case in Rajpore, where he was as good as a god, but here, at the Durbar, he was very nearly insignificant, a minnow amidst an ocean of sharks. Even each of these guppies, little fish though they were, could swallow him whole, a realization which left him with rather a quandary. How could he question them if they were not afraid of him in the least?

How could he intimidate them? Where was the leverage?

"Enough!" Captain Campbell snarled. His voice was commanding enough to bring an end to the caterwauling, silencing the Guppies immediately.

"This is the Maharaja of Rajpore, not some *chammar*. You shall treat him with respect, is that clear?"

"Ah, the royal bastard speaks!" It was Fruity Metcalfe who spoke up. He offered Sikander a tight smirk. "Has he told you his tragic story yet? Our friend the Captain likes to pretend he has noble blood, but I think he is a charlatan. His father is probably a poxy sailor, and his mother a tuppeny whore, haw haw."

Campbell's jaw tensed, the tendons clenching so tightly that Sikander could hear them creak. Sikander could not help but feel sorry for him, accompanied by the briefest flicker of admiration. Any other man would have turned tail and run, but Campbell stood his ground, as indomitable as Gordon of Khartoum.

"Noble blood or not, I promise you, if you do not do exactly as Mr. Singh says, I will give each and every one of you a hiding you won't soon forget. Is that clear?"

"You can't talk to us like that," the Pelham brothers exclaimed almost in unison.

"You insolent dog," Cholmondeley growled, clenching his fists. "I ought to give you a whipping."

"You can certainly try, boy," Campbell gave him a cold smile, "but I think you will find I am not quite as easy to trounce as the fags at Eton."

"Hold on, lads." Boy Hardinge stepped forward, trying his very best to seem menacing, but the best he could manage was to look somewhat constipated. "Do you know who my father is?"

"Oh, I do, indeed. As it happens, I met with him not one hour ago." Sikander gave the boy an affable smile. "In fact, now that you mention it, I cannot help but wonder how he would react if it was brought to his attention that his son, his heir, has taken to patronizing places like this."

Boy Hardinge paled, his lip quivering.

"Just who do you think you are, eh?" Grenville Peek, who had maintained a taciturn silence so far, came to his rescue.

"Oh, I am a veritable nobody, just a minor king from a tiny principality of which I am sure you have never heard." Sikander let out a theatrical sigh. "I am neither as rich as the Nizam, nor quite as influential as the Gaekwad. However, if there is one thing that makes me interesting, it is that I own shares in, what is it? Four…no, five newspapers." His smile widened. "Can you imagine the scandal, Mr. Peek, is it, if word was to leak out that you gentlemen like to lurk around brothels and gambling halls? A sternly worded missive, I think, about how deplorable it is that the young hopefuls of the Empire have been corrupted here at the Durbar."

Pausing, Sikander glanced straight at Battenberg, who had put down his cards and was now watching him intently.

"I know, it may not seem like such a dreadful thing, given how permissive times have become, but coupled with the King's impending arrival, and with all the press *wallahs* lurking around? I doubt His Majesty would take kindly to having the limelight usurped from him on the eve of his crowning moment, so to speak. What do you think, Mr. Battenberg? He is your cousin, after all. You know him far better than I."

"Damn you!" Metcalfe vaulted to his feet, his face darkening to match his jacket as he slammed his hands down so hard that the table almost gave way. "How dare you threaten the Prince so openly, you cur?"

"Calm down, Fruity." Battenberg grinned for the first time, and gave Sikander a fleeting salute. "Well played, Mr. Singh! Well played, indeed. Go on then, ask your questions."

Sikander leaned forward. "I believe you gentlemen enjoyed quite a performance yesterday, a private show by a *nautch* girl at the King-Emperor's camp."

He let his eyes play across the faces of each of the boys in turn. They all reacted quite differently. Cholmondeley's brows beetled with suspicion, and the elder Pelham brother sucked in a guilty breath. The younger Pelham and Grenville-Peek both seemed somewhat embarrassed, while Fruity Metcalfe let out a slow, shuddering breath, before sinking back down onto his chair without another word. As for Boy Hardinge, he looked troubled, even wary, as if he was worried by Sikander's line of questioning.

Only Battenberg remained calm, quite as emotionless as a mannequin.

"And what business is that of yours?" he riposted. "Is this a professional interest, or a personal one?"

Sikander smiled. Battenberg's reputation for cleverness was well earned, it seemed. It was a fine question, clearly intended to draw him out. Sadly, it also betrayed the boy's greatest weakness, his inexperience. It had taken Sikander a lifetime to learn that sometimes the key to winning any battle of wits was to hold one's tongue, and that was precisely what he chose to do, watching the boys once again, letting his eyes drift from one to the next, wondering which of them would be the first to crack this time around.

To his bemusement, it was Boy Hardinge who piped up.

"I arranged it." He shook his head shamefacedly. "I overheard my father talking about the girl, that she had been gifted to His Highness and was being lodged at the Imperial Camp. I mentioned it to the others, and we decided we wanted to see what the fuss was all about."

"Cost a pretty penny, let me tell you," Grenville-Peek added. "Sadly, it turned out to be quite boring, really, rather a damp squib."

The younger Pelham, Sackville, nodded eagerly. "She was a beauty, all right, but other than that, it was a bloody awful waste of time. Frankly, I didn't care much for the dancing, all that heaving and flailing about and eye-blinking. And that godawful music!" He shivered. "What a caterwauling, like they were strangling a bag full of cats!"

"Hear hear!" his brother piped in. "And not an inch of skin on display." He let out a horsey laugh. "The silly bint wouldn't even have her kit off, no matter how much lucre we offered her."

"Ha ha! You tried hard enough," Cholmondeley chirped, "didn't you, Charlie? Any more, and you'd be a damned rapist!"

"You forced yourself on her?" Sikander's voice grew so cold it was almost brittle.

"Oh, nothing like that! I just thought it would be fun if she would show us a bit of tit. Ain't that what these dancing girls are supposed to do? Anyway, she wasn't having any of it, and stamped right off, the uppity slag."

"That she did!" Sackville nodded once more, in agreement. "And she wouldn't even give us our money back. What a gyp!"

"And you gentlemen left immediately after she departed?"

"Yes," Boy Hardinge retorted. "Fruity here had a line on a game of whist, and we decided it would be a better evening than watching all that *nautch* nonsense."

Battenberg, who had maintained a stoic silence, finally spoke up. "Well, not all of us. That colonel fellow stayed behind, didn't he?"

"What colonel fellow?"

Battenberg glanced at Fruity Metcalfe, who was studiously staring down at the table, expertly shuffling and reshuffling a deck of cards with one hand.

"Fruity brought him along. We had never seen him before. Who was he, Fruity?"

Metcalfe gave Battenberg a pained look, as if to inquire if he really had to answer. He saw no sympathy there, and finally, after a defiant pause, his shoulders slumped, and he placed the cards on the table, before saying, "He's a distant cousin of mine. In the employ of Mysore, I believe. He commands his irregular cavalry. Anyway, I bumped into him at the Officer's Mess the day before yesterday, after a game of polo, and happened to mention the girl to him, and he insisted on attending the performance." Once more, he offered Battenberg a wounded shrug. "What could I do? I had to let him tag along. How could I say no?"

"And he stayed behind? Do you have any notion why?"

"He said he wanted to talk to the girl," Fruity Metcalfe said. "I guessed he probably wanted to try his luck with her, maybe proposition her for a bit of rough and tumble, which is why I didn't object. None of us did," he insisted, looking at his friends sulkily.

"Say," Grenville-Peek interjected, "what is this all about exactly? Has something happened to the girl?"

Sikander pursed his lips, his fingers absently drumming the surface of the table. He did not have to be Sherlock Holmes to sense this interview was drawing to an end. He had squeezed all he could out of these boys without divulging that Zahra was dead. True, he could always take a more aggressive tack, and resort to making blatant accusations, but not only did he doubt the potential efficacy of such an approach, he was also quite sure that none of these lads were capable of keeping a secret— not to mention the fact that he was almost certain that none of them was the killer he was seeking. They were inexperienced, yes, and rude, and about as spoiled as week-old milk, but they were not cold-blooded killers, not quite yet. What the future held, unfortunately, was something only time would tell.

Sikander hauled himself to his feet, and offered the Guppies a genial, if very insincere, smile. "Might I offer some advice, gentlemen? I was like you once. I lived for pleasure, for the indulgence of my senses and desires. But as I grow older, I have come to realise that a man must aspire to something greater than the pleasures of the flesh, some higher meaning. The thing about privilege is that it ruins a man. One needs adversity to flourish, the crucible of suffering. That is what ennobles a man, makes him more than ordinary. You are all still young, your lives ahead of you, terra incognita waiting to be explored. If you have an ounce of good sense, you will find something to believe in. Seek a cause, gentlemen. Embrace it. Armor yourself in purpose. You will find life far more meaningful if you do."

He turned, but before he could leave, the Prince spoke up.

"I have a feeling, Mr. Singh, that we will meet again."

"I sincerely hope we do not, Mr. Battenberg. I am not sure I can take the excitement."

With that remark, he retreated toward the exit, followed by Campbell who asked, "Do you believe them?"

"Why don't you answer that? You know them far better than I do."

The Captain considered this question carefully before shaking his head.

"No," he said, "I don't think they are lying. They are not clever enough…well, except Battenberg. Although, I don't like that fellow Metcalfe, not one bit."

"I don't think he is the Metcalfe we have to worry about? Tell me, have you heard about this cousin of his, the colonel who serves the Maharaja of Mysore?"

"As a matter of fact, I have."

"What can you tell me about him?"

Campbell's mouth twisted. "He's not a real colonel, for one. Until two years ago, he was a lowly lieutenant with the Grenadier Guards. Rumor has it he got caught cheating at cards and was forced to resign his commission or be drummed out of the service. He went south and entered into Imperial service." He laughed, a disdainful snort. "Answered an advertisement of all things, I believe, and settled down in Mysore in royal style, living it up like a proper nob. He is said to be the Maharaja's problem-solver, sir, a man with the ability to get things done, but I think what he really is is a jumped-up thug, a glorified mercenary."

"You obviously have a low opinion of him."

"Oh, I can bear the fact that he's as unpleasant as a mule,

but what I cannot abide is that he is said to cheat at cards." Campbell rolled his eyes. "Tell me, what sort of gentleman cheats at cards? It is simply unforgivable."

"I think we should track him down and ascertain exactly why he stayed behind to chat with Zahra. Do you have any idea where we can find him, at this late hour?"

Captain Campbell's face hardened. "Actually, now that you mention it," he said, "I think I can guess exactly where he is."

Chapter Nine

Silently, without offering another word of explanation, the Captain led Sikander out of the Golden Bough, retracing their steps across the road, before heading westwards. He did not stay on the crowded avenue for long, instead turning abruptly down a deserted side street. Sikander followed him warily, trying not to grow disconcerted as the alleys grew narrower and narrower, the houses packed so densely on both sides that the only sky visible was directly overhead. He was blessed with an excellent sense of direction, but as Campbell made turn after unpredictable turn, the maze of gullies grew ever more bewildering, until he could not help but feel hopelessly lost. Campbell, on the other hand, seemed to know exactly where they were headed. He forged ahead, silently maintaining a steady, mile-eating trot that soon had Sikander a little out of breath, despite the fact that he endeavored mightily to keep himself in good trim.

They must have traveled for the better part of fifteen minutes before, to Sikander's relief, the Captain came to a brusque halt in a small cul-de-sac, an enclosed courtyard just a stone's throw from the Jama Masjid.

"In here." Campbell strode up to a decrepit-looking *haveli* with crumbling unpainted walls. "This is where we will find Metcalfe, I believe."

"What is this place?"

Campbell's face hardened. "They call it the Apothecaries Den, sir, and this is where most soldiers come to forget. Give me a gold coin, will you?"

"Whatever for?"

"You'll see soon enough."

Shaking his head at the man's deliberate attempts at playing it cryptic, Sikander pulled a sovereign from his pocket and handed it to Campbell, who leaned forward and tapped it against the door, one sharp rap of metal on iron.

Immediately, a peephole snapped open, from which a pair of hostile eyes stared out. "What do you want?"

The Captain flipped the coin up, tossing it in a lazy spiral. After a minute's pause, the door creaked open with a squeak of unoiled hinges, and a plump Mussulman with a carefully hennaed beard stepped out, holding out one hand, palm upwards.

"We are looking for an Angrez, a tall officer with spectacles." Campbell dropped the coin in his palm.

"Inside," the doorman mumbled, and Sikander saw that he had no front teeth, guessing that they had been knocked out in a brawl. "In the last alcove. That is where you will find him."

"Come along, sir," Campbell said, surging onward, elbowing past the Durban. Inside, it was pitch dark, with windows that had been boarded up. The walls were painted a dull shade of off-white, and on either side, a row of niches stretched towards the distant wall, each obscured by flimsy, slatted doors made of cheap plywood. The air was thick, pungent with a fugue of stale smoke, but it was not tobacco. It took Sikander a moment to recognise the heady odor, before it dawned upon him exactly what this place was. He had expected a brothel, or a drinking hole, but to his surprise, this was an opium den.

Sikander cast a wary glance around his surroundings. Even though he was quite aware of the popularity of the drug amongst the working classes, he was shocked to discover an establishment flouting the law so openly. This was the very reason the British had enacted the Opium Act of 1878, to curb the sale of opioids without a doctor's prescription. For the duration of the Durbar, the Viceregal edict had been quite clear. All opium dens within a ten-mile radius had been ordered to be shut down, forcibly if needed, and any soldiers caught in possession of opium, even in laudanum form, within the confines of the encampments would be reduced in rank immediately.

"Hurry up, sir," Campbell interjected, cutting short his musings. "This way!"

He strode to the very last niche. Without further ado, the Captain rammed one shoulder into the door. It slammed open to reveal an incongruous sight. Inside, on a low *charpoi*, a naked girl lay supine. She was facedown, her copper skin glistening with sweat. Behind her, a middle-aged Englishman sat on a wicker stool, a tall, slender specimen with lank blond hair and a louche moustache. He was clad only in a pair of ratty long johns tucked into muddy riding boots, his mouth twisted up into an expression of great concentration as he leaned over the girl to daub out a swirling design on her bare back and buttocks with a horsehair paintbrush and what seemed to be henna dye. By his side stood a tall hookha, burbling gently. In his other hand, he held its spout, stopping occasionally to inhale from it deeply.

Was this the man they were seeking? Sikander cast a side-long glance at Campbell who nodded in affirmation.

"Colonel Metcalfe, I presume?"

The man ignored him, as if he wasn't there. He did not bother to look up, pausing from his labors only to exhale, a fragrant puff of what Sikander recognized as a blend of raw opium and Turkish tobacco leaf.

"I am the Maharaja of Rajpore. We need to talk."

This time, the man let out an audible hiss. He squinted up at him, obviously annoyed by the intrusion. Sikander noticed he had a predator's eyes, very pale, almost yellow. Though he was wearing a pair of thick tortoiseshell eyeglasses, it was obvious, even through the lenses, that he was intoxicated, evident from the way his pale eyes struggled to focus.

"I do not care if you're Queen Victoria herself, risen from the grave. Just bugger off, won't you? You're ruining my mood."

A frisson of rage swelled inside Sikander, but before he could compose a scathing reply, Campbell, who had been watching patiently, spoke up.

"May I have a go, sir?"

Sikander frowned, reluctant to let him take over, but the Captain gave him a wink.

"Trust me. I know what I am doing."

"Very well! Do your worst."

Campbell stepped forward and held out a hand to the girl, who was sitting up by now, cowering on the edge of the bed, her dazed eyes flicking from one man to the next, quite obviously terrified.

"Run along, dearie," he said. "It would be best if you left now."

The girl obeyed, swaying to her feet unsteadily. She tottered toward the door, the pattern on her back beginning to run, curiously reminiscent of blood.

Metcalfe slouched upright, grabbing for her hair, trying to wrest her back. "Hold on a minute! I have paid for her, I have."

With blinding speed, the Captain's hand darted out, landing squarely on his chest, pushing him off balance. Metcalfe swayed, and then fell backwards, collapsing onto the stool with a gasp.

"How dare you?" he wheezed.

"Shut your mouth!" Campbell said evenly.

"Who the bloody hell do you think you are?" The colonel started to object, but the Captain forestalled any further words by leaning forward and giving him a slap, one swift swipe across his face with the back of his hand. It was so sudden, so unexpected that even Sikander winced, taken entirely by surprise as the man's head snapped back with such force that a crack starred across one lens of his spectacles.

The colonel let out a groan, utterly stunned. It took him a

minute to gather his wits before he managed to give Campbell a poisonous glare.

"Have you lost your mind? Laying hands on a superior officer, I shall have you shot."

"Lay hands on you?" Campbell shrugged, doing such a good job of feigning ignorance that Sikander could not help but grin. "I did no such thing."

"What? You just slapped me!"

"Me? Slap you? Oh, no! I fear you must have imbibed far too much opium, Colonel, and are imagining things." The Captain reacted with a wounded expression, turning to Sikander.

"I saw nothing," Sikander snapped. He was beginning to understand why Malik Umar had picked Campbell for the job. Whatever else his flaws, he certainly had a flair for getting things done, and that with admirable alacrity.

"This is preposterous."

"Perhaps, but let me make two things very clear. First, you are not in uniform and therefore not my superior. As far as I am concerned, you're nothing more than a jumped-up bounder. Secondly, my friend here is going to ask you several questions. If you do not cooperate and answer him with absolute honesty, I might be forced to lose control." He gave the colonel a stiff smile. "You will not enjoy that, do you understand?"

Metcalfe nodded, by now quite sober, judging by the wary look he offered Sikander.

"Excellent! We are all on the same page at last." Campbell gave Sikander a genial wave. "I think you will find the colonel more pliable now, sir. Please, go ahead!"

Sikander gave the colonel a frown. "I believe you witnessed a dance performance last evening, a young *nautch* girl at the King Emperor's camp."

"What of it?" Metcalfe replied sullenly.

"We were told that you were not on the original guest list, that you invited yourself along. Tell me, why you were so eager to see this girl?"

"I had heard about her, that she was an exquisite dancer," he swallowed, his Adam's apple bobbing up and down, betraying the fact that he was lying. "I have always had a keen interest in the Arts."

"Is that so? Is that why you stayed back even after the other gentlemen had departed, to discuss the intricacies of *nritya-shastra*?"

The colonel clenched his jaw, realizing he had been caught out.

"Answer the question," Campbell hissed, his voice taking on a dangerous edge.

It seemed to work. Metcalfe shuddered visibly, before whispering, "I was on an errand."

"For whom?"

"I cannot say," he replied, shaking his head obdurately.

Sikander let out a sigh. "Captain, if you would you be so kind?"

Campbell nodded, tilting his head slightly as if to study Metcalfe speculatively. Very quickly, his fist darted out, a blindingly fast jab to the man's nose that made his head snap back like it was on a spring.

"Stop!" Metcalfe wheezed, his nostrils beginning to drip blood. "Please, I will tell you everything." His shoulders slumped, all the fight gone out of him. "It was the Maharaja of Mysore. He asked me to go and speak with Zahra on his behalf."

Sikander's brow knitted as he considered this revelation. Of all the people he had imagined consorting with a *nautch*-girl, the name of Krishna Raja Wodeyar was very close to the bottom of the list. From what he knew of the Prince of Mysore, he was a straitlaced, almost saintly Brahmin of a man, said to be cut from the same cloth as Lord Rama himself. It was difficult to imagine him sending an envoy to a woman of low reputation, no matter how comely she may have been. Could he have been trying to buy her favors, and had dispatched Metcalfe to arrange a surreptitious rendezvous? Or was something more nefarious afoot?

"What message did the Maharaja wish you to convey?"

The colonel sucked in a slow breath, contemplating defiance once more, but when Captain Campbell made a great show of cracking his knuckles with a grim smirk, that was more than enough to change his mind.

"The girl was trying to blackmail the Maharaja sahib. It seems he has a bit of an infirmity that she had found out about."

"Is that so?"

Metcalfe nodded, touching his face gingerly.

"Here you are," Campbell offered him a handkerchief. Metcalfe took it rather reluctantly, looking at it suspiciously, as if it was poisoned before dabbing at his nose with a pronounced wince.

"Some years ago, the girl's mother, she was a *nautch* girl too, she performed for the Maharaja. He was younger then, and much more hot-blooded, and decided to proposition her, offering her a very generous sum to enjoy a brief sojourn in her company. However, when the appointed hour came, the Maharaja, for lack of a better turn of phrase, was quite unable to come."

Sikander let out a chuckle, which was echoed by Campbell. It certainly was a fine turn of phrase, especially for a man under duress.

"In any case, as you can imagine, if such a tale was to be circulated publicly, it would irrevocably damage His Highness's reputation. He is well known as a virile, vital man in the very prime of health. As a result, the mother was paid a handsome sum to hold her tongue."

"Until she died?"

"Yes, the matter was thought to be forgotten once she was dead and buried, but then, some weeks ago, we received a missive from this young girl, claiming that she was in possession of a sworn affidavit testifying that the Maharaja was incapable of consummation."

"Let me guess, she offered you this document in exchange for a small gratuity."

"Not so small," Metcalfe replied. "She wanted one thousand guineas, to be precise." Campbell let out a low whistle. "Naturally, the Maharaja was quite irate at being confronted by such an outlandish demand, and he asked me to intervene on his behalf."

"So you decided to call on the girl and threaten her?"

"Not quite! The Maharaja was willing to pay, but he wanted proof that the document was genuine. I went there to try and reason with her, but she refused to be reasonable. And then, when I asked her to show me the document, so that I could verify its veracity, she started to grow rather vexed. That was why I let her have it, a bit of the old rough and tumble."

"You assaulted her?"

"It was just a love tap," he said peevishly. "She was too bloody shrill, the silly ninny. I thought it would shut her up, but instead, she just started screaming her lungs out!"

Beside him, he saw Campbell clenching his fists, but before the man could wreak bloody havoc, Sikander stilled him with one upraised finger.

"What did you do next?"

"I bloody left, of course. I thought I would come back another time, and try to talk some sense into her when she wasn't menstruating." His eyes narrowed as he realized for the first time he was being interrogated. "Say, what is this all about? Are you trying to finger me for something, eh?"

Sikander gave the man a glare, resisting the urge to belt him squarely in the mouth. He was a dimwit, and an utter scoundrel, but Sikander doubted he was a killer. Not only had he admitted to hitting the girl, he had no clue that she was dead, as was evidenced by his admission that he intended to visit her later. True, blackmail made for a fine motive. What was the old mnemonic: love, lust, lucre, and loathing? The Maharaja of Mysore could have ordered Zahra removed, but from what he knew of the man's reputation, not only was he no murderer, he was as deathly afraid of scandal as a Puritan.

Besides, what purpose would it have served him to have her killed? It was obvious that the document in question still remained in her possession. Why would Mysore have her removed, only to leave the incriminating testimony to be found by another blackmailer? That is, he thought, if such a document had existed in the first place. It was possible that the whole scheme had been a wild goose chase, but the fact that Metcalfe had no clue as to the document's location made it quite impossible to pin him for the crime.

Suddenly, the room felt too small for Sikander, the noxious fug too thick to breathe in.

"Come along, Captain, let us away! He is not our man."

Even as he turned to leave, Campbell dawdled. "Give me a minute, sir! I wish to bid Colonel Metcalfe a proper farewell."

Sikander nodded, striding out of the alcove. Behind him, he heard a shrill squeal followed by the sound of several dull thuds. In spite of his tiredness, a smile played across his lips. He was beginning to like Captain Campbell. True, the man was a bit of a mad dog, and much too quick, both with his temper and his fists, but this once, he would happily have traded places with him. Metcalfe deserved every bruise he got, and more. How dare he assault a woman! The very thought of it made Sikander's blood boil.

At the front door, Sikander was intercepted by the Durban once more.

"Are you sure you would not care to stay longer, huzoor? We have just had a consignment of hashish from Bokhara which is rumored to be quite exquisite."

"I think not." Pulling out another coin, he waved it at the man. "If anyone asks, we were never here, is that clear?"

"Of course! The Mussulman snatched the coin from him greedily, his mouth splitting into a gummy grin. "I have a terrible memory, huzoor. Why, there are times when I cannot remember my own name, much less yours.

Chapter Ten

Outside, Sikander shivered. At some point while they had been inside the opium den, the night had taken a turn toward the frigid. A dim mist hung in the air, obscuring the moon and stars above. Each breath he inhaled was so crisp it made him want to cough. In a way, the turn in the weather perfectly mirrored the somber change in his mood. This had been the easy part, he realized, the preliminary investigation, where the obvious leads had presented themselves. Everything that came now onwards would be an uphill struggle as motives grew murkier and the suspects more complicated. And then, of course, there was the deadline the Viceroy had insisted upon, hanging over his head like the sword of Damocles. He had a day, a day and a half at the best, a thought that sent a tremor down his spine.

About ten minutes elapsed before the Captain made his return.

"I am sorry to have kept you waiting," he said, wiping at his hands with his handkerchief. Sikander saw that his knuckles were bruised and bloody.

"There is no need to apologize, Campbell," Sikander said grudgingly. "That was well done in there. Perhaps you aren't quite useless after all."

If he had been expecting this lopsided compliment to elicit a response, Sikander was sorely disappointed. Campbell didn't say a word. Instead, he merely shrugged, his raffish smile absent for once as he led the Maharaja back through the maze of alleyways toward where they had parked the Standard.

"Should we go roust up the Maharaja of Mysore?" Campbell asked listlessly.

"I think not. The hour is far too late to go visiting the native encampments, not without raising everyone's suspicions. Not to mention the fact that I really am quite exhausted. No, take me back to the Majestic. We can resume the investigation early in the morning."

Sikander had expected Campbell to object to this command, to resist, but to his surprise, the man capitulated as meekly as the Sultan of Zanzibar.

"As you wish," he said with a shrug, throwing the car into gear and steering it northward up the Esplanade Road.

Eyeing him askance, Sikander was unable to keep himself from feeling a flicker of concern for the man, a hint of empathy. Although he had been quick to brush off the epithets the Guppies had hurled at him, it was apparent from the sullen set of his shoulders and the morose expression on his face, that the insults had caused him more heartache than he was willing to admit. True, he was quite tiresomely eager, and rather too confident for his own good, but despite the fact that he had been saddled with him like Sisyphus' rock, Campbell was growing on him, even though it pained him to say so.

"Is something wrong, Captain?" he inquired. "You seem rather glum."

"I am fine, sir." His smile was bitter, more a rictus than a grin. "Tired, that's all. It's been quite a day, hasn't it?"

He lapsed into silence. Sikander did not press him further. That was the first rule observed by a good investigator. You had to let people speak at their own pace. When Campbell was good and ready, he would divulge what exactly was bothering him. All Sikander would achieve by pushing him would be to make him even more despondent.

Instead, he leaned back, watched the city flicker by as they rattled along, taking a turn at the Chandni Chowk, driving past the Edwardian edifice of the Town Hall and then paralleling the Rani Bagh until the Railway Station hove into view.

"I have heard it all before, but it still rankles." The Captain broke his silence as the vehicle clattered over the railway tracks. "Why is it, Mr. Singh, that a man's blood is more important than his deeds?

"I take it Mr. Hayat Khan told you my story. However, I doubt you are aware of the whole saga. The truth is my mother never told me who my father was. Oh, I knew I was illegitimate, that I had been born out of wedlock. I was shunned, mocked, derided. Even the priests refused to bless me or grant me communion. It was made clear to me from a very young age that I was a mistake, a sin come to life, not worthy of love or respect.

"I decided from boyhood, sir, that I would not let the circumstances of my birth cripple me. I would prove myself. I would make my way in the world on my strengths, and my merits, and that was what would define me, not my illegitimacy. In many ways, that was why I became a soldier, why I chose to enlist in the Army. I welcomed the brotherhood of the regiment. They became my family, the brethren I had never had. On the field of battle, Mr. Singh, a man's birth does not matter, only his courage.

"But then, some four years ago, my mother took ill. Pneumonia, the doctors told us. I took a leave of absence and traveled back to see her, and it was then that she decided, on her deathbed, to reveal to me who my father was. Can you believe it, that I, an unlamented bastard , should turn out to have the noblest of noble blood? Of course, I refused to believe her, but she insisted it was the truth, right until her last gasp."

His face stiffened. "After I buried her, I was ready to forget it all, but my mother, she had been quite determined that I should not be denied my birthright. As it turned out, before her demise, she had sent my father a letter, revealing my existence to him, of which, it seems, he had been entirely unaware."

Before them, the Mori Gate loomed out of the shadows, like a ghostly mouth.

"Three months later," Campbell sighed, "I was visited at my barracks by three gentlemen, two Barons and a high and mighty Earl. They informed me that I was a charlatan and threatened to have me cashiered from my regiment. I was ordered to answer their questions, and they asked me all kinds of rubbish, at the end of which, the Earl told me that I was going to be transferred from the Black Watch to the Coldstream Guards and raised to Captain. He also told me that my benefactor wished to endow me with two hundred pounds a year, under two conditions, the first that he remain anonymous, and the second that I drop all pretensions and claims to my parenthood."

"Did you take it?"

"Of course. It was like a boon from high above. I thought my ship had come in, that I would finally be somebody." He shuddered. "I was wrong, damned wrong. In the Black Watch, I was respected for my abilities, my battlefield prowess. But when I reported for duty to the Coldstream, I knew had made a mistake. I was informed, very politely, of course, that I would spend my term of service on detached duty, which was a polite way of saying that I was not to travel to England. And even here, when I was assigned to the Viceroy's Guard, I was treated like a pariah. A hundred whispers followed me, that I was not a gentleman, that I had won my spurs because I was a royal bastard, that I was a parade ground mannequin, not a real soldier. Once again, in spite of my stellar record, my blood had damned me."

A long, low groan escaped his lips. "How is it fair, sir, that a man like me is mocked, while deviants like Metcalfe are lauded, even celebrated?"

He looked to Sikander for sympathy, but instead, the Maharaja let out a sardonic laugh.

"Fair, Captain? Since when has anything in life been fair?" Sikander' face was as hard as granite. "You speak of being damned by your blood. I think you are mistaken. I think it is your blood that is your greatest asset."

"But I am a bastard, sir. How can I ever escape that stigma?"

"Perhaps one half of your heritage is illegitimate, but the other half, you bear the bloodline of a proud and ancient family. Tell me, have you heard the legend of Aengus Og?"

"I haven't, I am afraid."

"What kind of third rate Scotsman are you, that you don't know your history? Aengus Og was born out of wedlock, just as you were. His mother was a Campbell, with the very same blood as you. His father was John of Islay, the Earl of Ross, who was accused of signing a secret treaty with England's Edward the Fourth and stripped of much of his land and power by King James the Third. Aengus refused to accept this and overthrew his father, and went to war with just about everyone in Scotland."

"Did he win?"

"For a brief while, yes. He wrested back his ancestral lands and even seized control of the port of Inverness, but then, he was murdered in his sleep. However, before he died, he was declared the last of the Lords of the Isles, who answered to no man, not English King nor Scottish laird.

"Stop the car here, will you?" Sikander said as the car drew up in front of the Majestic's gateway. "Do you know what the motto of Clan Campbell is? *Ne Obliviscaris*. Never forget! They can belittle you, they can curse you, and mock you, but only you can forget who you are."

With that declaration, Sikander threw open the door.

"Thank you, sir," Campbell said as he dismounted, his voice thickening with gratitude.

"Do not thank me, Captain. I have told you nothing but the truth. Honestly, I have no respect for men who speak of blood. As far as I am concerned, it is an excuse for men who have no strength, and no character."

Sikander continued, "Look at Chandragupta Maurya, or

Babur, both of whom carved an empire from nothing. Look at Sher Shah, at Ranjit Singh, at your Clive. These are the men I admire, not your blooded swine who sit in the club and drink sherry and talk of Empire."

Sikander offered the captain a nod. "This is India. Here, a man is what he makes of himself."

Chapter Eleven

As the Captain drove off, Sikander felt himself gripped by a sudden listlessness. The phrase Campbell had used resonated through his mind. "Damned by my blood." In many ways, Sikander was equally damned by his own blood. While he would truly have loved to have been a professional sleuth, a deducer by trade, his birth had doomed him to be a Maharaja. And, true, while he enjoyed the trappings that came with the throne of Rajpore, the wealth and prestige, the only time he felt truly alive was when he was on the chase.

Arching his back like a cat, he spared a long moment to stretch his tired limbs. Above, he saw that the clouds had cleared. It was a cold, startlingly clear night. Sikander squinted, spying his favorite constellation, Orion, the hunter, visible in the far distance. He had always felt an affinity toward it. It was the lodestone for detectives, he had always believed, the guiding star for all those who set out to decipher mysteries. Seeing it now was strangely reassuring.

Sadly, his appreciation of the mysteries of the cosmos was truncated as a car came rolling up, a Vauxhall A-Type, by the looks of it. It screeched to a halt in front of Sikander, throwing up a shower of dust and gravel that temporarily blinded him. The front door slapped open, disgorging a duo of brawny troopers, Rajputs, he inferred, by the way they had tied their *pugrees*.

"Sorry for the presumption, huzoor, but please get in the car," the first of them said.

"I most certainly will not," he started to say, but before he could finish voicing his objections, they each seized one of his arms.

"What in God's name do you think you're doing?" Unfortunately, his outrage had no effect whatsoever on his assailants, who bundled him bodily into the back of the car and slammed shut the door behind him.

As the vehicle lurched into motion, Sikander realised he was not alone. A man sat poised on the opposite seat, sneering at him. Maharaja Ganga Singh of Bikaner was the very epitome of the martial Rajput, from his polished jackboots to his carefully coiffed moustache, which was so sharp-edged it could have sliced through armor. His only shortcoming was that he was rather short, even smaller than Sikander, and his nose was much too arrogant, precisely the sort of appendage designed to look down at others over, a skill he had mastered at a very young age.

Bikaner was one of the largest states in Rajputana, famed for two things, fine camels and even better warriors. It was said of the Rathores that there was no one better to guard your back in a battle. Sikander, however, had a different theory. He thought they made such valiant soldiers because they were thoroughly unimaginative, a humorless bunch who cared about only two things, honor and duty, which made them great warriors in wartime but utterly boring once the trumpets had sounded.

True, honor and duty were important, but then, so was a bit of fun every now and then. Unfortunately, Ganga Singh's idea of fun was a round of polo followed by an hour or two of pig-sticking, essentially anything that involved copious amounts of sweat and public displays of masculinity. That was tiresome enough, so it didn't help that he was as straightforward as any man could be, with no capacity for either subtlety or subtext, a quality which had always made his relationship with Sikander rather rocky.

"Hello, Ganga Singhji," Sikander said. "What has it been, eight years, or is it nine? The last time I saw you was at my coronation, wasn't it?"

"You know, I really do not like you, Sikander Singh. You represent everything I despise," Ganga Singh hissed, his moustache bristling with disdain. "Your father was a proper man, a *pukka* Maharaja. He carried himself with dignity, with grace. Why, he would never have been caught traipsing about in the middle of the night in, what is that, your bathrobe?"

His jaw clenched with disgust. "Unfortunately, it looks like I am stuck with you. I must think of the greater good, of what is best for King and Empire, even if it means working with an overconfident lout like yourself."

"Perhaps it is because I have had a very long day, Your Majesty, but I am feeling rather slow on the uptake. Do stop beating about the bush, won't you, and explain why you have abducted me?"

Ganga Singh let out a snort. "As it happens, I know what is going on, why you were at the Royal Enclosure earlier today, everything!"

"I have no idea what you mean," Sikander said, but the Maharaja of Bikaner cut him off with a savage slash of one hand.

"Enough! Do not take me for a fool! The Viceroy told me himself." He fixed Sikander with one eye, squinting. "Lord Hardinge asked me about your suitability for the job at hand. While I was reluctant to give my blessing, even I had to admit you have some small modicum of talent for poking your nose in other people's affairs." His face looked like he had swallowed a bitter lemon, to give Sikander a compliment, however infinitesimal. "Unbecoming though it is for a man of your antecedents and breeding to go skulking about like a *havildar* looking for clues, in this case," he admitted grudgingly, "we need someone like you.

"I warn you, though, if you dare to embarrass the King in any way, I will not rest until I have broken you. Is that clear?"

He waited for Sikander to confirm with a nod before continuing.

"Good! So, as it happens, I have a tip that may be of help to you. As you know, I have a widespread network of spies and informers." He offered a saturnine smile. "One can never have too much information, can they? One of my sources has been keeping a close eye on a Nationalist named Bahadur Rao. Perhaps you have heard the name?"

Sikander shook his head once more, this time to signify the negative, a denial which managed to send Ganga Singh into a veritable paroxysm.

"Good heavens! Could you be any more ignorant? You know the name of every wine in France, no doubt, but about the things that truly matter, you remain utterly clueless." He was practically foaming at the mouth by now. "These Nationalists, they are our truest enemy. Like a fungus, they have spread everywhere, sinking into the very foundations of our homes, taking root and rotting every square inch until all that is left is dust and ash. Mark my words, it will be them or us. If they are allowed to flourish, if they prevail, we will be pulled from our thrones and offered up as sacrifices. Just you wait and see!"

"You were about to tell me how your man was shadowing this Bahadur Rao," Sikander reminded Ganga Singh gently, before he could lose himself fully in this flood of invective.

"Yes! Of course! As I was saying, this Nationalist has been heard declaring several times, in public in fact, that he intends to ruin the Durbar somehow. What do you think of that, eh?"

Sikander shrugged. "I am sorry to disappoint you, but that isn't actually anything new. The Durbar Committee probably receives half a hundred threats each and every day, and most of them turn out to be rubbish."

"Ah, but that is not all!" Ganga Singh grinned triumphantly. "Just the day before yesterday, my informer happened to follow Bahadur Rao as he went to pay a visit to one of his agents. Can you guess his destination?"

"Not the King's Camp, surely." Sikander sat up.

"Exactly!" Ganga Singh leaned back, twirling his moustache proudly. "And can you deduce who he called upon while he was there, for almost half an hour?"

The answer to that question was really quite obvious, even if Sikander had been a rank amateur. It took him only a minute to put two and two together, to fit this intriguing snippet of information into what he already knew. This must have been the so-called uncle that Sergeant Macgregor had mentioned, the older man who had called upon Zahra. But why? What was the real reason Bahadur Rao had gone to meet with her, and that, too, under an assumed identity? How were they involved? Whatever the case, it certainly made the Nationalist a viable suspect, at least worthy of a visit.

"How sure are you of this, Ganga Singh-ji? Do you trust your man?"

"As a matter of fact, he is unimpeachable. He would lay down his life for me and for the glory of the Empire."

"Very well then. Thank you for the lead. I shall look into it, I assure you."

"Do that," Ganga Singh said, "and make sure you keep me apprised of your progress. We wouldn't want any surprises, would we?"

"Not at all," Sikander said. "I despise surprises, especially unexpected ones," but the irony in his tone was wasted upon Ganga Singh, who merely leaned forward to knock on the partition that separated the passenger seat from the driver, a signal to stop the car.

"So be it. Now get out, will you? And go do something useful!"

Sikander grinned, and hastened to obey. Even as the car clattered to a halt, and he prepared to dismount, Ganga Singh stretched out to give him a quick pat on one shoulder, a surprisingly intimate gesture.

"Do be careful, Sikander. You are a little fish in a pond filled with sharks. One wrong step, and they will not hesitate to gobble you up."

Even though the metaphor was about as mixed as could be, Sikander could not help but be absurdly touched. It was quite unlike Ganga Singh to play the caring patriarch, but the very fact that he was issuing such a warning, served to remind Sikander exactly how precarious the path he was taking.

"I solemnly swear I will be on my best behavior." He gave Ganga Singh a nod. "I am just glad you care about my welfare, my friend. Why, it is bringing a tear to my eye!"

"Stop being cheeky!" The Maharaja of Bikaner scoffed. "Really, one of these days I am going to have teach you some manners, you clown!"

"I look forward to it. Perhaps you can come by the Majestic this weekend and have a bottle of champagne with me. I have a case of very fine Laurent-Perrier Grand Siècle I have been saving for just such a special occasion."

"I'll try to find the time," Ganga Singh replied. In spite of the disapproval in his voice, the faintest of smiles touched the corners of his lips. "And do try and dress a little more appropriately, will you, Sikander?

"You're letting the side down."

Chapter Twelve

Watching the Vauxhall speed away, Sikander shook his head, barely able to believe that Ganga Singh had just abandoned him in the middle of nowhere.

He cast a wary glance about, trying to take stock of his precise location, looking for recognizable landmarks. It took him a few moments to get his bearings straight. To his left, he saw what seemed to be the gleaming lights of Curzon House and, to his right, the towering figure of John Nicholson's statue was visible in the distance, which led him to conclude that he was somewhere on the Delhi Club Road. If that was correct, his hotel was nearby, perhaps fifteen or twenty minutes away by foot.

Well, he thought, there was only one way to find out. Stuffing his hands into his pockets, he set off at a brisk trot in what he hoped was the correct direction. It had been a long time since Sikander had walked anywhere alone. Somehow, it felt liberating, and to his surprise, he found he was quite enjoying himself.

His mind wandered to what Ganga Singh had said about the Nationalists and how they were active at the Durbar, in spite of all the security preparations the English had arranged. Personally, Sikander did not care one way or another about the putative Independence Movement, if one could call it that. As far he was concerned, all this talk of armed insurrection was just rabble-rousing, the work of clever demagogues whose sole interest was to further their own interests. He was no great supporter of the English, but even he could not deny that their rule had been beneficial to India, what with the great advances in science and education and law, not to mention the vast progress they had engineered for women and the lower castes. Besides, he possessed enough foresight to realize that without the English, India would soon dissolve into a mess of internecine conflicts. It would be Hindu arrayed against Muslim, rich against poor, high caste against low, modernist against traditionalist. And who would pay the price? His kind, of course. It was the Princes of India who stood to lose the most if the Nationalists prevailed. Even a fool could see that.

Just as he was beginning to work up a sweat, he heard the rumble of an approaching automobile. Halting, he saw a pair of glowing headlights advancing towards him, which resolved out of the shadows into a very handsome vehicle. It was a Packard, he guessed, one of the new Type Six limousines, painted a very elegant combination of purple and yellow. Sikander gave it an admiring once-over as it came to a halt not far away, the passenger door opening to reveal a stout, bearded man, dressed in a pristine white tunic with purple jodhpurs.

"Sikander Singh, isn't it?" The man called out. "How delightful to bump into you so unexpectedly! What a coincidence this is! We were just on our way to see you at your hotel."

Sikander wracked his brain, trying to recall if he knew this man. He did seem somewhat familiar, but when he tried to recollect where they had met before, he drew a blank. He was on the wrong side of fifty, a Mewari, by the looks of his bushy beard, which was parted neatly in the middle. This inference was confirmed when the man emerged from the car and Sikander saw the push dagger tucked into the red sash that encircled his midriff. It was a Bundi *katar*, particularly favored by the inhabitants of Malwa.

"I do not believe we have met before," Sikander said. "Who might you be?"

"Me?" the man's face curved into a scornful expression. "I am merely someone who would like very much to have a quick word with you, if you could spare a moment. Perhaps we could give you a lift?"

"I think not." Sikander turned, about to resume his hike, but before he could take another step, the Rajput drew a pistol, a stubby-nosed Browning Model 1910.

"I am afraid I must insist," he said, his tone making it clear he would not brook a second refusal.

Sikander clenched his fists. His heart-rate raced considering the choices available to him. He could try and reach for the gun in his *banyan* pocket, but no, the Rajput had the draw on him. He could rush the man, and try to overpower him, but once again, from the looks of him, Sikander doubted he could be quick enough before the man managed to get off a shot. That left him only one option. The car was on his left, which meant he would have to go to his right, a dive to the ground and perhaps a half-roll, and he would be close enough to try and sweep the man off his feet, hopefully fast enough to take him by surprise.

Before matters could escalate toward any unpleasantness, a voice ended their standoff.

"Oh, put that away! The Maharaja of Rajpore is an old friend."

The vehicle's other door swung open, and another man emerged, waving one hand at Sikander in greeting.

At first glance, Sayaji Rao of Baroda looked more like a cowherd than the King of a twenty-one-gun state. In fact, that was exactly where his dynasty's traditional patronym, the Gaekwads, was derived from. Translated from Hindustani, the word quite literally, meant "the guardian of cows." Ironically, it applied particularly well in this instance, because long before he had been chosen to take on the mantle of Maharaja, Sayaji Rao had spent his childhood as the son of a poor farmer. When the previous Gaekwad, Khanderao, had died without a male heir, the British had briefly allowed his brother Malharrao to assume the throne of Baroda. Unfortunately, Malharrao had proven to be a man of weak character, given to vast expenditures and of a cruel, selfish nature. His spending habits had quickly made him fall afoul of the English, a situation exacerbated when he had tried to poison the Resident to forestall an audit of his finances. As a result, Lord Salisbury had ordered him deposed and forced into exiled to Madras, left to die in ignominy.

It had then fallen to Khanderao's widow, Maharani Jamnabai, to choose the next Gaekwad. She had sent for all the branches of the family, however minor, commanding them to assemble at Baroda. Among them had been Sayaji Rao's father, Kashi Rao, who had walked six hundred kilometers with his sons, to present himself at court. Legend had it that each possible heir was asked the same question by Jamnabai—"Why have you come here?" And to that, Sayaji Rao, then just a boy of twelve, had replied, "I have come to be a King," an answer that had so impressed the Maharani that she had chosen him to become the next Gaekwad of Baroda.

It had been a sensible choice, Sikander had to admit, because Sayaji Rao had proven to be one of the finest and most progressive rulers in Princely India. This was a man Sikander truly admired, not only because he was the very epitome of an enlightened monarch, the sort of man who put the welfare of his citizens before his own comforts, but also because he was incapable of falsehood or duplicity.

Sikander studied his old mentor. It was obvious that something was weighing heavily on him, for the Gaekwad seemed exhausted, wearier than Sikander had ever seen him, his shoulders hunched, as if the world itself rested upon them.

"How are you, my dear boy?" Sayaji Rao held out one hand. Although ordinarily Sikander eschewed physical contact, finding it somewhat distasteful, on this occasion he took his hand readily, bringing it to his forehead with a deference that was most unlike him. With a fleeting smile, Sayaji Rao patted his cheek, an almost paternal gesture. He was the same height as Sikander, but more rotund, with deep-set eyes and a bushy toothbrush moustache that made him seem older than he was. Still, there was a gravitas about him that always gave Sikander a chill, an imperiousness of bearing mingled with an utter sincerity that he trusted immensely.

"I am very well, Your Majesty, although I must confess, I certainly did not expect to bump into you in such unexpected circumstances."

"Forgive my manners!" the Gaekwad said, his eyes twinkling. "Come, let us take a walk, and I will explain everything."

Sikander hesitated, unsure whether this was a request or a command, but only for a heartbeat. He owed the Gaekwad far too much to refuse to oblige him, and as Sayaji Rao turned and began to amble slowly in the direction of Nicholson's statue, Sikander followed.

As for the Rajput, he decided to come along, too, giving Sikander a nonchalant shrug by way of apology as he put his pistol away, and fell into step beside the two of them.

"By the way," Sayaji Rao said, "this is Fateh Singh of Mewar. I do not believe you two have met before."

Sikander's eyes widened. So that was why he had thought the man so familiar. He had seen his picture often enough in the broadsheets. Why, this was none other than the infamous Maharana of Udaipur, the chieftain of the Sisodias, one of the oldest and most powerful clans in Rajputana, entitled to nineteen guns, which put his standing just below Baroda, Mysore, Kashmir, and the Nizam.

In a way, he was Sikander's distant cousin, because Phul Singh, who had founded the Phulkian houses of Punjab had been a Sisodia as well. However, unlike his family, who prided themselves for being forward thinking, the Mewari Sisodias were said to be very old-fashioned, firm believers in tradition, still adhering to archaic practises like *purdah* and *jauhar*. Fateh Singh in particular was said to be as fractious as a Puritan, and lived his life trying to emulate the very model of the abstemious warrior king, supposedly shunning any and all vices, whether it be women, wine, or luxury.

In fact, Sikander thought, he was also supposed to be boy-cotting the Durbar, the only Maharaja brave enough to openly defy the Viceroy, although the English had spread the word that he was in ill health. But now, to see him strutting about, could only mean one thing. There was something sinister afoot, and somehow, with unerring accuracy, Sikander had managed to land himself right in the midst of it.

Biting back the many questions crowding against his lips, he held his tongue, choosing instead to show the Gaekwad the courtesy of letting him have the first words.

"We were just on our way to see you."

"So the Maharana said," Sikander murmured, giving Fateh Singh a sidelong frown. "While I am always happy to see you, Gaekwad Sahib, what is this about?"

"There is a rumor that something happened in the Imperial Camp this morning. Some sort of trouble about a dead girl? And I believe you have taken it upon yourself to investigate the case. Is that true?"

"I cannot confirm or verify anything, Your Majesty," Sikander said, very careful to keep his features composed, unwilling to show how surprised he was by this question.

His reply managed to elicit a voluble snort from Fateh Singh. He was about to say something, to chastise Sikander, but before he could, the Gaekwad stayed him with a firm shake of his head.

"How long have we known each other, Sikander?"

"A very long time, Your Majesty."

"And you trust me?"

"Of course! You have never steered me wrong."

"Then listen to me now." He paused, giving Sikander the

most earnest of frowns. "I need you to cease your investigations. Immediately!"

Of all the favors he could have demanded, this was one Sikander just could not have anticipated. What possible motive could the Gaekwad have to dissuade him from investigating Zahra's murder? Could he be involved in some way, and Fateh Singh, too? His mind reeled, considering this possibility. No, he thought, dismissing it outright, Sayaji Rao would never have anyone murdered, especially a hapless woman. He was much too honorable for that. Still, that did not diminish his intuition that he was involved with Zahra in some way. But how?

"Enough of this nonsense!" Fateh Singh exclaimed, finally losing his patience. "Why are we being so polite to this…this upstart?" He fixed Sikander with a baleful glare. "You will do as you're told, is that clear? Or else you will face the direst of consequences!"

"That will not work with Sikander," the Gaekwad interrupted. "He will not be swayed by threats or intimidation. He is that rarest of creatures, a man of principle." His tone wavered between envious and sarcastic, and Sikander could not tell if he was paying him a compliment or making a critique of his character.

"Why, sir? Why is it so important that I abandon my investigation?"

"What nerve!" Fateh Singh stared daggers in his direction. "What makes you think we have to explain ourselves to the likes of you?"

"Enough, old friend! I think Sikander deserves a bit of honesty." Sayaji Rao let out a slow, cold sigh. "Tell me, my boy, have you changed your political views? Do you now support the British Dominion of India?"

Sikander responded with a chuckle. "You know how I feel, Your Majesty! I do not care one way or the other as long as they leave me and Rajpore well enough alone."

Rather than being amused, this earned another dark glare from Fateh Singh.

"I thought you said he was wise. He's just a callow fool."

Sayaji Rao shook his head. "Be honest, Sikander. Surely, you cannot be in favor of the Angrez? Look at how they think they can treat all of us, like second-class citizens in our own homeland! Take this damn circus of a Durbar as an example. People are dying of plague and famine, and all the British can think of doing is spending a fortune to put on a wasteful display of pomp and circumstance. It is abominable. While our subjects suffer the abjectest of poverty, we are forced to gather here, the most powerful men in India, compelled to sit and wait like lapdogs, and why? To appease the ego of a third-rate King. How is that admirable?"

Sayaji Rao paused, gathering a breath. "As you know, Fateh here is boycotting the Durbar publicly. Sadly, my seniority means the English will not let me do the same, and I am being forced to attend, much as it irks me. However, I will not let this moment go to waste. I intend to make a statement, to strike a blow, as it were, for our cause.

"I cannot divulge more, but let it suffice to say, there are things in play here, my boy, plans unfolding behind the scene that are much more complicated than you can imagine. And your investigation, Sikander, will put our scheme in grave jeopardy, which is why I ask again, will you oblige me? Will you let sleeping dogs lie?"

Sikander's mind reeled. Could this mean that Sayaji Rao and Fateh Singh had hatched some sort of plan to sabotage the Durbar, to undermine the King's grand entry? But how was Zahra involved in all this? That was what he could not peg out—unless, of course, she had been working for the two of them. Could that be it?

"I cannot help you, sir," Sikander said, his voice thick with regret. "Much as I wish I could, I gave the Viceroy my word."

Sayaji Rao held his gaze for a long time, before nodding curtly. "So be it. I cannot say I am not disappointed. But I understand your decision, Sikander."

"Is that it?" Fateh Singh's face burned a bright crimson, like he was about to combust spontaneously. "What if he goes straight to the blasted English and blabs everything?"

"No, he will not. If there is one thing Sikander cares about even more than his damned curiosity, it is his honor." Sayaji Rao sighed. "It always comes down to a man's honor, and that is one quality this boy possesses in excess. Come on, Fateh, let us leave before someone sees you. Sikander, I trust you will manage to find your way back to your hotel on your own."

As the Gaekwad turned and returned toward the car, Sikander could not resist the urge to call after him. "This is a dangerous path you are treading, sir. Be careful."

"Someone has to make a stand, my boy. Sometimes, a man does not have the luxury to choose his duty. Sometimes, his duty chooses him."

With that, he clambered into the passenger seat of the Packard. Fateh Singh followed, but not before pausing long enough to offer Sikander a disdainful scowl.

"If you dare breathe a word to anyone, I will track you down, I swear it on my honor."

"I wish I could say it was a pleasure to meet you, Fateh Singh-ji, but I would be lying."

The Rajput snorted and slammed the door. A moment later, the car growled into life, but before it could move away, the Gaekwad leaned out of the rear window to peer at Sikander one last time.

"I will leave you with this warning, my boy. Sooner or later, you will have to pick a side."

"What if I choose not to? What if I wish to remain neutral?"

"You cannot," Sayaji Rao said mournfully. "We have no choice, Sikander. Our time is ending. A new world awaits, a new order, and there is no place for gilded peacocks in that age. Either you are for India, or the English. You cannot hope for both, or you shall belong to neither."

Chapter Thirteen

Shadows.

He is drowning in shadows.

They surround him, viscous, eddying like smoke. He tries to move, but his limbs are frozen. He cannot move, his flesh has petrified to stone.

His eyes widen with horror as he realizes the shadows are alive. They writhe, and creep toward him, sharp tendrils, reaching out for him. He opens his mouth to scream, but no sound emerges, only a dull chattering of his teeth. The shadows are as frigid as ice, and wherever they touch his skin, it burns, and he weeps, bleeding not droplets, but frozen shards, of blood.

And then the smoke coalesces, hardening, lips first, then the vague shape of a nose and a sinuous neck, the suggestion of matted strands of hair, undulating like eager fingers, and then, last of all, those dreadful eyes, as black and opaque as tar. It is her, the dead girl. That wreck of a mouth opens, her swollen tongue emerging to lick his lips, tasting him.

"It is your fault," she whispers. He can smell the grave on her, as bitter as spoiled meat.

"You killed me."

"You let me die."

She smiles. He sees that her teeth are impossibly sharp, curved, gleaming like scimitars. She leans forward and grazes his mouth with her own, delicate, a lover's first kiss. It is surprisingly erotic,

*and his heartbeat quickens. But then, there is a rending, a tearing,
as she bites him, ripping a gobbet from his mouth and swallowing
it, his blood smearing her mouth like a nightmarish rouge.*

Gasping, Sikander sat up, to find Charan Singh's shaggy
face looming over him, wearing its characteristic expression of
one part amusement and two parts disapproval.

"Are you having a heart attack, huzoor? Shall I fetch the
doctor?"

"Oh, do go away, you oversized baboon!"

"It would be best if you arose, Sahib. There is a message
from Malik Umar Hayat Khan. He has arranged an appointment for you to meet with the Nizam in an hour. If you do not
hurry, you will be late."

Biting back a curse, Sikander forced himself to sit up as
hastily as he could manage. A familiar ennui brushed against
the edges of his consciousness. It was never far, a despondence
that ebbed and rose like a tide. On most mornings, it was easily quelled, but on some days, like this one, it assailed him as
relentlessly as a sickness, an ache in his bones that made every
movement, however minor, an ordeal.

"What time is it?" he asked, staggering to his feet.

"Just after eight, huzoor. I have taken the liberty of laying
out an appropriate suit." The big Sikh gave Sikander a stern
frown. "You must look the part if you are visiting someone as
important as the Nizam. And, for once, try to be on your best
behavior, will you? Whatever you say or do, it will have a bearing on your reputation, and on Rajpore's."

That imprecation was precisely what Sikander found himself contemplating as he bathed and dressed. Of all the proverbial jewels in England's Imperial crown, the Nizam-ul-Mulk
of Hyderabad was undoubtedly the most resplendent. To milk
the metaphor for all it was worth, he was a flawless diamond,
a veritable Kohinoor. In comparison, Sikander was a garnet,
perhaps, or a topaz, semi-precious in value at best, and rather
undistinguished in quality.

Interestingly, the origins of the Asaf Jahis were exceedingly humble. The founder of the dynasty, Mir Qamar-ud-din Khan , had been a minor Turcomani general who had been elevated to the position of Governor of the Deccan by Aurangzeb's successor Farrukh-siyar, only to usurp power in the wake of Nadir Shah's sack of Delhi, thus starting the decline of the Mughal domination of India. His sons and grandsons had proven to be even more politically adroit, allying first with the French against the English, and then switching sides to support the English against the French. As a result, even as the embers of Seringapatam smoldered, Hyderabad had eclipsed Mysore to emerge as the preeminent power in Southern India, encompassing an area roughly the size of France.

A century later there was no prince more exalted than the Nizam, nor any wealthier. The current holder of the title, Osman Ali Jah, had assumed the throne just some months previously, when his father had succumbed to an unexpected stroke of paralysis at the youthful age of forty-six—caused, no doubt, by the excess of good living for which he had been renowned. If rumor was correct, he was said to be the richest man in the world, with a fortune exceeding a billion pounds, a sum so monumental that even Sikander, who was a very prosperous man himself, simply could not envision it without shuddering involuntarily.

Naturally, this immense disparity in status left Sikander, who was ordinarily as intrepid as a Jason, feeling rather nervous. How was he to proceed? If it had been Jind or Nabha or one of the Sisodia lads, someone who was at roughly the same level as himself, he would not have spared a second thought about showing up unannounced under the pretext of making a social call. But one did not just drop by to see the Nizam of Hyderabad without an invitation. Not only was that tantamount to social suicide, but Sikander doubted if Osman Ali Khan even had any inkling who he was, or even exactly where Rajpore was located.

It was a peculiar sense of helplessness for Sikander, indeed. Ordinarily, he was accustomed to using his rank and power to intimidate potential suspects into cooperating with his investigations. But, this once, it seemed he was the littlest fish in the pond. Much as he would have love to resort to his favorite tactic and try to bully the Nizam into submission, Sikander was wise enough to realize that there was no way a prince with a mere eleven-gun salute could push a twenty-one-gun *nawab* around, not without causing a serious diplomatic incident.

With this realization weighing heavily on his mind, just as he was putting the finishing touches to his dressage, the door creaked open, and Captain Campbell strode in, whistling merrily.

"Ah, excellent!" he exclaimed. "I feared I was late, but, thank heavens, I am just on time. I stopped for breakfast, you see. Have you had breakfast yet, sir? No? Then you shall have to interview the Nizam on an empty stomach, for we have no time to waste."

Sikander bit back a groan. To his chagrin, he had managed to forget all about the Captain. Unfortunately, the man was even more persistent than a missionary, it seemed, and was absolutely determined to stay attached to Sikander's side, quite as cumbersome as a limpet.

"There is no need for you to accompany me, Captain. I am more than capable of managing this interview by myself."

"I have no doubt of that, sir. Unfortunately, sir, my orders are unequivocal." He offered Sikander a beaming grin. "Besides, I am quite looking forward to seeing you in action. How are you going to do it, if I might ask? What approach are you planning to take?"

Sikander gave him a withering look. The man's incessant cheerfulness was beginning to grate at his nerves. Not only was it much too early in the morning to be quite so upbeat, but unknowingly, the Captain had managed to remind Sikander of how nervous he really was at the prospect of interviewing the

Nizam. How on earth was he expected to interrogate the most powerful of India's princes, without giving irrevocable offense? And how was he supposed to carry out an effective investigation without mentioning the crime that had been committed?

It was a trepidation that grew and grew. Mixing in his stomach with the sour acid of half-digested alcohol and the pangs of barely suppressed hunger, it rapidly mounted toward nausea as they took a seat in the vehicle that Charan Singh had prepared for the occasion—a green Silver Ghost with carriage-work by Barker's of Mayfair. Thankfully, the journey from the Majestic to the Hyderabad encampment did not take too long. Given the Nizam's exalted status, quite naturally, only the finest of locations had been granted to him. It was situated at the very forefront of the Native Chiefs quarter, bordered on one side by the Najafgarh Canal, and on the other by the Coronation Road, a stone throw's away from the Commander-in-Chief's camp and the cul-de-sac that housed the Royal Enclosure.

Unlike the other Maharajas, the Nizam had chosen to eschew ostentation in favor of muted simplicity. Instead of a grand archway, a simple pebbled path flanked by potted shrubs led to an elegant gateway flanked by four minarets, in the style of what was known in India as a Chaumakha *darwaza*, not unlike the famous Charminar. As Sikander's vehicle drew up before it, he noted with bemusement that there were no soldiers on guard dressed in regimental finery, no regimental band waiting to break into salutation each time any dignitary chose to make a visit.

He gave his driver a quick instruction to remain with the Rolls before turning to saunter through the archway, followed closely by the ever-obtrusive Captain Campbell. A quick glance at his gold Breguet told him he was exactly one half hour early, an observation which managed to elicit a tight smile. Punctuality was very nearly a mania with Sikander, and in his opinion, there was no worse way to offend someone than by showing up late for an appointment.

Beyond the arch, to his right, he saw that eight whitewashed buckram tents were arranged in a lopsided U. Opposite them, on his left, a large, resplendent open-sided *shamiana* had been erected in Imperial purple silk embroidered with gold braid, about the size of a circus marquee. Next to it stood a small reception pavilion, a gazebo with a peaked roof surrounded by finely carved ivory *jalis*, each about seven feet high.

Outside this enclosure, a servant waited, an elderly *khidmutgar* clad in spotless white silk who was watching them with a rather assertive half-smile.

"What do you want?" The man asked rather too pointedly, making no effort to bow or genuflect as Sikander approached him.

"I am here to see the Nizam sahib."

"The Nizam sahib is not in residence here. He is staying in the Old City," the man said rather too self-assuredly for Sikander's taste.

"I am well aware of that. However, he made an appointment to see me here, at half past nine."

"Is that so?" With one raised eyebrow, he held up a silver hunter. "According to my watch, you are much too early."

"I will be happy to wait," Sikander snapped, annoyed by the man's' impertinence. He had never admired impudence, particularly from other people's servants.

The man pursed his lips, looking Sikander up and down with a sneer, as if to suggest this was an entirely unreasonable suggestion.

"I shall check," he said, and vanished into the pavilion without offering another word of explanation. A good fifteen minutes drifted by, time Sikander spent trying not to lose his temper, clenching his fists so hard that his fingernails left raw red crescents in the skin of his palms, before the man returned, popping his head back out to say, "Well, are you coming? Or would you prefer to stay out here?"

Holding open the entrance to the tent, he beckoned

Sikander to enter. Giving the servant an exasperated scowl—
which was completely wasted, for his supercilious grin did not
waver—Sikander moved forward. In his wake, the Captain
began to follow, but the servant forbade him with a brisk wave
of a hand. "You will remain here!" he said.

He pointed at Sikander. "The Nizam wishes to see only him,
not you."

The Captain hesitated, looking to Sikander for affirmation.

"I don't see what choice we have," the Maharaja said with a
shrug, trying not to let his exultation show, secretly delighted
to be rid of the albatross around his neck.

"Very well," Campbell said reluctantly, "I shall wait by the
car." He spun on one heel and marched away.

Sikander followed the cocky servant into the pavilion.
Inside, he found himself in a sitting room so opulent it was
very nearly garish, all silk tapestries and Charles X antiquities.
The *khidmutgar* barely gave barely him time to spare one glance
at his surroundings before hurriedly ushering Sikander onward
as if he were a recalcitrant chicken, shooing him through a
nearby doorway into a private meeting room.

Unlike the previous parlor, this room's décor was spartan.
Just a single Louis XVI gilt armchair flanked a rather handsome
French rosewood *bijouterie* table. Behind the chair, an Art
Nouveau four-panel screen bisected the room, its façade painted
to depict a naked nymph rising from an ocean of pearls. No
refreshments awaited atop the table, as was customary. Instead,
its sole occupant was an Ormulu clock, featuring Athena as
Winged Victory.

"Sit over there," the impertinent servant commanded,
pointing at the solitary chair. "His Eminence will be with you
when he is ready."

With that, he held out one hand, to indicate he had the
gall to expect a tip for such completely impolite behavior. All
Sikander gave him was a very frosty glance, before settling into
the chair with stiff hauteur, leaving the man to retreat with an
insultingly noisome sniff.

The minutes dragged by. Five, then fifteen, then half an hour. The appointed time came and passed, but still the Nizam did not appear. Sikander closed his eyes and tried to slow his breath, like a yogi, trying to quell his impatience. Unfortunately, even this old technique, which normally did the trick, failed him miserably on this occasion. Not only was he coming perilously close to the boiling point at being kept waiting like a common supplicant, but the ticking of the clock was beginning to grate on his nerves. Amidst the still silence of the room, it seemed much too loud, a steady tick-tocking that only accentuated the passage of every second, so tiresome it made his teeth grind.

Added to that, his irritation was intensified by his mode of dress. The outfit chosen by Charan Singh was entirely the antithesis of his customary black *sherwani*. It was the military uniform of a Colonel of the Rajpore Cavalry, a navy-blue worsted wool tunic with red piping, paired with pale-blue breeches and buff Hussar boots, topped by a *pugree* in red silk. While it made him look quite resplendent, the outfit was made for parading on horseback, not sitting in a chair, and it was only a matter of time before the high collar began to chafe at his neck and he found himself sweating rather too much, a condition intensified by the mugginess of his surroundings, which were sadly bereft of any ventilation whatsoever.

Finally, he could endure it no longer. Sikander sprang to his feet, and impatiently, began to pace back and forth. Five short steps and then a spin on his boot-heel, and then five more, to repeat the whole thing over and again. He lost track of how long this went on, a steady circuit that had very nearly begun to wear a groove in the expensive Hereke carpet underfoot, before the servant returned.

"Where is the Nizam?" Sikander snapped. "I have been waiting over an hour."

Ignoring his complaints, the servant proceeded to fold the screen back, to reveal that there was another chair on the other side, a twin to the one Sikander had so recently occupied. In it sat a rather nondescript man, enjoying what seemed to be a cup of tea while perusing a copy of The *Times of London*, which he folded and put away before leaning back to offer Sikander a sardonic smile.

This was the wealthiest man in the world! Sikander thought, trying not to scoff. Why, judging by the way he was dressed, he looked more like a teacher of Naskh calligraphy than a king. The previous Nizam, Mahbub Ali Khan had been famous for being a dandy and a sybarite. It was said that he had devoted a whole wing of his palace to his wardrobe, and refused to ever wear the same outfit twice. Sikander had seen him once from a distance while attending a state dinner, a handsome greyhound of a man with old-fashioned whiskers in the style made famous by Albert Victor, clad impeccably in a *sherwani* embossed with filigree of gold. To Sikander's boyish eyes, Mahbub Ali Khan had epitomized the very quintessence of an Indian monarch, as magnificent as something out of the pages of a history book.

The gentleman who confronted him now could not have been more different. Unlike his father, Osman Ali Khan was a pale whisper of a man, short, with a cadaverous face and bulbous eyes and a bristling moustache worn *en brosse*. He was clad in a tattered, somewhat slovenly, damask dressing-gown and a pair of comfortable slippers, with a woolen scarf wrapped around his neck and a Rumi topi perched on his narrow skull.

The only thing betraying the vastness of his power and wealth was the cold reptilian eyes which watched Sikander disdainfully, waiting, almost inviting him to lose his cool. Sikander's own eyes narrowed to mere slivers. From the mocking expression decorating Osman Jah's face, it was obvious the Nizam had been seated there for some time, which could only mean that he was playing some sort of game with Sikander. But what was he trying to achieve? Was this personal, intended only for his benefit? Had he offended the man in some way, even though they had never met before? No, he concluded after a moment's consideration, this was obviously a rather adolescent way to remind Sikander of his place, just another way for him to show off his power, like the supercilious servant, a means for the Nizam to amuse himself at someone else's expense.

Sikander found himself recalling a story he had once heard about the previous Nizam. He had chosen to keep the Resident of Hyderabad, the senior-most Englishman in the south, waiting for four hours after making an appointment to see him. When he had finally deigned to grace the man with his presence, the exasperated Resident had asked why he had been kept him waiting for so long.

"Because I felt like it," the Nizam had replied, "and there is nothing you can do about it."

The son, it seemed, Sikander thought, his cheeks reddening, had inherited his father's bad habits, if not his sense of style. It took much of his self-control to contain his exasperation, to force himself to still his naturally waspish tongue. He knew only too well that he could not afford to alienate the Nizam. Not only could the man buy and sell Rajpore a hundred times over, but Sikander needed to stay on his good side, if for no other reason than to question him. That was why, instead of giving the man the full broadside he so righteously deserved, Sikander made a great effort to maintain his *sangfroid*.

"Your Eminence!" Very deliberately, he offered the Nizam the mildest of nods, a tremor of his neck so infinitesimal it was as good as an insult. "It is an honor to meet you, at long last."

Osman Ali Khan's gaunt features split into a smile, obviously delighted by Sikander's effrontery, muted as it was.

"Which one are you? Kapurthala, is it, or Nabha?"

"Neither, actually. I am Sikander Singh of Rajpore."

"Is that so?" The Nizam shrugged, a dismissive gesture. "Forgive me! You know how it is. You minor kings from Punjab, you all look much the same."

It was a calculated insult, obviously another test designed to get a reaction from him, which was exactly why Sikander strained to maintain his equanimity. He had no intention of letting the Nizam have the satisfaction of getting the upper hand quite so easily.

"This is for you," Sikander said. "A small token of my admiration. Thank you for finding the time to see me."

Solemnly, he held out a small gift-wrapped parcel. *Take him a present*, Malik Umar had suggested, *that should loosen his tongue. Osman Ali Khan is a magpie. He loves things, especially shiny ones, much more than he cares for human beings.*

He had been right on the money, because the Nizam snatched the proffered gift as greedily as a child at Christmas. Impatiently, he tore away the gift-wrapping to reveal an ivory snuff box inlaid with mother of pearl and tortoise-shell.

"It is from Ottoman Turkey," Sikander explained, "the Süleymaniye era, to be exact. The dealer I purchased it from assured me that it belonged to Roxelana herself, the Hurrem Sultan."

Unfortunately, if he had expected the Nizam to be dazzled, his hopes were dashed. Rather than being beguiled, Osman Ali Khan gave the snuff box little more than a cursory glance, before shoving it roughly into one of his pockets.

"Oh, do sit down," he carped, "my neck hurts from looking up at you."

Trying to hide his dismay, Sikander obeyed. Returning to his chair, he settled into it and crossed his legs before extracting a sterling silver cigarette case from the inner pocket of his tunic.

"Would you care for a cigarette?" he asked, offering the Nizam the case. Leaning forward, Osman Ali helped himself to not just one, but a handful of Sikander's hand-rolled Fribourg & Treyer Sobranies. They disappeared into another of the pockets of his dressing gown, except for the one which he broke carefully in two, placing one half between his lips and tucking the other away behind his ear.

Stifling a smirk, Sikander leaned forward and lit it for him, before proceeding to ignite his own.

"Very nice." The Nizam took two satisfied puffs, and held out his hand. "Might I see the case?"

When Sikander handed it to him, he examined it carefully, his eyes lighting up with barely concealed greed. "Can I keep this?"

Sikander hesitated. The cigarette case had been a birthday gift from his long-suffering mistress, Helene, a handsome solid silver Imperator made by Cartier, embossed with the Rajpore crest. While he was loath to part with it, quite naturally, how could he refuse the Nizam without seeming churlish?

"By all means," he said, realizing he had no choice.

"And the lighter, if you please?"

Osman Ali held out one gaunt hand, and as soon Sikander handed over the matching lighter, a fine Flaminaire engraved with his initials, both items disappeared into the Nizam's pockets as quick as a prestidigitation.

"Excellent!" Osman Ali Khan smiled, baring yellow, tobacco-stained teeth. "Would you care for a drink, Sikander Singh of Rajpore, was it?"

"Actually, Your Eminence, I was hoping to have a chat—" but before he could conclude the sentence, the Nizam let out a shrill whistle.

In reply, the insolent servant returned once more, bearing a golden salver upon which two plump goblets of wine waited. With a wink, he offered one to Sikander, who had sat down, and then the other to his master, before retreating.

Sikander studied the decanter for a moment, his eyes widening with disbelief. It was made of pure gold, beaten by hand into the shape of a lotus blossom. No wonder the Nizam had remained unmoved by his gift. Compared to this cup, the snuff box was a mere bauble. The elaborate Kutchi filigree that inlaid its surface, a scrolling pattern of foliage and flowers, told him it was very old, from the early Mughal era, he guessed, which meant it was worth a fortune, and here the Nizam was using it like it was just another china cup. Was this an affectation, yet another display intended to humble and impress him, or did the man really have so much money to spare that he could not care a jot for appearances?

Bringing the cup to his lips, Sikander took a tentative sip. It took all his resolve not to wrinkle his eyes and gasp. No wonder Osman Ali Khan was quickly earning a reputation for being a miser—while the cup was a veritable treasure, the wine within was quite as sour as vinegar.

Stifling his disgust, he put the cup down on a nearby table, and turned back to the Nizam, only to realize he was being watched very carefully.

"You look like your mother."

"I was not aware you knew her."

"Oh, yes, I met her once, a long time ago. A wonderful, beautiful woman! She gave me a handful of boiled sweets. Did you know my father once made an offer to take her as his fourth wife and she refused?" Those reptilian eyes bored into Sikander's own, one eyebrow curving archly, as if to challenge him. "She chose your father instead. It was a mistake, of course. He was not good enough for her, not by a distance."

The Nizam's smile grew wider, as if to taunt him. "Your father was a fool, as spineless as a worm. In fact, that is the problem with you Punjabi princes. You are all vulgar, just a bunch of upstarts, little more than glorified landlords."

Sikander did not need to be a detective to deduce that Osman Ali Khan was baiting him yet again. Nevertheless, in spite of his resolution to remain calm, his pulse quickened, his hot Sikh blood rising in response to the Nizam's jibes about his family.

"I am not at all like my father, Your Eminence," He whispered through gritted teeth. "For one, I am not so easily intimidated."

The Nizam gave a derisive snort. "Is that why you are here, to talk about what you are and are not? If that is the case, then you should turn right around, and leave the way you came."

"Actually, I am here, Your Eminence, at the express command of the Viceroy himself, and it would be in your best interest if you heard me out."

If Sikander had thought that such blatant name-dropping would impress the man, he was sorely mistaken. The Nizam's reaction was quite the antithesis of what he had expected. Instead of being cowed, he let out a shrill laugh.

"Is that so?" He raised one eyebrow, "And why would I want to waste my time with the likes of you? You are nothing, nobody, as insignificant as a gnat!"

Biting his lip, Sikander contemplated this declaration. The Nizam was quite right, of course. Ordinarily, he was accustomed to being the ascendant, to dominating his suspects, but here, now, it was only too apparent that gambit would not work on Osman Ali Khan at all. It was rather a reversal of roles. What incentive could he offer the Nizam to cooperate? Money wouldn't do the trick, nor aggression. What option did that leave him then? It had to be something he wanted, he needed. The answer came to him in a flash. It was obvious Osman Ali Khan liked to play games. So, what better to inveigle him than by turning his interrogation into a game?

"I can assure you, sir," Sikander said, "you will find what I have to say quite amusing."

That remark, albeit innocuous, seemed to do the trick. Osman Ali Khan's lips twitched imperceptibly.

"Very well, boy!" He said after a long pause, "You have managed to persuade me. I will humor you, at least until I am bored. Go on, ask your questions."

Sikander resisted the urge to roll his eyes at the condescension of the Nizam's tone. Boy, indeed! The sheer gall of the man was astounding! He was nearing forty, and the Nizam was at least ten years his junior, if not more. Still, money, as the old saying went, bought privilege, and Sikander had no intention of picking a fight he could simply not afford to win, at least not just yet.

"You paid an unscheduled visit to the King Emperor's camp yesterday. Don't bother to deny it, Your Highness. I have several witnesses who can corroborate that fact, including the officer of the day."

"I wasn't planning to deny it."

"Very well, in that case, tell me why you happened to drop by."

"Do you really believe I have to explain myself to you?" Osman Ali Khan straightened up, his smile replaced by an expression of domineering disdain. "You dare to question me, as though I were a mere criminal?"

For a moment, Sikander was caught entirely on the wrong foot. He shivered, distressed that he had made a fatal misstep and bungled the interview even before it had begun in earnest, but then, thankfully, after the passage of three heartbeats, the Nizam let out an immense guffaw.

"I am only joking. Oh, you should see your face!" He clapped his hands together delightedly. "As it happens, I am on the Durbar committee, and I decided to stop by to view the *parure* necklace the Maharani of Patiala intends to gift the Queen…to make sure it was suitable. You see, I have two great passions in life, Sikander Singh. Jewels and beautiful women."

"Is that why you met with the girl?" Sikander's lips curved into a wicked smile, pleased that the Nizam had blundered so easily into his trap. "Let me refresh your memory, sir. I am speaking of a *nautch* girl named Zahra, seventeen years old, a delicate little thing. Do you recall her?"

Sikander had expected a denial, a protest, another feint, but to his surprise, the Nizam merely nodded.

"Indeed, I did meet with her! As a matter of fact, I made her a proposition."

Such a blasé admission managed to throw Sikander off balance for a moment, but he recovered admirably, barely revealing a hint of discomfiture.

"What manner of proposition?"

The Nizam pursed his lips, as if debating the good sense of speaking any more candidly than he already had.

"I have rather curious and unique tastes," he said at last. Pausing, he pulled the second half of the cigarette from behind his ear, lighting it with Sikander's lighter, which he turned over in his hands appreciatively before placing it on the table next to the discarded glass of wine.

Sikander struggled mightily not to fidget, straining to keep his impatience in check as the Nizam made a great show of puffing away, once, twice, thrice, before coughing phlegmatically and letting out a slow sigh.

"When you are as wealthy as I am, you can afford to indulge your whims, to explore the darker aspects of human nature. You see, in my youth, I enjoyed amorous pursuits as much as the next man. I have had hundreds of beautiful women, thousands," he boasted unabashedly, "but now, as I approach my middle age, I find my interest in physical sensuality fading. I find myself coming to dislike intimacy, to find it tiresome. No, what has come to excite me now is the sense of the voyeuristic. To watch is infinitely more tantalizing to me than to indulge myself." He quivered noticeably. "The screams and moans of a woman being pleasured, the groans of a man in the throes of carnal ecstasy, the sweat and the scent of musk, that is what arouses me, far more than sex itself."

In spite of the fact that he considered himself a man of the world, this confession left Sikander red-faced. What a dreadfully lecherous creature! he thought, Why, the Nizam was even more depraved than Bhupinder, who was said to make love to his concubines at least a dozen times each day!

"Is it not true that you have a very comely French mistress?" The Nizam continued shamelessly, entirely unaware how deeply he had managed to perturb Sikander. "Yes," he leered, "perhaps the two of you can be my guests one of these evenings."

"That's a very kind invitation, Your Eminence," Sikander said, inwardly cringing at the thought of introducing Helene to Osman Ali Khan, "but she has chosen to return to Paris for a few months, ever since the Viceroy decided to prohibit unofficial consorts from attending the Durbar."

"Another time, then, after the Durbar is over and done. You can come and visit me at the at the Faluknama Palace, perhaps even make a holiday of it."

It took all of Sikander's wherewithal not to wince. "If I may return to what we were discussing, you admit you approached the young *nautch* girl concerning these, ahem, diversions you enjoy."

Osman Ali Khan nodded. "As I was leaving the Viceregal tent after viewing the Patiala *parure*, she caught my eye, so to speak. I convinced the gentleman escorting me to make an introduction, and when she was brought to my presence, I made her a gift of a necklace of pearls and asked if she would care to visit me in Hyderabad once the Durbar had concluded."

"And how did she respond to your overture?"

"She refused." His face darkened, with barely repressed exasperation. "She returned my gift and told me that she could not indulge me."

"Was this before or after you told her of your special…" Sikander struggled to find the right word, "…propensities?"

"Actually, I did not say a word about my preferences. She made it very clear that she had no interest in obliging me, not for any price, even if it was only to perform for me. That is why I bid her good afternoon, and departed."

"Really? You let her insult you so openly, and then you just left?"

The Nizam nodded. Sikander resisted the urge to break into a triumphant smile. For all his game-playing prowess, Osman Ali Khan did not even realise that he had painted himself into a corner. Unbeknownst to him, he had just given Sikander a very palpable motive. It was obvious the Nizam was as proud as he was wealthy, accustomed to always having his own way, and for such a man to be rebuffed by a mere *nautch* girl, rejected like a callow teenager, he would certainly not have just walked away, not quite so easily. But was he really that reckless, that unabashedly arrogant, that he would murder someone merely out of pique?

As he considered how to broach that question, the Nizam began to chuckle, a squall that quickly swelled into a storm.

"You are said to have quite a reputation for being an intelligent man, Sikander Singh of Rajpore, but I see now that this notoriety is entirely misplaced. I thought you had inherited your mother's wit, but you are as much of a dunce as your father ever was."

Osman Ali Khan leaned forward, so close that Sikander could smell his stale breath. "I am the Nizam of Hyderabad. I have eyes and ears everywhere. Did you really think I would not know that the girl is dead?"

"Did you kill her?" Sikander asked, dropping all pretense at subtlety.

The Nizam sneered. "That is entirely the wrong question. What you should be asking is, would the Nizam of Hyderabad do his dirty work himself?" He shook his head. "I think not. All I have to do is snap my fingers and half a hundred men would jump to do my killing for me, if I so desired it." Osman Ali Khan rolled his eyes. "Not to belabor the fact that I am not a madman, Sikander Singh. Really, if I intended to revenge myself for such minor slights, why, then half the people in India would be dead and buried."

Sikander had to admit that this explanation made a great deal of sense. True, the Nizam had a motive, but at best, it was a flimsy one. And he certainly could not accuse the man of any impropriety publicly, not without an excess of proof, and even then, he ran the risk of inspiring an even bigger scandal than the Viceroy had expressly prohibited him from causing.

"I suggest, boy, that you find a way to speak with the Maharaja of Kashmir."

This suggestion took Sikander by surprise. It was well known that Hyderabad and Kashmir were the bitterest of rivals, constantly jockeying for prestige. Could Osman Ali Khan be trying to take advantage of the situation to try and embarrass his *bête noire*, or was he aware of some secret Sikander did not know? Was there any truth behind this suggestion, or was it just a case of blatant misdirection?

"Why should I believe you? I mean, it is well known that you abhor Partap Singh, that you believe that it is you who should be ruling over Kashmir since it has a vast population of Mussulmans and you perceive yourself as their spiritual leader."

"An interesting conjecture! Nonetheless, regardless of my personal disregard for the Dogra Raja, I assure you, he is a more than worthy suspect for you to investigate."

"What makes you so certain of that?"

"As it happens, when I arrived at the camp, who should I see but Kashmir's *munshi* leaving in a buggy. When I made a discreet inquiry to ascertain what he was doing there, I was informed that he had come to deliver a private letter. The officer of the day, a rather taciturn sergeant, was most reluctant to divulge who it was intended for at first, but after a small gratuity—" he loosened his tongue soon enough. Can you guess who was the recipient of the letter?"

The answer was obvious enough. "The girl," Sikander said hoarsely. "It was addressed to Zahra."

"Well done!" The Nizam made a great show of feigning mock approbation. "Perhaps you Sikhs have half a brain after all."

"But why?" Sikander murmured. "Why would Partap Singh of Kashmir send a private letter to a *nautch* girl?"

"A fine question," the Nizam echoed. "Now why don't you go off and ask him that, eh, and stop wasting my time?"

Clapping his hands together, he summoned his rude *khidmutgar* yet again.

"You may show Mr. Singh out," he commanded. "He has begun to bore me."

Chapter Fourteen

As Sikander made his exit from the Hyderabad camp, Captain Campbell came rushing up to accost him.

"Well, what did Old High and Mighty have to say for himself?" Campbell hopped restlessly from foot to foot, as nervous with excitement as a schoolboy.

"He is not involved," Sikander retorted, refusing to elaborate any further.

"Are you certain of that, sir? The Nizam is well known for being rather a clever sort."

Sikander gave him a derisive glare. "Just because I said a few kind words to you last night, Captain, does not give you permission to question my judgment."

"I meant no insult, of course," Campbell hastily apologized. "It's just that this has been an utter waste of time, hasn't it?"

Inwardly, Sikander had to agree. The Nizam's interview had left him with considerably more questions than answers. For one, it was dismaying to think that news of the girl's demise had already begun to spread through the native encampments. That only made his position more precarious. One whisper in the wrong ear, a single misstep, and a scandal of epic proportions would erupt. And who would be blamed? Him, of course. At best, he concluded, he had a little less than a day left, to find Zahra's killer before the King made his grand entry. And while it was true that he had acquired ample fodder for gossip, some rather startling and embarrassing secrets about the new Nizam's boudoir habits, he had no intention of sharing what he had learned with the Captain, who was, by all apparent signs, blessed with lips as loose as a platypus'.

"So, whatever shall we do now? Back to the Majestic with our tails between our legs?"

Sikander scowled, his hackles rising. It was bad enough he had been forced to drag Campbell along everywhere, but to have to put up with his incessant questions and his decided over-familiarity, it was quite enough to make him want to scream.

"I think, Captain, it is time we paid a visit to the Maharaja of Kashmir, and offered our respects."

Conveniently enough, the Kashmir camp was located very near the Hyderabad enclosure, about halfway up the Coronation Road. For a change, Sikander decided to leave the car behind, and make the walk across instead. As he strode along, rather than engaging in conversation with the Captain, who insisted on sticking doggedly to him, he considered what he knew of the Maharaja of Kashmir and his antecedents.

As far as the hierarchy of India's princes went, Kashmir was right at the very top, second only to the Nizam of Hyderabad. Along with Mysore, Baroda, and Gwalior, these were the five most powerful states, each entitled to a salute of twenty-one guns. Territorially, the kingdom of Kashmir encompassed a vast tract of land, stretching from the alluvial plains of the Jhelum and the Pir Panjal in the south, to distant Gilgit and the vast wall of the Pamir Mountains in the north. Its history was as ancient as India itself. This was where the fabled Silk Road concluded, where every invader who had ever marched into the subcontinent had left behind bloody footprints, from Alexander the Great and Kanishka, to Taimur the Lame and Mahmud of Ghazni, until at last it had been annexed by the Mughal Empire. That had come to an end in 1540, when Nadir Shah had sacked Delhi, and Kashmir had briefly come under Afghan dominion, ruled over by the Durranis until it was conquered by Maharaja Ranjit Singh and the Fauj-i-Khas, and assimilated into the kingdom of the Sikhs.

Still, in spite of the immense size and ancient history of the kingdom, Sikander felt little but disdain for the current rulers of Kashmir. Why? Quite simply because they were in the truest sense of the word, *arrivistes*. Unlike his own family, which traced its origins back to the ancient Aryan tribes that had settled the plains of the Indus, the Dogras were second-rate Rajput adventurers. Although they were always quick to assert that they were descendants of Surya, the god of the Sun, the founder of the dynasty, Gulab Singh, had begun his career a mercenary in the service of Maharaja Ranjit Singh. He had been sent to subjugate the original rulers of Jammu, but then, when the English had arrived, had betrayed his master and sat back and twiddled his thumbs while the Anglo-Sikh wars took place. And then, when Ranjit Singh had died and the English had annexed Punjab, he had quite literally purchased his throne from them, for the sum of seventy-five *lakh nanakshahi* rupees.

The very thought of buying a title was enough to make Sikander sneer. It was about as *nouveau riche* as one could get, but then what could you expect from a bunch of jumped up horse-herders? As if that wasn't bad enough, he had heard the stories of how Gulab Singh had managed to amass such a dazzling sum. Though his family liked to say that they had won their wealth as spoils of war, the truth was that he had been a slaver, plain and simple, who had made his fortune selling Yousufzai women and children to the brothels of Lahore and Multan, as had his son, Ranbir Singh, who had been famous for commanding his men to spare the lives of Yasin women during his campaigns against the Afghans so that they could later be put on the block to be auctioned as concubines.

Why, he thought, as their destination hove into view, one had to look no further than the entrance to the Kashmir camp to discern that Partap Singh, the current Maharaja, was at heart a *parvenu*. Naturally, being a senior Maharaja, just like the Nizam, he had been allocated an enviable location for his camp. However, unlike Osman Khan, Partap Singh had to decided to broadcast his importance by making a spectacle of his camp. The entire frontage of the Kashmir encampment had been enclosed by a wall wrought from fretted walnut panes, each seven feet high and three feet wide, carved with floral designs in the traditional Gatha style. At the very center of this elaborate palisade, in imitation of the Pandrethan Temple, a massive triumphal gateway had been erected, manufactured from slabs of gleaming *sheesham*, with each gatepost standing some thirty-five feet tall, intended to be visible from a great distance to anyone who traveled down the Princes Road.

Partap Singh had been very quick to declare he was trying to bring attention to the skill of traditional Kashmiri artisans, but to Sikander, who was well versed with princely egos, it was only too obvious that he was trying his best to show off. In fact, far too many of the Maharajas had come to think of the Durbar as a way to show off. Bahwalpur had thrown up an arch to rival Titus' Gate, and Jind had a sandstone gateway fit to put the Bulund Darwaza to shame. That was another of the reasons Sikander had chosen to take up residence at the Majestic. He had neither the patience nor the stomach for such petty pursuits, and while his peers sweated it out here under the winter sun, scheming and plotting to outdo one another, he was perfectly content to sleep swaddled in silk sheets beneath a proper roof, rather than buckram or canvas.

His musings were interrupted by a hoarse cough behind his shoulder.

"Yes?" he said, turning to the Captain, who was eyeing him with an expression of intense trepidation.

"How well do you know Partap Singh of Kashmir, Your Majesty?"

Sikander furrowed his brow. *Not well at all*, he thought. He had met the man only once, years ago, when his mother had hosted a gala for the Punjab princes to celebrate his coming of age. What he recalled from that occasion was a dull, rather stodgy man, old beyond his years, with all the personality of one of the Hangul for which his state was so renowned.

"Only very vaguely. Why do you ask?"

Campbell hesitated, choosing his next words very carefully. "There are rumors, sir, that he is not quite loyal to King and Country."

Sikander had heard several such unsavory stories himself, perhaps the most persistent of which was the rumor that Partap Singh had been flirting with the Czar. In fact, in 1889, long before he had assumed the throne of Rajpore, Kashmir had become embroiled in scandal when the then-Resident Colonel Nisbet had accused Partap Singh of treason and corresponding with enemies of the British Empire, after which he was stripped of most of his powers and reduced effectively to a mere figurehead, a puppet in the truest sense of the word.

Even though almost two decades had passed since that deplorable incident, Sikander was not surprised to find that the rumors of Partap Singh's disloyalty remained as pervasive as ever. Of course, he knew from personal experience not to pay too much attention to such hearsay. Why, at any given moment, there were a dozen stories about himself doing the rounds: that he was illegitimate, that he was a spy for the Germans, that he had murdered his mother and father and usurped the throne of Rajpore from the rightful heir, Lal Singh, and strangest of all, that he was a dabbler in dark arts and black magic.

"I am quite aware of Partap Singh's picturesque reputation. I am also aware that a great many of the stories about him are entirely unsubstantiated."

"Indeed, but as the old adage goes, where there is smoke… and so on." Campbell frowned. "That is exactly why we shall have to proceed very carefully. We cannot afford to offend him."

"We? There is no we, Captain." He gave Campbell a scornful look. "As far as I am concerned, you are excess baggage, and

I would suggest you imitate a trunk and keep your lid shut. No matter how ripe the urge to act smart, you will hold your tongue. Is that clear?"

The briefest flicker of fury flashed across Campbell's face, no doubt for being given a talking-to like a recalcitrant school-boy, but he recovered quickly, his anger replaced by his familiar grin. "Your wish, my command," he said with a nod, stepping aside so Sikander could enter the Kashmir enclosure.

Thankfully Partap Singh's staff were far better trained than the Nizam's uncouth servant. The Durban recognized them, and immediately led them to the reception pavilion, which was handsomely decorated with a distinctly Kashmiri theme, more fretted wooden *jallis*, hand-knotted woolen carpets, a pair of carved chinar sofas, and a silver chandelier polished to a sheen.

They were not kept waiting long. In a matter of minutes one of Partap Singh's myriad *vakeels* came trotting out, a handsome Sikh in a sky-blue *sherwani* who wore his beard parted down the middle, in the Mewari style.

Sikander smiled as he performed the ritual *namaskar*, joining his palms and bowing low at the hips respectfully. He recognised the man. His name was Sant Singh and he was one of his manservant's many relatives, a second cousin or some such, although it was difficult to be sure since Charan Singh's relatives were as numerable as mice in a paddy field. Still, to encounter one here simplified his task immensely.

"I would like to speak with Partap Singh, if he could spare a moment."

"Of course," the man replied smoothly, without a blink. "I shall inquire if His Highness is available, if you would be so kind as to wait."

"Thank you. I am in your debt," Sikander reached into his pocket to extract a small silk purse filled with coins which he offered to Sant Singh, but the man refused this gratuity with a dignified nod.

"There is no need, huzoor. It is my honor." He offered

Sikander a cheeky grin. "I have heard much about you from my cousin, almost all of it complimentary."

He retreated, leaving Sikander and Captain Campbell to settle into a pair of matching rococo-style chairs. Barely had he exited when the curtain obscuring the entrance-way to the pavilion parted, and a pair of lissome handmaidens entered. They were twins, perfectly identical in every way, clad in matching silk *phirans* that came to their knees. Below the knees, their legs were bare, revealing shapely ankles weighed down by strings of silver anklets which made the most delightful sound as they swayed into the room, a clink-chinking that made Sikander smile appreciatively.

The first girl bowed low and offered Sikander a tray bearing a pair of warm towels perfumed with amber and musk. Meanwhile, the other girl crossed to a table at the distant corner of the pavilion, where a copper samovar waited. Uncovering it, she poured out two thimbles of *kahva*, which she served to Sikander and Campbell with a shy smile.

"Well, this is certainly civilized," Campbell said, giving the girls an appreciative glance as they exited as silently as they had arrived.

Sikander had to agree. After Hyderabad's rudeness, he thought, enjoying the taste of the saffron and cinnamon with which the tea had been flavored, it was nice to be treated with princely courtesy.

As he put down his cup, the curtain parted once more, but it was not Partap Singh who entered to greet them.

Instead, to his dismay, it was the Maharaja of Kashmir's elder brother, Amar Singh. While Sikander did not know the younger, he was only too familiar with the elder. Amar Singh had been one his father's oldest friends, a frequent visitor to Rajpore during his childhood. The years, it seemed, had not changed him much. Other than a swath of gray in his hair, he still looked much the same as he had the last time Sikander had seen him very slim with a pronounced hunch that quite ruined the cut of the silver *sherwani* he was wearing, and a face surmounted by the hook nose of the Dogras, which gave him a hawkish countenance.

Sikander could not help but shiver. His task, which was difficult enough to begin with, had now been complicated immeasurably. While he had been quite confident that he could outmaneuver Partap Singh, Amar Singh was a far more astute opponent. If Partap was the puppet, then here was the puppet-master. This was the real power in Kashmir, the Richelieu to his brother's Louis. This was the man who ran the Regent's Council, and if rumor was to be believed, the very person who had betrayed Partap Singh to the English, turning witness against his own blood so as to consolidate his hold on the throne.

"Well, if it isn't young Sikander Singh," Amar Singh exclaimed expansively. "How lucky we are that you have chosen to call upon us this morning!"

Sikander tried not to frown. He could not tell if Amar Singh was being genuine, or if he was playing with him. The man was a cipher. His mouth was smiling, but his eyes remained absolutely emotionless, as dark and still as a moonless night.

"Amar Singhji," he responded, hiding his turmoil of emotions and offering the man a wary bow.

"Oh, stop being so formal!" Amar Singh surged forward, taking Sikander by surprise as he enveloped him a tight hug. Sikander struggled not to squirm, thinking it rather too intimate. He was not at all fooled by the man's avuncular act. Amar Singh was a consummate Machiavellian, so clever he could have outwitted Mephistopheles himself. Nothing he said, nothing he did, could be taken at face value. Every word, every gesture was intentional, as carefully plotted out as a master fencer seeking out his opponent's weakness with a series of feints.

"How you have grown since the last time I saw you! What was it, ten, twelve years ago?" He gave Captain Campbell a genial smile, indicating at the chairs they had so recently vacated. "Please, do sit down." He waited until Sikander and the Captain had taken their seats, before pulling up another armchair and sinking down opposite them. "Tell me, how may I be of help to you?"

Before Sikander could respond, Amar Singh clapped his hands, and the comely twins returned to offer him a cup of *kahva*, before refilling Sikander and Campbell's glasses as well, with a pair of identically coy smiles.

"My nieces," Amar Singh explained. "Beautiful creatures, are they not?" He smiled. "Tell me, Sikander, are you married yet?"

"This is Captain Campbell," Sikander hurriedly changed the subject as the Scotsman let out an involuntary chuckle, doing a very poor job of trying to disguise it as a cough. "We were hoping to see your brother."

"Might I inquire why?"

"Oh, just a social call!" Sikander said, feigning a broad smile. "Actually, I was hoping to speak to him about the possibility of transplanting a few hundred acres of Hunza apricots to Rajpore. It could be very lucrative for both of us."

Amar Singh's eyebrows lifted, just a whisper, but it was as mordant as a laugh.

"Come now, my boy. Really? Apricots! Is that the best you can do?" His face hardened, and for a moment, Sikander could discern exactly how formidable an opponent he was, as unyielding as granite. "Please don't take me for a fool! You are not the sort of man who makes unannounced social calls, and certainly not in the company of Captains of the Coldstream Guards. No, this visit, I suspect, is about that poor, dead whore who was found in the royal enclosure last evening, is it not?"

The Captain let out an audible gasp, which he quickly tried to choke down, leaving him sputtering. Sikander, however, was not quite as shocked. Of course, Amar Singh would know about Zahra. If Hyderabad knew, then how could Kashmir not?

This was an army camp, after all, and nothing could be kept secret with half a million ears and eyes listening and watching. And most of them, Sikander guessed, were probably on Amar Singh's payroll.

Actually, the fact that Amar Singh knew what had happened made his job somewhat easier. Now that the truth was out in the open, there was no further need to keep obfuscating. To his relief, he could stop beating about the bush, and, as was his preferred habit, go straight for the jugular.

"You are correct, Amar Singhji. A *nautch* girl was found murdered in the royal reception pavilion yesterday. The Viceroy himself has tasked me to find out who was responsible for her demise."

"And how, pray tell, is this connected to Kashmir?"

"Well, it has been brought to my attention that one of your exalted brother's *vakeels* was seen visiting the King's camp yesterday to convey a private message to the very girl who was found dead. Would you care to explain what he was doing there?"

"Tell me, Sikander, do you have a copy of this message?"

"I do not. However, Captain Campbell can confirm that your *munshi* was present at the camp, as can the officer of the day, a Sergeant Mackenzie."

"Really? That is, of course, if you can prove beyond a doubt that the person who carried the message was indeed one of ours! Do you have the man in custody? Have you questioned him? Has he admitted to being one of our envoys? If not, then what do you have, my boy, but rumor and hearsay, yes?"

Sikander's heart sank as he realized how easily Amar Singh had managed to put him squarely on the back foot, without even breaking a hint of a sweat.

Unfortunately, Captain Campbell chose that precise instance to disobey Sikander's express instructions and try his hand at playing detective.

"There are several rather distasteful rumors, Mr. Singh,

about your brother. It is said that he has been cosying up to the Russians." He leaned forward, trying to intimidate Amar Singh with his height. "Is that why your envoy was visiting the girl? To try and entice her in some way to pay her to ruin the Durbar? Or were you trying to recruit her as a Russian agent, hoping to get her to spy for you perhaps, to gain access to confidential information? For that matter, perhaps your man was the one who murdered her so brutally. Perhaps he was sent there for that very reason, to get to her by pretending to be a messenger and then killing her, if only to sabotage the King's Coronation celebrations." Campbell turned to Sikander, preening as triumphantly as a peacock. "Think about it, sir. What could benefit the Russians more than managing to gravely embarrass King and Empire at this juncture, when the whole world's eyes are fixed squarely on the Durbar?"

Sikander resisted the urge to roll his eyes. What a rank amateur! The dunderhead was just grasping at straws, without an ounce of proof to back up a single one of these assertions. That was the very first rule of an effective interrogation. Never make an accusation without enough evidence to back it up. Was Campbell really naïve enough to think he could bully someone as cunning as Amar Singh? It was highly unlikely, not unless pigs had somehow learned to defy Newton's law of universal gravitation.

As he had predicted, Amar Singh was not unduly nettled by Captain Campbell's aspersions. In fact, he let out a sly little chuckle.

"An interesting theory, Campbell, was it? You have a very fertile imagination. Perhaps when you retire from the service, you should consider writing dime novels, as the Americans call them." He turned to Sikander. "Sadly, I hate to dash your friend's hopes, but I can think of several more likely suspects. Jey Singh of Alwar, for one, or Scindia. You may not be aware of this, but there was a bidding war for the girl when she was being auctioned. Alwar and Scindia both tried to purchase her, as did Idar and Nabha. However, it was your friend, Kapurthala, who won her, by a very narrow margin, I believe."

"Is that so?" Both Jey Singh and Madho Rao had immense egos, as Sikander knew from personal experience. Both gentlemen had been his contemporaries at school, and from what he remembered of them, there was no way either would have viewed such a public defeat as anything other than a grievous loss of face. But of the two, it was Alwar who made for a better suspect, he thought. True, Scindia was a hothead, but he was also a careful man, at least when it came to his reputation. Jey Singh, on the other hand, had always treaded perilously close to the line that separated sanity from derangement. There were times when Sikander had thought him very close to mad, that behind his handsome exterior, another, more savage creature hid, not unlike Robert Louis Stevenson's monstrous Mr. Hyde.

Amar Singh's next words more or less confirmed these suspicions a moment later. "Naturally, you know how Alwar is. He was not at all amused at being trumped by Kapurthala, and he swore he would get revenge. I believe his exact words were, 'If I cannot have her, then no one will.'" He gave Sikander a level look. "And now she is dead. What a convenient coincidence!"

Sikander pursed his lips, perfectly aware that Amar Singh was taunting him. Still, if there was one thing he did not believe in, it was coincidences, especially when it came to cases of cold-blooded murder.

"Why are you helping us? Why are you so eager I go and talk to Alwar?" Sikander asked, his eyes narrowing with suspicion.

Amar Singh smiled, but it was not the amiable grin he had displayed before. This was more unsettling, like watching a predator trying to seem human.

"There are several reasons, my boy. First, like you, I do not like loose ends. Plus, I have a vested interest in seeing you find the girl's killer. The last thing I wish is to see the English embarrassed in any way. In that regard, I am a loyal subject of his Majesty, a patriot, at least as long as it does not interfere with my ambitions and my plans for my son. Do you understand me?"

Suddenly, like a punch to Sikander's gut, comprehension dawned. The messenger had not been sent by Partap Singh. On the contrary, it was Amar Singh who had dispatched him. But what had been the contents of the missive? An offer, Sikander thought. It was he who had tried to recruit the girl, but for what reason? To spy for the Russians?

No, that made no sense, unless... The answer came to Sikander like a bolt of lightning. It was a classic case of misdirection, just like a thimblerig game, where a hustler tricked his mark into looking at one hand while he should have been watching the other.

It was obvious that Amar Singh had his eye on the throne of Kashmir. The only obstacle that lay in his path was his brother. And the only possible way to get rid of him and ensure that he, Amar, remained blameless was by discrediting him.

That was where the girl came in. What better way to embarrass his brother than by recruiting a spy in his name, and then exposing her to the English? The ensuing scandal would undoubtedly finish the job that he had started all those years ago—getting Partap Singh out of the way once and for all. But who stood to gain from such a course of events? Not Amar Singh himself, who was already the head of the Regent's Council that ruled Kashmir. If he had wished it, he could have seized the throne years ago, and declared himself King. No, if anything, this had to be a deeper gambit. His son—Sikander sucked in a slow breath. It was his son who would supplant Partap Singh and become the new Maharaja of Kashmir. That was what Amar Singh had been working toward all these years, to steal the *gaddi* and hand it to his son.

Sikander resisted the urge to applaud the man. Bravo! What a clever bastard he was! And talk about playing a long game! Of course, if he was right, that pretty much put paid to the theory that Kashmir was behind Zahra's death. The last thing Amar Singh wanted was any threat to the stability of British rule in India. He had spent the better part of two decades winning their confidence and turning them into his staunchest allies, and he needed them kept in power at all costs. Why? Quite simply, because without the English, there was no way he could depose his brother, not without revolt. Violence might win his son a crown, but the only way he would inherit loyalty was if the throne was given to him, not taken. That was why he needed the girl. She was only useful to him as long as she remained alive. With her dead, Amar Singh had no leverage, no way to get his plan rolling.

"You really are a very clever man, Amar Singhji," Sikander said admiringly, "almost too clever for your own good."

"I will take that as a compliment."

"Please, do not! I intended it as a warning." Sikander's face hardened. "Being clever can be a dangerous thing, because someone cleverer is bound to come by sooner or later, and then you find yourself mired in trouble you cannot think your way out of."

Rather than being intimidated, Amar Singh seemed amused.

"You style yourself as somewhat of a scholar, don't you, Sikander? Tell me, have you heard the story of the Fishes That Were Too Clever?"

"I cannot say I have."

"It is from the Panchatantra. A fine little parable." Amar Singh stretched his neck, let out a brief yawn, and began reciting.

Once, in a pond, there lived two fish, and a frog. The fish were named Satabuddhi, and Satsrabudhi, and they were both very intelligent, constantly swimming in circles and discussing the meaning of the Universe. The frog, alas, was named Ekbuddhi, and he was really quite average, preferring to spend his days doing what most frogs do, which is catch flies and sleep beneath a shady leaf.

One day, a fisherman was walking by and saw the pond. When he spied the fish swimming about, he exclaimed, "What a fine meal these fish would make! I shall return tomorrow with a net and catch them all."

After he strode away, Ekbuddhi the frog approached his piscine friends and said, "What shall we do? If we do not flee, he will catch and eat us."

"Do not fear," Satabuddhi replied, "we are very intelligent and know a hundred secret ways to evade a net."

"No fisherman will ever be able to catch us," Satsrabuddhi added. "We are much too smart for him. Between us, we have the knowledge of a hundred thousand men."

"Well, I am a simple frog," Ekbuddhi replied, "and I have only the knowledge in my head. That tells me to run away, and that is what I intend to do."

That very night, even as the fishes swam around in circles, the frog fled to another pond, taking his wife with him. When morning came, the fisherman returned and cast his net. For a while, the fishes managed to avoid him, but finally, he grew tired and decided to drain the pond itself. Taking a shovel, he dug a deep trench, and when the water drained away, it left both Satabuddhi and Satsrabuddhi high and dry, flopping around gasping for breath.

Immediately, the fisherman snatched them up. Placing Satabuddhi atop his head, and slinging Satsrabuddhi from his shoulder by a rope, he set off for his home.

As he passed Ekbuddhi's new pond, whistling jauntily, the frog turned to his wife and said, "Look, there goes the wisdom of a hundred men atop that fisherman's head, and the knowledge of a thousand men hanging from his shoulders. But I, who has so little knowledge, am still sitting here, having the last laugh."

Captain Campbell's brow wrinkled, unable to grasp the moral of the story, but Sikander saw the point of it immediately.

"That was a charming tale. Amar Singhji. I have only one last question to ask. Tell me, am I one of the fishes or the frog?"

"That, I think, remains to be determined, Sikander." With that pronouncement, Amar Singh rose to his feet. "This has been an entertaining diversion, but now, sadly, I must bid you a good-day. Go speak to Alwar, my boy, and to Scindia. I am sure they will have more answers for you than I have."

He held out his hand, and in spite of his disdain for personal contact, Sikander took it readily.

"I would wish you luck, but luck is for the uninspired. Men like you and me, we make our own luck, don't we?"

Chapter Fifteen

"What a terrifying man!" Campbell said as they exited the Kashmir camp. "You know, I could not tell for one tick if he was telling the truth or lying."

Sikander had to agree. Amar Singh was blessed with a lawyer's tongue, which was capable only of half truths and misdirection. Even though he had pointed the finger squarely at Jey Singh of Alwar, Sikander reminded himself to take the accusation at face value. Most likely it was a feint, a tactic designed to deflect attention from himself and his scheming. Still, he thought, as suspects went, Jey Singh was certainly a compelling one. Not only did he have a notoriously spotty reputation, but then there was the fact that he had been present in Bikaner, all those years ago, when Zahra's mother had been killed. Two *nautch* girls, two identical murders—surely that had to be something more than a coincidence.

"I must say, this investigating is a deuce of fun. I see why you enjoy prowling about so much."

Sikander stiffened. "Are you hard of hearing, Captain, or have you a recurring battlefield injury that makes it difficult for you to understand me?"

"No, of course not!"

"Then why do you insist on trying my patience? I commanded you to hold your tongue, but still you insist on butting in. Was I not clear enough?"

Campbell looked abashed. "Forgive my presumption, sir. I will not make the same mistake twice." He offered Sikander a contrite smile. "Well, where are we off to next? Shall we go see this fellow Alwar?"

"Not just yet," Sikander replied. "Let us go pay our respects to Jagatjit Singh first, and find out exactly what induced him to send the King-Emperor such an unlikely gift."

The Kapurthala camp was within walking distance of Kashmir's monstrous gateway, about halfway up the Princes Road. Sikander paused as they approached its entrance, casting an appreciative glance at the exterior. Unlike Kashmir, Jagatjit, who was as ardent a Francophile as Sikander, had chosen to go for understated elegance. The perimeter of his camp was marked by a simple wrought-iron fence capped by ornamental *fleurs-de-lis*, and the gate was a miniature version of the arch Septimius Severus had built in the Roman Forum, the very same structure that Napoleon had copied for the gate to the Tuileries Gardens, only one-fourth in size. The end result was very dignified, an exercise in good taste and elegance that made Sikander hum with approval.

"Are you familiar with the Maharaja of Kapurthala, sir?" Campbell inquired.

"In a manner of speaking, yes, I am."

"He is said to be rather a colorful character."

Sikander stifled a smile. That was an understatement if ever there was one. Jagatjit Singh of Kapurthala was more than colorful. He was the entire spectrum of the rainbow and then some, a man with a nature as capricious and mutable as a storm.

They could not be more different from each other. Sikander was gaunt, Jagatjit rubicund to the brink of being Rabelaisian. Sikander's habits were ascetic, Jagatjit was a sybarite who could put Caligula to shame. Sikander was careful, cerebral, private, while Jagatjit was loud, talkative, flamboyant, a man of vast and constant appetite, who was always in a hurry—to drink, to laugh, to live.

There was no explicable reason why two such dissimilar people should end up such close friends, especially since Jagatjit was a good deal older than Sikander, very nearly his father's age. Of course, a disciple of Sigmund Freud's quackery would have been quick to point out that what Sikander was really seeking was a paternal surrogate, given that his own father had died very young. Sikander had often wondered if that was indeed why he was so fond of the man. It was not in his nature to care deeply for people. He thought of them as commodities, other than a rare few, like his manservant, and his mistress, Helene. They were his family, and his love for them was unconditional, unconstrained by their usefulness to him. But friends, no, Sikander had never been the sort of person who made friends easily. Acquaintances, yes, but he rarely dropped his guard with anyone, only when he had come to trust them deeply and absolutely, which made it even more surprising that he should get along with someone quite as feckless and unreliable as Jagatjit Singh.

The only other explanation he could come up with was a very simple one. Jagatjit was bloody great fun. While there were Maharajas who had more wealth, and many who possessed greater rank, there were none who could lay claim to a grander sense of style. Though the Phulkians, especially Bhupinder Singh, were quick to dismiss him as a glorified landlord, growing rich off the rents he collected from the estates the British had granted him, the truth was that Jagatjit Singh was a very cultured, well-traveled man.

It was exactly this consideration which haunted Sikander, leaving him more than a little confused. It was difficult to imagine Jagatjit as a murderer. He was a talker, not a doer, and to strangle a woman in cold blood, to commit a crime so intimate, took a heartlessness he lacked entirely. But, still, Sikander could not prevent just the faintest pang of doubt from aching at his gut. Jagatjit was a wild card, the Joker in the pack, and it was that very unpredictability that made him so difficult to dismiss as a suspect outright.

Upon entering the camp, they were immediately intercepted by a portly Sikh dressed in a French footman's livery, a pale yellow waistcoat with silver frogging and knee breeches with silk stockings and buckled shoes.

"Your Majesty," he said, offering Sikander a traditional *kornish*, before turning and giving his manservant an even deeper bow.

"Charan Singh-ji, it is good to see you."

"Dalip," Charan Singh replied with a broad grin. "How are you, my boy?"

"The battle goes on," the man said, and they clasped hands briefly.

"Another of your brethren?" Sikander inquired.

Charan Singh let out a laugh. "My nephew, huzoor, on my wife's side."

"I should have guessed it." He rolled his eyes and turned to the porter. "We are here to see Jagatjit, obviously."

"I regret to say, huzoor, the Maharaja Sahib is not here at present."

"Damn!" Sikander cursed. He had taken a chance making an unannounced visit, hoping that Jagatjit would be loitering around this early, probably only just rising from his slumber, but now this looked to be a wasted trip.

"When will he be back, do you know?"

"Not long, sir. We received a telephone call that he is on his way." He held out his hand, inviting Sikander to a nearby tent. "If you would care to wait."

"Yes, of course." Sikander followed Dalip as he ushered them into a formal waiting room done up in the style best described as Punjabi Rococo. The roof had been cleverly hung with silk panels to mimic a dome, and the walls were festooned with gilded mirrors, making the enclosure seem larger than it actually was. The furniture was a bit modish for Sikander's tastes, a rather heavy Louis XV *encoignure* in one corner, and a Louis XVI armoire in the other, with three mismatched Chippendale chairs arranged around a marble-topped pedestal table.

"Would you care for some breakfast, sir? Some sherbet perhaps?"

"Not for me, thank you," Sikander said, choosing the chair nearest the door, with the Captain settling opposite him and Charan Singh taking up position just inside the entranceway. "But do have someone bring us a pot of coffee, will you?"

"Of course, huzoor."

"If you would like, sir," Campbell piped up as soon as the footman had left, "I would be happy to take a shot at questioning the Maharaja when he gets here. That is, you know, if you are uncomfortable interrogating your friend."

Sikander frowned, studying the Scotsman intently. He could not tell if he was merely brash, or if he was deliberately trying to inveigle himself into the investigation. Part of him still didn't trust the Captain, even though he was proving quite useful, as Malik Umar had said he would. Nevertheless, there was something about the man that managed to make Sikander suspicious, which made him wonder if he had been sent not to help him, but rather to complicate and obfuscate matters. Was he working for someone, O'Dwyer perhaps, someone who wanted Sikander to fail, or was this just his natural manner, to be overly inquisitive?

Before he could make up his mind, his musings were interrupted by a sudden din, a staccato clacking, like the volley of a Vickers gun.

"What on earth is that?" Captain Campbell exclaimed.

"Let's take a look." Sikander sprang to his feet, and moved to the rear of the tent, parting the exit flap slightly to peer outside. To his surprise, he saw that the racket was coming from a small open space not far away, a paved courtyard positioned between the tents, where a woman stood, loudly clicking her heels on the ground. She was Caucasian, not much taller than himself, with wavy coal-black hair bundled into a tight chignon, and a black ruffled dress with a flared hem, beneath which she was wearing a pair of block-heeled shoes. It was from these that the sound Sikander had heard had originated, the peculiar clattering which had startled him so.

He watched curiously, wondering what she was up to, as the woman raised her arms above her head, an elegant flourish, and clapped her hands, once-twice-thrice. In response, a servant who was seated cross-legged nearby began to crank the handle of a gramophone. Immediately, a mournful dirge of music poured forth from its spout, hissing and crackling. It took Sikander a moment to place what it was, a solea from Cadiz, and he leaned forward, realizing that the woman was about to perform.

She began by clapping her hands again, first hard, then soft. This was the *palmas*, the marking of the rhythm. Next came the *golpe*, where she stamped down on the pavement, a resounding rat-a-tat. Once that preliminary was past, she began to dance in earnest, launching into what was called an *escobilla*, a series of blindingly fast movements to show off her virtuosity with her feet. Even though he was not an aficionado of the flamenco, Sikander thought he recognized a few of the complicated steps, a *planta*, a *tacon*, another *planta* followed by a *punta*, one, two, three *chuflas* and then a blindingly skillful *talon*.

It was almost as intoxicating as a glass of *orujo*. She was transformed into something fantastical, a thing of pure *duende*, as the Spaniards called it, a spinning, shimmering blur so ecstatic he could not tell where she ended and the music began. So this was Jagatjit's Spanish Maharani, Sikander thought, the woman who had turned his head so completely. Anita Delgado, or Maharani Prem Kaur, as she now styled herself, had caught Jagatjit's eye while performing the flamenco at a café in Madrid. He had fallen in love with her instantly, and had pursued her relentlessly until she had consented to become his fifth wife. It had caused quite a scandal, but as always, Jagatjit had chosen to fly straight in the face of tradition and custom, regardless of how many tongues it set wagging.

Sikander thought he recognized what had enticed Jagatjit so

entirely. The slim poetry of her arms as they wove their complex symphony, the curve of that proud neck, the sinuous sway of her hips; she was nothing less than spectacular.

Her performance came to a conclusion all too soon. With one last clap of her hands and one final stamp of her feet, she arched her back into a question mark before letting out a loud "*alla*"! Immediately, the servant ceased his cranking, and with a drawn-out groan, the music tapered away, lapsing into a sullen silence.

Some primal instinct must have warned her that she was being watched, because abruptly, the Spanish Maharani turned directly toward Sikander. Their eyes locked into each other, and her face stiffened, as if to convey she resented being spied upon. She pulled her shawl close around her shoulders, before striding toward him as determinedly as a Pamplonan bull at the charge.

As the Maharani drew closer, the illusion she had woven while dancing was quickly dispelled. What finally came to a stop before him was rather a sweaty, stout creature, with the beginnings of a dour jowl and the faint shadow of a moustache darkening her upper lip.

"And who are you?" she scowled. "How dare you spy on me?"

"My apologies, Madam. My name is Sikander Singh, and I am a friend of your husband's."

Her brow knitted, those hirsute eyebrows coming together like two caterpillars mating.

"See-kan-dar." She pronounced each syllable carefully, as if she was trying to place the name. "Ah, *el hurón*!" She let out a laugh as recognition dawned. "I know who you are. Jagatjit speaks of you often, and of your predilection to poke your nose in other people's business. In Andalusia, where I was born, that is what we call a creature who is always sniffing about. Oh, what is the English word? Ah, of course, a weasel! You are the royal weasel, no?"

Sikander gave her a diplomatic nod. If he could have understood her better, he might have been more offended, but her accent was very thick. It was quite obvious that English was not her first language, and even to his ears, which were finely attuned to variations in dialect, he found the drift of her consonants rather incomprehensible.

"I must complain to you," she said, "about your friend. He has been neglecting me dreadfully."

"Jagatjit is an important man, Madam. He has many responsibilities to fulfill."

The Spanish Maharani let out rather an indelicate snort. "Nonsense! He is a wastrel who spends all his time drinking and chasing women. If I had known that, I would never have consented to be his wife."

Sikander resisted the urge to retort, *"Yes, you would, because you only had eyes for the Kapurthala jewels, not Jagatjit's virtues or lack thereof."* Instead, he bit his lip and tried to play the conciliator, a role that was entirely unfamiliar to him.

"I fear you are being unfair, Madam. Jagatjit is a good man. It is just that he is prone to occasional bouts of melancholy. You must bear with him. He means no harm."

"Is that so? Then why is he being unfaithful to me?" She stamped her foot, as though to punctuate this declaration. "Don't try to defend him. I am sure of it."

Sikander blushed, as did Campbell. Both men were visibly embarrassed to hear such private matters being aired publicly.

"Madam, this is not an appropriate conversation."

The Maharani's face darkened to an outraged crimson. "Oh, I see! You are one of those fellows who disapproves of women who speak their minds."

This accusation caused his face to redden again, but Sikander bit back the acerbic reply that sprang to his lips, not because he was afraid to offend, but because she had hit uncomfortably close to the truth. He did disapprove of her, but it was not because of her forthrightness. No, his gift, if he had one, was to see to the core of people, and what he saw inside her was greed, a cold-hearted calculation, and that made him dislike her instinctively, rather than some misplaced sense of misogyny.

"You Indians, you are such cavemen. Your friend expects me to stay hidden from the world, cowering obediently behind a veil, but I will not. I will be free." She tossed her hair tempestuously, a marvelously theatrical gesture. "I *will* dance."

For once, Sikander found himself entirely at a loss for words. He gave Campbell a sidelong look, but the Scotsman's only response was a sardonic grin followed by a noncommittal shrug.

Thankfully, before the Maharani could work herself up any further, Jagatjit Singh made a dramatic entrance.

Sikander let out a sigh of relief as his old friend came staggering into the tent. Quite obviously, he was returning from a night of carousing, judging by the stink of gin coming off him, and the state of his *achkan*, which was a crumpled mess.

When he saw Sikander, Jagatjit's mouth curved into a delighted smirk. However, a heartbeat later, when he noticed his Maharani glowering at him, this grin wavered, a bloom withering in the face of winter.

"Anita, how nice that you have met Sikander at last!" The words came out flat, obviously forced. Rather than mollifying the Spanish Maharani, it served to aggravate her even more, and with a contemptuous sniff, she spun on one heel and stormed away.

As she departed, Jagatjit flung himself into the nearest chair. "Charan Singh, would you be a dear and bring me a cup of hot tea?"

"Of course, Your Majesty. I am happy to serve."

Sikander studied his old friend. He had not seen Jagatjit for almost a year. The poor fellow looked a proper mess. In his youth, he had been rather heavyset, but recently, it seemed, he had managed to shed a goodly amount of weight, giving him quite an emaciated look, which was added to by the fact he had not shaved that morning, leaving his cheeks covered with greying stubble.

"You look terrible," Jagatjit said, as if he had read Sikander's mind. "Have you not been getting any sleep?"

"I could say the same thing to you. Where on earth were you all night?"

"I have been trying to avoid the apple of my eye." A long, weary sigh escaped Jagatjit's lips. "She is on the warpath."

"What did you do this time?"

"I haven't done a thing." His voice was almost a whine. "Damn her Iberian blood! I should have been more careful before I fell in love with her."

"She thinks you are having an affair," the Captain chimed in.

Jagatjit's good humor evaporated. Turning to Campbell, he asked, "And who are you?"

"Ah, yes! I am Campbell of the Guards. I am assisting Mr. Singh for the next few days."

He held out his hand, but Jagatjit pointedly ignored it. "Go away, won't you?"

"I beg your pardon?" Campbell's eyes widened, obviously alarmed by such brusque treatment.

"Make yourself scarce. I wish to speak to Sikander privately."

"Much as I would love to oblige, sir," the Captain said, glancing at Sikander, as if to solicit his support, "but I am afraid I have my orders."

"Go ahead, Captain," Sikander said. "Give me a few moments with Jagatjit. I will catch up with you later."

"But…but…" Campbell struggled to object.

"Now, please. I insist," Jagatjit repeated.

"Very well, I shall be waiting just outside." He stood and reluctantly, left the tent.

Jagatjit waited until he had departed before asking, "Who is your shadow? Are you in some kind of trouble, Sikander?"

"I'll explain later. But first, what was it you wanted to speak to me about that the Captain simply could not be permitted to hear?"

"Ah ,yes!" His smile rekindled, as giddy as an adolescent. "I am in love."

"Aren't you always?"

"Don't be facetious. This time, I really am serious."

"That's what you insist every time." Sikander grinned, and made a great show of rolling his eyes. "Who is the unlucky woman, might I ask?"

"Her name," Jagatjit said with a groan, "is Zahra."

Immediately, Sikander's face hardened. "Do you mean the *nautch* girl you sent to the King as a gift?"

"I did not send her to him." Jagatjit frowned. "That was a mistake."

He looked deeply chagrined, almost embarrassed. "Let me explain exactly what happened. The truth is that I purchased her contract for myself. I was going to woo her, ask her to be my sixth wife, or is it the seventh? Never mind! It's the Spanish hag who sent her away. When she found out about Zahra, she threw an absolute fit, and when she confronted me, on the spur of the moment, I made up a lie that I had bought her as a gift for the King." He shook his head. "The next thing I knew, she had packed her off in the middle of the night, sent her away to the King Emperor's camp."

"Is that why you went to see Zahra the day before yesterday, to try and persuade her to come back to you?"

"Yes," Jagatjit replied, not even realising he was being questioned. "I offered her any sum, anything her heart desired as a dowry, but she spurned my overtures. She said she was flattered, but she had found someone else."

"Another man?" Sikander's ears pricked up. "Did she mention who he was?"

"She did not." He shook his head. "What a lucky devil, though! Oh, Sikander, if only you could see the girl perform! She is breathtaking, like some celestial *apsara* come to life, as wanton as Menaka herself."

Sikander winced. "There is something I need to tell you, my friend." He gazed at Jagatjit solemnly. "The girl is dead. She was murdered the night before last."

He watched Jagatjit very carefully, to see precisely how he would respond to this revelation. His sorrow was nothing short of spectacular, his face crumpling with utter dismay. He let out an anguished gasp, unable to conceal his shock. It was almost astonishing, to see him so emotional, considering how adept he was at hiding what he was thinking behind a playful mask. That was when Sikander knew Jagatjit was not the murderer. Only a master actor could falsify such pain, such absolute and unequivocal regret, and while Jagatjit was a man of many parts, that was not a role he was gifted enough to play.

"Who did it?" His voice was thick with despair.

"I do not know, but I have been tasked by the English with investigating the case."

"What a waste!" Jagatjit's mouth stiffened into a scowl as sadness turned to fury. "Whoever killed her, Sikander, you have to find him. You must track him down."

"I intend to, Jagatjit. I assure you of that. I have no intention of letting him get away."

"Good!" His fingers folded into a fist. "And when you do, before you take him to the English, bring him to me. Promise me you will do that much for me, old friend."

Chapter Sixteen

"You have to stop excluding me, sir. The Viceroy was quite explicit. You must include me in every facet of your investigation."

Sikander gave the Captain a warning look, as if to remind him that he did not take kindly to being berated.

"I understand you are reluctant to have a partner, sir," Campbell continued, adopting a more circumspect tone. "I shall endeavor to stay out of your way, but if you continue to ignore me, I shall be forced to make a report. I am sorry, but that is how it must be."

The Maharaja bit back a rude comment. He was tempted to send Campbell packing, but he knew he could not, if only for the sake of expediency. He simply didn't have the time to get mired in a battle of wills, especially with the odds stacked so firmly in the Captain's favor.

"Very well," he said coldly, "I shall try my best to involve you forthwith. However, if a suspect is unwilling to speak to me in the presence of an Englishman, there is nothing I can do about that."

"I can live with that." Campbell rubbed his hands together. "Might I inquire, what did old Kapurthala have to say for himself?"

"He is not our man."

Sikander had expected the Captain to dispute him, to

question his veracity, but to his surprise, Campbell accepted his statement without a word of dissent.

"That's too bad," he said with a shrug. "I thought we had a proper lead here. So, who is next on your list, sir?"

"Bharatpur first, I think, and then Patiala. Let us go and see why exactly they each paid Zahra a visit, shall we?"

Bharatpur was firmly a middle-tier kingdom, a seventeen-gun state located some fifty kilometers west of Agra, encompassing a quadrilateral roughly the size of Luxemborg. It was rather a desolate, wild place, bordered in the west by the Banganga, and in the East by the foothills of the Vindhyas, best known for tigers and sugar cane of the highest quality. Although technically a part of Rajputana, it was ruled over by a family of Jats, the Sinsinwars. At the end of the seventeenth century, as the Mughal hold on power had weakened, Badan Singh, the descendant of a minor *zamindar*, had been quick to expand his territory. It was he who had seized much of ancient Karauli and built the stronghold after which the dynasty was named—the fort of Bharatpur, whose towering walls had earned a reputation for being very nearly as impregnable as Golconda. His nephew, Suraj Mal, had expanded the kingdom even further, briefly conquering Agra, and even subduing Delhi itself. After that zenith, however, the Sinsinwars had fallen into decline, earning a reputation for being quick to change allegiances, playing the Mewaris against the Marathas and the English until finally Lord Combermere had invested the fortress and forced them into submission in 1826.

There was an old saying in Punjab: "A Jat is your friend as long as there is a stick in your hand." There were few finer illustrations of this adage than the Sinsinwars, who had become renowned for displaying a fickleness of character and political adaptability that would have put the most brazen of Borgias to shame. True, while in previous generations this had been a benign, self-serving trait, with the previous Maharaja, Ram Singh, it had chosen to manifest as an utter disregard for normal behaviour, a disinhibition that came close to what Esquirol had described as monomania. He had been very nearly a lunatic, given to the consumption of vast amounts of liquor, and public displays of intemperate rage that had almost bordered on madness.

Sikander had only met the man once, when Ram Singh had traveled to Rajpore to attend his Coronation dinner. During the mutton course, had flown into a rage when a waiter had mistakenly dribbled a few drops of champagne onto his hand while trying to top up his glass, and in a fit of rage had very nearly beaten the man half to death with a soup spoon.

This penchant for quick violence and utter lack of self control had increased as he had aged, until one day Ram Singh had decided to shoot his barber to death, apparently because he had been displeased by the man's efforts to trim his beard. The ensuing scandal had forced the British to depose him and force him into exile, instead placing his infant son on the throne. As a result, the real power in Bharatpur had fallen into the hands of his wife, Maharani Girraj Kaur, who ruled in all but name as the Regent.

Sikander wracked his brain, trying to recall what he knew of her, which was lamentably little. She was the Maharaja's second wife, a relatively young woman who was said to be ruthlessly single-minded, concerned only with preserving her son's legacy, and trying to restore her husband's good name. She also shunned the public eye, refusing to attend any of the social functions affiliated with the Durbar and rarely left the confines of the Bharatpur enclave—all of which led Sikander to ruminate on a germane question: What had the Maharani then been doing meeting with a *nautch* girl, and deep in the heart of the British quarter? Whatever the reason, it was enough to set his every instinct on edge.

The Bharatpur Camp was located near at the far end of the Rajputana enclosure, abutting the Dahirpur Road. It was nondescript, in keeping with the Maharani's reputation for maintaining a low profile, its sole exception to ornament a rather demure *badshahi* gate made entirely of polished teak.

Upon entering the reception pavilion, a handsome space decorated with woven tapestries that chronicled the history of the Sinsinwar Jats, they were greeted not by a manservant, but by a woman butler, a middle-aged Anglo-Indian matron dressed not in the traditional Rajput *lehenga*, but rather a proper evening suit, complete with a bow tie.

It made for quite a striking change, and the Captain goggled at her, surprised no doubt, by the sight of an Indian woman in long trousers.

"If you would be so kind as to wait just a moment," she said as Sikander introduced himself. "Ma Devi is bathing. She will be with you shortly."

She clapped her hands, and a trio of comely servers came striding in. Once again they were all female, dressed identically in tie and tails, bearing a panoply of trays. The first offered steaming thimbles of what appeared to be mint tea; the second, tall decanters of what smelled to be pear cordial; and the third, a varied selection of local sweetmeats made from *jaggery* and *ghee*.

Sikander refused all three, and Campbell followed suit.

"What do we know about the Maharani?" he inquired, waiting until the seneschal and her minions had left them.

"She is a bit of a nonentity." Sikander replied, settling into a nearby chair and picking up the latest edition of the *Lahore Daily News*. "She keeps to herself. After her husband's shenanigans, I don't really blame her. She is said to be a good Regent, though. The English support her rule, which is surprising, because normally, they prefer to supplant female heirs with Resident Officers."

"Do you think she had anything to do with the girl's unfortunate fate?"

Before Sikander could reply, a child came traipsing into the room, skipping merrily through the entrance. The Maharaja studied him, unsure whether to smile or shudder. He was about ten or eleven years old, and perhaps the least lovable creature he had ever set eyes upon. Rather than being chubby, he was thin to the point of being almost skeletal. His face was gaunt, his hair oiled and combed back to expose a wide brow, beneath which a pair of deep-set eyes gave him the look of a rodent. This incongruous aspect was only complicated by the fact that he was dressed, inexplicably, in a sailor suit, complete with a beribboned hat, in a pale blue shade that seemed odd contrasted against his skin, which was very dark.

The boy paused first in front of Campbell, looking him up and down with a pronounced sneer.

"Your face is very red," he exclaimed in a singsong voice.

"It's the sun," Campbell replied. "It is very unkind to English complexions…" but the boy had already lost interest in him. He turned to Sikander, squinting his eyes and examining him very carefully.

"And who are you supposed to be?"

"I am the Maharaja of Rajpore," Sikander replied, offering the child a cool smile.

The boy responded with a florid snort. "Well, I am the Maharaja of Bharatpur, and I have seventeen guns. Rajpore only has thirteen, which means that I am much more important than you."

With that declaration, he stuck his tongue out at Sikander, before holding up one grubby hand.

"Give me your ring! I want it."

"I think not," Sikander said. It took all his wherewithal not to put the boy over one knee and give him a spanking. That was what he needed, a little discipline. *It would do his character wonders in the long run*, he thought, imagining the sort of base tyrant he would turn into without proper guidance.

The boy's face turned crimson. "You dare to refuse me," he screeched. "I shall have you killed, you cur."

"Guards! Guards!" He screamed, stamping his foot. In

response, three soldiers came rushing in, two *pehradars* led by an aging Colonel, a well-built Rajput with carefully coiffed moustache that curled halfway up his cheeks like a pair of angry caterpillars.

"Rathore," the boy commanded the Colonel, "I want you to kill him now." He pointed at Sikander. "Shoot him and get me his ring."

The Colonel looked from his master to Sikander, his expression apologetic. Obviously, he was accustomed to such tantrums, because rather than obeying the boy's orders, he offered Sikander a conciliatory nod.

"Forgive us, sahib. He is just a boy."

"I am not a boy," the little Maharaja shouted. "I am your King. I am your god." Dashing forward, he directed a well-placed kick at the Colonel's posterior. The man flinched, but rather than objecting, he fell to his knees, prostrating himself even as the boy gave him another kick—to the head this time, unsettling his *pugree*. From the practiced look of suffering on his face, it was obvious to Sikander this was not the first time he had been subjected to such a histrionic assault.

"I am putting you all on my list. Just you wait! When I am King, I will have you all killed."

He turned on Sikander, crouching in preparation for trying to kick him, but before he could follow through, a cold voice spoke up behind him.

"Behave yourself, Kishan Singh. Do not forget who you are, not for a moment!"

It was the Maharani. She stood framed in the doorway, a small woman, not more than five feet tall, but with a presence that made her seem larger than life. She was clad simply, wearing a purple sari in the Rajput style, the *pallu* pulled up to cover her head. Unlike most Maharanis, who favored an excess of jewelry, she wore a single *demi-parure*, a pair of diamond earrings and a matching necklace. Other than that, her only concession to ornament was a pearl the size of a quail's egg, decorating her parting, beneath which a crimson *tikka* was emblazoned, as striking as an exclamation mark. It was a very masculine touch, which on most women would have seemed ostentatious, but with her, it only added to her already regal bearing, an observation that Campbell agreed with wholeheartedly, it seemed, for he let out an appreciative exhalation of breath.

"He started it," Kishan Singh squealed, pointing one petulant finger at Sikander. "All I wanted was his ring. He wouldn't give it to me, the bugger."

"Go and play with your toys," the Maharani exclaimed. "Colonel Rathore will accompany you."

"But I don't want to play." The boy wrinkled his eyes and clenched his fists, in what were the early stages of an undoubtedly monumental tantrum.

"You will do as you're told. Is that clear?" the Maharani hissed. It was like a slap to the child's face. Immediately, he quieted down, and allowed the Colonel to lead him away, but not before stopping to give Sikander one last murderous scowl.

"I will remember you." He stuck his tongue out at Sikander once more. "Bugger! Bugger! Bugger!"

Sikander watched the boy scamper off, unsure whether to be appalled or astonished. He cast a dismayed glance toward his mother, who reciprocated with an indulgent smirk, apparently unconcerned by her child's lack of decorum.

"He is the son of a great man, and one day, he will grow into one," she offered by way of apology.

"Maharani-ji, This is Captain Campbell of the Coldstream Guards, and I am—"

"I know exactly who you are, Sikander Singh," she said, cutting him off. Clapping her hands, she called for her majordomo, who hurried to offer her a cup of pear cordial. The Maharani took a perfunctory sip before crossing to the center of the room to seat herself on a throne-like chair.

"I knew your mother," she said to Sikander.

"Really? I was not aware of that."

"Oh, yes! We met once, on the eve of my betrothal. Your mother was a guest at the nuptial ceremonies. I was very nervous, and she reassured me." The Maharani fixed Sikander with a steely gaze. "That is the only reason I have taken this interview. Because you are said to be your mother's son, I will grant you ten minutes. What do you want?"

"I thought I would come and pay my respects," Sikander started to say, but for the second time, she held up one hand, forestalling him.

"Do not waste my time, Sikander Singh! Your charms will not work on me. Come right out and tell me what you want, or consider this interview at an end!"

Sikander sat back, unexpectedly stymied. Next to him, he could see that Campbell was equally nonplussed. Beneath her comely exterior, this woman, it was apparent, was as hard as stone. It would be pointless to try and be clever with her. She was too direct, and besides, from what he had seen and heard, she had no interest in making small talk, which really left him only one approach to take.

"I believe you made a visit to the King's camp yesterday."

"I did," the Maharani replied with a nod.

"And while you were there, you decided to see a *nautch* girl, didn't you, named Zahra?"

The Maharani's mouth stiffened. "Who sent you here? Are you working for the English?" Her gaze shifted toward Campbell, blazing with distrust.

"We are here, Madam, at the express orders of the Viceroy—"

This time, it was Sikander who interjected, interrupting the Captain before he bungled everything up.

"I am the Maharaja of Rajpore, Madam. I answer to no man but myself."

She narrowed her eyes, evaluating him for a moment. "Yes, I have heard that about you. Sikander Singh, the last of the gallants, Sir Lancelot without a lance." Smiling suddenly, she swayed to her feet. "Come, will you tour the camp with me?"

"If you wish," Sikander said, standing. Campbell made to follow, but the Maharani stopped him with one twist of a slim wrist.

"If you would be so kind, Captain, I wish a private conversation with the Maharaja."

Campbell's brow knotted as he realized he had been backed into a corner. Much as he wished to decline, to contradict her, evident from his obstinate expression, there was no way he could do so without seeming a boor.

"Of course, Your Highness!" he said, feigning graciousness with some difficulty. "Please take as long as you need. I shall wait right here."

"Wonderful! I shall have my bearers bring you some melons. They are freshly picked, by my own hands."

"That's very thoughtful of you," he said through gritted teeth.

Leaving him chafing at the bit, the Maharani led Sikander out of the tent. "You may take my arm," she said imperiously, holding out one slender limb. It was more a demand than a request. Sikander complied. She steered him toward a nearby paddock, where, under the watchful eye of Colonel Rathore, the young Maharaja was apparently putting a piebald mare through her paces, whooping and screaming each time the horse took a step.

The Maharani paused to watch her son, her face suffused with obvious pride. As for Sikander, he watched the Maharani. There was something about her that reminded him so much of Helene. The two women could not have been more different, not just in appearance, but also in their origins. Helene had been born in the roughest quarter of Paris, and grown up amidst terrible poverty, struggling every single day. The Maharani had been born to wealth, and had probably never had to struggle a day in her life, not until her husband's fall, but still, both women shared the same diffidence, a calm strength, a resolute sense of equanimity, that Sikander had always found very intoxicating.

"When the English deposed my husband," the Maharani said, "they did not wish me to become the Regent. Simla," she spat out the word, her voice stiff with disdain, "intended to appoint a Political Officer to take over. However, I would never, could never, allow it. The English are like termites. If you ignore one and let it take nest, five more arrive, then five hundred, all ravenous, eating up everything in sight."

"How did you ever manage to dissuade them?" Sikander asked, genuinely interested.

"They sent out an officer to evaluate the situation, a fat Colonel, I cannot recall his name. It was easy enough to change his mind, to beguile him into doing exactly as I desired and appointing me the Regent." She looked at Sikander, her expression wavering between diffidence and triumph. "That is what your mother taught me all those years ago. I did not wish to be married, but when the offer came from the Maharaja sahib, my father left me no choice. For him, it was a matter of honor, but for me…I contemplated running away, even taking my own life. I think your mother sensed my unrest because she took me aside and tried to console me. I complained that it was unfair that we women were denied the right to choose our own destiny, and that made us powerless. She laughed and explained to me that I was being naïve. While it may be our fate from birth to become wives and mothers, that does not make us weak. On the contrary, that is where a woman's real strength lies. A strong woman does not view her sex as a curse. She uses it as a weapon, to bend men to her will. That is the truest form of power there is."

"Are you so very hungry for power, Madam?"

Those smoky eyes turned to him. Even though Sikander considered himself a man of the world, he could not help but feel a sense of vertigo.

"You misunderstand me, Sikander. I care not for power, not one bit." Her gaze returned to her son, who was now pretending to be a cowboy, mock-shooting at the Colonel with his thumb and forefinger and roaring uproariously each time the man pretended to twitch and dance. "Everything I do is for Kishan. The British may have stolen the throne from my husband, but I will not let them do the same to him. I will die first."

"Is that why you went to see the girl?" He leaned forward, looming over her. "I think I have been able to put together most of the story. Tell me if I am correct. You deeply resented it when the English supplanted your husband. Not only was it a blow to your prestige, you feared the same fate awaited your son someday. As you mentioned, that is your paramount concern, to protect the *gaddi* for him, to keep his throne safe.

"As a result, when you heard of the *nautch* girl contracted to perform for the King, you saw a chance to get even. You visited her, and offered her money, I am guessing, to cajole her into some sort of scheme. What was it exactly? To go to the press, perhaps. Or was it to sign an affidavit of some sort? One that said the King forced himself on her or some such thing. Regardless, the end result you desired was the same. You wanted to foment a scandal, one that would blacken the face of the British Establishment publicly. It was only fitting, wasn't it? Through scandal, your husband was damned, and so through scandal, you would have your revenge."

Sikander had expected her to react with surprise at such a forthright accusation, dismay, even outrage, but to his awe, the Maharani responded with considerable composure.

"Well done! I can see your reputation for intelligence is well earned. Sadly, you are only half-correct. My husband is a boor, a brute. I owe him nothing. I have only one allegiance, to my son." She gave him a defiant scowl. "Yes, I admit it, I did offer the girl money. Yes, I did have a scheme, but not why you think. It was not vengeance I wanted, but rather leverage to ensure that my son's throne was kept safe." A tremulous sigh escaped her lips. "It was all for naught, though. The girl refused to assist me. There, the truth, you have it. I have made myself vulnerable to you," she shuddered, as if the mere thought of being in a man's power was an entirely unfamiliar, altogether unbearable feeling. "What do you intend to do, Sikander? Are you going to betray me to the English?"

Sikander contemplated her testimony. Could she be lying? It was certainly possible, even though his every instinct told him she was telling the truth. Yet there was one fact he simply could not ignore. She needed the *nautch* girl alive, not dead. Alive, Zahra was a pawn she could manipulate. But dead, she served no purpose to the Maharani at all, which was the very thing which absolved her of suspicion.

"You are walking a dangerous path, Madam," he replied. "Much as it would profit me to expose you, I cannot bring myself to do it. I fear my mother would not approve."

His reward was a delicate smile. "You intrigue me, Sikander Singh." The Maharani's voice was throaty. She was close enough that he could smell her, a physical sensation, the tendrils of her musky perfume fanning against his nostrils, as sensuous as a caress. "It has been a long time since I have thought of anything other than my duty to my son. But now, after meeting you… perhaps you can come visit me in Bharatpur someday?"

Sikander was almost tempted. For a moment, he wanted to kiss her, take her up in his arms, even though they were standing in plain sight of everyone. She was formidable, as beautiful and deadly as a Borgia, and though he knew it could only end badly, some part of him, the reckless half that was always hungry for adventure, wanted to take her up on her overture. But then, unbidden, Helene's visage sprang to mind, her faithful eyes, her knowing, indulgent smile, and Sikander knew he could never betray her, not even for this oddly enticing creature.

"You are magnificent, Madam, but sadly, you terrify me."

Her brow furrowed and for a heartbeat, he thought he might have offended her, but then the Maharani laughed, a graceful flash of white teeth against dusky skin.

"Another time then," she said, releasing his arm. "In another life, perhaps."

"You can count on it, Madam."

Chapter Seventeen

The origins of the kingdom of Patiala could be traced back to the seventeenth century, when the Sikh guru, Hargobind, had blessed a poor Jat boy named Phul Singh, prophesying that he would grow to be a man of great distinction. It was from this very child that the kings of Patiala, Nabha, and Jind were descended, the clan known as the Phulkian, who had risen to become preeminent amongst Punjab's princes.

Phul Singh's son, Ram Singh, had been baptised as one of the Khalsa by Guru Gobind Singh, and his son, Ala Singh, had distinguished himself as a fine soldier and fought along-side Banda Bahadur, before striking out on his own to capture much of the territory belonging to the Bhatti Rajputs. It was he who had built the Qila Mubarak, the ten-gated fort, and founded the city of Patiala, named quite literally for his pillow, for in Punjabi, that is what *pati* meant, the pillow whereupon Ala had rested his weary head.

Even as Ranjit Singh had consolidated power and the great Sikh Empire had spread from the banks of the Sutlej to the mountain wildernesses of Afghanistan, Patiala had remained an insignificant backwater until 1808, when Sahib Singh, Ala Singh's great grandson, had turned his coat and entered into an alliance with the British. It was this very decision that had cemented Patiala's fortunes, and they had stayed loyal to the sahibs in Calcutta through the Rohilla wars and the Great

Mutiny, their star rising as the Raj had flourished, promoted from minor vassal to most favored British ally, and endowed with a personal salute of seventeen guns.

Sikander's own family was closely connected to Patiala. His mother, Amrita Devi, was the previous Maharaja Rajendra Singh's youngest sister, which made Bhupinder, the current occupant of the *gaddi*, his first cousin. However, despite this bond of shared blood, Sikander had never quite managed to get along with his cousin. Part of the reason was that Sikander was cerebral, preferring a good book or his piano to perspiration any day. Bhupinder, on the other hand, was ribald, one of those overly virile types who was forever bludgeoning something or the other with a bat or a stick. Sikander was spartan in his habits, Bhupinder so indulgent he could have made Epicurus blush. Even physically, they were opposites. While he had inherited his mother's slightness of frame, Bhupinder was gargantuan, standing six and a half feet tall in his socks, and weighing over a hundred kilos.

As if these differences were not enough to set them at odds, it did not help that Sikander was very possibly the only living person in the world who could lay claim to the dubious distinction of having made Bhupinder Singh of Patiala cry. It had been a long time ago, of course, when they had been mere children, and Bhupinder had tried to bully him, only to have Sikander trounce him squarely and leave him with a bloody nose. And while it was said that time healed all wounds, he doubted that his cousin, who had an ego the size of Kanchenjunga, would either have forgotten the incident or forgiven Sikander for such a debacle.

Other than the pending showdown with Alwar, this was the interview he had been dreading the most. There was no earthly reason that Bhupinder would cooperate with him. Not only was he far senior to Sikander in rank, but he was exactly the sort of petulant man-child who would refuse to help merely out of spite. Sikander was tempted to avoid the interview altogether. Despite of Bhupinder's many infirmities of character, he found it very difficult to believe that he could be involved in cold-blooded murder. True, he did have a marked weakness for beautiful women, as was amply testified to by the fact that he possessed more than three hundred concubines, but was he capable of homicide? For that matter, why? No murderer acted without a motive. What could be the motive here? Not profit, surely, nor revenge. That left only two other plausibilities: Rage, *à la crime passionel,* or what Philippe Pinel called mania—madness without delirium. Sikander shivered. Yes, Bhupinder was capable of great rage and, given the right circumstances, perhaps even madness, which was why he could not be sure of his innocence, not until he looked his cousin straight in the eye.

Patiala's camp also had a prime location. The plot immediately adjoined the Nizam's enclosure, bordered on one side by the Coronation Road and the other by the Najafgarh Canal. However, unlike his more discreet neighbor, Bhupinder had gone the whole nine yards. No expense had been spared, an army of architects and craftsmen hired to make sure that Patiala's encampment, however temporary, was as lavish as any palace.

An ornately carved wall enfiladed the entire camp, the frontage distinguished by a panoply of arches decorated with white and gold lions, flanked by gilded cannons that were lit up at night, like lanterns. The entrance to the camp was an enormous ceremonial gate, beyond which lay an elaborate garden and a massive reception *shamiana* wrought from gold silk and silver satin. To the left of the marquee stood a smaller pavilion where the Granth Sahib lay ensconced, and past it, four lesser archways, each embossed with the Patiala coat of arms, led to the interior of the camp, where an array of tents had been arranged in a neat square around a miniature wood and marble palace, where Bhupinder had taken up temporary residence.

Upon entering, Sikander was greeted by a middle-aged

Sikh gentleman with a scarred face and one blind eye. This was Major Ram Singh, the Maharaja's long-suffering personal secretary. In many ways, he was Bhupinder's equivalent of Ismail Bhakht. A veteran of two wars, he had been reduced to keeping his master out of trouble, a job he did with great equanimity and skill. And, conveniently enough, he happened to be Charan Singh's eldest brother, which made Sikander only too familiar with him.

"Your Majesty, salutations! May the gods bless your every breath." Giving Sikander a vast smile, Ram Singh performed an elaborate *kornish*, sweeping one hand from his brow to his lips and heart.

"And may the fates never disappoint you, my dear fellow!" Sikander reciprocated, offering him an uncharacteristically respectful bow. He had nothing but the utmost regard for Ram Singh. He had been of great help to Rajpore on more than one occasion, and while, of course, he would always put Patiala first, as far as he was concerned, the Phulkian blood in Sikander's veins, diluted though it may be, was deserving of more than a modicum of loyalty.

"What brings you to us this afternoon?" Ram Singh said, giving his brother a brisk nod. "Is this not normally the time you are resting, sahib?"

Sikander sighed. Behind him, he heard Charan Singh and Captain Campbell both stifle chuckles. That was another thing Ram Singh had in common with his oversized brother; they both were far too cheeky for comfort.

"I want to see my cousin, if it is possible."

Ram Singh's smile faltered, his demeanor sobering at this request.

"I think today is not a good day. I regret to say, huzoor, that the Maharaja sahib is somewhat overstimulated at the moment."

Sikander rolled his eyes. When was Bhupinder not over-stimulated? Most likely he was drinking or cavorting with one of his innumerable concubines, or something equally salacious.

Before he could continue, unfortunately, Captain Campbell took it upon himself to chime in. "This is a matter of the utmost importance," he declared, stepping forward. "We are here at the behest of the Viceroy himself."

Ram Singh's face hardened at the Captain's cocksure manner, all vestiges of hospitality evaporating. Hurriedly, before Campbell managed to alienate the man completely, Sikander shot him a withering glance. Thankfully, Campbell was not quite so dense that he did not get the hint, and immediately, he held his tongue.

"It would be in Bhupinder's best interest, Ram Singhji, and Patiala's, if you could arrange for me to speak with him for just a few minutes."

The scarred Sikh's eyes widened. He knew Sikander well enough to grasp that he would never make such a statement unless circumstances were truly dire. Pursing his lips, he gave his brother a searching glance, to which Charan Singh responded with a slight nod of his own, as if to confirm that his master was deathly serious.

"Very well, follow me, sir. Right this way."

Instead of leading Sikander toward Bhupinder's palace, he steered him in the opposite direction, skirting the reception *shamiana* and heading to the rear of the camp, where the stables lay, adjoining a small, open *maidan*. Here, an ersatz wrestling ring had been marked out, roughly forty feet in diameter, its boundary bordered by slate stones arranged in a rough oval.

At the center of an open-faced pavilion abutting the ring, Sikander's his cousin's immense form perched atop an ivory chair so covered with gilt it could have been a throne. Even though he was seated, his turbaned head towered above the usual motley of hangers-on who surrounded him, hanging on his every word, like jackals nipping at a lion's heels. They were all strangers to Sikander, with one exception, a familiar English face who turned to greet him with an expansive grin.

Brigadier-General Charles Granville-Bruce was a broad-shouldered, brushy-moustached bear of a Welshman, the Commandant of the legendary Gurkha rifles. In Sikander's opinion, he was undoubtedly the best kind of European—a bluff, generous fellow with no capacity for subterfuge, who loved India and respected her people. He was the quintessential man's man, forever engaged in some manner of physical pursuit, a great fan of the pugilistic arts and undoubtedly one of the best climbers Sikander had met. That was what had brought them together, a shared love of the high, lonely places of the world, particularly the far reaches of the Himalayas. Sikander had dabbled briefly with mountaineering in his youth, and had first met Granville-Bruce while making an ascent of Ben Nevis during his Cambridge days. And though he had let this passion lapse upon ascending the heights of his throne, Granville-Bruce's passion for climbing had only grown with the passage of time. Already, in the company of his faithful Gurkhas, whom he loved like his own children, he had made attempts to peak Karakoram and Nanda Parbat, and rumor had it that he intended to be the first man to climb Everest, and was outfitting an expedition out of his personal income.

"Sikander, you snake, how have you been? You certainly look fit." Coming forward, he gave both Charan Singh and his brother a pair of respectful nods, and spared one long minute to look Campbell up and down.

Sikander reciprocated the Brigadier's earnest grin with one of his own, reaching out to lightly punch him in his belly.

"You're getting fat, Charlie. Too much mutton, and not enough exercise."

"Oh, do shut up!" Granville-Bruce scowled, sucking in his gut. "Are you here for the match?" He nodded toward the ring. "Bhupinder's champion, Kikkar Singh, is scheduled to fight Kallu Pahelwan this afternoon in a challenge match at the Badshahi *mela*. He is the younger brother of the fabled Ghulam of Amritsar, who Kikkar Singh defeated some years ago for the Punjab championship." He let out a throaty laugh. "It's going to be bloody well spectacular, a good old-fashioned grudge match. You must come and watch as my guest."

"I am afraid that I cannot, my friend. I am just here for a quick word with my cousin."

"Good luck!" Granville-Bruce snorted. "He's in a bit of a snit today."

"So I was told, but I have to try." Turning to Ram Singh, he nodded. "If you would be so kind, Ram Singhji? Quick as you please. Time is of the essence."

"Of course, huzoor!" Indicating that Sikander should wait a moment, Ram Singh marched up to the pavilion, and leaned over to whisper in Bhupinder Singh's ear. The Maharaja of Patiala paused briefly, turning from his entourage to eye Sikander coldly before shaking his head dismissively and waving Ram Singh away. However, rather than retreating, the scarred Sikh persisted, remonstrating with his master until finally, Bhupinder lumbered to his feet and advanced to confront Sikander.

He loomed over him, towering over even Charan Singh. Unlike the old Sikh, though, who was as slim as a rapier, Bhupinder was very nearly as fat as an elephant, with a large belly hidden behind a red cummerbund and the petulant face of a brat always accustomed to having his own way. Sikander ran an amused eye over his outfit. He was overdressed as always, in one of his customary white uniforms, a General of Cavalry on this particular day, festooned with enough gold braid to make Lord Wellington himself envious.

"Well well, if it isn't my beloved cousin. What do you want, crow?" Bhupinder sneered, purposely using the childhood nickname Sikander had so loathed, a calculated insult. "Why have you come skulking around here, like a bird of ill omen?"

As if on cue, his sycophants burst into giggles. Sikander bridled, his face reddening with embarrassment. Typical Bhupinder! This was how he had always been, even as a boy, brash, so self-involved he believed he could treat everyone like they were his servants. Of course, deep down, it was not his fault. He had been bought up that way, his every whim indulged from childhood, brainwashed from the cradle into believing that he was better than everyone else. Still, that did not give him the right to be rude, especially since Sikander was his elder.

He gave his cousin a forced smile. "I need a minute. It is a matter of the utmost imperative."

"Oh, go away! I haven't the time for your nonsense, not today. You will bring me bad luck."

Once again, Campbell forgot his manners and stepped forward, to Sikander's chagrin.

"We are here, sir, on behalf of the Viceroy," he started to say, but Bhupinder cut this futile effort off in mid sentence.

"I do not speak to English with ranks less than that of Colonel."

With that imprecation, he turned away to focus his attention back on the wrestling arena, clapping eagerly as his champion stalked into the ring. *So this was the famous Kikkar Singh*, Sikander thought. He was a veritable mammoth, with muscles bulging from every inch of his oiled body, like a titan of yore come to life. After bowing to Bhupinder, he proceeded to lift a tree trunk off the ground and press it above his head as effortlessly as if he were lifting a bale of dirty laundry to which the delighted crowd responded with a symphony of cheers.

"Kikkar Singh cannot be beaten," Bhupinder boasted.

Sikander was tempted to disagree. In his youth, perhaps, he might have been a force to reckon with, but to his sharp eyes, it was obvious Kikkar Singh was well past his prime. He seemed strong enough, at first glance, but anyone with half a brain could see that his knees were unsteady, and judging by how he was already breathing heavily just from the effort of warming up, it was quite apparent that he had lost his wind.

That realization inspired an idea, the faintest notion of a

scheme. "I take it you are supporting the champion."

"Of course." Bhupinder cheered, clapping enthusiastically. "He is going to kill the Lahori, just you see. I am sure of it."

"What do you say to a wager then?"

Exactly as he had hoped, Bhupinder took the bait. The tactic had worked well enough with the Guppies, but with Patiala, it was even easier. Not only was Bhupinder an egotist and a snob, but his consummate faith in his own superiority made it impossible for him to resist the lure of a bet.

"What sort of wager?"

"A sparring match. Charan Singh against your champion. One fall. If my man is able to topple your behemoth, you shall answer my questions."

Bhupinder's eyes narrowed. "And if he loses?"

"Then you can have my latest acquisition," Sikander said. "It is the new Rolls-Royce, the Corgi, with a limousine chassis in ivory and gold by Pullman. It is due to be delivered in six weeks. Consider it your property if Charan Singh takes a fall."

A long moment passed as his cousin weighed the bet, before he let out a shrill laugh.

"You are a fool, Sikander Singh, and I shall use your car for a garbage scow once I have won it, so that all of Patiala will always know how chock full of shit you are."

Sikander ignored this jibe, turning instead to face his manservant.

"Well, old man, what do you think?" he inquired, one brow curving into a question mark.

The big Sikh rolled his eyes, studying Kikkar Singh with pursed lips for a long minute, before giving a shrug and beginning to unbutton his tunic with unhurried nonchalance.

"Why is it, sahib, that when you set out to investigate a case, I am the one who always ends up getting a hiding?"

"Oh, come on, you can take him easily. It will be simpler than trying to get a kiss from your wife."

"That's easy for you to say, sahib. Not only are you unmarried, but you don't have to grapple with this monster. Besides, my wife is worth the trouble, unlike this brute."

Stripping down to his singlet, he unraveled his *pugree* carefully and handed it to Captain Campbell for safekeeping, before giving first Sikander and then Bhupinder a deep bow. As he turned and strode out of the pavilion and descended into the wrestling ring, Sikander could not help but be struck by the contrast between the two men. His manservant was taller by a few inches, his carefully oiled beard giving him a leonine air. In spite of his advancing age, he remained as well muscled as a prizefighter, his physique obviously having lost none of its strength. Nevertheless, Kikkar Singh seemed to dwarf him, making up for this discrepancy in height by sheer girth. Not only was he almost twice as wide as Charan Singh, he was at least forty kilos heavier, with simian arms and a hairy belly which made him seem more like a gorilla than a man.

It was obvious Kikkar Singh thought he had this match in the bag, because when Charan Singh came to a stop in front of him, he let out a laugh before turning to jabber at his entourage, pointing and laughing as he rattled off a string of colorful insults.

Charan Singh ignoring his heckling, and began to stretch, raising his arms over his head and smoothly leaning forward to touch his toes. This impressive display of elasticity did not awe Kikar Singh at all. In response, he bunched his massive chest, slapping his hairy belly as he rolled his shoulders, making the muscles of his trapeziums jut out like boulders. Calling out for a nearby servant, he snatched up a mug of cool milk and guzzled it down in one vast gulp, before letting out an immense belch in Charan Singh's face with a insolent sneer.

"Go home, Papaji," he hissed, "This is not an old man's game."

Charan Singh responded with a snort. "Has anyone told you that you smell?" he replied, wrinkling his nose. "When was the last time you took a bath?"

The champion's sneer dissolved into a scowl. "I am going to

enjoy hurting you."

Charan Singh feigned a yawn, and reached up to cinch his hair into a tight topknot, so that it would not unravel. "Do your best, fatso."

Kikkar Singh quite obviously had no interest in subtlety. Instead of taking the time to circle his opponent, and suss out his strengths and weaknesses, he merely lowered his head, and gave a grunt, before lumbering straight forward, like a rhino at the charge.

To his credit, the old Sikh did not back away, not one inch. Most men would have quaked in their boots at being confronted by such a behemoth bearing down with bloody murder writ on his face. Charan Singh, however, remained unflappable. Even as the champion swung one fist at his chest, the Sikh sidestepped him, demonstrating an impressive speed.

"Is that the best you have?" he inquired, even as Kikkar Singh blundered to a stop, his expression thunderous.

Letting out an irate growl, the wrestler charged forward again, crouching low this time, trying to sweep Charan Singh off his feet. Once again, the Sikh dodged away, leaping backward with a young man's agility.

"Stand still, blast you!" Kikkar Singh grunted, breathing heavily, already visibly winded. "This is a bout, not a damned dance."

"Very well!" Charan Singh responded. Cracking his knuckles, he held out one hand, offering it to Kikkar Singh. The wrestler's mouth curved into a feral grin, recognising this gesture for what it was, the traditional challenge inviting him to a test of brute strength.

With a guffaw, he enveloped the old Sikh's hand in one hirsute paw. It was obvious he was convinced he could easily overpower the older man, crush his fingers as if they were but kindling. However, to his dismay, Charan Singh did not even blink. Instead, he held resolute, even as the champion squeezed down with all his might, exerting every ounce of power he could summon, the veins in his forehead bulging as if he was having an apoplexy.

A minute passed, then two, before Charan Singh reached out to grasp Kikkar Singh's shoulder, a move the champion quickly reciprocated, until they were leaning into each other, like two mighty elephants, each trying to push his opponent off balance. Kikkar Singh's massive shoulders bunched, his face reddening as he struggled to bring his superior weight to bear, trying to overpower Charan Singh by sheer burden of mass. It almost worked. Slowly, Charan Singh took one step backward, then another, but then, his jaw clenched, and he brought Kikkar Singh to a stop. The champion's eyes widened. He let out the faintest of sighs as he realised he was being outmatched, his arms shivering as Charan Singh's vise-like grip held him firmly in place for a moment.

The big Sikh remained expressionless, his forearms bunching like pistons as he began to push his opponent backwards, inch by tortuous inch. The champion writhed, trying to resist, but Charan Singh proved inexorable. Kikkar Singh's back slowly arched, until he was bent almost at an angle of sixty degrees. Just as he was on the very brink of losing his balance, the old Sikh exclaimed, "Hah!" and with blinding swiftness, turned one hip, tossing Kikkar Singh cleanly off his feet, using his own momentum to send him crashing to the ground in a disgruntled heap.

A stunned silence descended, the spectators unable to believe what they had just witnessed, until Sikander let out a triumphant laugh.

"Well done!" He clapped his hands delightedly. "Perhaps you still have some good years left after all, you old goat."

"I am glad that you enjoyed the show, huzoor," Charan Singh retorted. He exited the ring, leaving Kikkar Singh lying prone amidst the dust, watching him with an expression of unmitigated awe, unable to believe that he had been manhandled so easily. Retreating to the pavilion, he approached Captain Campbell, who returned his tunic and *pugree* with an admiring smile. "Now, if you will excuse me, I shall make myself presentable, if you please."

"Of course," Sikander said expansively. "Take as long as you need. You have earned it."

Leaving the old Sikh to seek out a mirror so that he could re-tie his turban, Sikander turned to his cousin, utterly unable to resist the urge to gloat.

"Well, it looks like my man won, doesn't it?"

Bhupinder was not at all pleased, his brows merging into one bushy glare. "The old fool cheated. He used some sort of judo. The bet is off."

"Is it?" Sikander turned to the Englishman, seeking his opinion. "What do you say, Brigadier?"

Granville-Bruce responded with a shrug. "You did say one fall, Your Majesty. No other conditions were specified." He gave Sikander a comradely wink. "I am afraid that you will have to acknowledge defeat to the Maharaja of Rajpore after all."

"Bah!" Bhupinder offered Sikander a poisonous scowl. "If your oaf has hurt my champion and he loses against the pahalwan from Lahore, I will hold you personally responsible." Snapping his fingers, he summoned a bearer carrying a silver claret pitcher filled with what appeared to be pomegranate cordial. Without offering a drop to either Sikander or the Brigadier-General, he quaffed the whole jug in one enormous swallow, before crossing to his throne and settling into it with an expression of absolute irritation on his bearded face.

"Go on then, crow, ask your blasted questions. Make it quick. I am a very busy man."

"I believe you paid a visit to the Imperial camp yesterday?"

"What of it? I am on the Durbar Committee, aren't I?"

"So you were there on official business?"

"Of course. We are gifting a very handsome parure to Her Imperial Highness, my wife and I, on behalf of the Council of Maharanis. I went to make sure it was ready for presentation."

"Then you did not happen to pay a visit to a *nautch* girl named Zahra?"

"What business is that of yours, eh?" Bhupinder growled, even more belligerent than usual. His eyes narrowed, and he sat up, looming over Sikander. One could almost hear the cogs in his brain, ticking away, as he tried to put two and two together, to ascertain why Sikander had bought up the *nautch* girl. "Wait a moment! Did you try to buy her as well? Were you one of the fools Kapurthala beat out? Is that why you have come to me, to try and ask me for help to get that wench?"

Sikander hid a smile. For all his worldliness, Bhupinder was as predictable as a child. The only two measures he could conceive of were money and sex, and quite typically, he had assumed that it was those two things that had brought Sikander to his door, a misapprehension that Sikander was only too happy to exploit.

"You have seen right through me," he said, giving Campbell a nod, to remind him to hold his tongue and play along. "I am here about the girl."

"Of course, you should have thought twice before trying to put one over Bhupinder Singh of Patiala." His cousin puffed up his immense chest, sounding even more self-satisfied than usual. "Still, let me give you a warning, Sikander, because I was fond of your mother, may the Gurus protect her soul. The girl is a waste of time, a dead end."

"Why do you say that? Is she not quite as comely as they say?"

"On the contrary!" Bhupinder's eyes lit up, a gleam which Sikander had only ever seen when he was speaking of horses or women. "She is breathtaking, a *houri* come to life. In fact, that was the very reason I paid the camp a visit. You see, I had heard of Scindia, Alwar, and Kapurthala's bidding war, and I wanted to see if this particular courtesan lived up to the legend. As it turned out, she was every bit as ravishing as rumor had it. In fact, I decided I wanted her for myself, so I made her an offer on the spot."

"You tried to buy her?"

"Oh, no. I told her I would marry her."

"You did not?" Sikander's mouth fell open in disbelief.

"Yes, I offered her the opportunity to be one of my lesser *begums.*"

"Don't you have enough wives already, Bhupinder?"

His cousin's face stiffened, his eyes flashing with scorn. "What a pompous little creature you are, Sikander. You think yourself better than me. You call my little pleasures vices, and imagine I am weak, venial. But you are the one who is wrong, not I." He leaned forward. "Tell me, what is the point of living if you do not take pleasure from your senses? Why wake up each morning if not for the delights of taste and smell and touch? I have no interest in being like you, cousin, in drinking myself to a stupor each evening and coming alive only when someone drops dead. I want to live, damn you. I want to suck the marrow from every moment of every day. Is that so wrong?"

"Tell me, how did the girl react to your proposal?"

"She refused," Bhupinder grimaced, brimming with outrage. "Can you believe it? She dared to reject me."

Sikander pursed his lips. It could be a possible motive. Bhupinder was well known for having a short temper and was undoubtedly unaccustomed to being rebuffed, especially by courtesans—but was pique enough of a reason to strangle someone? He had to admit it seemed like quite a stretch, a recognition that Bhupinder affirmed just a moment later.

"She said her heart belonged to another." He turned to the Brigadier. "If she had taken my offer, she would have had everything, comfort, wealth, status, but instead she chose love. Ha! What a load of codswallop! I told her as much, didn't I, Granville-Bruce?"

"You did, indeed."

"You were with him when he visited Zahra."

"I was." Granville-Bruce frowned. "A lovely child, but rather naïve, I think, to have rejected such a generous overture."

Bhupinder let out a vast snort. "She'll change her tune, sooner or later. Mark my words, the moment she realises what is best for her, she will come crawling to me, begging to take my offer."

This declaration served to confirm what Sikander had suspected all along, that Bhupinder was not involved in Zahra's murder at all.

"One last question, cousin. Did you happen to notice anything out of the ordinary when you visited with Zahra? Anything suspicious?"

"What is that supposed to mean?" Bhupinder gave Sikander a piercing look, beginning to realise perhaps that he had misread his intentions. "What mischief are you up to now?"

Rising to his feet, he stabbed one corpulent finger at Sikander's face. "I have no more patience for your nonsense. This interview is over. Both of you, get out."

Chapter Eighteen

Upon emerging from the Patiala pavilion, Sikander saw Charan Singh engaged heatedly in discussion with his brother.

"What is wrong?" he asked the big Sikh. "Is there a problem?"

"Ram Singh has some information for you," Charan Singh replied. "Will you speak to him?"

"You go and fetch the car," Sikander commanded, offering his manservant a nod. As he lumbered away to fulfill his orders, Ram Singh approached Sikander, clearing his throat pointedly.

"Could I have a moment, huzoor?"

"Of course, Ram Singh. What is the matter?"

"In private, if you please." He offered Campbell an apologetic look. "I mean no offense, Captain sahib."

"And none is taken," Campbell said gallantly. "Actually, I will ask you to excuse me as well, Your Highness. I need an hour to myself."

Sikander was taken aback by this unexpected *volte-face*. Until now, Campbell had insisted on obeying his orders to the letter, sticking as close to him as a rash. But now, he seemed almost eager to get away, a reversal that left Sikander nothing if not curious.

"Are you unwell, Campbell? A touch of the croup perhaps?"

"Not at all, sir." He gave Sikander a hesitant smile. "Actually, I think I have a lead I would like to follow."

"Is that so? Do tell!"

"Not just yet, sir. Let me see if my hunch pans out." He gave Sikander a brief bow. "I shall see you a bit later."

As soon as the Captain departed, Sikander turned back to Ram Singh, who had been patiently waiting for him to conclude his conversation.

"Tell me what is bothering you?"

"There is a rumor, huzoor, that someone was murdered in the Imperial Camp. Is that why you are here?"

Sikander stiffened. "I cannot speak of it, Ram Singh, even with you."

"I understand. I have only one question, sahib. Is Bhupinder Singh-ji a suspect?"

Sikander pursed his lips, tempted to refuse to answer. However, when he saw the concern in Ram Singh's eyes, he could not help but feel a pang of empathy.

"I think it is safe to say that he is not. My cousin is overly self-indulgent and much too selfish, but he is not a criminal, of that I am sure."

"Excellent!" Ram Singh's shoulders sagged with visible relief. "I try my best, sir, to keep his wilder urges restrained, but the Maharaja Sahib does not always choose to listen."

"You are a loyal man, Ram Singh. Bhupinder is lucky to have you."

Ram Singh's face softened at these words of praise. "I am grateful for your candor, sahib. Perhaps I can repay you with some information." He glanced around, as if to ensure they were not being overheard. "When we arrived at the Imperial camp to see the *nautch* girl, she was not alone. A gentleman was leaving her quarters when I went there to inquire if she would spare a moment to speak with my master."

"Is that so? Did you recognise this gentleman?"

"As a matter of fact, I did, huzoor. It was the Maharaja of Indore."

This revelation took Sikander entirely by surprise. Indore was not on the list the Scottish sergeant had disclosed, nor had his name come up with Zahra's entourage. What could have compelled the Holkar to visit Zahra, and in secret? Whatever it was, Sikander thought, knowing Indore's reputation, it had to be somewhat nefarious.

"Are you sure, Ram Singhji?"

"I am willing to stake my good name on it. I have nothing but the greatest respect for the Holkar sahib, which is why I was so taken aback to chance upon him in such questionable circumstances." He bit his lip, looking very troubled. "He seemed somewhat angry, sir. I tried to greet him, but he stamped past me without a word of acknowledgment. It looked to me that he was quite furious with the young woman for some reason."

Sikander frowned, unsure what to make of this testimony. It was hearsay of the most tenuous kind, but he knew Ram Singh well enough to accept the man at his word. Not only was he Charan Singh's kin, but he was a truly honest man.

"I do not mean to cast aspersions, huzoor. I just thought you might find this information useful."

"Thank you, Ram Singh. You have done very well. I am exceedingly grateful for your help."

"It is my pleasure, sahib. Call on me if you need anything else. I am always glad to be of service."

A moment later, the Rolls came trundling up. Sikander was about to climb aboard when the Brigadier emerged from the pavilion and waved at him urgently.

"Hold on a minute!" He hurried up to the car. "Can you give me a lift, old man?"

"Of course." He held open the door, and the Brigadier hopped on board, as agile as a macaque. Sikander followed after, a lot less gracefully, settling into the passenger seat with a sigh. "Where can we drop you?"

"Maiden's Hotel, if it is not too much of an inconvenience."

"Not at all. I am at the Majestic myself, just a stone throw's away. Drive on," he said to Charan Singh, smiling as the Englishman pulled out a sterling silver hip flask and uncorked it.

"Here, try that," the Brigadier said, offering him the flask.

"God in heaven!" Sikander took a small taste, only to choke and cough uncontrollably. It was raw liquor, as harsh as turpentine, so pungent it brought tears to his eyes. "What on earth is that?"

"The Nepalis call it *raksi*. They brew it from millet and rice. It is not unlike Japoni *sake*, only rather less fashionable." He took a long pull, and smacked his lips. "I have acquired quite a taste for it."

He held out the flask once more, but Sikander refused with a vehement shake of his head.

"Well, my friend, how long has it been since I saw you last—two, no, three years?"

"Can we skip the small talk, and speak honestly?" The Brigadier gave Sikander a scowl. "What is this really about? You are not the sort of man who has his head turned by a *nautch* girl, no matter what Bhupinder may choose to believe."

Sikander squirmed. He should have guessed that Granville-Bruce would see through his ruse. Beneath the bluff exterior, he was a taciturn man, and it was only natural he had smelled a rat even if his cousin had failed to do so. Unfortunately, that managed to put Sikander in rather a bind. He considered his options. He could refuse to answer, but that would offend his old friend deeply. He could try to lie, but he doubted he would be able to put one over on the Brigadier quite so easily. That left him with only one choice.

"I cannot divulge any details," he said after a long pause, "but suffice it to say, I am on Imperial business."

"I thought as much." The Brigadier sank back into the upholstery. "That is exactly why I am taking you to Maiden's. We are going to see Palanpur."

"Really?" Sikander's eyes narrowed. "I happen to know the Nawab Sahib quite well. He is a fine, if somewhat old-fashioned, gentleman. Certainly not the sort of man to be involved in"—he checked his words before he said too much—"any sort of scandal."

"Not the father," the Brigadier explained, "the son. That is who you need to speak to." He leaned forward. "Yesterday, while your cousin was fluffing about, I happened to bear witness to a most unexpected scene. The Sahibzada of Palanpur— Yaru Bhai, I believe he calls himself— turned up unannounced and created quite a bit of doolally."

"Did he now?"

"Yes, he kept raving on and on." The Brigadier rolled his eyes. "I think the boy was quite pickled, to be honest, ranting away like a bloody buffoon. Naturally, the lads on guard, four of my Gurkhas, mind you, sent him off with his tail between his legs. But not before he cried all sorts of bloody murder, let me tell you, harping on and on about how he would have what was his, no matter who dared to stand in his way, and such balderdash. What a goon!"

Sikander wrinkled his brow, contemplating this unforeseen lead. He had heard of this Yaru Bhai, if only by reputation. He was said to be the worst of the young princes, a brat who was also a bit of a boor to boot. Could he have been in a relationship of some kind with Zahra? Were they lovers, perhaps? Could she have jilted him, and broken his heart? That was a motive Sikander always liked to work with—What was that old line from Shakespeare? "Lilies that fester smell far worse than weeds."

Stop speculating, he told himself. Yaru Bhai's reason to come calling had to be something palpable, given that he had made a scene in public. The only way Sikander would know exactly what had elapsed, what exactly had compelled the boy to embarrass himself, was by cornering him and getting the truth out in the open.

"Now that I have helped you out, old chap," Granville-Bruce interjected, "perhaps you can do me a bit of favor?"

"Of course! Anything in my power!"

"I am in love," the Brigadier sighed.

Involuntarily, Sikander let out a laugh. "Forgive me," he

said. "Aren't you a little too, umm, seasoned to be lovelorn, my friend?"

"Don't be cynical. A man is never too old to hope." His eyes glazed over, mooning like a schoolboy. "I met her the day before yesterday at the Hussars' Camp. What sensible shoes she was wearing! And such excellent posture! He gave Sikander a serious frown. You do know what they say about women with good posture, don't you?"

"Do enlighten me," Sikander said, hiding a smirk.

"They make fine climbers. You need a straight back if you want to be a good mountaineer."

"Is that so?" He was just a little disappointed, briefly tempted to share the two dozen things he thought that women with good posture could do far better than climb mountains.

"You have to help me find her, Sikander." The Brigadier's voice was urgent, almost desperate.

"Of course," Sikander replied. "It should not be too difficult. What can you tell me about her? Did you happen to ask her name?"

"No," he looked sheepish, bashful, "I did not speak with her. I was too afraid."

"You, afraid? Surely you can't be serious, Brigadier?" Sikander rolled his eyes. "Well, worry not! All is not lost. Sikander Singh is on the case. I shall find your mystery woman, I promise you."

"Thank you!" The Brigadier beamed, grasping his hand and pumping it so eagerly Sikander thought he might pull his arm from its socket. "I knew I could count on you."

Maiden's Metropolitan Hotel was much larger than the Majestic, a handsome establishment located directly opposite the Delhi Club, some seven miles north of the Old City. Compared to Sikander's hotel, it was a far more creditable establishment, with marble flooring and hot and cold water in each room, and a fine restaurant—not quite the Savoy, but certainly the best accommodation to be had in Delhi. Actually, Sikander had tried to engage a floor for his own use, but unfortunately, for the occasion of the Durbar, the entire establishment had been rented out to the Maharaja of Mysore.

Sikander spared a moment to admire the neoclassical edifice and its whitewashed Palladian arches that reminded him vaguely of the terraces surrounding Regent's Park. In London perhaps, it would have been rather ordinary, but here in India, it was triumphantly vulgar, incongruously elegant amidst the heat and dust.

Before they could enter the hotel, a rather officious-looking Lieutenant clad in the blue and red of the Mysore Infantry held up a manila folder to forestall their passage.

"Might I have your names, gentlemen?"

"This is the Maharaja of Rajpore, and I am Granville-Bruce of the Gurkhas."

"Ah!" The man opened the folder, to reveal a typed list, which he scanned with one deliberate finger. "Here we are! You may enter," he said to the Brigadier, but to Sikander, he gave a rather supercilious sneer. "You, however, are not on the list."

Before Sikander could react to such a curt dismissal, Granville-Bruce let out a growl.

"Nonsense! Step aside! The Maharaja is my guest."

The Lieutenant took one hesitant step backward. Who would not, confronted by a man of the Brigadier's rank, not to mention his girth? "I am afraid that the Maharaja of Mysore was quite specific, sir," he said, his voice wavering. "He is hosting a formal banquet, and only the people on this list are to be permitted entry."

"I am sure you can make an exception," Sikander explained. "I am not here to spoil the Maharaja's lunch. I am here on Viceregal business. It should only take a moment or two."

Sadly, before the Lieutenant could be persuaded, they were interrupted by none other than the host himself, the Maharaja of Mysore, who came striding up, surrounded by his usual entourage of assistants.

Krishna Raja Wadiyar was an unassuming creature with the look of a clerk about him, a small, rather portly man with a drooping moustache and a back that had grown prematurely bowed, no doubt from having to bear the burden of such a magnificent title. Sikander knew him very well. They had undertaken a journey to Europe some years previously on the same vessel, and Sikander had found the man an utter bore, uninterested in either wine or conversation.

What was thought virtue by some was often considered sanctimony by others, and the truth of it was that the Wadiyar was rather too pompous by half for Sikander's personal taste, not to mention far too quick to align with the English. But then what else could you expect from a man who was essentially a British puppet? The Maharajas of Mysore were quick to extol their history, claiming descent from the Yadavas of Dwarka and Krishna himself, but in reality, the current dynasty had far more modest antecedents.

True, the original Wadiyars had ruled the fiefdom of Mysore during the glory days of Vijayanagara, but their fortunes had waned as the star of Tipu Sultan had ascended. It was only with the fall of Serangipatam that the Wadiyar clan had regained the throne of Mysore, and then merely as figurehead monarchs, forced to pay a healthy annual tithe to the English. In fact, the current Maharaja's grandfather had once been deposed for defaulting on these annual payments, his adopted son restored to power only when he agreed to hand over every facet of governance to a British Commissioner who handled all real administration in his name.

In spite of being pedantic to the point of blandness, the gentleman who faced Sikander now had managed to acquire an enviable reputation, considered by many to be the finest king in India, a veritable Rama reborn. The English adored him, calling him the epitome of the platonic ruler, but Sikander could not help but loathe him just a little. Unlike the Gaekwad, who was a pragmatist, Krishna Raja Wadiyar was an idealist of the worst kind—a man too rich to be contradicted, who genuinely believed wisdom came from the pages of a book, not from the crucible of reality. He dreamed of creating the perfect state, but what he failed to comprehend was that perfection was innately inhuman, achievable only if one ignored the basest instincts of human nature.

That was where Sikander differed from him so fundamentally. He was at best a Stoic, who understood that civilization was only a thin veneer, a veil behind which humanity's true capacity for savagery hid. In fact, it was that very baseness that excited Sikander, that tantalized him, that drove him to seek out the most depraved of crimes and the darkest of criminals. But in Krishna Raja's world view, there was no place for crime, for murder or lust, for jealousy or greed. In short, there was no place for men like Sikander, as was evident by the expression of absolute scorn that decorated Mysore's fleshy countenance.

"Sikander Singh! I do not remember inviting you."

"As a matter of fact, I am here as the Brigadier's guest."

Mysore let out an imperious snort that amply conveyed his disdain. "What a disappointing creature you are! Like a rodent, always sniffing around for gossip, trying to ferret your way into other people's business."

Sikander was not unduly ruffled by such obvious hostility. In fact, if anything, he was quite used to it.

"Speaking of gossip, Your Majesty, I heard rather a fine snippet just yesterday, from an acquaintance of yours, a Colonel Metcalfe. He had some very interesting things to reveal about you."

Sikander raised an eyebrow. "I was feeling rather *listless*, I confess. My spirits have been *flagging* lately, but after chatting with Metcalfe, I must say, my interest was *aroused*, so to speak. It really was quite an *uplifting* conversation, if you know what I mean."

He knew he was being rather cruel, not to mention somewhat excessive with the double entendres, but it was the Wadiyar who had started it by calling him a rodent, he reminded himself.

To his delight, his sally hit home hard, exactly as he had intended. The Wadiyar colored a deep carmine, and dissolved into a fit of coughing.

"Excuse me," he said hurriedly, wiping at his mouth with a silk kerchief. "I must look to my guests."

"But sir," the obtrusive Lieutenant piped up, "what about this gentleman? What am I to do with him?"

"Let him in, of course. Please, enjoy yourself, Sikander Singh," he said, with a poisonous glare, as if to promise him he would receive his comeuppance at a later date.

"What was that all about?" The Brigadier inquired as the Wadiyar beat a hasty retreat.

"Never underestimate the power of suggestion, my friend," Sikander laughed. "Well, while I always enjoy getting under Mysore's skin, let us go and find the man we came to locate, shall we?"

They made their way into the hotel, entering the main banquet room, where a long damask-covered table had been laid out, around which Mysore's guests were seated, enjoying a round of cocktails. Sikander recognised a few of them. There was the Begum of Bhopal, veiled, as always, in a blue silk burkha, and next to her, the Khan of Kalat, who looked rather like a villain from *Arabian Nights*. Seated across from them was the somewhat startling figure of the Saopha of Yaunghwe, who seemed to be wearing a Burmese pagoda as a hat. At the other end was the Maharana of Dungarpur, a handsome fellow who was said to a fine spin-bowler, deep in conversation with the legendary Ranjitsinghji, the Jamsaheb of Nawanagar, who was arguably the finest batsman in the world.

"There he is," the Brigadier exclaimed, pointing at a young man seated near the distant end of the table, a slender fellow with shaggy sideburns that merged into his moustache *à la Souvarov*, who looked to be in heated argument with one of the Dewas Rajas—Junior or Senior, Sikander was not sure.

The kingdom of Palanpur was not so distant from Sikander's own capital. Like Rajpore, it was a thirteen-gun state, located at the cusp of Gujarat and Malwa. The ruling family were the descendants of Pathan adventurers who had migrated westwards in the twelfth century, and carved out a kingdom from one dun corner of the central Indian massif. The founder of the dynasty, Malik Khurram Khan, had been renowned for being extraordinarily comely, a trait he had passed on to his heirs. The current nawab, Sher Muhammed Khan, was an elegant hawk of a man, and his son, Taley, the heir apparent, was famous for being a heartbreaker and a skirt-chaser, whose innumerable conquests rivaled those of Jagatjit of Kapurthala. Why, it was said he had never met a white woman he had not tried his level best to seduce!

This fellow had inherited neither his father's elegance nor his brother's *savoir faire*. It was obvious that the flamboyant moustache was intended to disguise his weak jawline and make him seem more imposing. Sadly, all it managed to achieve was to make him look even more chinless, which when combined with his bulging eyes and hunched posture, gave him rather a turtle-like air.

"What do you know about him, Brigadier?"

"Oh, he's a bit of a gay dog! A courser, so to speak. There isn't a skirt in Simla he hasn't tried to chase down, with little success, I might add. But you so have to give the boy credit for persistence. Also, he has quite a reputation for having a short fuse. He was educated privately because Mayo wouldn't have him. I knew one of his old teachers, a fine fellow called Moorcroft. He used to describe him as an unmitigated terror."

"Well, then, let's go talk to him, and find out if there is any truth to the rumors, shall we?"

Sikander approached the young man; the Brigadier followed at a more sedate pace, pausing briefly to exchange pleasantries with one of the other guests.

"Are you Yawar Husain Khanji, the Nawabzada of Palanpur?" Sikander asked by way of introduction.

Dewas Junior gave him a grateful nod, as if to suggest he was glad for this opportune interruption. Hurriedly, he rose and sidled away, leaving the boy to swivel his neck to look Sikander up and down, an examination so sullen it was almost a challenge.

"And what if I am?" His face twisted into an insolent sneer. "What is it to you, eh?"

From the combative set of his stance, Sikander could see that Yaru Bhai was one of those men who firmly believed that belligerence and masculinity were directly proportional to one another. Typical, he thought, a boy play-acting at being a man, trying to make up for inexperience by pretending to be worldly. His plan had been to take his favorite tactic with him, but he could see now that intimidation would only make Yaru Bhai even more aggressive. How was he to break Yaru Bhai? How was he to question him without it devolving into an argument?

The answer came to him in a flash. All it would take was a little play-acting of his own, a touch of cleverness to outmaneuver the boy.

"Oh, thank the heavens!" Sikander allowed a carefully orchestrated expression of relief to sprawl across his face. "We have been looking for you all morning. I am here on behalf of the Viceroy himself. We have urgent need of your help."

"My help?" The boy echoed, his aggression evaporating, replaced by bewilderment.

"Yes! The Empire needs you, Yaru Bhai. Unless you assist us, the Raj, the Durbar, the King himself, will be in dread jeopardy."

It occurred to him that he was laying it on a bit thick, but to his relief, it looked like Yaru Bhai was hooked. A rapturously self-important look fluttered over his features. He seemed to puff up visibly, swelling, not unlike a toad.

"If the Empire needs me, very well! You can count on me. What is it that you need?"

"Excellent! I was told you would be cooperative." Sikander pulled up a chair and sat down, leaning forward until he was very close to the boy. "Last night, a woman went missing from the King's camp, a *nautch* girl named Zahra. I believe you were familiar with her."

"I was." His brow knitted with the onset of sudden suspicion. "Hold on a minute! How can I know you are who you say you are? Do you have some identification?"

"Here is Brigadier Granville-Bruce of the Gurkhas," Sikander said, pointing at the Englishman, beckoning him to come closer. "He shall confirm what I am saying."

As the Brigadier gravitated toward them, Sikander gave him the discreetest of winks, to warn him to play along. The man was a bit slow on the uptake, but after a brief pause, he grinned and held up one thumb in approval.

"Oh, yes! I will vouch for Mr. Singh. You can trust him completely."

Yaru Bhai looked at him with glazed eyes, obviously dazzled, overcome by hero worship.

"My father speaks of you very highly, Brigadier," he said. "He calls you the boldest man in India."

"I take it, then, that the Brigadier's assurances will suffice?"

"I guess so," Yaru Bhai responded, but his tone was still surly, wary.

Sikander lowered his voice to a whisper. "Let me lay my cards on the table. We believe the girl has been spirited away. Obviously, a man is involved, and we were hoping to find out if you happened to see anything or anyone out of place when you were at the King's camp the day before yesterday. You did pay the girl a visit, didn't you?"

"I did," he admitted, more a murmur than a declaration.

"Might I ask why you went to see her?"

Yaru Bhai hesitated. "It was a personal matter."

"Could you please elaborate? It could be vital to locating her."

The boy's brows darkened. "She was my property. I went to claim her."

"I'm not sure I understand."

Yaru Bhai let out a solemn sigh, deciding to speak freely. "Some months ago, I was in Lahore and happened to see her perform. A friend had retained her services for the evening, and when I saw her dance, I was absolutely entranced. I cannot describe it, I do not have a way with words like my brother. Let me just say, I am not a drinking man, but I imagine that is what a stupor is like, the way I felt as I looked at her.

"When I returned home, I happened to mention her to my father." Beneath the moustache, his mouth curved into the tiniest of smiles. "We have a tradition in Palanpur. When a boy becomes a man, when he comes of age, his father gifts him his first concubine, so that he can be initiated in the ways of love. When my father heard about my passion for this girl, he decided he would purchase her to gift to me on my birthday, which is next month."

"But your bid was defeated by Kapurthala," Sikander said, finally seeing what had driven Yaru Bhai to make such a scene in public.

"Yes. We had already settled on a price with her to visit us at Palanpur for the season, but then Kapurthala swooped in and offered to outbid us, the snake!" He frowned, as petulant as a child from whose hands a toy has been snatched. "It just isn't fair. She was supposed to be mine. We had an agreement, for god's sake."

"So you went to confront her?"

"Yes!" His face was mulish with outrage. "I was going to demand she honor her contract with my father and come back with me immediately. But the damn guards would not even let me in to see her. The nerve of those *jemadars*, they sent me packing like I was some bloody *boxwallah*."

Sikander studied him, biting his lip. The boy was a thug, that much was for sure. And it took only two small steps to go from resentment to indignation and finally to frenzy. Still, Sikander remained unconvinced. True, he had a palpable motive, but it was doubtful he possessed the temperament to commit such a brutal crime. He was too young, too credulous, too easily enslaved by emotion. It took a ruthless, savage man to strangle a woman with his bare hands, a man accustomed to killing, inured to the taking of life, not a callow, overindulged brat of a boy.

"You say she has gone missing? You must find her, I insist." Yaru Bhai leaned forward, and gave him a sickly smile. "And when you do, bring her to me, not to the English."

That clinched it. The boy was not even aware that Zahra was dead. That meant this was yet another dead end. Sikander stifled a curse. What a waste of time! he thought, another detour that brought him no closer to solving Zahra' s murder.

"Promise me you will bring her to me," the boy continued to wheedle, so caught up in himself he did not even notice that Sikander had lost interest in him. "Return my property to me, and I will reward you well, I swear it. My father will fill your pockets with gold."

"Excuse me," Sikander said brusquely, rising to his feet. Before he could take a step, though, the boy vaulted up as well, and grabbed him by the shoulder.

"Hold on a minute!" Yaru Bhai exclaimed. "Aren't we going to go find the girl? What do you need me to do? I can have my father's men form a search party. We can offer a substantial reward for information about her whereabouts. You have to help me. I'll pay you for your time. How much do you want? Name your price."

"You really are clueless, aren't you?" Sikander shrugged off the boy's hand with a restrained vehemence. "Grow up, Yaru Bhai, and do it quickly, before someone less scrupulous than myself decides to take advantage of your naïveté."

He strode to the door, pausing only to bid the Brigadier a fulsome farewell. Outside, Charan Singh was waiting for him patiently, the car already cranked over, its engine ticking away as smoothly as a metronome.

"I take it the Nawabzada was not your man," he said.

"No, he is a buffoon. But a murderer, I think not."

"Well, then, where to next, huzoor? Would you like to question Prime Minister Asquith perhaps, or maybe the Queen?"

"Stop trying to be witty, old man." Sikander let out a vast yawn. "Back to the hotel, I think. We have enough time for a quick lunch and an even quicker drink."

"Are you sure?" Charan Singh made no effort to disguise his misgivings. "Didn't you say you were running short of time? Wouldn't it make more sense to carry on with your investigation?"

"Patience," Sikander said with more confidence than he felt. "We have several palpable leads, and besides, after the morning I have endured, I really could do with a pick-me-up."

Chapter Nineteen

By the time they returned to the Majestic, Sikander's earlier despondence had returned twofold.

It would have been only too easy to dismiss this melancholy as an affectation, the sort of *mal du siècle* which the Romanticists were known to affect. But Sikander had always believed it was something more, an innate dissonance that was endured by all people of above-average intelligence. The Germans had a wonderful word to describe such a condition–*sehnsucht*, which translated roughly as a missingness, the innate dissatisfaction a man feels when he comes to understand that reality can never quite be as satisfying as his imagination, a deep, intense longing that consumes him for something more, something inexplicable.

Charan Singh, who had grown finely attuned to his master's changes in mood over the years, was quick to realise that Sikander had no appetite for food.

"Shall I bring you a bottle of absinthe, sahib?" he asked instead.

"No, a magnum of Bollinger, I think, the 1884. I am feeling festive this afternoon." Sikander let out a sigh, and stretched his neck. "And one more thing, old man. What do you know about a nationalist named Bahadur Rao? Have you heard of him?"

"Only by reputation," Charan Singh replied, his face

souring. "He is said to be a rabble-rouser, the worst kind of demagogue."

"I want you to find him. Pick him up and bring him in for questioning."

"That might be difficult, huzoor. He has many followers."

"Then be discreet about it, won't you?"

The old Sikh snorted. "I will see what I can arrange."

"Good! Now go away! I am tired of looking at your ugly face."

As Charan Singh strode away, Sikander settled at his piano. At first he did not touch the keys. Instead, he squeezed shut his eyes and began to clench and unclench his fists, breathing deeply, first a long inhalation, then a series of short exhalations. It was an old Tantrist's trick he had learned many years ago from a traveling yogi, a ritual to clear the mind of all thoughts and attain that rare state of emptiness called *sunyata*. It took almost ten minutes before he felt a peace settle over him. Only then did he commence to play, the first hesitant notes of Chopin's "Étude," but as his fingers warmed up, Sikander quickly grew more confident. The day's frustrations began to melt away, metamorphosed into music, pouring from his fingers in a flood.

Sadly, before he could lose himself in this sibilant symphony, once again the door crashed open and Captain Campbell came hurtling in. Close on his heels, Charan Singh followed, offering his master a sheepish apology.

"I tried to stop him, huzoor, but he was very insistent. And you did say that he was working with you?"

Sikander gave first him, and then Campbell, a brace of equally poisonous scowls.

"What is so urgent, Captain, that it has made you forget your manners yet again?"

"Well, sir, as it happens, I have been able to find you a clue."

"Is that so?"

"Indeed!" Campbell exclaimed. "As a matter of fact, I have

been able to deduce the identity of the women who paid a visit to our *nautch* girl."

"Have you now?" Sikander could sense how excited he was, buzzing with restless energy. "How did you manage to pull it off?"

"Oh, I took a page from your book, sir. I *investigated*." He grinned. "I recalled what the Sergeant said about our young woman being a redhead accompanied by an older woman who always stayed by her side. On a whim, I decided to pay a visit to the Army and Navy Store and inquire if such a mismatched duo had made an appearance there, and sure enough, it seems a Miss Eleanor Cavendish visited the store three days ago to purchase a pair of *chukka* boots and a tropical hat, accompanied by her chaperone, a Miss Eaton."

Despite the man's unvarying ability to show up at exactly the wrong time, Sikander could not help but be somewhat impressed by Campbell's initiative.

"Well done," he said, "perhaps you are of some use after all, Captain." Sikander eased the piano lid shut, stretching his fingers until his knuckles cracked audibly. "I shall have my man track down this young *memsahib's* whereabouts, and then we can go visit her."

"There's no need for that, sir. Actually, I took the liberty of visiting her already, to suss her out. She is staying with the Hussars, as it turns out, with their Colonel, who is her uncle." His smile grew even more raffish. "I happen to know him rather well, so I decided to pop by, so to speak."

"Did you now?" Sikander said coolly. Once more, he felt his blood pressure rising, whatever newfound affinity he felt diffusing as quickly as it had kindled. Who did Campbell bloody well think he was? How dare he question one of his witnesses without his permission? Did the man have no sense at all, or was he just that callow?

"Oh, yes!" the Captain forged on, barely noticing the brittleness of Sikander's tone. "She is a real peach, let me assure you. As lovely as Lillie Langtry, and an heiress, to boot. Quite a catch, really, just the sort of girl a poor soldier dreams of landing!" He let out a very masculine chuckle, in appreciation of the absent *memsahib's* ample assets. "I happened to mention that I knew you, and offered to make an introduction. Naturally, she was rather excited at the prospect of meeting a genuine Maharaja, and jumped at the chance."

Taking out his hunter, an expensive Breguet, he brandished it at Sikander. "In fact, we are scheduled to meet her for tea and scones in precisely forty minutes."

Sikander's irritation subsided. He realised he had misjudged Campbell, and quite gravely, he had to admit. The man was not callow after all. He was on the contrary, very clever, and not inconsiderably subtle. As a native, it would always have been difficult for him to solicit an interview with a *memsahib*, particularly one who was a stranger. He certainly could not visit the Hussars' Camp and accost the lady in question, not without seeming a lecher. Nor could he dispatch Charan Singh with an invitation asking her to call upon him at the Majestic, not unless he wished to gain a reputation as a cad. However, by inviting the young woman to a neutral location, under the guise of making a formal introduction, the Captain had managed to solve both of these dilemmas, and rather neatly at that, to Sikander's delight.

"I shall need just a moment to make myself presentable."

"Very well! I will have the car brought around."

A little over ten minutes later, time which Sikander had used to change quickly into a pale white *bundhgula* paired with a rather rakish scarlet *pugree*, and to take a quick gargle with a thimbleful of Bollinger, they departed in the Silver Ghost. Charan Singh's son Ajit had been deputed to drive, with the Captain riding pillion. Seated comfortably in the passenger seat, Sikander leaned back, feeling much more like himself. His mood, he found, was uplifted considerably, not just because of the prospect of meeting this Irish peach with whom the Captain seemed so smitten, but also because he was more than a little amused by the prospect of questioning a suspect over high tea.

Their destination was at the northern edge of the Lothian Road, not far from St. James Church. It was here that an enterprising widow from Simla had opened a small tea pavilion in the style of Lyon's famous Ludgate Street establishment. Mrs. Flander's eponymously named Tea Room was housed in a small postal bungalow with a green tin roof and a wide verandah. From the looks of the crowd congregated at the tables out on the lawns beneath an assortment of gaily colored umbrellas, it was doing booming business, serving six types of tea and a variety of homemade cakes and biscuits.

The Major led Sikander into the bungalow itself, explaining he had booked a private room for their rendezvous with the Irish *memsahib*. This turned out to be a rather dimly lit cubicle at one corner of the parlor protected from prying eyes by a thick muslin curtain, behind which stood a marble-topped table adjoining an arched window that overlooked a very woebegone bougainvillea bush.

Upon entering they found somebody already seated at the table, a middle-aged woman with a prim hat and a disapproving frown who seemed to be waiting for them to arrive.

Sikander struggled to disguise his disappointment. This was Captain Campbell's ravishing heiress! She was forty if a day, with pinched lips accustomed habitually to scowling, and the sort of scathing squint a spinster gets when she has surrendered all hope. If this was what Campbell found attractive, Sikander thought, then perhaps the man needed a pair of spectacles even more than he needed a wife!

"You're Miss Cavendish," he exclaimed, unable to hide his surprise.

"No, this is Miss Eaton," Campbell said, "the chaperone."

"Of course it is!" Sikander offered her his very best smile. To his dismay, she remained impervious, her disapproval deepening to palpable distrust.

"I thought it best we have a brief word before you spoke with my ward," Miss Eaton said with a sniff. "I have heard of you, Mr. Singh, and your reputation as a womanizer."

"Madam!" Campbell interjected. "You are being unfair."

"Perhaps I am. Forgive my forthrightness. Nevertheless, I must warn you, I will not allow you to beguile my ward. You are to limit yourself to topics that are respectable. Is that clear, sir?"

Campbell blanched pale, utterly appalled by such a grievous breach of manners, but Sikander was amused, rather than offended.

"I assure you, Madam, this is not a seduction. I give you my word, as a gentleman."

Miss Eaton did not seem convinced by such a declaration, heartfelt though it was, but she could not contradict him, not without adding injury to insult. "Very well, I shall fetch Eleanor, but remember, I have my eye on you."

With that admonition, as imperiously as a Romanov, she marched away. Sikander waited until she was well out of earshot before letting out a long, low whistle and shaking his head in disbelief.

"What a terrifying creature!"

"If little labour, sir," Campbell said with a chuckle, "little are our gains." His face brightened and he nodded toward the front door. "Here she is now!"

Turning, Sikander was greeted by the sight of a very attractive young woman advancing toward him. She was every bit as lovely as the Captain had insisted, albeit a bit slender for his taste, very tall, with a diffident straightness of posture, elegantly dressed in an ankle-length silk dress he recognized as a Delphos, in a charming shade of soft silver that seemed to evoke the shimmer of moonlight when she moved. It perfectly matched her hair, which was indeed red, not the brazen ginger of the Celtiberians, but rather a very deep russet, so dark it was almost auburn.

"Miss Cavendish, I presume." He offered her a courtly bow. "I am Sikander Singh, the Maharaja of Rajpore."

He had expected her to blush and be somewhat at a loss for words. Sikander was accustomed to overawing women, especially Europeans, who could not help but become agitated by his hawkish good looks and piercing eyes. But Miss Cavendish was no wilting willow. She managed to surprise him, holding his gaze frankly, very sure of herself, with a quiet confidence he found rather alluring. Her mouth quirked into a half smile as she held out her hand for him to shake, very like a man.

"Please," she said, "call me Eleanor."

Reluctantly, Sikander gave her hand a perfunctory pat. Her grip was strong, her skin cool, and she smelt of sweat, he realised, and leather, which made him infer she must have arrived on horseback, rather than by car.

"I have heard a great deal about you, Mr. Singh," she said, her voice a delicate contralto. "I believe you know a dear friend of mine, Lady Sarah Wilcox."

It took Sikander more than a moment to place the name. An ex-lover, he thought, almost forgotten except for the remembrance of a pair of sapphire eyes and a very athletic disposition, particularly after a magnum of champagne.

"All lies, I assure you," he responded. "I am an exceedingly simple man."

"Is that so? Sarah was very flattering, I assure you," she said, a hint of suggestion in her tone.

"Would you care to sit down?" Campbell hurried forward, scraping back a chair.

"Thank you." She rewarded him with a resplendent smile. "I am very grateful for your kind invitation, Captain. This is such a delightful place, don't you think?"

Campbell flushed, as red as a brick. Sikander rolled his eyes, unable to hide his amusement. One kind word from an attractive woman, and the hero became as gormless as an adolescent.

Just as he was about to sit down himself, from behind them, Miss Eaton let out a rather forceful sniff, to remind him and the Captain that they had quite managed to forget her. With a wry smile, Sikander offered her his own seat, which she took with the habitual arrogance of a woman accustomed to being ignored by men.

"Well," he said, hailing a nearby bearer, "what would you ladies care to try?"

"I have taken the liberty of ordering, Your Majesty," Campbell said, as the waiter approached, offering a bottle of Pol Roger for the Maharaja's approval.

"Well done! I could certainly use a glass of something fizzy to clear the dust from my throat."

Sikander pointed at the *memsahibs*, indicating that the bearer should offer them the first glasses, as good manners dictated.

"I think not." Miss Eaton's voice was as cold as steel. "We will take a kettle of tea, and make sure it is *pukka* stuff. Earl Grey, do you hear? None of your Darjeeling rubbish. Cream, not milk. And serve the sugar on the side, not in the kettle, do you understand?" As the waiter backed away hurriedly, she gave Sikander and the Captain a haughty nod. "You have to be stern with these fellows, or they will muck everything up. Now, Mr. Campbell, what is it you wanted to talk to Eleanor about, eh?"

The Captain offered the two ladies a sheepish smile. "I confess, Madam, I had an ulterior motive to invite you to tea today. You see, the Maharaja here desired to have a chat with you."

Miss Eaton bristled visibly, shooting him a warning glare as if to forestall what she mistook to be a romantic overture, but curtly, before she could launch into another tirade, Sikander cut her off.

"I believe you visited the Royal Camp the day before, Miss Cavendish. Might I inquire why?"

"Please, do call me Eleanor." The *memsahib* smiled and

arched one well-plucked eyebrow, before holding up her wrists suggestively. "I have heard about your reputation, Your Majesty. Am I being interrogated? Don't you need to manacle me first?"

"Another time, perhaps," Sikander retorted, ignoring Miss Eaton's muted growl of disapproval at such banter. "For now, how about answering my question, if you please?"

"Well, as it happened, I have been rather bored, waiting for the Durbar celebrations to ensue. There really is not much here for a young woman to do, and so, when my uncle's *aide-de-camp*, Lieutenant Pelham, suggested we make a tour of the Imperial camp, I was only too eager to jump at the opportunity." She sighed, accompanied by a magnificently contrived toss of that startling hair. "I came to India thinking it would be the greatest of adventures. But all everyone here at the Durbar seems to want to do is parade about and march endlessly in circles. To be honest, I find myself sorely in need of some diversion. Perhaps one of you fine gentlemen might care to remedy that."

A less worldly man might have been beguiled by such a brazen attempt at being disarming. Captain Campbell certainly seemed captivated, entranced by Miss Cavendish's poise and beauty. But Sikander was rather less easy to win over. He had encountered many beautiful women along the course of his life, and if there was one truth he had learned along the way, it was that the more flirtatious a woman acted, the harder she was trying to hide something.

"I do not believe you, Miss Cavendish. I think you are lying to me."

Both Campbell and Miss Eaton let out identical gasps of dismay.

"Mr. Singh, this is just inexcusable. Stop haranguing the poor child."

"I have to agree, Your Highness. Steady on, won't you?" Campbell added.

Sikander ignored them, keeping his eyes fixed squarely on

Miss Cavendish. She uttered a little laugh. "I must confess, Your Majesty, I am rather disappointed by you."

"Is that so?"

She nodded her assent. "After all the praises that Lady Wilcox had sung, I expected more. I had imagined you would be a modern man, but I see now you are just as backward thinking as all the others, precisely the sort of man who thinks he can bully a woman. However, I must warn you, sir, you will find that I am not the sort of woman who is easily intimidated."

"I am not trying to intimidate you, my dear Eleanor. I assure you, I mean you no harm."

"Don't you?" Her voice was as scathing as raw acid. "Your breed always does. You are threatened by any woman who is unafraid to speak her mind, who wishes to make her own way in the world. You are no different from my father, or my brothers, who would rather have me wedded and bedded than allow me to travel, to see the world."

It was a masterful monologue, one part emotion, two parts accusation. Sadly, it left Sikander entirely unmoved. This was not the first time he had been accused of misogyny, nor did he suspect would it be the last. It was easy enough to mistake his brusqueness for loutishness, but the truth was somewhat simpler. It was not that he disdained womankind. On the contrary, Sikander had nothing but the utmost respect for what in his opinion was often erroneously described as the weaker sex. If anything, women were far stronger than men, if not physically, then at least emotionally.

The problem was that, at heart, Sikander was a misanthrope. He despised most people. Those few he counted as friends, that rare handful he admired, were individuals who had managed to rise above their basest instincts, who aspired to something more meaningful than the material. All others, men and women alike, he preferred to keep at an arm's length, not out of irascibility, but because he found them altogether too venial.

"I think, Madam, that you are being rather too theatrical,"

Sikander murmured, "and while I certainly applaud your attempt to change the subject quite deftly, the truth of the matter is that you went to the Imperial camp to meet with a *nautch* girl named Zahra, didn't you? If we were to summon this Lieutenant of yours, I am sure he would corroborate that, wouldn't he?"

Miss Cavendish's only response to this accusation was a stony silence, accompanied by an equally obdurate scowl.

"Tell me, dear Eleanor," Sikander said, leaning forward, "how long have you been a follower of Miss Pankhurst?"

This really was the final straw for Miss Eaton. Like a jack-in-the-box, she sprang to her feet.

"That is utterly unacceptable, Mr. Singh! Miss Cavendish is a respectable young lady. She has no truck with the likes of those…those…" Turning to her ward, she held out one hand. "Come along, Eleanor, let us away. We do not have to endure such boorish behavior a moment longer."

"Please, Madam, hold your tongue!" Sikander snarled. "I have had quite enough of your interruptions."

The elderly woman let out a squawk of disbelief, as shrill as an overwrought chicken. Her face darkened, flustered by such contemptuous treatment. She darted a quick look at Captain Campbell, seeking his support, but all she received was a non-committal shrug.

"It is all right, Miss Eaton," Miss Cavendish said diffidently. "Please sit down. As it happens, the Maharaja is entirely correct. I am indeed a suffragette."

This admission elicited another gasp, even more voluble than the last, and Miss Eaton all but fell back into her chair, fanning herself frantically with her handkerchief.

"Oh, my dear! What have you done? How are we ever going to find you a husband now?"

"I do not want, or need a husband," Miss Cavendish declared vehemently. "Why must a woman need a man to be considered worthwhile? Why can we not have an identity of our own?"

She gave Sikander a defiant look. "It was Sarah who introduced me to the Women's Social and Political Union. She hosted a meeting for them some years ago, and I had the privilege of attending and hearing Miss Pankhurst herself speak about the liberation of women. That was what changed my life forever. Until then, I had thought something wrong with me, a flaw deep within in my character, that I was dissatisfied by the very things that so preoccupied young women my age. I had no interest in knowing the latest fashions, or practising polite conversation, or being presented to eligible bachelors like a cow for sale. It was only when I heard Miss Pankhurst speak so eloquently of how women were the equals of men that I came to understand it was not me who was at fault, but society at large."

Her voice rose to a shrill crescendo, and with each successive exclamation, Miss Eaton let out a new groan, as if she were being flayed by her ward's words.

"That is the greatest ill of our times, Mr. Singh, the gravest injustice, that we women, who are strong enough to bear sons, to raise them to be stalwart soldiers of the Empire, are dismissed as too fragile, too nervous to have an education, to hold a job, to cast a ballot. That is what Miss Pankhurst wishes to remedy, to give a woman the right to be more than a mere vessel, to allow us to be the same as men, if not better."

"Is that why you went to see Zahra, to try and liberate her?"

"No, not quite. That is not what happened exactly." She sighed, and massaged her brow tiredly. "I was indeed bored, and only too happy to accept Lieutenant Pelham's invitation when it came. Of course, I was quite aware he was trying to woo me, but I had no intention of reciprocating his advances. I just needed a diversion, as I mentioned, and he was as good as any.

"When we arrived at the camp, Pelham was showing us around, raving on and on about the décor and so forth. Oh, what a lot of hot air! I was beginning to quite regret my decision to accompany him, when Mr. Urban happened to let on that there was a *nautch* girl being held in the camp."

"Hold on just a moment! Who is this Mr. Urban?"

"Oh, didn't I mention him? He is a filmmaker from America, here to chronicle the Durbar. He came out with us from London on the *Maloja*, and made my acquaintance while we were on board. Quite a cheeky fellow, actually. He told me I should be an actress, ha!"

"He was at the King's camp when you arrived there?"

"Yes, scouting for local color, he said, accompanied by two of his cameramen."

"And he was the one who told you about Zahra? He had been to see her?"

"Yes, he had tried to film her, I believe. Anyway, when I heard, I just knew I had to find a way to have a word with her. So I came up with rather a hasty plan." She smiled, her cheeks dimpling mischievously. "I feigned a fainting spell, and told the Lieutenant and Miss Eaton that I was feeling intemperate. They suggested I rest briefly, and while Pelham scurried off to try and scrounge up a car to take us back to the Hussars' Camp, I asked Miss Eaton to try and find me a nice cup of tea and some smelling salts. As soon as she left me alone in the reception tent, I snuck straight out and quickly tracked down the young lady. Pelham had mentioned she was being kept in the servants' quarters, and I tipped one of the *bhistis* who was watering down the walkway to show me the way."

"And you just barged right in, without any formal introductions whatsoever?"

"Of course! I was on a mission, Mr. Singh. I had to help the child. That is what Mrs. Pankhurst always says. Deeds, not words. That is how we will win our battle, not by posturing, but through action." She shuddered. "Poor thing! What kind life is that for a girl? To be bought and sold like a brood mare, and forced to dance for the entertainment of men, who drool over her like she was a piece of meat. No, I could not, in good conscience, leave her to such a fate."

"So you offered to rescue her?"

"Yes! I told her I would be happy to spirit her away to a safe refuge, to liberate her from a life of servitude and the curse of being a man's chattel to be used and discarded at a whim. I have a dear friend in Madras, one of the Governor's nieces, who is always keen to help those less fortunate. I told her she could easily get a job there as a maid, or maybe even a seamstress, if she was willing to work hard and learn a trade."

"But she did not wish to be rescued, did she?"

Miss Cavendish grimaced. "Not at all. On the contrary, she laughed at me." Her voice wavered with incredulity—or was it wrath? "She called me a fool, and said that a woman should know her place in the world!"

"Did that make you angry?"

"Of course! It is women like that who are setting back our cause." She ground her teeth so loudly that Captain Campbell winced. "How dare she call me a fool!" Her voice grew heated, her cheeks reddening with emotion. "If we could be rid of all such women, such weak and docile creatures, our cause would be advanced immeasurably, I tell you."

Sikander pursed his lips, contemplating this outburst. On one hand, it gave Miss Cavendish a compelling motive, at least theoretically to want Zahra dead. As she had admitted with her own words, her cause would be immeasurably advanced. On the other, would she really be so forthright now if she had caused the girl any real harm? Would she make such an incriminating statement if she really was a killer? And then there was the matter of the physics of it. He found it difficult to picture her strangling someone. She was tall enough, yes, but her slender build and slim hands lacked the strength to have throttled Zahra so brutally and then strung her up like a prize.

"What happened next? Did you try to reason with her, to remonstrate that you were acting in her best interest?"

"No," Miss Cavendish shook her head. "I could see that I

was wasting my time, and I felt like a fool for having even tried, so I left. Besides, I had to hurry back before Miss Eaton here found out that I was gone." Her face stiffened. "I must ask, what exactly is this about, Mr. Singh? Has some ill fate befallen Zahra?" Her eyes gleamed, like cabochons. "Has she run away? Absconded with a man perhaps?"

"Now why would you say that?"

Miss Cavendish lowered her voice. "She has a lover, I am sure of it. That was the impression I got when I spoke with her."

Miss Eaton's handkerchief-fanning grew still more outraged, until Sikander was afraid she would take to the air, like some demented bird.

"What makes you so sure of that?"

"Oh, a woman knows! She was in love, that much was written on her face. In fact, I am quite certain that is why she turned me down." She exhaled, a sympathy of breath. "I can only hope she is happy, wherever she is, the poor misinformed thing!"

Sikander sat back, intrigued by her suggestion that Zahra had been hiding a secret lover. Bhupinder had insinuated much the same thing, as had the Nizam. Who could this elusive Lothario be? Was he Indian or Caucasian? And was he the one who had murdered Zahra?

He realised that Miss Cavendish was watching him very intently, waiting for some measure of a response to her earlier question.

"It has been a distinct pleasure to meet you, Miss Cavendish," he said, keeping a proverbial poker face. "And, for the record, I have no dispute with women being equal to men, so long as they are quite as exceptional as you."

"How gallant! But who is the one being evasive now?"

"Good-day, Madam!"

"Very well!" Rising, she shook her head. "You can keep your secrets this once. And you, too, Captain," she said as Campbell stood up as well. "I would suggest you gentlemen stay out of trouble, but I get the feeling I would be wasting my breath."

"It was my pleasure, Madam," Campbell said. "Might I have permission to call upon you, at the Hussars' Mess tomorrow?"

This overture finally caused Miss Eaton to spark up, having recovered enough of her composure to regain some semblance of her previous prudishness.

"You are presumptuous, sir, and much too forward."

Even as she made that declaration, a startling thought occurred to Sikander, induced by Campbell's fleeting mention of the Hussars' Camp. Could Miss Cavendish be the woman that Brigadier Granville-Bruce had mentioned earlier, the object of his newfound affections?

"There is a ball later this evening, Madam, at the Indore Camp, hosted by Lord and Lady Bute. It would be my honor if you would deign to attend, as my guest. If you wish it, I shall have a car sent for you, and for Miss Eaton. Shall we say about six-thirty?"

"I should think not." Miss Eaton rose to her feet with stately disdain. "I have no intention of allowing dear Eleanor to become involved with you and your schemes. Come along, child. We shall find a more respectable way to spend the evening."

She marched away, as regal as a Tudor. As for Miss Cavendish, she chose to linger, just long enough to give Sikander a comradely wink.

"Don't mind Miss Eaton. She will come around." Her eyes twinkled. "I shall see you this evening, gentlemen. You can count on it."

"What a woman!" Campbell observed as she walked away.

"Indeed!" Sikander agreed, calling for the waiter to settle up the bill. "Too much woman for you, though, I fear, Captain."

When they departed the tea house, Charan Singh was waiting to greet them.

"I have done it, huzoor. Once again, I have cracked the case."

"What are you looking so self-satisfied about, you old baboon?"

"As it happens, sahib, I have found your Nationalist."

"Where is he?"

"My sources inform me that there is a gathering this very afternoon to protest the Durbar. This Bahadur Rao will undoubtedly be there."

The Captain looked stunned. "Are you certain of this information? We haven't heard of any such meeting."

"That is because it is a secret, sahib." Charan Singh's voice could not have been more patronizing. "Some Gujarati named Gandhi has called for a boycott in South Africa, and the Nationalists are gathering at one of the *maidans* near the Lahori Gate to show their support."

"And how did you come to know this?"

Charan Singh's only reply was a noncommittal shrug. Sikander resisted the urge to delve further. The old man's private life was his own, and he had no intention of intruding.

"I'll inform the Commissioner and ask him to put a flying squad together," Captain Campbell said.

"Hold off on that. The last thing I want is to spook our quarry." Sikander bared his teeth, delighted by the thought of a bit of action.

"No, we'll handle this ourselves. Let us go and net ourselves a fish."

Chapter Twenty

From a very young age, Bahadur Rao had decided he wanted to be an important man, a somebody. His father had lived and died as a nobody, working his fingers to the bone in a mine in Raniganj, his eyes and tongue stained permanently black by coal dust. And it was deep in the bowels of the earth that he had died, just one man among four hundred-fifty others who had perished when the roof had caved in, remembered only by his son and none other.

Bahadur Rao refused to live like that, struggling to eke out a meager, insignificant life. He wanted so much more—to travel, to drink and eat and suck the very marrow from life. But most of all, he craved to be someone, a man who counted, who was more than just a statistic.

Luckily, he had realized early in life that he had that rarest of gifts, an innate charisma. People liked him at first sight. More than that, they trusted him. It helped that he had grown into a handsome man, tall, well-built if somewhat on the portly side, with a booming laugh and a face that strangers found easy to relate to. Added to that, he had been gifted with a silver tongue, the ability to beguile people with his words, like a snake-charmer entrancing a cobra.

Coupling this with his natural cleverness, he had managed to win a scholarship to attend university in Lahore, where he had graduated with a degree in history. He had then taken the

Civil Service Entrance examination and done well enough to travel to England for higher studies. There, unfortunately, the very outspokenness which had made him so remarkable in India had won him no friends, and he had endured exceedingly shabby treatment from the students and professors alike. And then, when he had dared to complain, he had been labeled a troublemaker and expelled, forced to return to India with nothing to show except a heart filled with resentment against the English, an emotion which had slowly hardened over time into a vehement hatred.

Over the ensuing years, Bahadur Rao had tried his hands at many things. He had been a shill, a salesman, a speculator, a *vakeel*, an *aumildar*, a *boxwallah*, a *dalal*, a trader, a money-lender, a *munshi*, a confidence trickster, and a guru. But it was only in his fifties, when he became involved with the nascent Nationalist Movement, that he had truly found his calling.

The Congress had welcomed him with open arms, for he was a born demagogue. When it came to rhetoric, he was a virtuoso, capable of manipulating his listeners with consummate skill, taking their emotions, their despair and hunger and resentment and stoking it to the very brink of madness. It was said Bahadur Rao could foment a revolt with a hundred words, such was his skill at whipping crowds into a frenzy.

That was what had drawn him to Delhi, and to the English Durbar. It was here that he intended to make himself a household name. By the end of this day, he thought with a grin, the English would know who he was, as would their lackeys, those damnable Maharajas. By the time the sun set, he would be recognized as the foremost amongst the Nationalist leaders, greater even than Tilak, Gokhale, or the Lala.

The venue chosen for his assembly was a small square at the distant end of the Sadar Bazaar, not far from the Lahori Gate. His followers had been circulating amidst the crowded by-lanes for weeks, assiduously spreading word of his arrival. As a result, quite a large crowd had gathered to hear him speak, more than enough people to fill the square almost to overflowing.

Bahadur Rao was a large man, and it took two attendants to help him climb onto a temporary stage made from a cart. From atop this makeshift dais, he gazed down at the sea of brown faces surrounding him. Some were cynical, some eager, but all attention was fixed squarely upon him, a realization which made him tremble, not with nervousness, but with anticipation. Most of the people in the crowd were poor laborers, carters and herdsmen, farmers and serfs, unsophisticated villagers who had come to see the Durbar celebrations. But to a man like him, they represented the rawest of clay, putty in his hands, waiting to be manipulated. Like all rabble-rousers, this was what he lived for, to face a crowd and incite it to hysteria with nothing but his words. That was his greatest thrill. For him, there was no more potent ecstasy to be had, not money, nor love. Power. That was what Bahadur Rao was craved most of all.

He took a deep breath and began to speak.

"How long will we wait?

"How long will we let the English mistreat us?

"How long will we let the Maharajas grow fat while we starve?

"How long will we be slaves?

He paused after each declaration, giving the crowd time to react. As he had expected, they hung on every word, enraptured.

"No more!" With practiced skill, Bahadur pitched his voice upwards several octaves, amplifying it into a thunderous monotone that boomed across the square like thunder. "We will take it NO MORE!"

A palpable susurration swept through the crowd, a barely repressed rage accompanied by a hundred whispers of agreement. Bahadur Rao stifled the urge to smile, gloating inwardly, knowing then at that moment he held the crowd in the palm of his hands, that they were willing puppets to his voice, ready to dance to his whims as he tugged at their strings.

"Rise up," he declaimed, shaking his fist in the air. "Cast off your chains. *Swaraj* is not a dream! It is our birthright!"

A loud clamor greeted this announcement, a roar followed by a scattering of applause.

"Rise up," he exclaimed, almost dizzy as a wave of adulation swept out of the crowd and washed over him, as intoxicating as a drug.

Stifling a groan, he prepared to make one final declaration, but before he could continue, a cacophony of whistles echoed tinnily through the air, shattering the spell he had begun to cast.

"It's the police," one of his attendants squealed. "Hurry, Bahadur sahib, you must get away!"

If there was one talent he had other than oratory, it was the ability to know when the game was up. Turning, Bahadur Rao immediately vaulted off the cart in spite of his girth. Desperately, he tried to make a beeline in the opposite direction from the police whistles, trying to melt into the crowd, lose himself in its stampeding midst. But it was to no avail. The crush of bodies was too thick, and whichever way he turned, his passage was impeded by a frenzied throng.

He quickly lost sight of his handlers, who were swept away by the rush of people. Behind him, the whistles grew shriller, drawing closer with each passing second. A shudder ran through Bahadur Rao's portly frame. Had his luck run out at last? He knew he could not let the police to get their hands on him. After all that he had said and done to undermine and sabotage the English, he had a feeling that it would be less than healthy for him if he allowed himself to be apprehended.

His salvation presented itself in a most unexpected fashion. As he struggled to push his way free of the crowd, a man materialized in his path—a giant Sikh dressed in a nondescript black *achkan* and a red *pugree* who towered over him by a head and a half.

"This way," the man beckoned, without bothering to offer a word of introduction.

Bahadur Rao paused, unsure of how to respond. On one hand, he was positive he did not know the man. If they had met before, he certainly would have remembered a specimen quite so massive. On the other, he knew it could only be a matter of minutes before the police cut off any hope of escape. Opposing instincts warred against each other in his mind, suspicion pitted against panic, as he struggled to make up his mind. In the end, self-preservation won out over caution, and Bahadur Rao gave the man a nod, to indicate he would follow him.

Unlike his own feeble efforts, the big Sikh wrestled his way through the crowd effortlessly, slowly making his way toward a nearby alley. Bahadur Rao fell in behind him, trying to keep up as the man loped along, moving with admirable speed for someone so elderly.

He breathed a voluble sigh of relief as they finally broke free of the mob.

"Who are you?" he asked. "I cannot thank you enough for coming to my rescue."

The Sikh ignored him, and Bahadur felt the first faint flicker of worry. Nonetheless, he permitted the man to lead him into the gully, which seemed to be deserted. Now that they were free of the encumbrance of the crowd, the Sikh quickened his pace, settling into a brisk trot that soon had him huffing breathlessly.

Just when he thought they had made a clean getaway, the giant Sikh came to an unexpected halt.

"Here," he said, turning to face him, holding up what seemed to be a cloth bag. "Put this on."

"What is the meaning of this?" Bahadur exclaimed. "I thought you were here to help me."

He tried to retreat, but before he could take more than two steps, the Sikh had clapped one hand on his shoulder, his grip as unyielding as iron. Bahadur Rao let out a squeal of outrage as he was manhandled to the ground, the sack draped across his face, obscuring his vision.

"My master would like to have a word with you," the Sikh explained, and then one immense fist lashed out and caught Bahadur Rao squarely on his chin, knocking him into a stupor.

What followed was a blur, a disjointed collection of half-conscious impressions. The hood over his head made everything hazy, as immaterial as a dream. He had a sense of being lifted bodily and bundled into the back of some sort of automobile, followed by a bumping and shaking when it trundled into motion. It traveled for some time, and he was shaken and jostled until his teeth felt loose in his head before the vehicle came to an abrupt stop. Then, once again, he was roughly dragged out and then carried for some distance before being dumped into the back of another vehicle, pushed so hard that he let out a squawk of pain as his already bruised ribs were subjected to further mistreatment.

Abruptly, the sackcloth hood was whipped away. Bahadur Rao squinted, trying to adjust to the sudden change in brightness. He found he was in a sumptuously decorated limousine, lying akimbo atop a very luxurious seat. Opposite him, a short, gaunt-faced Indian sat, watching him.

"Mr. Rao," he announced, "what a pleasure to meet the man behind the myth!"

"Who are you?" Bahadur Rao croaked. "Where am I?"

"Both, of course, are valid questions." The man leaned forward. "I am Sikander Singh, the Maharaja of Rajpore. Perhaps you have heard of me?"

Bahadur Rao's eyes widened. He had, indeed. Some said he was a devil, and others, a genius. He was said to be one of the better Maharajas, a noble benefactor who genuinely cared for the welfare of his people, and was no supporter of the English, but then why had he disrupted the Nationalist demonstration? What was his agenda?

"This is Captain Campbell." He pointed to the Englishman seated next to him, who gave Bahadur Rao a wink. And I believe you already met my manservant, Charan Singh?" As if on cue, the door opened, and the enormous Sikh who had assaulted him so grievously lumbered into the vehicle and sat down next to Bahadur Rao, causing him to recoil.

"Why have you brought me here?"

"That's simple enough. I am going to ask you several questions You will answer them as honestly as humanly possible." The Maharaja smiled, which made his face even more ominous. "If you lie or refuse to cooperate, my man here will be forced to hurt you. Is that clear?"

Bahadur Rao's mouth lolled open. He looked from one man to the next, unable to believe what he was hearing.

"I am an important man," he shrilled. "I have followers. You cannot just kidnap and threaten me like this. There will be consequences."

Sikander's face hardened into a scowl. "Very well, if that is how you wish to play it." He turned to Charan Singh and gave him a nod. "See if you can persuade him. I give up!"

The big Sikh's hand shot out with blinding speed, slapping Bahadur Rao once, twice, thrice, a trio of crisp backhands across his plump face that left him gasping.

"Are you ready to cooperate now?" Sikander inquired. He had expected that, like all talkers, the Nationalist would have no stomach for physical violence. But Bahadur Rao managed to surprise him.

"Never!" The man exclaimed, showing that beneath his flabby exterior, there hid some genuine steel. "You can torture me, even kill me, but I will never betray the cause. I will gladly go to my grave a martyr."

Sikander rolled his eyes, unimpressed by such unnecessary dramatics. Still, one thing was obvious. The direct approach would not work with Bahadur Rao. Not only was he a fanatic, it was obvious he was much too thick-skinned to be intimidated, no pun intended. No, it was time to try a different tactic.

"If you don't talk to me, Bahadur Rao, you *will* have to speak to the English. They shall not be quite so civilized, I assure you. Do you really want me to hand you over to them?"

He gave Campbell the briefest of nods, but it was quite enough for him to grasp the situation.

"What would happen, Major, if I handed him into English custody?"

Campbell shrugged, taking up the skein effortlessly.

"I can't be sure. Transportation, most certainly, to Port Blair, but after some of the rubbish he has been spouting, most probably I think they will just hang him and be done with it."

"You can't do that." For the first time, Bahadur Rao looked scared, his eyes widening with dismay.

"Oh, the English can do whatever they want. Who's going to stop them?"

Sikander feigned a shudder. "Hanging, my goodness, that's a dreadfully uncivilized way to die. Have you ever seen a man being hanged, Bahadur Rao? The bowels go first, and you shit yourself, like a baby. And more often than not, your neck doesn't break. Instead, you just dance about until you slowly choke to death."

He could see his words were having the desired effect. Bahadur Rao looked positively green at the gills. "Is that what you want? To dance the dead man's jig at the gallows?"

Sikander offered the man a sympathetic smile. "I will make you an offer. Speak to me now, and you can go free. Refuse, and the English shall have you. It is your choice."

Bahadur Rao considered this dilemma. He was nothing if not a pragmatist, and it took him just a minute to weigh his options, and come to the conclusion that there really only was one thing he could do.

"I will answer your questions."

Sikander's smile widened, pleased to have coerced the man quite so easily. "A few days ago, you visited the Viceregal camp. You were in disguise, pretending to be one Bansi Lal, and you attempted to visit a *nautch* girl, a young woman named Zahra, claiming that you were her uncle? Am I correct so far?"

"Yes," Bahadur Rao gave one curt nod of assent.

"I thought as much." Sikander leaned forward. "The question that I need answered is why, Bahadur Rao? Why risk such a ruse, and chance arrest to sneak into the most heavily guarded camp here? Was it for some mischief connected to the Nationalists, something to disrupt the Durbar, perhaps? Was the girl working for you? Or was there some other reason you were lurking about trying to gain access to her?"

Bahadur Rao let out a long, slow breath. "I was there on a personal matter," he said, looking Sikander straight in the eye. "I had met the girl some years ago, when I was in Baroda teaching at the orphans' school there. She was one of my best students, a bright child blessed with a great deal of natural intelligence, not to mention almost unlimited promise. I took a liking to her, and decided I would help her make something of herself. I did not know of her past at first, how her mother had died, but then when she confessed everything to me, I knew I had to assist her however I could. To tell the truth, I admired seeing such strength of character in someone so young, to have come from such dismal origins and still have the bravery to try and leave it all behind and make something of herself, forge her own way in the world. As a result, I pulled every string I could to try and find her a job, and finally managed to secure a position for her as a seamstress in a factory in Lyallpur."

Bahadur Rao frowned. "That was the last time I saw her, until now. I thought of her often, I admit, wondering what had become of her. I hoped always that she had prospered. But then, when I heard she had lapsed and become a *nautch-wali*, I was very disappointed. That is why I decided to pay her a visit, to ask her why she had given up on her dreams and taken up the very profession that had robbed her of her mother. I wanted to plead with her, make her see reason. I wanted to help her. Is that so wrong?"

It was a heartfelt story, and Bahadur Rao told it well, with just enough emotion to make his words believable. He almost managed to get away with it, too, but Sikander was not quite so easy to dupe. He was far too proficient at reading body language and, unbeknownst to Bahadur Rao, he was betrayed by what card-players called a tell. Each time he mentioned the girl, he blinked not once, but twice, very rapidly, an involuntary gesture that told Sikander he was nervous, which could only mean one thing.

"You're lying," he said

"I am not. I am telling the truth. I swear it."

"Very well! If you insist on being difficult." He shrugged. "Captain, he's all yours."

"Wait!" Bahadur Rao let out a sigh. "I did know her, and try to help her, but you're right, that is not why I went to see her."

"What was the real reason for your visit then?"

"I had a message for her. I went to deliver it."

"Let me hazard a guess," Sikander said, leaning forward. "This message, was it an invitation to work for you Nationalists?"

The man's eyes widened in shock. "You are a *shaitan*, a devil," he hissed. Hurriedly, he made the sign of the evil eye, apparently to ward off Sikander.

"Oh, do grow up. You are an educated man, Bahadur Rao. Do try and act like one." Sikander wrinkled his brow. "I think I see the scheme now. You intended to use her to blackmail the English, didn't you? What was the plot? Were you going to try and entrap the King? Make Zahra swear an affidavit that she was molested by him, that he forced himself on her. No, that doesn't work. He would merely deny it, not without proof of some kind. Wait, I have it! You wanted to set it up so that you could take a photograph of them together, catch the King *in flagrante delicto*, so to speak. And for that, you needed Zahra to agree to seduce him. But she refused, didn't she? She sent you packing."

Bahadur Rao shook his head, his voice hoarse. "You have it only half-right. Yes, we wanted her to help us ruin the Durbar by exposing the King. I had a press *wallah* all ready to interview her, an Irish journalist who is a sympathizer of our cause. He was all set to break the news that the King was consorting with courtesans and that the taxpayers were footing the bill, but unfortunately, I was unable to get to her in time." He paused, before deciding that he might as well put all his cards on the table. "I managed to cajole my way to her tent, but when I got there, it turned out that she was entertaining someone else at the time."

"A gentleman?"

Bahadur Rao nodded. "He was like you."

"What do you mean, a Sikh?"

"No, not a Sikh. A Prince. I do not know which state, but he was definitely a royal."

"What makes you so sure?"

"He had the same demeanor as you do, the exact manner." Bahadur Rao's mouth curled into a sneer. "Strutting around like you own everything, like everyone has been born solely to serve your ridiculous whims."

"You cur," Charan Singh swore. "How dare you speak to the Maharaja with such insolence?" His hands curled into fists, and he looked ready to cuff Bahadur Rao again, but Sikander, who was not at all put out by the Nationalist's hostility, forestalled his manservant with a wave.

"Can you describe this man for me?"

"He was very ordinary looking, quite short, dark, on the fat side. Also, he had a moustache."

"That could be any one of four dozen Indian monarchs," Sikander said, struggling to hide his impatience. "Is there anything else you recall? Anything odd?"

"Well," Bahadur Rao said, frowning, "he was wearing rather a funny hat." He sketched a shape in the air with his hands. "It was red and shaped like a cylinder. And it had a rope hanging from it, like a donkey's tail."

Could he mean a fez, a tasseled cap, like the ones they wore in Turkey? That could be a viable clue, Sikander thought excitedly. It was rather a distinctive piece of headwear, and shouldn't be too difficult to find.

"You say Zahra was entertaining him? Do you mean romantically?"

"No, not at all. On the contrary, they were arguing about something. Or at least he was, haranguing her as loudly as a fishwife."

"Did you happen to overhear what he was saying?"

"No, I did not. He was very irate, though, whoever he was. And when I entered the room and interrupted him, he nearly bit my head off. I tried to explain I had a message for Zahra, but the man snapped at me like I was a third-rate *chuprassy*. He told me to make myself scarce, and when I tried to argue, he had two of his guards escort me away."

Bahadur Rao shook his head. "What choice did I have? I couldn't hang about, not without looking suspicious, and I could not leave my message for someone else to deliver, given the sensitivity of the topic. As a result, I had no choice but to leave the camp, and go back to my master to explain that I had failed to carry out his orders."

Even as he said those words, his eyes widened with dismay. Bahadur Rao let out a curse, biting his tongue when he realized that he had inadvertently revealed far too much information.

Sikander's heartbeat quickened. So here was the truth of it at last, he thought. Bahadur Rao was merely a catspaw. The real puppet-master was someone else altogether.

"Your master, you say," he said, quick to pounce on Bahadur Rao's misstep. "Now that is an interesting development. Tell me, who is he? Who do you work for?"

"I cannot." His face stiffened, turning as obdurate as a Sphinx. "I have said all that I am willing to say."

"Have you now?" From the determined cast of his shoulders, Sikander could tell Bahadur Rao was deathly serious, that he had no intention of cooperating any further. "Very well, in that case, you may arrest him now, if you wish, Captain."

"With pleasure," Campbell said. Leaning over, he clamped

one hand on the Nationalist's shoulder. "Come along, my friend. You have an appointment with the Assizes, and I wouldn't want you to miss it."

"But," Bahadur Rao recoiled, "you said you would let me go."

"Did I?" Sikander gave the man a pitiless glare. "I said if you cooperated with me fully, I would consider it, but you are the one who is refusing to divulge the identity of your master. Sorry, Bahadur Rao, but you have left me no choice in the matter."

He nodded at Campbell, who opened the car's door, but Bahadur Rao moved with unexpected speed. Breaking loose, he turned on Sikander. His face was so red that for a moment, the Maharaja thought he intended to assault him, but instead, he pursed his lips and spat in his direction, a gobbet of phlegm that only narrowly missed him, splashing to the carpet between his boots.

"You are not done with me, Sikander Singh," he raved. "We will have our day. Very soon, the English will be forced to leave India, and when they go, you and your kind will be thrown off your thrones. Your ivory palaces will be pulled down, and your titles stripped from you. And we shall rise, we, the commoners, the nobodies. We will usurp all that you own. You will be a pauper then, a nothing, just you wait and see, Sikander Singh. I curse you, and your white masters who you serve so loyally, like a slave."

This tirade was just too much to take, enough to test even Sikander's patience.

"I am no man's slave," he thundered. Even before he knew it, he had surged forward, his hand bunching the man's shirt, his face suffused with fury. But then, just as soon as it had crested, this wave of passion receded, leaving Sikander feeling dirty, like he had betrayed himself somehow by allowing himself to give in to such a base onslaught of emotion.

"Just take him away." He released Bahadur Rao, rubbing at

his hands, as if he could not get them clean.

Charan Singh obeyed, dragging the Nationalist bodily out of the car, but not before Bahadur Rao managed to get in a parting rejoinder.

"You have chosen the wrong side," he snarled. "Sooner or later, India will belong to us Indians, you can be sure of that."

His words stung at Sikander, as sharp as a razor. He stiffened, but it was not rage that gripped him this time around. It was realization. The wrong choice, Bahadur Rao had said. Sikander had heard those words before, that very phrase, repeated not twenty-four hours past.

In a flash, he knew exactly who the man's elusive master was. The Gaekwad of Baroda. That was who Bahadur Rao had to be working for.

If that was indeed the case, then it also meant he could not be the one who murdered Zahra.

Why? Because Sayaji Rao would never resort to murder, especially not that of a woman.

He was far too much of a gentleman for that.

Chapter Twenty-one

About a kilometer due west from the Royal encampment, very near the junction where the Kingsway intersected with the Princes Road, the English had razed several acres of farmland to create a vast open *maidan*. At the southern end, playing fields for hockey, football, and cricket had been demarcated, but the majority of the space was dedicated to the game of polo, of which the King was said to be an ardent devotee. Two full sized-greens had been laid out, with the stables and the paddocks adjoining the distant end, and the area between used to erect rows of stands for spectators, flanked by a handsome clubhouse done up in Tudor style and a row of matching pavilions.

When the Rolls came to a stop outside the entrance to the clubhouse, it seemed a *chukka* was just drawing to a close. Sikander disembarked, strolling over to lean on one of the fenceposts that bordered the green. Shielding his eyes with one hand, he peered out at the players, trying to pick out his quarry.

"Which one is Jey Singh?" Campbell inquired, coming up behind him.

"Over there, the man on the white Arabian, wearing blue and red."

"I have heard some rather sinister things about him," the Captain said with a shiver. "Is is true that he is a pederast?"

Sikander replied with a grimace. "The princes of Alwar are complicated."

Located at the border of Rajputana, Alwar was roughly the size of Montenegro. It had been founded by a Kachawwa Rajput named Partap Singh Prabhakar, a soldier of fortune who had conquered the ancient Kingdom of Mewat. Compared to its neighbor, Jaipur, it was a relatively minor principality, entitled to only fifteen guns. However, it was very wealthy, due mainly to the famed slate and sandstone mines located at the fringes of the Aravalis. However, in recent times Alwar had become most notorious for the unbridled eccentricity of the ruling family, who had long enjoyed a reputation for being somewhat unhinged.

Jey Singh's grandfather, Sheodan Singh, the first of the clan to be anointed Maharaja, had been as erratic as a tornado, so unpredictable that the British had pushed him aside and taken over management of Alwar's affairs. When he had died, ironically, of brain fever, with no legitimate heirs, an adopted son, Mangal Singh, had been placed on the throne. Unfortunately, he had turned out to be an alcoholic, another victim of the Alwar curse.

If rumor was to be believed, this infirmity of character had been passed on to his son, Jey Singh, the current bearer of the title. There were half a hundred stories about his peculiarities: that he had built himself an Italian villa and then refused to live in it because a black cat had walked past its entrance; that he loved practical jokes so much that he had once had one of his ministers arrested and sentenced him to death, only for it to turn out that he had ordered the crossbeam sawed through so that it would snap precisely when the man was hanged from the gallows. It was rumored he bought three new automobiles every year and had his old cars buried in unmarked graves after full state funerals, and that when his guru had died, rather than cremating his corpse, he had it pickled. There were darker stories as well, that once he had doused a polo pony with kerosene and set it aflame merely because it had bucked him, that he used the babies of villagers as bait on tiger hunts, and that he was a sadist and a pederast and a sodomite who enjoyed having his concubines seduce young British officers so that he could then coerce them into sexual liaisons, threatening them with scandal if they refused.

Of course, looking at him, it was difficult to detect even a trace of insanity. Sikander was reminded of the story of Jekyll and Hyde. It was as if two people inhabited the same body, one urbane and calm, the other savage and animalistic. On the face of it, Jey Singh was handsome, a man of unsurpassed wit and elegance, gifted with the silver tongue of a Cicero. As far as the English were concerned, he was a thorough gentleman, not to mention that he was widely considered the best polo seat and rifle shot in India. But those who knew him personally understood that this was a carefully cultivated façade. Jey Singh wore sanity like a mask. Beneath it, he was deeply deranged.

Which Jey Singh was he about to encounter? Sikander wondered. The affable version, or the lunatic? It was that very thought which remained uppermost in his mind as he preceded Campbell into the pavilion. Inside, it was like something straight out of Kipling. No effort or expense had been spared to perfectly recreate a planter's clubhouse, right down to the rattan furniture and the bamboo bar in the corner, not to mention the preponderance of potted palms spread around the room, giving the place a vaguely jungle air.

"Come, let us get a drink," he said, allowing a white-jacketed *khidmutgar* to usher them over to a cane-and-glass table, flanked by a pair of wicker armchairs.

"We shall have a bottle of Pol Roger." Sikander settled into the chair facing the entrance, leaving the other vacant for Campbell.

"We haven't time for this, sir," Campbell insisted, looking rather out of sorts.

"Patience, Captain! Here comes our suspect now."

He swiveled his neck toward the door, where Jey Singh had just made a triumphant ingress, accompanied by the usual crowd of hangers-on. He was a striking man, almost as tall as Bhupinder, so slender he seemed almost effeminate, and very dark, with sunken, inscrutable eyes and a perpetual smirk that gave him the air of a Rupert of Hentzau.

When he saw him, unbidden, a memory sprang to Sikander's mind, the recollection of a sunny afternoon, many years long past, when he had chanced upon a young boy sitting in a secluded corner of the school dormitory, laughing uproariously even though he was all by himself.

"What are you doing?" he had asked curiously.

"They die so easily," the child, who had been none other than Jey Singh had replied, holding up his hands, which had been filled with the corpses of butterflies. "Do you think they feel any pain when I pull off their wings?"

A chill ran down his spine now, a tremor of dread, and Sikander took a deep breath before raising his arm.

"Jey Singh!" he shouted. "Over here!"

Alwar's neck swiveled toward him, studying him with a quizzical, almost hostile frown, before recognition dawned. His mouth broke into a faint smile. Altering his direction, he sauntered to their table.

"Is that Sikander Singh, as I live and breathe? What an unexpected surprise! Since when did you take an interest in polo? I thought all you cared for was mystery stories!"

"Actually, I came to see you."

"Did you now?" He whistled to the waiter who approached him warily, dragging up a well-upholstered chair.

"You, boy, bring me oysters, two dozen of them, and make it quick."

It was obvious his erratic reputation had preceded him, judging by the speed with which the *khidmutgar* hurried away to fulfill this command. Languorously, Jey Singh sat down, crossing one leg over the other and casting an appreciative glance at the boy's retreating backside before turning his attention to Campbell, eyeing him carefully, an examination so discomfortingly lascivious that it was almost an assault.

"Well, aren't you going to introduce me to your handsome friend?"

"This is Captain Campbell of the Coldstream Guards."

"Is he now? Tell me, Captain, have you even considered leaving the Army and entering private service? We at Alwar are always on the lookout for a few good men." He tittered, amused by this unexpected *double-entendre*. "With posture quite as admirable as yours and those wonderful eyes, you should be a Colonel, at the very least."

The Captain blushed a deep scarlet. Luckily, that was when the waiter came to his rescue, returning with the requested oysters and champagne. Losing interest in Campbell entirely, Jey Singh attacked the platter with immense gusto, cracking open the shells and shoveling their slippery innards into his mouth greedily. Sikander sat in silence, watching him, trying to keep his gorge from rising.

"I adore oysters," Jey Singh said, grinning. "They are wonderful for a man's virility." Tendrils of pink meat hung from his teeth, and he smacked his lips which were slick with ichor at Campbell. "Do try one," he offered the plate to Sikander, who refused with a scowl.

"I think I will stick to the champagne, thank you," he said, helping himself to a generous measure of Pol Roger.

"Aren't you going to pour me a glass?" Jey Singh said. Sikander obliged, and Alwar paused from his molluscian genocide long enough to take a delicate taste.

"That is bloody awful," he pulled a face, and let out another, even more shrill whistle, which brought the waiter scurrying back. Jey Singh fixed him with a glower and then, without warning, flung his glass squarely at the man's face. Luckily, his aim was off, and it missed its intended target, bouncing off the waiter's chest and falling to the floor, but not before his tunic was quite inundated.

"How dare you serve us warm champagne?" he squealed. "Go fetch a properly chilled bottle immediately."

Squirming with embarrassment, Sikander shifted in his seat, aware that the entire pavilion had fallen silent, every eye now fixed squarely upon them. Jey Singh, on the other hand, indifferent to the fact that he was making a spectacle of himself, returned instead to his oysters as if nothing at all had happened.

Oblivious to Sikander's discomfort, Jey Singh said, "How long has it been since we last met. Ten years, is it?"

Sikander's spirits rose, seeing his opportunity. "Twelve, I believe. The last time was in Bikaner. We were both guests of Ganga Singh for the grouse season. Don't you remember?"

"I don't, I am sorry to say."

"Are you sure? Jagatjit arranged for us to watch a *nautch* girl perform, don't you recall, a bewitching creature named Wazeeran? In fact, if my memory serves correctly, you were very taken with her, weren't you?"

For the first time, Jey Singh's smile wavered, and a shadow fell across his features. "I have no idea what you are talking about."

"Come on, how can you have forgotten Wazeeran? She was exquisite! And didn't she have a daughter, what was her name?" Sikander snapped his fingers theatrically, making Jey Singh flinch. "Ah, yes, Zahra! That's what it was. I wonder what happened to her."

Whatever else his flaws, Jey Singh was not stupid. Like a predator sensing a trap, his face stiffened, his smile melting entirely away.

"Well, this has been interesting," he declared. "I would love to stay longer, but I really should make sure my horse has been stabled properly.

As he stood, Sikander nodded at Campbell, who moved quickly to place himself squarely in his way.

"Let me lay my cards on the table, Jey Singh. I am here because the *nautch* girl I just mentioned to you, Zahra, was found murdered yesterday in the King Emperor's camp, and

I have been entrusted by the Viceroy with the task of finding her killer."

This declaration was met by the slightest widening of Alwar's eyes, accompanied by a grim sparkle of interest, but Sikander could not quite identify what emotion it signified. Was it guilt or something else, pleasure perhaps, the vicarious thrill of a voyeur?

"What does any of that have to do with me?" His expression remained deadpan, as emotionless as a cadaver.

"Did you not bid for her contract in Lahore, only to lose to Kapurthala? Did you not, upon failing to engage her services, publicly swear that if she would not be your property, then you would not permit her to belong to anyone else? And finally, did you not pay her a visit the day before yesterday, which ended with her asking you to leave her alone?"

"You are grasping at straws," Jey Singh replied with a nonchalant smirk. That was when Sikander saw it, the madness in his eyes, barely held in check.

"Does it not strike you as strange, that this girl should be killed in exactly the same way her mother was murdered all those years ago in Bikaner? And that you just happened to be present on both occasions?"

Most normal men would have been ruffled by such questions, but Jey Singh remained as unflappable as a Hessian. In fact, he seemed to be enjoying himself, judging by how readily his smirk deepened into a wicked grin.

"I could say the same thing of you, couldn't I? What if you're the murderer? You could be trying to implicate me to deflect attention from yourself, for all we know."

"That's very clever, Jey Singh, but this is what I believe happened. I think you killed Zahra's mother all those years ago. I always suspected it, but I was unable to prove anything, which is why you got away scot-free. Or so you thought until you encountered Zahra again. She recognised you, didn't she? You knew she was the only witness to her mother's death, and you grew terrified that she would expose you to the English. That is why you tried to buy her contract, to get her in your grasp, but when she evaded your clutches, you decided to pay her a visit. What was your plan? Did you offer to pay her off, to buy her silence? Or did you threaten her?"

He knew he was goading the man, but that was exactly his intent, to push Jey Singh to his breaking point. And it worked. In the blink of an eye, his composure fell apart. With an involuntary twitch of his lips, the reckless smile collapsed, replaced instead by a snarl.

"I do not have to listen to this rubbish." His face reddened, his voice rising to a screech so shrill that it echoed through the pavilion. "How dare you accuse me, you…you upstart? I have had men beaten to death for less."

This was the real Jey Singh, Sikander realised. Now that he had lost control, the inner savage stood revealed in all its dark glory, his teeth bared, his hands clenched into claws, flecks of spittle flying from his lips like froth.

"Calm down, sir," Campbell said, trying to reason with Jey Singh, but he ignored Campbell like he did not exist. His focus remained fixed on Sikander and he took one angry step forward, as if intending to assault him physically.

Most men would have fled in the face of such overwhelming fury, but it was not in Sikander's nature to retreat.

"You do not scare me, Jey Singh." Sikander stared him down. "When Wazeeran was murdered, my hands were tied, but this time around, I have no intention of giving up. If I find a single piece of evidence connecting you to Zahra's death—one hair, one fingerprint—I will not rest until I bring you down. You can count on that."

To his surprise, Jey Singh's response was a complete turnaround. Rather than becoming further incensed by such a naked threat, he let out a cackle.

"What a fool you are, Sikander Singh!" Unexpectedly, he lunged forward, seizing his shoulders. He was surprisingly strong, those seemingly slim arms corded with muscle from hours spent swinging a polo mallet. Sikander was not accustomed to being manhandled, but effortlessly, Jey Singh enveloped him into a parody of an embrace.

"Do you want the truth, you foolish boy? Then here it is." He leaned in so close that Sikander was terrified the man was about to kiss him. "Yes, I killed that whore all those years ago. I wanted to bed her, but when I made a proposition, she dared to rebuff my advances. She insisted she was only a performer, not a courtesan. I cannot stand to be rejected and so, in a fit, I strangled her with my bare hands. There, now you know the truth. And there is nothing you can do about it. There is no evidence, is there? And, without evidence, there is no crime. Even I know that."

His voice was matter-of-fact, devoid of a single shred of regret or remorse. Sikander clenched his jaw so hard that his head hurt. Unfortunately, Jey Singh was right. It was far too late to get justice for Wazeeran. The trail had long since gone cold. If he took what he had to the Viceroy, at best it would be his word against Alwar's, and that was a fight Jey Singh would always win.

"You bastard," he hissed.

"A bastard I may be, my dear fellow, but I am one who has an alibi cast in iron."

Jey Singh took a step back, raising his voice. "There is no way I could possibly have killed your *nautch* girl. I was at the Fusilers' Ball from seven till two in the morning. You are welcome to check with their commanding officer, Colonel Gordon. I am sure he will be happy to vouch for me. As a matter of fact, you can check with his wife, as well, although she may not be quite too eager to corroborate my whereabouts, considering some of the things we did to each other bordered on the illegal."

Alwar giggled, as shrill as a cuckoo. "Once again, I win, Sikander Singh. And just like all those years ago, there really is nothing you can do about it."

Chapter Twenty-two

Jey Singh's laughter bit at Sikander, as painful as the lash of a whip.

"You think you are better than me, don't you, Sikander Singh? But the truth is that we are one and the same. We are both barbarians, excited only by the iniquity that hides behind the thin veneer of civilization, the violence and the cruelty of human nature that other, lesser men are afraid to confront." His lips curled into a snarl. "The only difference between us is that I revel in my darkness, embrace it. But you, you poor fool, you try to deny it. That is why you will never get the better of me."

With that declaration, Jey Singh gave him a parting wink before striding back to join his company. Sikander could do nothing but seethe. It took all his wherewithal to hold back his rage. Part of him wanted to kill Alwar, to reach out and strangle him on the spot, just as he had throttled Wazeeran, to choke the life from him until that supercilious smile was wiped away.

Unfortunately, while it was anathema to his nature to allow a killer to go free, he knew there was nothing he could do to Jey Singh, not just yet. Perhaps at a later date, he would be able to give the man a rightly deserved comeuppance, but for now, his hands were as good as tied. This was the feeling Sikander despised most of all, the sensation of helplessness that gripped him. What made it infinitely worse was that he knew, deep down, that Alwar was right. There was indeed a darkness inside him, a void that he could never quite fill. That was why he was drawn to the perverse and the profane, because he found what others considered normal boring. The only time Sikander felt truly alive was when he was confronted by death and sin and blood. Did that make him as bad as Alwar? For once, he found he was afraid, terrified of even trying to answer that question.

"What's wrong, sir?" Campbell piped up. "You seem terribly out of sorts."

"It's nothing, just a headache coming on."

"Would you like to return to your hotel?"

"No, I still have to question Holkar and Scindia." Sikander gave Campbell an apologetic shrug. "You cannot come with me, I'm afraid, Captain. Lady Bute's ball is by invitation only."

Campbell did not seem unduly ruffled. "That will be fine, sir. I have to make a report anyway to the Viceroy, update him about our progress. If you would be so kind as to drop me off at the Bombay Camp, I am scheduled to meet him there at six o'clock."

"Of course! Once he has dropped me off, my driver will take you wherever you need to go."

Upon returning to the Rolls, Sikander struggled to compose himself, to regain some measure of his equilibrium and prepare himself for the upcoming ordeal. Although the Captain tried to strike up a conversation several times, he held his tongue resolutely, refusing to be engaged. Instead, he leaned back, and let the vibrations of the road seep into his bones, lulling him into a state of half-sleep.

The venue chosen by Lord and Lady Bute for their extravaganza was the Indore camp, which was located directly opposite Patiala's enclosure. While there had been a great many formals and fêtes hosted by the English over the preceding weeks, this was intended to be the *pièce de résistance*, the last party before the King arrived and the actual Durbar celebrations began full-tilt.

Sikander only knew the hosts very vaguely. He had met the

Marquis at Ascot a few times, and recalled him as a shy, rather self-effacing Scotsman with a fine pair of whiskers who was mad for shooting and Baroque architecture. As for his wife, he had never encountered her personally, but she had a reputation for being rather formidable. Augusta Crichton-Stuart was said to be a relentless woman, both in temperament and ambition. She was renowned for being what the French called a Rastignac, a determined social climber.

Ordinarily, Sikander went to great lengths to avoid such gatherings. He found them tedious, not just the ostentation and the inane competitiveness, but also the crowds. The raucous din of hundreds of voices talking at the same time, the press of bodies surrounding him to the point of suffocation— not to mention the smells of perfume and sweat and gingivitis, all mingling into one noxious stench, just the very thought of which was quite enough to make him nauseous. However, on this occasion, he had broken from habit for one reason alone. He had heard that both Indore and Scindia would be in attendance, which meant he could tackle two of his remaining suspects at the same time. And it was time that was most paramount, for that was the commodity which was most in short shrift, as Sikander was well aware.

Abruptly, the Rolls slowed almost to a crawl. Sikander leaned out to find that there was a long line arrayed outside the camp's entrance, moving forward with tiresome slowness as each vehicle and carriage paused to disgorge grandee after gaily dressed grandee. Rather than waiting his turn, he waved farewell to Campbell and dismounted early, choosing to walk the rest of the way to the gate, which was a massive domed *chattri* across which a white banner had been furled, emblazoned with the words "Long live the King."

After presenting his invitation, he was escorted into the camp by a page, where an ornate *shamiana* had been erected for the festivities. Around it, an array of Chinoiserie screens had been arranged to create a promenade, illuminated by myriad paper lanterns hung at strategic intervals, giving the whole place an atmosphere of shadowy glamor. Grudgingly, Sikander had to admit Lady Bute had managed to do an admirable job, for the end result was exceedingly elegant, very much to his taste.

Inside the tent, he found that the Hussar Band had been tasked with providing the evening's musical entertainment. They were in the midst of mangling one of Chopin's mazurkas, belting it out with rather stilted bonhomie. Sikander paused, studying the room. It seemed to be peopled by a preponderance of white faces. A few of them he recognized. There was Earl Mar and Kellie, done up in his customary green and gold, accompanied by his wife, Violet, who had once made a pass at Sikander, and who now gave him a saucy grin as she flounced by. Behind them, he saw Lord Cadogan, a doddering old gent who had caused quite a scandal by marrying his cousin, a beautiful young redhead with an impressive prow. She was chatting with an old friend of Sikander's, Beatrice Forbes, the Countess of Granard, who was the most prominent of the American "dollar" princesses. On her right, stood the grande dame of London society, Evelyn James, who was deep in conversation with one of the Rothschilds and the famous Australian soprano, Nellie Melba.

Out on the dance floor, a giggling covey of young duchesses—Norfolk, Hamilton, and Montrose—were taking a turn under the watchful eyes of their glowering husbands. Behind them, he saw his hostess, a handsome woman done up in purple tussar, who held his gaze briefly, and then dismissed him when she recognized he was not a senior potentate.

At the far side of the tent, Sikander saw the Brigadier waving at him frantically, trying to catch his attention. He looked very out of sorts, dressed in an ill-fitting evening suit for a change rather than his customary uniform.

"My goodness, Brigadier," Sikander greeted him with a warm smile, glad to find a friendly face. "Don't you clean up well?"

"Oh, stop being snide." He shrugged, very nearly splitting the seams of his jacket's shoulders. "I received your invitation, here I am, though I still cannot understand why you have called me here, into this den of overdressed monkeys."

"Ha!" Sikander laughed, realizing that Granville-Bruce had made a rare witticism. "Well done! As to why I asked you to come, here is the reason now." He gestured toward the entrance, where Miss Cavendish was making an arrival, escorted, as always, by her chaperone. Sikander smiled appreciatively. She looked radiant, dressed in a simple Callot Soeurs cocktail dress, in a very becoming shade of metallic green which perfectly offset her fiery hair. Beside her stood Miss Eaton, overshadowed, outfitted in a heavy satin gown which made her seem even more pugnacious than normal.

"You found her," the Brigadier gasped, his mouth falling open with surprise.

"I did. And might I say, my dear fellow, you have exquisite taste. Why, if I did not have Helene in my life, I might be tempted to take a pass at the *memsahib* myself."

Granville-Bruce blushed a deep crimson, fidgeting with his tie nervously. "Introduce me, won't you?" His voice quavered. It was quite funny, Sikander thought. Here was a man who felt no fear charging into the midst of a rampaging horde of Afridis, but now, confronted with a beautiful woman, he was reduced to being as gormless as a griffin.

"Come along then." Crossing the floor, he greeted Miss Cavendish with a wave. "How wonderful to see you, Madam! And you, too, Miss Eaton." He nodded at Granville-Bruce, who was cowering behind him, pulling at his moustache. "This is Brigadier Granville-Bruce, the hero of Nepal. He has been waiting to meet you very eagerly."

"My dear," Granville-Bruce said as he bumbled forward. Much to Sikander's surprise, he held a hand out, not to Miss Cavendish, but to Miss Eaton. "Would you care to dance?"

For once, Sikander found himself utterly at a loss for words, goggling as Miss Eaton took the Brigadier's outstretched hand with a shy smile, allowing herself to be shepherded out onto the dance floor.

"Isn't that wonderful!" Miss Cavendish exclaimed, clapping her hands together in delight. "It seems that Miss Eaton has found an admirer."

"How very unexpected!" Sikander murmured as Granville-Bruce proceeded to lead his partner into the first steps of a spirited Viennese waltz, moving with a surprising elegance for a man his size. Sikander could not help but shake his head bemusedly. Even if he were floundering as a detective, he thought, it seemed his career as a matchmaker was certainly flourishing.

"I did not realise the Brigadier could dance quite so well."

"Can you, sir?" With an impish chuckle, Miss Cavendish looped her arm into the crook of his elbow. "Come along, let us find out."

Even though she was being rather too forward for his liking, Sikander allowed himself to be herded along. They faced each other, Sikander placing one hand very lightly on her elbow, maintaining a respectable distance as he swirled her gracefully across the dance floor. She was a tall woman, but he handled her effortlessly, as if she weighed nothing. Miss Cavendish beamed, leaning into him, almost resting her forehead against his chest, so close he could smell her scent, oleander and vanilla underpinned by a hint of amber.

Inexplicably, this cachet reminded Sikander of Helene. It had been some weeks since she had departed for France, and he had almost forgotten how reassuring it felt to hold a woman close to him. Sikander let out a sigh, an inchoate sense of regret tearing at him as he realised how deeply he missed Helene. Dancing with her had been effortless, like a wisp of wind. With Miss Cavendish, it was very different. She kept trying to take the lead, and rather than holding her tongue and losing herself in the music, she kept chattering on, trying to make small talk.

Sikander tuned her out, instead using their circuit to glance around the room to see if he could pick out any of the people he had come to interview. Abruptly, he felt an itching at the base of his spine, some primal instinct warning him that he was being watched. Swiveling his neck, he saw that he was being observed rather keenly by none other than the other host of this soirée, the Maharaja of Indore.

Indore was a nineteen-gun kingdom, located in the heartland of Central India encompassing an area roughly the size of Sicily. Like Gwalior, Nagpur, and Dewas, it was yet another of the principalities established after the collapse of the Maratha Empire. Its founder, Malhar Rao, had been one of Peshwa Bajirao's most valiant generals, and after his demise, had slowly consolidated power until he controlled most of the Plateau of Malwa. His descendants had initially opposed the English in the three Anglo-Maratha wars, but finally, in 1818, in typical Maratha fashion, they had turned coat and become a British protectorate.

Along with this talent for political adaptability, the Holkars had inherited a reputation for never quite having lost their wild roots. The previous Maharaja, Shivaji Rao Holkar, had been famous for his cruel temper. It was well known he had been somewhat unhinged, given to beating his servants and often riding them like horses, and it was said he had once emptied a basket of night-soil on a Brahman's head before whipping him half to death. This propensity for violence had grown more and more overt until at last, the British had become convinced he was insane and had been ready to depose him and annex Indore. Luckily, he had chosen to abdicate in favor of his son, and thus preserve the dynasty's rule.

Not that the current Holkar was much of an improvement on his mad father, Sikander thought with a grimace. He knew Tukoji Rao the Third only too well. They had undertaken a sea journey together some years previously, sailing back to India from the continent on the same vessel. The irony was that Sikander had come to quite like Holkar. He was a clever, interesting fellow, and Sikander was only too happy to call him a friend. However, there was something about him that Sikander had always found unnerving, even unsettling. The reason was difficult to explain. Though he was as handsome and urbane as Lancelot, Sikander could sense that beneath this charming mask, a more sinister creature hid, the sort of amoral man who would smile in your face even as he stuck a dagger in your back.

With one last swelling surge, the music tapered to a close and Sikander took a step back, relinquishing his hold on Miss Cavendish's arm. "If you will excuse me, Madam, I shall go and pay my respects to our host."

"Of course! I am rather parched. I think I shall fetch myself a drink." Her eyes twinkled. "Some champagne, I think. I have developed quite a taste for it." Her mouth curved into a seductive smile. "Try not to forget me, will you?"

"Never!" Sikander gave her a gallant bow. "You are unforgettable, Miss Cavendish."

"Ha! You are a terrible liar, Mr. Singh. Thank heavens you are an excellent dancer, or I might be offended."

With that comment, she glided away. Sikander took a moment to flatten his lapels and check that his turban was in order before he crossed the floor to approach Holkar.

Tukoji Rao was very tall, very dark, and very slender, cutting a dashing figure in pale blue brocade and golden trousers. He hadn't an ounce of fat on him, and wore his hair slicked back, fixed in a wave with a generous smear of pomade. His ears were comically large, like an Etruscan jug, and he favored a slim moustache which would have looked ratlike on most men, but on his face, was rather dashing. His eyes were deep-set, and he possessed an uncanny habit of staring into the middle distance while conversing, which made him particularly difficult to read.

"I believe congratulations are in order, Holkar," Sikander exclaimed, coming up behind him. "I heard the *burra* sahibs have confirmed a twenty-one-gun salute for you. Scindia must be absolutely livid."

Holkar turned, his mouth twisting into a sarcastic smile. "Why, as I live and breathe, Sikander Singh, you always manage to say the rudest things." He gesticulated, as if to encompass the room. "So, tell me, how do you like my little soirée?"

"It's very..." Sikander's brow wrinkled as he struggled to choose his words politically, "fashionable."

"What it really is is a damned waste of time and money, but a man must keep up appearances." Holkar let out a sardonic laugh. "Come along, let's have a drink. I have a bottle only you can appreciate."

Sikander followed him to the wet bar that dominated the far corner of the tent, where Holkar summoned the bartender, a thin Bengali in a white jacket, and whispered a muted command in his ear.

"Here we are," he said when the man reached under the counter and extracted a very dusty bottle, which he then offered to Sikander.

"This is a Saulnier Frères Grand Champagne Cognac 1789. This particular bottle has a double significance, because not only is it from the very year of the French Revolution, it is also the sole remainder of a cask which was served at George Washington's inauguration ball."

Sikander prided himself as a difficult man to astonish, but on this occasion, he gaped with awe, finding himself at an absolute loss for words. This was one of the rarest bottles of brandy in the world, and his mouth began to water, just at the thought of being in such close proximity.

"Shall we try it?"

Sikander could barely believe his ears. Surely Holkar was joking with him, some sort of elaborate prank, he thought. He would not waste such a magnificent bottle, not on someone as junior in rank as him. Unless, of course, there was an ulterior motive. Sikander's penchant for exotic vintages was well known. Was this meant to be a bribe? If so, then why? What was Holkar trying to hide?

As Sikander struggled to come up with an answer to this question, Holkar gave the bartender a nod, and the man opened the bottle, slowly easing out the cork with a reverent wince. His hand shook as he laid out two snifters and poured out a pair of generous measures.

Holkar offered the first to Sikander, who took it nervously. The brandy was the deepest amber, so dark it was almost bronze. He brought it to his nose, letting out a gasp as he inhaled its deep bouquet. It was very rich, almost as ripe as honey, so potent it made Sikander shudder involuntarily.

It took all his willpower to resist. Closing his eyes, he put the glass down, before fixing Holkar with a piercing frown.

"I think I saw you the day before yesterday, at the King's Camp."

"Did you?"

"Yes. I waved, but, sadly, you didn't notice. You looked dreadfully busy. Were you there on official business?"

"Oh, do stop trying to be clever, old boy. You really are a terrible actor." Holkar's voice remained cold, almost emotionless. "As it happens, I know all about the *nautch* girl and how the Viceroy has asked you to look into her death. You don't have to play coy with me. Just ask your questions. I will answer them truthfully."

Sikander paused, thrown off balance. First the Nizam, and now Holkar—did everyone know about Zahra? And why was Holkar being so cooperative? Obviously, he was intelligent enough to discern that he was a suspect, but most people would have responded to such a realization with antagonism, not equanimity. Besides, from what Sikander knew of Holkar, he was about as reasonable as a bull in heat, which could only mean two possible things. One, he was confident he had nothing to lose. Or, two, he just did not care.

"So you admit you went to see her?" he asked. "Might I know why?"

"Isn't it obvious? I simply had to see what had Scindia all up in knots, of course. You know he tried his best to acquire her contract, but was beaten to it by Kapurthala. I wanted to get a good look at what all the fuss was about." He laughed, a noise as raucous as a neighing horse. "She was all right. A pretty enough filly, which is why I decided I would trump Scindia at his own game. That is why I went to see her, to make her a generous offer."

"You tried to buy her?"

"Yes, I did. I collect *nautch* girls, my dear fellow, the way some men collect stamps or coins. As it happens, I don't have a Kashmiri girl in my stable at present. The last one decided to go and have a child, and it left her stomach dreadfully stretched out of shape, so I had to get rid of her." He shook his head, as if he were talking about a prize steer, not a person. "Anyway, this Zahra, she fit the bill just right. She was the right age, for one. I like my women young and petite, just old enough to feel like you are bedding a virgin. And then, of course, there was the added bonus of sticking it to Scindia." He grinned, a vicious twist of his lips. "Can you imagine the look on his pompous face when he found out I'd stolen his prize?"

Sikander mulled over this confession, trying to judge its veracity. "But she refused?"

"She tried to, the nerve! To think she could rebuff the Holkar of Indore. But you know how it is with these whores. It's a game. You have to show them you mean business."

"You forced yourself upon her?"

"Oh, don't be such a prude! I may have made an aggressive overture or two, but then she started to cry, the silly child. That put an end to my ardor very quickly, let me tell you."

"So you just left?"

"Yes! Is that so hard to believe? Why don't you go speak to Scindia? I believe he paid the girl a visit, too, a few hours after I left."

Sikander frowned. Obviously, Holkar would point a finger at Scindia. Their rivalry went back years. Both Daulat Rao

Shinde and Yeshwant Rao Holkar had been generals in the service of the Peshwa, and both men had believed themselves to be the right candidate to become the next Emperor of India after the Maratha Empire had collapsed into factions following its defeat at the third battle of Panipat. This had resulted first in the sacking of Ujjain by Holkar, which had led to the seizure of Indore soon after by Scindia, thus resulting in a long-simmering blood feud that had endured for four generations.

It had taken the British decades to curtail this strife, and they had absolutely forbidden any further skirmishes between the two clans. And though it had been years since Holkar and Scindia had faced off in public, Sikander knew very well that to even speak the name of Scindia in Indore, was as good as committing blasphemy.

As a result, quite naturally, when Holkar chose to point the finger at his greatest enemy, Sikander could not help but take it with a pinch of salt.

"Why? Why are you telling me this?" he asked, not bothering to hide his doubt. "What do you have to gain here?"

Before Holkar could reply, they were interrupted by Miss Cavendish.

"Mr. Singh, you have been neglecting me terribly."

Sikander's brow darkened, and he very nearly snapped at the *memsahib*, annoyed by this untimely intrusion.

"Aren't you going to introduce me to your lovely friend?" Holkar said, stepping forward. As smoothly as a shapeshifter, a change seemed to come over him. Abruptly, the saturnine twist to his countenance was gone, replaced by a very personable half-smile, as though he had switched his identity in a heartbeat.

"Miss Cavendish, this is Tukoji Rao of Indore. Watch out for him, he is a rogue and a scoundrel."

"And you, Madam," Holkar said, "are too lovely to waste time with someone like Sikander Singh. He only has time for books and dead people, the poor boy." Leaning forward, he pressed his lips to the girl's hand, before waving languidly toward the dance floor. "Shall we take a turn?"

Holkar at full blast was intoxicating, as potent as a drug. Naturally, Miss Cavendish was only too susceptible, as any woman would have been, easily overpowered by his charm. Blushing shyly, she looked to Sikander, to seek his permission. He replied with a shrug, urging her to go right ahead.

"It would be my pleasure." She placed her hand shyly in Holkar's, who paused only long enough to give Sikander a long, lingering frown.

"You really do have a problem, Sikander. You are much too suspicious to realise when someone is trying to help you out. Go speak to Scindia. He is your man. I am willing to stake my fortune upon it."

Chapter Twenty-three

As the band swung into a stirring rendition of "Blue Danube," Sikander pursed his lips, considering what he knew of the Scindia.

Like Holkar, his ancestor, Ranoji, had begun as one of Baji Rao's mercenary generals before seizing a vast tract of land for himself and established the Kingdom of Gwalior, which was roughly the size of Ireland. His descendant, Madhoji, whose name the current Scindia shared, had been one of the first Indian princes to sign a treaty with the English, the Agreement of Salbhai, which had guaranteed the East India Company authority over all territory north of the river Yamuna. As a result, Gwalior had been free to annex everything south of this boundary, and after a series of quick and brutal invasions, had emerged as the preeminent state in Central India, rivaled only by Indore.

The current Scindia, Madho Rao, was one of Sikander's least favorite people. In many ways, he represented everything Sikander despised about the princes of India. Not only did he possess a sense of entitlement that made him almost intolerable, he was cursed with what the Greeks had described as *hubris*, that impermeable belief that he was exceptional in every way, if for no other reason than his exalted birth. With most Maharajas, this was merely a form of egotism, but with Scindia, his pompousness had been refined to the point of megalomania. Why, the man was so vainglorious he had built temples to himself, within which were placed marble statues of his visage, that his subjects were expected to worship, to venerate as a god come to life.

It was precisely this quality which was bound to make him such a difficult man to question. That was the dilemma that haunted Sikander—how was he to approach Scindia? Guile was pointless, as was any attempt at cleverness, given that the man was quite as dense as cement. That left Sikander only two choices, either to confront him head on, or to play the fool and hope he would fall into a trap of his own making. Unfortunately, neither gambit seemed particularly likely to succeed, he thought, not unless he was rescued by a minor miracle.

Just then, Sikander noticed that the glass of brandy was waiting in front of him, still untouched. With a sigh, he picked it up, and quaffed its contents in one long swallow. A groan of absolute delight escaped his lips. It was even better than he had imagined, like fire in his veins, revitalizing him with fresh energy.

As he made a slow tour of the room, he noticed a very palpable divide between the Indian Kings and the English guests. As he had expected, none of the real luminaries had turned up, neither the Nizam nor Kashmir nor the Gaekwad. Instead, most of the Maharajas in attendance were the younger set, mainly of his age and rank.

There seemed to be several distinct groups. The first were congregated around his cousin Bhupinder, who was seated in a distant corner, holding court to a coterie of sycophants, mainly *zamindars* and merchants. A few metres away clustered the fast set, drinking and laughing and smoking cigars. At the center of it all, of course, was Jagatjit, who seemed to have recovered from his earlier disappointment well enough to try his luck with a well-proportioned young *memsahib* whose hair was cut boyishly short in the new fashion called the Marcel. When he saw Sikander, he gave him a pronounced wink.

Sikander rolled his eyes, and fixed his attention on the final group. These were the politically inclined, serious Maharajas. Sikander recognised one or two of them—the Maharaja of Sikkim, who was a good-natured, if somewhat meek, young fellow; and Bhagvat Singh of Gondal, who was a fully accredited Fellow of the Royal College of Surgeons; and next to him was poor, wilting Travancore, who always looked like he was half-asleep.

In their midst, he spied the very man he was seeking. Ordinarily, the sight of Scindia, who was about as pompous an ass Sikander had ever encountered, would have caused him to frown. This time around, though, he beamed when he saw the way he was dressed—done up in black *chasseur* trousers and a scarlet *zouave* jacket beribboned with an array of gilt braid so excessive it made Sikander's eyes water. On a tall man, the effect may have been electrifying but Scindia was diminutive in stature, and rotund to the point of being dumpy. At best, it made him look a little like one of Tchaikovsky's toy soldiers.

However, that was not what had managed to amuse Sikander. It was the fact that instead of the traditional turban, Scindia had chosen to pair this extravagant outfit with a very distinctive piece of headgear, a red *tarboul* fez, not unlike those worn in Morocco.

He was the one the Nationalist had been talking about, Sikander thought exultantly. Who else would be caught in public wearing a fez?

Even as his heart raced with excitement, he was disturbed by a discreet cough behind him. Turning, he was greeted by the Maharaja of Cooch Behar, Rajendra Narayan, who gave him an ironic smile and said, "What skullduggery are you up to now, Sikander Singh?"

The Kingdom of Cooch Behar was about as insignificant a princely state as they came, a minuscule inkblot on the map barely the size of a thumbtack bordered on the north by Bhutan and to the south by British Bengal. The history of its ruling dynasty was equally undistinguished. An offshoot of the ancient kingdom of Kamata, the Narayan Dynasty had long guarded their thrones by rapidly surrendering to whoever invaded their borders. Surviving first as a vassal of the Mughals, they had been quick to run to the East India Company, begging Hastings for help when they had been deposed by the Bhutias. Hastings had despatched an army which had restored them to the throne for the princely sum of a tribute of five horses, and since then, Cooch Behar had been a British vassal. Although entitled to the same gun salute as Rajpore, the Narayans had only won the right to use the title Maharaja in 1884, which made them little more than parvenus when compared to the more ancient houses of North India.

However, despite their modest origins, one thing was certain: the Narayans had style. King Nripendra, who had died just a few months earlier in England, had been an extraordinary man, the true epitome of the educated, enlightened monarch. His wife, Sunity Devi, considered one of the great beauties of her age, had been a classmate of Sikander's mother. He remembered her well from his childhood, an elegant, magnificently outspoken woman who had been an equal partner to her husband. Together, they had been a rarity, a truly modern couple he had respected immensely, with the sort of union he hoped to emulate himself someday—if he could ever find a woman foolish enough to tolerate his many and unrelenting eccentricities.

King Nripendra had left behind two sons, both of whom were amongst Sikander's closest friends. Rajendra Narayan, who had assumed the title, was the elder, a shy self-effacing fellow who Sikander had first met at Oxford. He was very clever, gifted with a quick, acerbic wit, and a melancholic temperament that caused him to drink excessively. Sikander liked him immensely, which was why he felt a twinge of dismay when he saw what poor health he seemed to be in now, as anemic as a wraith.

"You look terrible, my friend," he observed.

"I am dying, Sikander," Rajendra said with a cough.

"Oh, stop being so dramatic. It's probably just a touch of the croup."

"I wish it were that simple." Once again, he was assailed by a paroxysm of hacking so vehement he looked like he was about to choke, and when he dabbed at his mouth with a handkerchief, Sikander noticed it came away speckled with blood. "I do not have much time, old boy, but I need you to make me a promise. Take care of my brother when I am gone."

Sikander found himself gripped by a terrible sorrow, a sense of utter helplessness at the thought of losing his old friend. Why is it that the good always suffered, their sparks extinguished early, while villains like Alwar and Scindia would persevere to see a ripe old age? It just wasn't fair. But then, what was fair in life? He had long since given up believing in naïve notions like fairness and right and good. Justice—that was the only currency he preferred to place stock in, his only absolute.

"You'll be fine, Rajendra," he insisted, even though he knew it was a lie. "We will find you a good English doctor, and he will fix whatever is wrong with you."

"Listen to me," Rajendra snarled, and for a heartbeat, Sikander could see the core of steel contained within that weak chest. "Jitendra is not like us. He is just a boy, and still believes that people are good and kind-hearted and trustworthy. He needs someone to watch over him, to protect him from the English, before they eat him alive." His eyes were as hard as agates. "I need you to do this for me, my friend. He will never survive unless you watch out for him."

"I will do my best," Sikander replied solemnly.

"Good," Rajendra gave him a grateful nod. "That is all I can hope for." He raised one unsteady hand to point behind Sikander. "Go on, you had better go catch up with him. He has been waiting for hours for you to arrive."

Sikander's gaze shifted out to the dance floor, where the

younger Narayan sibling was cavorting gaily with a pair of very comely English twins. Jitendra was quite the opposite of his brother. A scamp, a wag, and a cad, as recklessly full of life as Rajendra was composed, he managed to be so eminently likeable that it was difficult to resent him, even when he insisted on doing something stupid, which was more often than not.

The moment he set eyes on Sikander, his face flowered into a vast grin. He broke away from the twins, pushing past them as if they had ceased to exist, and made a beeline straight toward him.

"My dear fellow," he exclaimed, "where on earth have you been hiding yourself? The party is almost over."

Sikander could not help but reciprocate his smile. Though he was as fickle as a rainbow, Jitendra was as beautiful as one as well, so devastatingly handsome that few women could resist him—and most men, for that. What made him even more exceptional was that, unlike most handsome men who tended to be as conceited as Narcissus, Jitendra did not possess an ounce of vanity, as was obvious from his shambling manner.

"I have some marvelous gossip for you," Sikander said, "which will make your ears burn."

"Oh, there will be plenty of time for that later. First, tell me, who is that heavenly creature?"

"Do you mean Miss Cavendish? Come along, I will introduce you. I do suspect she is on the prowl for a husband, though, so you had better watch out."

"No, not the redhead you were prancing about with. Who is that peach, right there, just behind Scindia?"

Sikander cast an eye in the direction Jitendra was pointing, toward a young woman standing in Scindia's shadow with a bored look on her face. She was young, not more than eighteen, with a slim neck and a complexion as pale as virgin snow. Though she was clad in a demure chiffon sari, it did nothing to diminish her exquisite beauty. Sikander frowned. Did he know her? She certainly seemed very familiar, something about the set of her shoulders and her stance made him think they had met before.

Even as he struggled to place her, she must have realized she was being watched. Her gaze locked onto him, studying him for a moment before darting over toward Jitendra. Immediately, when their eyes met, she blushed, her pale skin blooming with an eloquent blaze of color.

It came to Sikander then, exactly who she was. The Gaekwad's daughter. He had met her some years previously while visiting Baroda. She had been just a child then, in her early teens, which was why he had been unable to recognize her at first.

"You know her, don't you?" Jitendra said.

"That is Indira Devi, the Princess of Baroda," Sikander replied, "and please, will you stop making cow eyes at her? She is betrothed to Scindia, and if he catches you flirting with his fiancée, he will have you beaten to a pulp."

"Introduce me! Please, Sikander," Jitendra implored, ignoring this warning altogether.

"Absolutely not!"

"You must! I will die if I do not speak to her."

"Oh, stop being such a child," Sikander said, but as he made that rebuke, he realised here it was, the very opening that he had been searching for. This was the way to approach Scindia, under the guise of introducing Jitendra to Indira Devi. He would never even suspect he was being investigated. It was well nigh perfect.

As he contemplated this possibility, his conscience ached at him. He had just made a promise to Rajendra that he would protect his brother, but now he wanted to use him as a pawn just to further his inquiry.

"Very well," he said, stifling this uncharacteristic pang of guilt. "Come on, let us go and speak to her."

Jitendra very nearly sprinted across the room in his haste to meet Indira. Sikander preferred to follow at a more sedate pace. When they approached, Scindia was engaged in holding forth to the rest of his group, chattering away in a tiresomely nasal voice.

"Frankly, in my opinion, all this talk of nationalism is mere stupidity. There can be no India without the English. They gave us the rule of law, the civil service, the railways, our system of higher education, not to mention the fact that they have united us into one country. We would be nothing without them."

"They also gave us the caste system," Sikander interjected from behind him, "the Doctrine of Lapse, the principle of Divide and Rule, and that dreadful fellow Kipling. Let us not forget about that, shall we?"

Scindia turned to face Sikander, his features crinkling with antipathy when he realised who had interrupted him so egregiously.

"You?" He made no effort to hide his dislike. "What are you doing here, Sikander Singh? Shouldn't you be off poking that beaky nose in someone's private affairs?"

"As a matter of fact, I came over to say hello to your fiancée." He gave Indira a small bow. "My dear, I am an old friend of your father's. We met some years ago, but I wouldn't expect you to remember."

"Of course I know who you are," Indira said, smiling widely. She stuck out her hand, a gesture which earned her a disapproving glare from her fiancé, but she ignored him. Sikander found himself liking her. She had spirit, and even though he normally avoided handshakes, he took her hand and kissed it briefly, if for no other reason than to spite Scindia.

Indira blushed. Her eyes flicked across to Jitendra who had remained poised behind Sikander, smiling rapturously like a fool.

"Who is your friend?" she asked shyly.

"This is Jitendra Narayan of Cooch Behar," Sikander said. "He is a thoroughly disreputable sort, and if you know what is best for you, you will ignore him completely."

This jest fell on deaf ears. Neither Indira nor Jitendra reacted at all. Instead, they watched each other silently, caught up in each other completely, as if everyone and everything else had ceased to exist.

When he saw the way they were looking at each other, Sikander was overcome by a premonition of doom, a feeling that only intensified when Jitendra held out one hand, inviting Indira to take it.

"Would you care to dance?"

"Oh, yes," Indira replied much too quickly. "I would love to."

Scindia was too dense to notice it, but Sikander had felt the frisson of electricity between the two of them. A tremor of worry ran down his spine as he watched his friend steer the young princess out onto the dance floor. Sikander had seen this before; he had experienced the same emotion himself once, many years ago, in the naïveté of his youth. A *coup de foudre*, the French called it. The thunderbolt. It had struck Indira and Jitendra as surely as the plague, even if they did not know it yet.

He could sense Scindia glowering behind him, and turned quickly, hoping to distract him before he managed to arrive at the same conclusion.

"Actually, Madho Rao, I am glad to have a moment with you. I was hoping to have a quick word."

Scindia's mouth twisted into a sneer. "I think not, Sikander Singh. I have no interest in speaking with someone as insignificant as you."

"Are you sure? I heard that you have been consorting with dance girls lately. I just wanted to check if that was true."

He had pitched his voice rather too loud, purposely to embarrass Scindia. It worked, judging how brightly his cheeks colored, turning the same scarlet as his tunic.

"Not here." He grabbed Sikander by one arm and pulled him to a secluded corner. "Are you drunk?" he growled. "What is this nonsense?"

Sikander considered his next move. Kashmir knew about Zahra's death, as did the Nizam and Indore. It was only a matter of time before Scindia found out as well, which was why he decided to throw discretion to the wolves, and go straight after the truth.

"Zahra, the *nautch* girl you were so eager to buy, she was found dead the day before yesterday. I have been asked to investigate by the Viceroy. That is why I wanted to speak to you."

A panoply of emotions sprawled across Scindia's face. Shock first, then wariness, and finally, a taut flicker of outrage.

"Do you think you can just question me like a common criminal? How dare you? I am Scindia, while you are nothing but a jumped-up goat herder."

Sikander snorted, dazzled by the man's arrogance. "You're right, of course, but as fate would have it, I am a goat herder who owns a newspaper, my friend. I have it on good authority that you paid a private visit to the girl just a few hours before she was found dead, and that the two of you had rather a heated argument." He clucked his tongue, like an old woman. "Can you imagine the scandal if the tabloids were to find out? Or young Indira, for that matter? Oh, the ignominy of it! What will the King say? Why, it might even ruin the Durbar. I can see the headline now: *Famous Maharaja implicated in Courtesan killing.* Wait, no! Slaying, I think, that has so much more impact, doesn't it?"

"I was only trying to help her," Scindia snapped, his moustache bristling. He paused, biting his lip. "Years ago, she was employed in one of my factories as a seamstress. There was an unforgivable incident. One of my cousins forced himself upon her, against her will. Unfortunately, I was complicit in this crime as well. When the matter was brought to my attention, rather that punishing my cousin, I paid the girl off to keep her mouth shut, and had her sent away."

A shadow darkened his face, a flash of regret. "I had all but forgotten about her, until a few months ago, when I witnessed her perform for one of the lesser Lahori Nawabs. I could not help but think that it was my fault in some way that she ended up as a courtesan. Do not get me wrong. I did what was needed to protect my cousin and our family's reputation, but still... I was a young man then, and did not think of the impact my decision would have on the poor child. As a result, I decided I would buy out her contract and set her free, as amends for my mistake."

This was it, Sikander thought, the missing piece of her story, the reason why Zahra had embraced the livelihood that had robbed her of her mother.

"That is why you bid for her, to help her escape the life of a *nautch-wali*?"

He nodded. "I tried my very best but unfortunately, lost out to your friend, Kapurthala, who decided to give the girl to the King. Nevertheless, I decided I would make one last effort, and risked my good name to go see her, to offer to shelter her in Gwalior after her contract was concluded, or to provide her with enough funds to make a life for herself, wherever she chose to go. But she would not even speak to me. She refused to listen to a word I had to say, or to take a penny of my money."

Sikander could see it; Zahra's beautiful face set with determination, staring stonily at Scindia, refusing to forgive him for the grave injustice he had done her. Any other woman, or man for that matter, would have taken Scindia's offer. But not Zahra. It was not in her nature to surrender, and she was too strong a woman to let any man decide her destiny, as she had proven time and again. Abruptly, a pang of regret ached at his chest, a sense of heartfelt loss. What other path could she ever have chosen? She had been driven to this, first by his failure to apprehend her mother's murderer, then by Bikaner's injustice, and then finally, by Scindia's failure. We are all equally culpable for her demise, he thought sadly, for we created her. Without us, she would still be alive.

"It's a good story, Scindia," he said stiffly, "but why should I believe a word you are saying?"

It was entirely the wrong thing to say, he realised, when Scindia's already ruddy face grew even more suffused. "You dare to question my word? Who do you think you are, you vermin, you excrement, you scion of poxed horse-buggerers?"

"Steady on, old boy. Calm down before you give yourself a heart attack."

But Scindia was too far gone to turn back. His invective was in full flow, his jowls wobbling with disdain, his lips frothing as if he were a bulldog stricken with hydrophobia.

"Let me make one thing very clear, you jumped-up turd of a man. I do not like you. I think you are a vulture, a bottom-feeder, and I shall not stand here and take your insults lightly. I am Scindia, do you hear? Do not dare to trifle with me. I am the sun. My ancestors were gods, while yours were apes who were still learning to wipe their arses with leaves."

"Look, it would be in your best interest to cooperate with me. I have *carte blanche* from the Viceroy's office itself. I could make things very unpleasant for you."

"A threat! You dare to threaten me?"

Scindia knuckled his fists, so furious that Sikander was convinced the man intended to strike him, but instead, he barged forward, shoving him aside with one shoulder.

"You stay out of my way, Sikander Singh. I am warning you. If you don't, I am the one who will make things unpleasant for you."

Chapter Twenty-four

Scindia stalked away, shaking his head from side to side, very like an enraged partridge. Sikander gazed after him, trying to decide whether or not to follow. What good would it do? He had many unanswered questions, yes, but without leverage, Scindia would never cooperate. He was too pompous, not to mention that he despised Sikander thoroughly.

Out of the corner of his eye, he noticed that a more pressing crisis was developing, one that required his attention far more urgently. At the distant end of the room, Jitendra and Indira were getting much too close for comfort. They had retreated to the refuge offered by a very bushy potted fern, and his friend had one of her hands clasped in his own.

By the looks of it, he was about to try to kiss her. Sikander realized he had only moments to avert a scandal. With the greatest of alacrity, he crossed the room and swooped down just in the nick of time.

"Forgive me, but could I borrow Jit for a moment?" Placing one firm hand on his friend's shoulder, he pulled him backward, eager to dampen his ardor before it could get the better of him. "Perhaps it would be best if you returned to your fiancé," he said to Indira, "before he decides to come looking for you."

"Of course," the girl said, blushing deeply. "I had forgotten all about him."

She gave Jitendra one last longing look before turning and hurrying away in the same direction the Scindia had vanished.

Jitendra watched her with shining eyes. "Gosh, she's something, isn't she?" His face hardened with entirely uncharacteristic resolve. "Mark my words, Sikander, I am going to marry that girl."

"Oh, grow up, Jit," Sikander scoffed. "She is betrothed to Scindia, and you know it."

"A gem like that is wasted on an oaf like Scindia. He's a boor, an ogre, a pig. She, she's an angel."

The dreamy expression on his face made Sikander's heart sink. What madness had he managed to set into motion? Had he made a grave error by introducing the two of them? It was obvious that Indira had made quite an impact on Jitendra, but was this real, or was it just another one of Jit's passing fancies? The latter, Sikander found himself hoping, let it be an infatuation and nothing else. The last thing he needed was for one of his closest friends to mire himself in the middle of some sort of Shakespearean love triangle, not while he had a case waiting to be solved.

"Snap out of it, Jit," he said rather too harshly. "You cannot afford to make an enemy of Scindia."

"She deserves better, don't you think, Sikander? Indira deserves a man who will worship her, who will treat her like the goddess she is."

"Perhaps, but do you really think she would jilt the fifth most powerful man in India for a callow boy who is second in line to the throne of a kingdom the size of a postage stamp?"

Jitendra flinched, as if he had been splashed with a bucket of cold water. "You're right, of course. Why desire what you can never have?"

He looked so hangdog that Sikander could not help but feel a twinge of sympathy.

"Fret not, Jit! There are plenty of fish in the sea. Come, let me introduce you to Miss Cavendish. You will like her, I think. She is a redhead, and you know what they say about women with red hair, don't you?"

Jit reacted to this suggestion with a withering frown. "I thought you had a romantic soul, Sikander," he said. "I thought you, of all people, would understand."

With that, he staggered away unsteadily, almost as though he were in a daze.

Romance, Sikander thought cynically, Oh, you poor, naïve boy! He wanted to follow Jitendra, to shake some sense into him. There was no romance in the world, no love. Those were merely words, invented by long-haired poets desperate for meaning and purpose. There was only one indivisible truth about life, and that was the certainty of pain and suffering and ultimately death. No, Sikander had neither the time nor the patience for romance. He had seen far too much of mankind's depravity, too much degeneracy to believe in something quite so intangible.

The pensiveness of his reverie was interrupted by a familiar voice.

"Your Majesty, I am sorry to bother you," Captain Campbell said. He was in full uniform, shiny shako, whitened puttees and all, and, for a change, looked very serious, his face devoid of its usual half-smirk.

"Campbell," Sikander said expansively, "what an unpleasant surprise! I was not aware you had an invitation. Tell me, what brings you here? Have you uncovered yet another wild goose chase to lead me upon?"

This barb failed to elicit any response, other than a slight tightening of his jaw.

"If you have a moment, sir, the Viceroy would like a word."

"Of course! I always have time for Lord Hardinge."

"In that case, this way, if you please?" Campbell turned crisply, indicating that Sikander should follow him.

"What is this about?" Sikander tried to inquire, but the Captain refused to offer any further explanations. Instead, he held his tongue, silently leading him out of the Indore enclosure altogether, and then across the wide expanse of the Princes

Road. On the far side, about fifty metres from the camp, a car was waiting, half hidden behind a towering oak. Even though it was a temperate evening, its canvas roof was up, and the windows shuttered, obscured by thick linen curtains, as if the occupants within were trying to stay incognito.

Sikander recognised the vehicle instantly. It was the Viceregal Standard, the very same one that Campbell had commandeered to transport him to the King Emperor's camp. Had it only been a day and half earlier? God, Sikander thought wearily, it felt like a whole month had gone by.

"In here, sir." The Captain stepped forward and swung open the passenger door open for him. "And, might I say, good luck!"

Upon entering the vehicle, Sikander found it was occupied by the same quartet of gentlemen he had encountered at the King Emperor's camp. Lord Hardinge had the seat opposite him, looking even more morose than usual. Next to him the Great Dane languished, flashing him a smile. To his left sat O'Dwyer, very poised as always, and next to him, Commissioner French, who gave Sikander a sneer.

"Gentlemen," Sikander tucked himself into the seat, leaving as much space as he could between himself and O'Dwyer, "Isn't it a bit crowded in here? Why don't we head inside and talk over a nice glass of Bollinger?"

This suggestion was greeted by absolute silence.

"Good heavens!" Sikander quipped. "Why so serious? Has someone else died?"

Once again, this jest fell flat, with the exception of Lord Dane, whose mouth quirked into the slightest of smiles.

It was Commissioner French who asked the first question. "Have you gotten anywhere with finding the *nautch* girl's murderer?"

"I have been making every effort—" Sikander started to say, but O'Dwyer interrupted him before he could finish his explanation.

"Answer the question, Mr. Singh. Are you close to solving the case?"

"As a matter of fact, I have made some substantial progress. I have accumulated several suspects," Sikander replied, struggling to keep his voice calm, "and devised several theories to explain what happened." He directed this assertion at Hardinge, ignoring O'Dwyer altogether. "I just need a bit more time, that's all."

"Time is exactly what we don't have." O'Dwyer shook his head. "The King arrives tomorrow morning. We must bring this matter to a conclusion now."

"I must concur!" Commissioner French agreed. "We cannot afford to waste another moment."

The two men exchanged a surreptitious glance. At once, Sikander understood what was going on. While he had been running about trying to apprehend Zahra's killer, the two of them had teamed up and slowly but steadily, whittled away at the Viceroy's resolve until ultimately, they had prevailed upon him to reconsider his decision.

Hardinge frowned, his eyes swiveling toward the Great Dane. "And what do you think, old friend?"

Sikander gave him a hopeful glance. Surely Dane would take his side? He was a reasonable man, and would not be swayed quite so easily.

"Much as I would like to find the girl's assailant, I'm afraid I have to agree." Louis Dane offered Sikander a commiserative shrug. "I don't see what other choice we have in this instance. We can't risk even a hint of scandal, not with the King's arrival so imminent."

"So be it." Hardinge's frown deepened as he turned back to face Sikander. "You are to cease and desist your investigations, Mr. Singh. I regret to say that the young lady's murderer will have to be permitted to go free."

Sikander gasped. "You cannot be serious. I can catch Zahra's killer, sir. I will catch him. Just give me one more day."

"That is out of the question. You will drop the matter, Mr. Singh. From this moment forthwith, no more poking around."

Hardinge's face hardened, as obdurate as granite. "This is not a suggestion. If I find out that you have disobeyed me, there will be hell to pay. Is that clear?"

His tone was adamant, patently unwilling to brink any refusal. One look at his craggy face was enough to tell Sikander his mind was made up, and that any argument he tried to offer would immediately be shot down by O'Dwyer and the Commissioner, nipped in the proverbial bud.

"I take it we have an understanding," Hardinge repeated.

"Do I have a choice?"

"You do not. Mr. O'Dwyer, will you see that the girl's body is disposed of respectfully? A discreet cremation with a minimum of fuss."

"She was Muslim," Sikander interjected, dull-voiced, "of Kashmiri origin."

"Very well," Hardinge looked at him contemplatively, "a burial then, out of the public eye."

"Consider it done," O'Dwyer replied, but not before he took a moment to offer Sikander a triumphant look, as if to gloat over the fact that it was he who had won their battle of wits.

"Very well." Hardinge, glad to see this last loose end wound up, said, "Let us consider this affair closed." He gave Sikander a brusque nod. "Thank you for your help, Mr. Singh. I shall remember your valiant efforts, even if they have come to no avail." He turned to address the Great Dane. "Let us have Rajpore's salute upped to fifteen guns, shall we? That should keep you happy, eh?"

It was an obvious bribe, intended to entice him to keep his mouth shut, so overt that he was insulted. Sikander was tempted to refuse, to give Hardinge a proper piece of his mind, but he was astute enough to grasp that this was neither the time nor place to make his true feelings known. It would do Rajpore no good if he alienated the most powerful Englishman in India. That was the only reason he held back his pique, and managed to offer the Viceroy a slight smile.

"Thank you," he murmured, feigning a graciousness he did not feel. Opening the door, he stepped out of the car hurriedly before his self-restraint could crumble.

As the Standard departed, Sikander just stood there, silently simmering. A tumult of emotions assailed him. First came a terrible fury, a wave of resentment crashing against him, like a tsunami. How could Hardinge allow such a grave miscarriage of justice? Sikander wanted to rave, to scream at the top of his voice. Zahra had been a person, a miracle, living and breathing, wrought by God, by nature. How could they allow someone to just snuff her out, to extinguish all that she was, and then walk away unpunished? What was wrong with these damnable English?

It did not take long for his anger to turn to indignation. Failure was not a sensation Sikander was accustomed to. It ached at him to leave a mystery unsolved, especially one so personal. It was frustrating, to say the least. And with this frustration came guilt, a dreadful, all-consuming sense of despair. He had failed Zahra utterly. He had promised himself he would obtain justice, and yet again, he had been unable to keep his word. Years ago he had allowed her mother's killer to escape, and now, in a macabre repeat of history, it was his fault that her murderer also would go scot-free.

"Your Majesty, could I have a word?"

Once again, it was Campbell who had interrupted him. Rather than leaving with Hardinge and the others, he had elected to stay behind, and was watching Sikander patiently, waiting to speak with him.

"Oh, what is it now?" Sikander snapped. "What more could you people possibly want from me?"

"I only wished to thank you."

This declaration caused Sikander's fury to abate considerably. It would be exceedingly churlish, he reminded himself, to take out his frustration on Campbell. Not only had the man tried his best to help him unravel the mystery of Zahra's murder, but over the last two days, he come to like the Captain quite a bit. In spite of his cocksure manner and sometimes abrasive need to insert himself into every facet of Sikander's investigative process, his instincts were sound. If only he could learn to hold his tongue, Sikander thought, then he had the makings of a first-class detective.

"I am sorry things are ending so unsatisfactorily," Campbell apologized. "It has been a proper pleasure, sir, to assist you, however briefly."

"The pleasure has been mine, Captain." Sikander broke from character by offering Campbell his hand. "Take care of yourself, and remember, here in India, a man is what he is brave enough to make of himself, nothing more, and nothing less."

"I will try to keep that thought uppermost in my mind at all times." Campbell's face flowered into a comradely smile. "Good-bye, Your Majesty. It was fun while it lasted."

"No," Sikander said, matching his expression with a grin of his own, "this is not good-bye. We shall meet again, I am sure of it.

"If you ever decide to give up on the regiment, why don't you come down to Rajpore and seek me out? I am sure we can find some way to keep you entertained."

Chapter Twenty-five

"What's wrong, sahib?" Charan Singh inquired when Sikander returned to the car. "You look even more depressed than usual."

"I am sorry to say that we have been ordered by the Viceroy to cease our investigations."

"Oh, that's too bad, huzoor, especially considering that I have found you another clue."

"What clue?" Sikander growled. "Are you trying to be funny, you old goat?"

"Not at all," the old Sikh's face broke into a vast grin. "It just so happens that I, Charan Singh the master detective, has found your elusive picture *wallah*."

"You have?"

"Indeed, huzoor. His name is Charles Urban and he has rented a *haveli* near the Sadar Bazaar, very close to the Dariya Ganj."

Sikander's dudgeon faded. His mind raced as he contemplated his next move. As far as he could see, he had two choices. He could obey Hardinge's command and return to the Majestic with his tail between his legs, or he could defy him, and carry on with his investigation. It took him less than a minute to make up his mind. If he could find something useful still, he thought, maybe the Viceroy would not be put out too badly.

"Take me there," he said, "and make it quick."

"Of course, huzoor." Charan Singh gave Sikander a knowing

look. "I knew you would say just that, which is why I have already given Ajit Singh the proper directions."

Their destination turned out to be a compound not far from the Turcomani gate. It was here that the film *wallah* had taken two adjoining bungalows and set up shop. Charan Singh had made a few discreet inquiries about the man. Mr. Urban was an American, who had made a fortune off footage from the Boer War, and had opened a studio on Wardour Street. His company had attained some renown for its scientific shows at the Alhambra, and he had shot a documentary about the people of London that had been well received. Also, it was said that he had developed a new process to bring color to the screen that was said to be revolutionary, something called Kinemacolor, and that the King was a great aficionado of his work, which was why he had been assigned the honor of chronicling the Durbar for posterity.

Sikander considered him a modern man. He took pride in being open-minded, especially when contrasted with the attitudes of some of his peers in the Chamber of Princes, who were still so backward in their mentality as to be very nearly medieval.

However, if there was one technology that dismayed him, it was cinema. When it came to moving pictures, Sikander found himself distinctly unimpressed. It was an irrational antipathy, of that he was quite aware. He had been there that cold morning in 1896, seated in the audience when the Lumière Brothers had screened their film in the garden of Watson's Hotel in Bombay. Unfortunately, rather than thinking it a revelation, he had found it disappointing, little more than a parlor trick, a gimmick. As far as he was concerned, the cinema was just another form of voyeurism. There was no mystery to it, no soul. It was fickle, an illusion with no real substance. And while he could see how people were easily enticed by the lure of the moving image, entranced by what seemed almost to be magic, somehow, to him, it symbolized an entropy, the death of imagination.

No, he much preferred a good book. There was something deeply reassuring about a book that a moving picture could never possess, that tangible intoxication of dust and ink, the solace of paper, its smell and its substance.

Still, regardless of his opinions about the medium, Sikander could not help but feel his spirits lift as the Rolls trundled southward, his moroseness being replaced by that familiar euphoria he knew so well. He had thought the game over, but, thank the heavens, it was still properly in play.

By the time Ajit Singh slowed the car, Sikander was positively brimming over with nervous energy.

"The lights are off, sahib," Charan Singh said, peering out at the film *wallah's* residence, which was surrounded by a high wall topped by spikes and an ominous-looking wrought-iron gate. "I think, perhaps, the bird has flown the coop."

"Let us take a look anyway," Sikander suggested, hopping off to make a slow recce of the environs, before pausing in front of the gate, which was chained and padlocked.

"You cannot be serious," the big Sikh's eyes goggled. "That would be breaking and entering, huzoor."

"Don't be so dramatic, old man. We are on the Viceroy's business, after all."

"Are we?" Charan Singh inquired, smelling a lie, but it was too late. Sikander had already vaulted over the gate, as agile as an acrobat. Leaving his manservant to struggle after him, he strode up to the front door of the *haveli* shamelessly. Sikander rapped on it once, then twice, but there was no answer. He tried the handle next. It seemed to be locked, but that was no great obstacle, not to someone with his varied and somewhat picaresque skills. From his turban, he pulled out a pin, a sliver of metal about two inches long. He examined the lock with one eye. It looked straightforward enough, a simple Yale and Towne mortice that should be easy to defeat. Sikander licked his lips and bent the pin almost into a P, which he then inserted into the keyhole. He pulled the door toward him and jiggled the pin in a complicated maneuver up and around, and *voilà*, the lock clicked open.

"Hold on, sahib! This a very bad idea."

"Oh, come on. You always say that."

"And you never listen," the Sikh groused as Sikander eased the door open, and tiptoed in. Inside, it was very dark, and a distinct smell of ammonia hung in the air, mingled with something else, a bitter odor not unlike burned hair. Squinting, he tried to get a sense of his surroundings, but just as his eyes were beginning to become accustomed to the shadows, one of the electric lamps blazed to life, and he found himself confronted by a red-faced man advancing toward him, brandishing a saucepan as if it were Excalibur itself.

Sikander studied this apparition, unsure whether to be amused or befuddled. He was very short, perhaps an inch under five feet, but with broad shoulders and a hunched back. Sikander put his age around forty, although he could have been older, judging by his sideburns, which were flecked with gray. As for the rest of his head, it was perfectly bald, shaved as bare as a monk's, an impression accentuated by the fact that he was clad in a tattered bathrobe and a pair of threadbare long johns.

"Who are you?" he squawked, with a distinctly northern accent. "What in blazes do you think you're doing here, eh?"

Behind Sikander, Charan Singh came barging in, ready to charge into the fray, his fists clenched. Sikander gave him a subtle nod, to warn him to hold his ground.

"I'm sorry." He decided to play played the hapless dolt. "I am here to see Mr. Urban."

"He's not here, is he?" He spared one long moment to eye Charan Singh, looking him up and down, which was why he decided to hold on to his saucepan, although he did make the concession of lowering it, if only a few inches. "He's gone off to Bombay to film the King's arrival, he has." His eyes narrowed. "Say, how did you get in here, anyway?"

"Ah," Sikander feigned a shrug. "The door was open, so I

let myself in."

"Open, you say?" He frowned, offering Sikander a suspicious glare. "I am quite sure it was locked. The master did it himself, before he departed. I saw him, with my own two eyes."

Darting past Sikander, he peered at the door short-sightedly, raising one hand to scratch at his head.

"Why would he lock you in?" Sikander asked curiously.

"The master does not trust a soul. He is convinced that there are all kinds trying to steal his footage. He actually has us sleeping on the canisters, can you believe it?"

The man scratched at his greasy hair. "Say, you aren't with the press, are you? Mr. Urban was very specific about that. No visitors, and no press *wallahs*, most of all."

"No, I am not a journalist."

"You an actor then? I warn you, I can't help you with any casting. The boss makes all those decisions himself."

"I am not an actor either. Actually, my name is Sikander Singh, and I am the Maharaja of Rajpore."

"Blooming hell!" The man's mouth sagged. "Surely not! You're really one of them Maharaja blokes."

"Indeed, I am, and this here is my manservant, Charan Singh." He pointed at the big Sikh, who offered a surly bow. "And who might you be?"

"Ah, yes," the man performed an elaborate salute, very nearly managing to decapitate himself with his saucepan, which he seemed to have forgotten all about. "I am Jenkins, late of Aberystwyth, cameraman extraordinaire. Pray, how may I be of service to Your Highness?"

"I was hoping to have a brief word with Mr. Urban about the process, so to speak. I am great fan of the cinema, you see, and when I heard that you were chronicling the celebrations on film, I simply had to pay him a visit." He gave the cameraman the most innocent of smiles. "Say, Mr. Jenkins, I don't suppose you could help me out, could you, answer a few of my questions for me? I would be happy to compensate you for your time."

Beside him, Charan Singh must have read his mind, because he already had a purse ready, clinking it suggestively in one hand before offering it to the Welshman.

"It's just plain old Jenkins, sir." Taking the purse, he let out a low whistle when he examined its contents. "My father was Jenkins, and my grandfather before him. Not a Mister in sight. Tell me, what can I do for you, Your Lordship?"

"I believe Mr. Urban visited the King Emperor's camp the day before yesterday. Am I correct?"

"Indeed, you are dead right," Jenkins replied, his unfortunate choice of words causing Sikander's jaw to clench. "We were there shooting some stock footage, just a few odds and ends to use as transitions. In fact, I was running the camera myself."

"Is that so?" He offered Jenkins a comradely wink. "I believe you filmed a *nautch* girl while you were there, a real beauty."

"Aye!" Jenkins laughed. "That she was. A proper peach! But we didn't film her. The master dearly wanted to record some sequences of her dancing. He was foaming at the mouth to do it, but when he approached her, she refused to perform outright. I think she was scared of us, or something such. She certainly seemed a bit nervous, the poor thing. In any case, we ended up shooting some scenery and a couple of feet of soldiers on parade and that sort of thing." His face lit up with a grin. "Say, would you like to see it?"

"I'm sorry. What exactly would you like me to see?"

"The rushes, sir, the dailies we shot while we were there. I was just getting the film developed, if you would care to have a look."

"Of course," Sikander's heartbeat quickened, sensing he was on the brink of something vitally important. "I would love to have a look."

"Come along, then." Jenkins discarded his trusty saucepan, placing it on a nearby table before ushering Sikander through the back door of the *haveli*. He trotted across the courtyard, and carefully unlocked a shed about the size of a stable at the distant end of the compound.

"In here, sir. We have a screening room all set up."

Inside, it was very dark, except for the dull illumination cast by two narrow windows. The laboratory stink of mercury permeated the air, making Sikander cough. One wall was white-washed, the far one, which Sikander guessed was used as the screen. The rest of the room was bare of furniture, except for several rows of cast-iron bathtubs, each one carefully covered with wet muslin cloth. Sikander paused and eased back one of the sheets, to reveal a metal canister beneath, embossed with the name Pathé, ensconced in a bed of rapidly melting ice.

"Careful, Your Majesty!" Jenkins castigated him. "That's raw stock. It's made from cellulose and silver nitrate, sir, very nearly the same ingredients as gunpowder. It is extremely inflammable. That is why we keep it cold."

He pulled up a workbench, just two slats of wood nailed to a crossbeam.

"Have a seat, sir. I'll have us up and running in no time."

Crossing to the far corner, Jenkins swept away a grimy dust cloth to reveal a small Gaumont projector mounted on a table beneath. After carefully checking its lens as reverently as a devotee, he turned and approached a nearby steamer trunk banded with iron, slamming open its lid to reveal a stack of film reels stored within. Rifling through them, he pulled out one round spool.

"Here we are," he said, returning to the projector, and carefully threading the film into the requisite receptacles, handling it as dexterously as a master weaver. "Are you ready, sir?"

"Yes, go on."

Jenkins marched around the room, drawing closed each window's curtains one by one, leaving Sikander enveloped by twilight. Then, returning to the projector, he spat on one palm and grasped its hand crank, slowly starting to turn it clockwise.

Whirring and clicking, the machine came to life. A moment

later, the room lit up with an unearthly light. Where moments ago there had been flat nothingness, now a series of black-and-white images flickered in stark focus, like ghosts come to life. It was magical, but also equally unnerving, so real that they seemed tangible. But then, when Sikander lifted one hand to try and touch the images with his fingers, they broke apart, splintering into a rainbow of dust motes.

As Jenkins had explained, it was mainly footage of the Imperial Camp. First came a close-up of the Union Jack fluttering gently in some invisible breeze, and then a panoramic vista of the tents, their flat white roofs spread out as far as the eye could see, like an intricate puzzle. Then a shot of the Kings Road, following the route His Majesty would take during his procession, followed by a very clever sequence showing an automobile bearing down toward them like some primeval behemoth. Then came a shot of some camels being herded by their tenders, and an elephant being bathed, water trumpeting from his trunk as his child *mahout* swung from his tusks, and then, a polo match in full swing, before finally cutting to a march-past, a row of Hussars mounted on horseback, maneuvering perfectly in unison on parade.

Sikander quickly began to lose interest. It did not take long for his eyes to grow accustomed to the half light, after which the pictures seemed drab somehow, flat and insubstantial. And there was no sound, which made the experience even more unconvincing.

Just as he was beginning to lose patience completely, a shot of the King's Reception Pavilion flickered across the screen. Sikander leaned forward to get a better look. There, in the background, off to the left, was that Zahra? It was, he realised, as the camera zoomed in. A shiver ran down his spine. She was so beautiful, so vibrant, it was hard to believe she was dead. It was eerie, to say the least, so surreal he felt like a voyeur.

He watched as she turned to face him, her face blooming with joy, a smile flowering on her lips. The camera pulled back, to reveal that a man had entered the frame, approaching Zahra. He was tall, broad-shouldered, clad in a leather duster and a broad-brimmed hat. Sikander's eyes narrowed, trying to discern his identity, but it was no use. Not only was his back to the camera, but the angle was all wrong, leaving his face obscured, swathed by shadows.

Sill, there was something very familiar about him, causing a flicker of recognition to gnaw at Sikander like an itch he could not scratch. A moment later, it became apparent exactly why. The camera panned left, just as the man took Zahra's hand in his own, and brought it to his lips, to give her wrist the tenderest of kisses. In that instant, his face was partially visible, revealing a profile that Sikander knew immediately.

Behind him, Charan Singh let out an audible gasp, an exclamation of utter surprise.

"Thank you, Jenkins. You can stop now."

"Hold on, there's a bit more, Your Highness."

"There's no need." Sikander let out a grim laugh. "I have seen everything that I need to solve this case.

"I now know exactly who our murderer is."

Chapter Twenty-six

By the time Sikander arrived at the King Emperor's encampment, dusk had long since subsided into the ebony gloom of night.

This time around, he had chosen to come alone, leaving Charan Singh and his entourage of guards behind, in spite of the old Sikh's persistent objections. The camp seemed a changed place. When he had last visited, just a couple of days previously, it had been quite deserted. Now, in spite of the lateness of the hour, it was the scene of hectic activity. Every electric light was ablaze, turning night to day, and there was a dense crowd congregated along the Kingsway, a motley of carts and lorries and horse drawn wagons bunched together. Beyond, a scene of absolute bedlam was unfolding, as soldiers and laborers and scurried about like worker ants, laying any remaining last-minute preparations before the King's arrival the next morning.

There was a bit of awkwardness when Sikander trundled up in his Rolls Royce, only to be barred from entering by the sergeant of the Black Watch who was on sentry duty. Sikander tried to reason with him, but the man remained obdurate, as only a Sassenach can. No matter what expanation was offered, he refused to let him pass without an official invitation.

Just before matters could take an ugly turn, Campbell showed up.

"The Maharaja of Rajpore is working directly for the Viceroy," he explained to the dour Scotsman. "He is to have the run of the camp. Those are Lord Hardinge's explicit orders."

As the sergeant grudgingly raised the cordon, Sikander turned to Campbell and asked, "Have you done as I requested, Captain, and sent for the Viceroy?"

"I regret to say, sir, that Lord Hardinge is unavailable. Unfortunately, he has gone down country to meet the King's train at Jhansi."

"What about Lord Dane, and Malik Umar Hayat Khan?"

"I have dispatched runners to summon them. They should be here shortly." The Captain's brow knitted into a frown. "What is this about, your Majesty? Couldn't you at least give me a hint about what is going on?"

"All in good time, Captain. Let us wait for the others to arrive, shall we?"

"Of course," Campbell replied, though it was patent from his waspish expression he was not at all satisfied. "Shall we step inside?"

Turning, he led Sikander into the King's reception pavilion. Inside, it was much the same as it had been two nights before, although everything had been polished to a high sheen in preparation of the King's arrival. The tapestries and carpets had been brushed, every nook and eave dusted, each piece of furniture buffed with linseed oil. It felt surreal. Every remnant of Zahra's presence seemed to have been erased, all traces of her death sanitized. It was almost impossible to tell that any crime had even been committed in these hallowed confines, if not for the faintest scent of bleach lingering in the air.

Like a terrier, the Captain nipped at Sikander's heels as he made a slow circuit of the room before finally coming to a stop in front of the same chair where the Viceroy had been seated the last time around. Sikander sank down into its cushioned embrace with a sigh, crossing one leg over another. Leaning back, he settled in patiently to wait. Campbell, on the other hand, refused to sit. Instead, he paced back and forth restlessly. Sikander watched him, reminded of the clockwork automatons he had seen in Germany once, at the Frauenkirche in Nuremberg. The Captain moved with the same mechanical regularity, six short steps towards the door and then he would stop, before turning and giving Sikander a wary glance, and then repeating the whole process once more, only in the opposite direction.

"Calm down, Captain, before you give yourself a stroke."

"I'm sorry," Campbell replied with a smirk. "Would you care for a drink, sir? I can call for a bearer and ask him to fetch us some champagne."

"No, I think not. At least, not yet."

This reply only served to make Campbell even more agitated. With a visible shudder, he resumed his pacing. Sikander watched the man, trying to quell his irritation. He was tempted to chastise him, command him to sit down and stop fidgeting, but he restrained his tongue, wondering which would give first, his patience, or the Captain's knees.

Thankfully, they did not have too long to wait. Malik Umar was the first to arrive. He hustled into the tent with a harried scowl on his face, as if to suggest he was not in the least bit happy at being summoned in such a peremptory fashion.

"This had better be a proper emergency, Sikander," he snapped without bothering to offer any formal greetings. "There are a hundred details waiting for my attention, so I warn you, if this is a waste of time, there will be dire consequences."

"As it happens, my friend, I have made some real progress in solving Zahra's case."

Malik Umar's reponse to this declaration was a narrowing of his mouth, his lips compressing nearly to invisibility.

"Didn't the Viceroy specifically order you to cease and desist your investigations? He will not be happy when he finds out you have disobeyed his express command."

"I am sure he won't mind too much." Sikander's face split

into a triumphant grin. "You see, I have been able to deduce who killed Zahra."

"Is that so?" Malik Umar's eyes widened, a mixture of surprise and disbelief.

Next to him, Captain Campbell let out a choked gasp. "Who was it? Alwar?"

"No, while I certainly would love to pin the blame on Jey Singh, he is not our man. Oh, he is quite unhinged, I know, suffering from what Krapelin calls dementia praecox, a precocious madness under whose influence he is capable of committing the direst of crimes, even murder. In this case though, I believe he is innocent, if only because he lacked the opportunity to kill Zahra. As we know from our investigations, she was alive when he left her, and the alibi he provided has been verified, which exonerates him, much to my dismay."

"Was it Kashmir then? Or the Nizam?" Malik Umar asked.

"No, I fear they are both innocent as well. The Nizam has motive certainly. When he approached Zahra with amorous intentions, she turned him away, which would be enough to foment a deep resentment. The fury of the scorned and such! But would that be reason enough to want someone dead? Perhaps, yes; I have known murders committed for less, especially by men who are as arrogant as Osman Jah. However, it is that very arrogance that exculpates him in this case. As he pointed out, he would have hired someone to do his killing, rather than strangled her himself.

"As for Kashmir, his motive is an even more palpable one. He tried to recruit the girl as an agent, but she refused him. If she chose to expose his machinations to the authorities, that would only land him in hotter water than he already is. But that is exactly where Partap Singh's salvation lies. You see, it was his brother who hatched this elaborate scheme, and it was his intent, I believe for it to fail, precisely so that he could undermine the Maharaja and supplant him with his own son.

"That brings us to Kapurthala and Patiala."

"Surely you cannot be serious." Malik Umar snorted. "Neither Bhupinder nor Jagatjit are killers. They could no more murder a woman than you or I."

"Do not be so quick to jump to conclusions, Malik Umar. Lust drives men to do strange and terrible things." Sikander steepled his fingers, bringing them to his lips. "And that is what united Kapurthala and my cousin, that they both lusted for Zahra. However, when they made overtures to her, she refused them, which gives them much the same motivation as the Nizam.

"In Jagatjit's case though, I believe we can dismiss him outright. He loved Zahra, or at least he thought he did, in his own quixotic way. He could not have taken her life. As for Bhupinder, he is a much more complex creature than Kapurthala. He could have someone murdered yes, if the fancy struck him, but a woman, and for rejecting his amorous advances? No, he is a narcissist, not a madman, which is why I think we must eliminate him as well."

"What about Prince Battenberg and his coterie?" Campbell chimed in, a bit too shrill. "One of them could be our man. After all, they were amongst the last to see her alive, weren't they? Shouldn't that make them the most obvious culprits?"

"No, I think not. Your Guppies are brats of the worst kind, yes, but that does not make them murderers, not yet. Perhaps with time one or more of them may grow to do something heinous, but now, let us be honest, they just did not have enough of a reason to want her dead.

"Colonel Metcalfe, though, is a different kettle of fish. He was driven by profit, a calculating, callous man, and precisely the sort of suspect who would kill if the price was right. But in this case, I believe it would be premature to blame him for her death. He threatened her, yes, but it was too early for him to kill her, not until he had secured the evidence he had been sent to obtain.

"Who does that leave? Bahadur Rao? A foolish, arrogant rabble-rouser, but a murderer. I think not. The Scindia? An unpleasant man, but he wanted to help the girl, not kill her. The Maharani of Bharatpore? Holkar? The Prince of Palanpur? No, none of them quite fits the bill either, do they?"

"You seem to have run out of suspects, Sikander," Malik Umar observed mordantly.

"That is exactly what I thought, until I realised there was one person I had to failed to consider entirely, even though he was right under my nose the whole time." He glared straight at the Captain. "You, Campbell. It was you who murdered Zahra."

Sikander sat back, waiting for Campbell to react. He had expected blustering—You must be joking, this is ridiculous. Or denial—Why on earth would I want her dead? Or even outrage—I am offended by such an accusation!

Cambell chose none of the three. Instead, he merely offered Sikander one of his characteristically smug smiles.

"I almost had you, didn't I?" He shook his head sheepishly. "I almost managed to get the better of the legendary Sikander Singh."

"Good God," Malik Umar exclaimed, sitting bolt upright. "You mean to say he's right?"

"You were very convincing, Captain. You really should have been an actor, not a soldier."

"When did you figure it out? What was it that gave me away?"

"Actually, it was purely by chance. You had me properly fooled so completely, I never once suspected you. You almost got away with it, too, when the Viceroy ordered me to abandon my investigation. It was just your bad luck that I decided to disobey him, and decided to pay a visit to Charles Urban, the filmwallah who is chronicling the Durbar. While I was there, one of his assistants showed me some of the footage he had shot, and lo and behold, what should I see but the sight of you speaking to Zahra, face to face. I knew then it had to be you. After all, you were very insistent that you had never met her, but there you were, kissing her hand as clear as day, captured forever on celluloid."

"You win, Mr. Singh. I admit it, I was involved with her." Campbell shrugged. "We met over a year ago. It was quite by accident. I had been seconded to Lahore last year, before my transfer came through, and one of my mess-mates took me to a *kotha* one evening, where I saw her perform." He shuddered, overcome by a surge of barely repressed emotion. "I am not the sort of man to have his head turned by any woman, much less a dancing girl, but when I saw her, I was smitten. As was she, because it was Zahra who searched me out and made the first overture. It was folly, I know, for an officer to become involved with a native dancer. I knew my career would be over if we were found out, but how could I resist? She was so exquisite!"

"But then my promotion came through, and I was assigned here, to oversee the logistics of the King Emperor's Camp. It was my intention to make a clean break of it, but fate had something else in mind. Just when I thought I had left Zahra behind me, she turned up here, and that too under my very nose. I tried to avoid her, to tell her we could not see each other anymore, but alas, my blood was too weak to resist temptation."

"Did you love her?"

"I suppose I did, as much as I am capable of it. There were times when I wanted to marry her, to make a life in some distant town, just the two of us, starting with a clean slate. I thought about doing it secretly, but I just couldn't take the risk, not if I wanted a career in the Guards."

"Is that why you did it," Malik Umar hissed, "to be rid of her?"

"That is not how it happened, not at all." Campbell's voice caught in his throat. "It was all her fault. That night, I had every intention of breaking it off with her, but then, when we met, she told me she was with child. My child! A bastard's bastard." A bitter chuckle escaped his lips. "She was excited, delighted by the thought of bearing a son with me, but all I could think of was the fact that I was bringing another unwanted bastard into the world. I told her that she should go to one of the midwives in Lahore and have the child dropped. I even offered to pay for it, but she was appalled by the very suggestion. She began to cry, and so, I tried to console her. And then, I just don't know what happened, sir. One moment she was in my arms, the next she was at my feet, dead." He shook his head. "I cannot remember a thing. It was like a darkness settled over me. I recall imagining how easy it would be to kill her, to snap her neck, and then, when I recovered my senses, she was lying there, lifeless. I did not mean for her to die. I don't know what came over me.

"What else could I have done, sir? I couldn't afford the scandal of siring a child with a *nautch-wali*. I couldn't allow her to jeopardise everything that I had managed to achieve, my rank, my position, my reputation. No, I did not want to do it, but it is for the best that she is dead."

"But why the whole dog and pony show with her corpse? Why hang her up, like a trophy?"

"I thought it would deflect attention from me, that when they found her here, in the King's own reception tent, the burra sahibs would sweep the whole thing under the rug. It almost worked, but then, you came along. I never thought they would send for you, of all people, Mr. Singh. But when you turned up, I volunteered to be your shadow. I tried my best to steer you away from anything that would connect me to Zahra, but sadly, you are too damn clever for your own good."

As if by magic, a small pistol appeared in his hand, a snub nosed Webley Bulldog revolver.

Malik Umar gave Campbell an astonished scowl. "You cannot be serious, man. Do you really think you will get away with this? Where will you go? Where will you hide? There isn't a corner of the Empire where they will not hunt you down."

"I am sorry about this, but I don't see what other choice I have."

He raised the gun, bringing the barrel to bear on Sikander's chest. Sikander stiffened, bracing himself for the fatal blow.

Could this be it, the end of the road? He had always believed he would live a long, full life, and die an old man, unhappy in his dotage, but now, confronted with the spectre of imminent doom, to his surprise,he found that he was neither afraid nor filled with regret. Instead, a calm filled him, a detachment so complete it was almost a bliss. I will face this head on, he decided, as I have confronted every adversity in my life. In his mind's eye, he saw Helene's face. "I am sorry, my beloved," he whispered to himself. "I only wish we had more time."

Campbell held the pistol steady for one long moment, but then, with a groan, he let his arm fall to his side.

"I cannot do it. I can't shoot you down in cold blood."

Malik Umar sagged forward, letting out a long, slow sigh. Sikander remained motionless, struggling to slow his heartbeat, which was pounding, like a piston.

"Surrender yourself to me, Campbell," the Maharaja said softly. "I give you my word, I will do everything in my power to see you are treated fairly." He turned to Malik Umar and gave him a curt nod. "Malik Umar will testify on my behalf, that whatever else my flaws, I am and always will be a man of my word."

Malik Umar's brow knitted into a frown. Sikander feared he would refuse to play along, but after a brief pause, he shook his head grudgingly.

"Yes, it is quite obvious you were not in your right mind when you killed Zahra. It is MacNaughten's Rule. When you committed your crime, you were not cognizant of the nature and quality of the wrong you were doing. I will make sure the judge is apprised of that fact."

"I think not," Campbell replied. "I do not deserve leniency, sir. What I deserve is to be punished. She was an innocent, and I killed her, and my child with her."

He glanced down at the pistol in his hand. Campbell turned it over contemplatively, biting his lip before looking back up at Sikander, his face grim with regret.

"Could I have a moment alone, Your Highness?"

It took Sikander a moment to understand.

"Very well." He said with a sigh. "Come along, Malik Umar. Let us step outside, and give the Captain some privacy."

Malik Umar was a bit slower on the uptake. Several heart-beats ticked by before he managed to grasp what Campbell intended to do.

"Are you sure this is the path you want to take, Captain?" he asked gently.

Cocking the pistol, Campbell's mouth twisted into one last smile. It was resigned, almost nervous, entirely devoid of the cocksureness which Sikander had come to expect from him.

"At least this way, sir, I will save Simla a headache."

Squaring his shoulders, he let out a shuddering breath, and offered first Sikander and then Malik Umar a crisp salute.

Sikander reciprocated the gesture, bringing one finger to his brow before he spun and hurried from the room. Outside, he sagged against the nearest tentpost. A numbness assailed him, the full realisation of how close he had come to death. Fumbling his cigarette case from his pocket, he struggled to get it open. His hands would not stop shivering. Even when he bundled his fingers into a fist, trying to will them to be still, to his dismay, they kept shaking, like they had a mind of their own.

"What a damned mess!" Malik Umar said, coming up behind him. "Well, I suppose we should at least be glad it is over." He clapped Sikander on his back. "Congratulations are in order, aren't they? Well played, my friend! You found your murderer in the end. When I make my report to the Viceroy, I will make sure you get your due reward, don't you worry?"

Sikander turned to face his old friend, a bitterness swelling inside his chest. Ordinarily, when he concluded a case, it aroused a sense of achievement so potent it was nearly an exultation. But now, standing there, all he felt was an all-consuming weariness, accompanied by the urgent need to get away from it all, from Malik Umar, from the English, from the damned Durbar.

"I don't want your blasted reward," he was about to say, but before he could, a loud exclamation forestalled him.

"Mr. Singh, there you are!"

Glancing around, Sikander saw Lord Dane approaching, followed closely by O'Dwyer and the Commisioner.

"What seems to be the situation?" Lord Dane inquired, greeting him with a warm smile. "Why have you sent for us?

Before Sikander could reply, a gunshot rang out from inside the tent, a flat crack of sound that roused the ravens sleeping in the trees and sent them scrabbling into the the sable sky, an unkindness of angry, beating wings.

The Commisioner reacted first, fumbling his service Webley free from its holster, his eyes darting back and forth frantically as he searched for the origin of this unexpected report. O'Dwyer was a little more circumspect. He moved quickly to his left, seeking the nearest source of cover, which happened to be a large water barrel.

As for Lord Dane, he froze stiff, shooting Sikander a frantic glare.

"What on earth was that?"

"It is Captain Campbell, I am afraid," Malik Umar said, stepping forward. "He has had a dreadful accident."

Epilogue

My beloved Helene,

I pray this letter finds you in the halest of health. And I hope that even in Paris, where there are so many distractions to engage your attention, you think of me quite as often as I remember you.

I regret that I have not been able to write this past week. To my delight, and Charan Singh's undiminished dismay, a case cropped up, and most unexpectedly at that. I shall tell you more about it, all the gory details, when you return to Rajpore, but let it suffice for now to say, I was able to wrap everything up, and, that too very neatly, just in time for the King's grand arrival in Delhi.

About that, it turned out to be a truly damp affair. The Viceroy had arranged an elephant for King George, but he refused to ride upon it. Instead, he decided at the last minute to make his entry on horseback and that too in a Field Marshal's uniform, rather than in his robes of state. As a result, the pomp and circumstance we had all expected was greatly reduced. In fact, the King looked more a sweaty cavalryman out on patrol than the Emperor of India. It was rather funny, actually. We were at the very far end of the viewing balcony at the Red Fort, and when the King and his entourage cantered by, Jagatjit commented, "Good God, is that him? He looks like a doorman at the Savoy." I nearly fell over laughing, let me tell you.

The actual Durbar went much more splendidly. There was a grand battue of all the regiments, and we were made to line up to greet the King, all the Maharajas and Nawabs of India, as resplendent as peacocks in our gilded finery. It was surely the strangest queue the world has ever seen, and I doubt there shall be another to match its grandeur, at least not during my lifetime. Everything was staged, of course. We had been put through the paces twice before, each of us told exactly what we had to do, which was to approach the King and offer a bow and then retreat the way we came. Trust the English to plan everything to the last detail! It all went off exactly as practised, with one glaring exception. My old mentor Baroda has managed to cause quite a scandal. For some reason, he refused to bow properly, and then turned his back on the King while leaving. Needless to say, he now finds himself in the very hottest of water. I wish I could help him somehow, but Ismail Bhakht has been very specific. I am to stay away from him until the furor dies down, lest I find myself in the proverbial soup as well.

Speaking of scandals, another even more juicy one seems to be brewing, once again involving poor Sayaji Rao. It seems that his daughter, Indira, has decided to elope with my old friend Jitendra Narayan of Cooch Behar. It is all the talk of the Durbar camps. She sent a letter, I have heard, to inform Scindia that she was breaking off their engagement, which he in turn has forwarded to the Gaekwad asking, "Whatever does the Princess mean?" Poor fool! I am not an admirer of Scindia, as you well know, but what an unlucky fellow, to have your heart broken and your ego bruised all in one fell swoop. Why, it is almost enough to make me feel sorry for him! Well, almost, but not quite!

This very morning, I was summoned to meet with the Viceroy. I have come to admire Hardinge. He is a fair man, and while I do not approve of his politics, I must admit, I much prefer him to his immediate predecessors. There is no duplicity with him, no subtext. I find that rather refreshing. It has been a very long time since I have felt able to take an Englishman at his word, but with him, I think there is hope for India.

We enjoyed a brief supper together, and he was a most civil host. While he chose to take only leek soup, I was offered a fine magnum of Taittinger, and a quite superlative pâté, which his Lordship informed me had been imported from Vichy. I am enclosing the precise address. Perhaps you can pick up a case or two before you return so that we can enjoy it together.

Anyway, halfway through our meal, we had a surprise visitor. It was none other than His Majesty himself. When he turned up, you can only imagine my surprise. Up close, George Almighty is a singularly unimpressive individual, let me tell you, with about the same regal bearing as a mouse. Not only is he very short, with abominable posture, but he also has a very low voice, speaking almost in a murmur. I had to strain to understand even a single word, and I am sure the poor man is convinced I have a dreadful case of Saint Fiacre's curse, the way I kept leaning into him, like I could not bear to stand upright.

In either case, it turned out he wished to thank me in person for my efforts to keep the Durbar from being ruined. As a reward for my services, he has offered to raise my salute to seventeen guns, which is a quite unprecedented escalation. He also invited me to visit him at Windsor, and it was hinted that perhaps I might be knighted as an Officer of the British Empire when the New Year's Honours List is published.

I am tempted to accept, I confess it. Just the thought of the furious look on Bhupinder's fat face when he hears about my good fortune is reason enough. At the same time, though, I cannot help but be reminded of something that Baroda said to me very recently, that sooner or later, I shall have to pick a side between the English and India. I don't know if it is madness or pragmatism, my love, but I have decided to refuse the King's largesse. I am happy to stay Sikander Singh, plain old Maharaja of Rajpore, with my meager thirteen guns, so long as it leaves me free to pursue my passions. After all, what is that the old line from Faustus? "What profits it a man to gain the world, only to lose his soul?"

As you often remind me, I am not a romantic man, but this evening, as the sun wanes and the cool shadows of dusk settle around me like a shroud, I find myself thinking of you more than *ever. Memories of you haunt me, the remembrance of the way your eyes flash when you are angry, and how you bite your lip when you are trying to concentrate. There is an ache inside me, for the caress of your hair upon my cheeks, and the taste of your lips on mine. This emptiness, this absence, will only be assuaged when you return to me.*

I lack the eloquence to tell you how much I miss you, so I leave you with these words by Valery, that most poignant of your countrymen.

> *Si, de tes lèvres avancées,*
> *Tu prépares pour l'apaiser,*
> *À l'habitant de mes pensées*
> *La nourriture d'un baiser,*
> *Ne hâte pas cet acte tendre,*
> *Douceur d'être et de n'être pas,*
> *Car j'ai vécu de vous attendre,*
> *Et mon coeur n'était que vos pas.*

> *If, with your lips advancing,*
> *You are preparing to appease*
> *The inhabitant of my thoughts*
> *With the sustenance of a kiss,*
> *Do not hurry this tender act,*
> *Bliss of being and not being,*
> *For I have lived for waiting for you,*
> *And my heart was only your footsteps.*

Come back to me soon, my love.
Fondly,
your Sikander.

Author's Note

There were three Coronation Durbars held in India. The first was organised by Lord Lytton in 1877 to commemorate Victoria's ascension as the Empress of India. The second was in 1903, when Curzon was the Viceroy of India. The third and final Durbar was the grandest of them all, held in 1911 by Lord Hardinge to mark George V's rise to the throne. It was also the first time a British monarch visited the subcontinent, which made it doubly significant.

The British Government offered many justifications for spending a fortune on hosting such a lavish spectacle, given that the rest of India was wracked by famine and disease. Hardinge described it as a celebration of empire; Lord Dane called it a pageant of unity, a way to bring together the diverse citizens of England's many colonies through shared patriotic fervor. An editorial column in the *Pioneer* even went so far as to insist that it was the Indians who wanted the Durbar, that "it is impossible to see any reason for its discontinuance in the face of the loyal desires and expectations of the Indian people."

The truth, as it often tends to be, was somewhat simpler. Russia and England had been playing the Great Game for almost a century, each vying for control of Afghanistan and Central Asia. The British military's reputation for invincibility had also taken a bit of a battering, following the Zulu and Boer Wars, not to mention myriad indecisive conflicts ranging from the

Boxer Rebellion in China to the Mahdist conflict in the Sudan. In addition, the European powers, Germany in particular, were spreading the borders of their own empires aggressively, particularly in Africa. What better way then for the English to demonstrate their imperial majesty and wealth than by a public demonstration? That was what the Durbar of 1911 really was, a way for the English to 'show off' on a global scale, to intimidate old enemies and dazzle new friends. In many ways, it can be thought of as the last pyrrhic gasp of colonialism, because only a few short years later, the world would be engulfed by the First World War, and the age of Empire would begin its decline in the trenches of the Western Front.

For the record, while there was a princely state called Rajpur, Maharaja Sikander Singh is a figment of my imagination. Also, there was no murder preceding the Durbar of 1911, nor did the King consort with any nautch girls, at least according to public record. However, while Zahra may be entirely fictitious, the rest of the cast of this book are all real, as are most of the incidents chronicled.

There is no Englishman more reviled by Punjabis that Michael O'Dwyer. We meet him here as a young civil servant whose star is on the rise. A few short years later, in 1919, as the Lieutenant Governor of the Punjab, he would order the Jallianwala massacre, where the Army opened fire on a peaceful crowd in Amritsar and murdered over one thousand men, women and children. He was in turn assassinated by Udham Singh in 1940.

The Battenbergs are, of course, the Mountbattens, who changed their family name to hide their Germanic origins after World War 1. The Prince mentioned here who leads the Guppies is not Louis, who partitioned India, but rather his elder brother, George, whose sole contribution to history is a vast collection of pornography which he left to the British Museum, where it is hidden away in a private room, deemed unsuitable for general viewing.

The rest of the Guppies were an equally interesting lot, and none more so than Fruity Metcalfe, who would go on to become a close companion of Edward VIII, and end up at the very center of the abdication scandal when he abandoned his throne to marry Wallis Simpson.

As for Malik Umar Hayat Khan, he would go on to become the largest landholder in North India. He remained loyal to the British, even appearing on behalf of Michael O'Dwyer as a witness in a libel case. He died in 1944 in London.

Amar Singh of Kashmir would ultimately be successful in his scheming. His brother, Partap Singh, was removed from the throne for conspiring with the Russians, and his son, Hari Singh was elevated in his stead. He was destined to be the last Maharaja of Kashmir, and much of the current unrest in the valley is the outcome of his vacillating when India attained Independence.

I have taken some liberties with the character of Jagatjit Singh of Kapurthala, and made him seem a bit more of a libertine than he truly was. At the time of the Durbar, he was, indeed, married to Anita Delgado, a flamenco dancer of Spanish origin. She did attend the Durbar, and was quite furious with Jagatjit because she wanted to be recognised as his official consort, a request he was unable to grant because of protocol. She was prohibited from attending all official functions, and her pique, I imagine, is quite genuine, as was Jagatjit's weariness. If you would care to read more about that doomed romance, try *Passion India* by Javier Moro.

Bhupinder Singh's vast appetites are well chronicled, as is his passion for sport. He was a great patron of pehelwani in Punjab, and there was indeed a legendary wrestler by the name of Kikkar Singh Sandhu, who got his name because he enjoyed uprooting entire acacia (*kikkar*) trees out of the ground and pressing them above his head. At the Durbar, he fought a challenger named Kallu for the championship of the Punjab. It was a grudge match, and he lost badly, although it was no fault of Charan Singh.

History has not been kind to Jey Singh of Alwar. He has been much maligned, his eccentricities and extravagances reviled. He is held up as the worst of the Indian Princes, but much of his behavior, I believe, was caused by psychological instability. He is a fine example of what contemporary doctors describe as a sociopath, and he would ultimately come to an ignominious end, deposed and forced into exile, his habits proving too disgusting even for the *burra* sahibs to endure.

The character of Miss Cavendish is based on a real person, an Irish heiress named Lilah Wingfield. At the tender age of twenty-three, she decided to sail out to India to attend the Durbar, and left behind a diary chronicling her many adventures. It has been adpated into into a charming book, *A Glimpse of Empire*, by her granddaughter, Jessica Douglas-Home, and makes for a delightful afternoon of reading.

The Maharani of Bharatpur is remembered regettably as a nonentity. However, I believe that she must have been a formidable woman, who held the throne of her state as Regent for more than twenty years after her husband was deposed, no small feat for a woman in Rajasthan at the turn of the century. Sadly, her son would be the one to supplant her, and would in turn be deposed by the English in 1928 for mismanaging his state.

Tukoji Rao of Indore is one of the great romantic rogues of Princely India. In 1925, he would have a man named Abdul Kadir Bawla murdered by hired assassins in Bombay. The reason—Bawla was involved with a dance girl named Mumtaz whom Indore considered his property. When he was brought to trial, the Maharaja's only defence was that Bawla had besmirched his honor, his princely *izzat*. He refused to bow to the court, insisting that he was above the laws that governed men of lesser birth. In the end, he was acquitted but the ensuing scandal forced him to abdicate his throne in 1926.

The first meeting between Jitendra Narayan and Indira Raje is a well-documented one. They fell in love instantly, and she jilted her betrothed Mysore by letter. The couple would go on to become the darlings of European media, and her daughter, Gayatri Devi, who was the Maharani of Japiur for many years, is an iconic figure in Royal India, synonymous with dignity and grace.

At the Durbar, Sayaji Rao of Baroda would cause quite a hullabaloo by turning his back to the King. While this may have merely been an oversight on his part, there were many who took it to be a deliberate insult, intended to strike a public blow for the putative Independence movement. Gaekwad weathered the storm admirably, and ruled for the next thirty something years, and is today venerated in India as the most enlightened monarch of his age.

The Durbar was the first event to be filmed in color on a large scale. Charles Urban very nearly went bankrupt trying to keep his footage from being stolen by others, but when *With the King and Queen through India* was released in 1912, it was a runaway success. A copy of the film can be found online and is well worth watching.

Legend has it that the British considered holding another Durbar in 1937 to celebrate Edward VIII's coronation. Plans were rumored to be in the preliminary stages, but were abandoned when he abdicated the throne. With the outbreak of the Second World War, any further extravangazas were permanently shelved. Today, all that remains of the Grand Durbar of 1911 is the Gateway of India in Bombay, and a neglected park in one crowded corner of Delhi, which has become the repository for all the Colonial era statues that once lined Delhi's streets. Now, they lie in crumbling heaps,chief amongst then an effigy of King George himself, his stony visage bearing mute witness to the unyielding irony of time.

If anyone is interested in reading more about the actual Durbar, I highly recommend *Delhi Durbar 1911: The Complete Story* by Sunil Raman and Rohit Agarwal.

To see more Poisoned Pen Press titles:

Visit our website:
poisonedpenpress.com
Request a digital catalog:
info@poisonedpenpress.com